D1434215

A3 139 948 4

The Cypriot

This book is dedicated to my parents,
who made me a Cypriot,
and to everyone who loves Cyprus

My thanks to my brother Iacovos
for being with me every step of the way

and to Margarita
for putting up with me for so long

The Cypriot

ANDREAS KOUMI

dexter
haven
PUBLISHING

Published in 2006 by Dexter Haven Publishing Ltd
Curtain House
134–146 Curtain Road
London
EC2A 3AR

ISBN-10: 1-903660-01-7
ISBN-13: 978-1-903660-01-0

A full CIP record for this book is available from the British Library

Cover design by Ken Leeder

Cover images courtesy of Panos (front cover: main image),
Ken Leeder (back cover: graffiti illustration, harmonica; spine:
Aphrodite illustration), Cyprus Tourism Organisation/Helen
Silvester (inside cover: old door; front cover: shore), Luke
Finterham (back cover: thimble)

Typeset in Minion by Dexter Haven Associates Ltd, London
Printed in Great Britain by William Clowes Ltd, Beccles, Suffolk

Contents

Prologue

i
The Cypriot   *O Gibreos*

The cross spun through the air like a small silver propeller, catching the light of the winter sun on its smooth surface with each turn. Gravity pulled the cross down until it punctured the turquoise sea below.

'In the River Jordan, Lord, I baptise Thee,' chanted a bearded man dressed, as tradition dictated for such occasions, in blue.

The metal object sank, its shimmer still visible from above the waves. All at once the skin of the water was again ripped open as a young man plunged in. The sea was cold against his lean body, but his thoughts were on the task in hand. His eyes were fixed on the cross beneath him and, with the strength of youth in his limbs, he pushed himself downward in pursuit.

Deeper sank the cross, the sun's reflected glory diminishing.

Within seconds the agile young man was upon the cross, reaching out underneath it to break its fall. He gripped firmly and allowed himself a moment's satisfaction before kicking upwards to complete his mission. Finally, a triumphant fist broke the surface of the sea, clenching the silver prize.

ii
The foreigner   *O xenos*

I was on a Piccadilly Line underground train packed with fellow commuters heading into town. I'd managed to secure a seat for once and wanted to believe that today things might continue to go my way – maybe I'd get that pay rise. Most people on the train were hidden behind their newspapers. One man, standing in front of me and swaying from a handle, peered down at me occasionally. I noted he was dressed inadequately for the weather in an ill-fitting pin-striped suit.

At the next station a few more passengers squeezed into our carriage. They included an attractive young woman who, judging from the bulge in her overcoat, was pregnant. She ended up pressed against the man in the pin-stripes. Instinctively, I rose to offer the woman my seat, and there was relief and gratitude in her blushing face.

I found myself looking down and smiling at her as our train rattled into the tunnel.

1
The baptism *Do vaftisman*

The handful of people on the small fishing boat were relieved to see their hero emerge successfully from the water.

'Bravo, Andoni. Bravo,' they enthused, helping to pull him aboard and patting him on the back. It was unusually warm for the time of year but not warm enough to prevent Andonis shivering. The only woman present clambered over to him and placed a large white towel around his bare shoulders.

With salt water still dripping from his nose, Andonis stared into the woman's eyes, beaming with a boyish pride. So filled was she with emotion that, with the boat rocking to and fro, her feet became unsteady. He had to grab hold of her to prevent her from falling. Then he stooped to kiss her forehead, before reaching out from under his towel to present her with the cross.

'For you, mamma,' he declared with that handsome smile of his. The woman blushed and glanced anxiously in the direction of the bearded man in blue. She was mindful that he might disapprove of Andonis's improper gesture, presenting the cross to his mother instead of to his priest. She was relieved to see that the priest was preoccupied.

The boat party had now to negotiate its way back to dry land, and the two oarsmen were squabbling over who should row when, and whether to turn to the left or to the right. The priest, whose normally dark olive face had lost its colour, intervened. He issued instructions from a higher authority while endeavouring to keep his own balance.

Andonis viewed those on the beach awaiting the boat's return and raised a hand. Perhaps thirty people, some waving the blue and white striped maritime flag of Greece, mainly old, mainly female, nearly all Christian, had made the journey to witness this annual religious ceremony. Andonis was both pleased and a little surprised to see that one particular young woman, a non-Christian, was also in attendance. She and all the others would congratulate him, kiss both his cheeks and wish him a long life. Then all would return together to the village, to prepare for the evening's festival.

Andonis's mother waited for an appropriate moment to pass the cross back to the priest, bending down to kiss his hand as she did so. The touch of her lips filled the man of God with a heavenly love.

'God bless your child, Irini,' he declared, stroking the woman's greying hair.

She raised her head and peered into the priest's admiring black eyes. The sound of an army jeep could be heard in the distance. It was trundling towards the village, along the main road from the town. Andonis's youthful eye could just make out the red, white and blue of a tiny British flag on the bonnet, flapping in the wind.

Irini shuddered. 'And every mother's child,' she added.

2

The tailor   *O raftis*

It was already dark as I left work and strode up the iron stairs. I emerged shivering onto the narrow alleyway which led to London's Regent Street. It was spitting rain and unusually cold for the time of year. I had to stop a moment to pull the scarf I was wearing tighter round my neck. By this time of day my chin always had more stubble than most, and I could feel the scarf catch against it.

It was a short walk down to the tube station at Piccadilly Circus. A chilling headwind caught the lapels of my woollen coat and made them flap against my cheeks. Wide lapels were very much in vogue in the seventies, but to my mind you needed longer hair for wide lapels. As I was starting to go grey and receding slightly I preferred to wear my hair shorter. So I knew the coat wasn't quite right on me.

Still, as one of two master tailors in the alterations department of an exclusive gentlemen's outfitters, it would have been poor form not to try to maintain some semblance of style. And I could buy items from my employer at a reasonable discount. It was a staff perk, and there weren't many, so one felt obliged to take advantage.

I had a job adjusting and repairing suits for our well-to-do customers. We had a workshop down in the basement, directly below the ground floor of the store. The other staff often complained about how depressing it was, having to spend their working hours under flickering fluorescent tubes, with only a hint of daylight peaking through windows submerged below street level.

Earlier that day Dave, the other master tailor, had brought this up with me. He was generally a good sort, and I found his company pleasant enough. We worked quite closely so it was important to keep on friendly terms. Physically Dave and I were opposites. I was taller, darker, of average build and with a thick-set brow. He was shorter, paler, pot-bellied and with a full head of mousy brown hair.

Dave had asked if the lack of natural light ever got to me. I considered his question for a moment, before lifting my head and eyebrows as my way of indicating that I wasn't about to concern myself with matters I knew were beyond my control.

'But you of all people must miss the sunshine,' he pursued.

I shrugged. Dave gave me a look which I'd seen before. It was a mixture of sympathy and confusion.

'You're a strange one, Tony,' he declared, and I felt I had to smile. Dave smiled back before suggesting we meet for a drink that evening. I found myself accepting. After all, perhaps there'd be reason to celebrate.

Later that day, Mr Osborne, the alterations supervisor, had tapped me on the shoulder while I was hunched over a jacket and beckoned me into his office. As I followed Osborne, Dave looked up from his sewing machine and gave me that same look of sympathy and confusion. Sympathy because one was usually only summoned by our dour and demanding boss if one's work was below standard. Confusion because my skills as a tailor weren't really in question. Only the previous week Osborne himself had deigned to declare me the world's finest tailor after I had delicately repaired the fraying crotch of an agitated junior minister's favourite suit.

I couldn't help but feel a little apprehensive as Osborne pushed the door of his office shut behind us and invited me to sit down. I examined his grey eyes, looking for clues as to whether my request for a pay rise had been accepted.

It wasn't about the money. I managed to save enough. Unlike Dave, who was married with children, I lived alone in this country and had no dependants. Indeed, some years ago I'd made arrangements with the bank to send regular amounts back to the village. I avoided direct contact of course. I had to after all that had happened.

No, it wasn't about the money, although it had occurred to me recently that a little extra might enable me to find somewhere nicer to live. It was more a matter of principle. Recently, on a night out with Dave, he'd revealed that he was paid quite a bit more than I was. We were both in our late thirties, in the same job, with the same level of experience. I deserved to be on a comparable wage.

Osborne seemed self-conscious, and began to stroke the top of his bald head nervously. He spoke. 'Now, Tony. The directors and I have carefully considered your request.' Then he flushed and looked away. I was sure now what his answer would be. I shook my head.

He continued. 'I'm sorry. In view of the economic climate, we're not in a position to offer you an increase.' Then he added needlessly. 'At this time. You understand, don't you?'

I nodded. I understood only too well. Now was a bad time. The country had been experiencing weak government, soaring inflation, three-day working weeks, miners' strikes, energy shortages, even sugar shortages.

Osborne continued. 'Please don't get me wrong. We admire your abilities and certainly wouldn't want to lose you.'

I rubbed the bristles on my chin with the knuckles of my clenched fist. Then I turned conspicuously to look through the glass window of Osborne's office in the direction of Dave, still working at his Singer. Osborne grimaced.

'Come on,' he countered. 'It's not appropriate to discuss the remuneration of other staff. You know that.'

I nodded once more. I'd been around long enough to know what was and wasn't deemed appropriate. I folded my arms resolutely.

Osborne smiled. 'You're not going anywhere, Tony. I know you too well.'

My mouth smiled but my eyes couldn't. I got up and reached for the door handle.

'You don't know me at all,' I observed, before leaving Osborne's office and pulling the door shut behind me.

Now, as I and countless other commuters escaped the rain and biting London air, huddling together on the escalator leading down to the underground, I reflected once more on Dave's question about the gloomy basement where we worked. I breathed out a steamy sigh of resignation.

Far easier, I thought, to be numb to such an environment.

※ ※ ※

The Piccadilly Line train brought me to Turnpike Lane in north London. From here I would catch a bus up to Muswell Hill. But before doing so, I made a detour to the continental shop, a short walk from the station along Westbury Avenue. I wanted to buy a newspaper.

It had been a while since I'd been to a shop like this, a while since I'd bought this type of newspaper. By avoiding such contact I could avoid bad news from home. Hatred, violence, killings. I'd had my fill of those.

Once inside and out of the cold and rain, the once familiar sights, sounds and smells – of coriander and lemons, of olives and garlic, of aubergines and okra, of excessive hand movements and of needless shouting – seemed to calm me. Although I wasn't a regular customer, the shopkeeper smiled warmly in a gesture of recognition but resisted the temptation to open a conversation. He knew me to be a man of few words.

There was only one newspaper on sale here. I picked up a copy and went over to the counter to pay. In front of me was a large, middle-aged woman, filling her basket with a variety of delicacies, including, I noticed, some haluvas and some gubes. The woman appeared agitated and talked at the shopkeeper as he priced her goods and filled her shopping bag.

She spoke passionately, in a language I understood. Of bitterness and impending doom. Of dark forces. Of the young being brainwashed. Of how it was up to us to mobilise, to go back and resist the evil taking over our land. I listened with only half an ear, as I'd noticed some packets of ground coffee on the shelf near me. It was a coffee I'd not tasted for some time, and I decided to buy a packet along with my newspaper.

Her shopping now packed, the woman turned to me. 'What do you say, sir?'

I was unprepared for her question, and at first could do no more than offer a shrug. But her stare demanded an answer.

'What can be done?' I uttered eventually, a little self-consciously, in a language I now rarely spoke. I added after a moment that I felt it better not to concern myself with matters which I knew were beyond my control.

The woman closed one of her eyes slightly as though to examine me more closely. Now even here, in this shop, I felt a foreigner. I looked back at her meekly, and she eventually gave me a nod.

'Perhaps you're right,' she conceded with a sigh. But the woman had not yet done with me. 'Which village are you from?'

I could do no more than stare back into those probing brown eyes. They looked vaguely familiar. Like so many eyes I'd once known.

The shopkeeper intervened. 'You must understand, madam. The man prefers not to talk about the past.'

The woman looked at us both with disdain. 'The past was bad, sirs, but, mark my words, the days yet to come will be far worse. Your health!' she exclaimed dismissively before picking up her shopping and bustling out of the shop.

The shopkeeper gave me an embarrassed look, which I returned. I paid for my goods in silence.

✳ ✳ ✳

On the bus up to Muswell Hill I opened the community newspaper I'd bought and began to leaf through. I noticed that the outside pages were touching the window, causing condensation to soak into them, but I wasn't too concerned. They were full of news on the deteriorating situation of which the woman in the shop had spoken. Instead I searched for rag-trade recruitment ads. I was hoping to find a new position at one of the clothing factories in Kentish Town, Seven Sisters, Holloway or Harringay.

There were a number of possible options, and I felt better. I would make some calls and see where fate might take me. I was about to shut the newspaper when I noticed a familiar though older face staring back at me from the obituaries page. It was someone I'd known years ago. Vasos, owner of the village coffee-shop. A friend of my father. The best of men. I read that he had died of a heart attack. His funeral was next week, at the Orthodox church in Camden Town.

I took a series of short and ever-deeper breaths and had to close my eyes.

On arriving at my lodgings, a room in a large converted house off Muswell Hill Broadway, I immediately cut open the packet of coffee and breathed in its pungent, bitter-sweet aroma.

Before even taking off my coat and scarf or lighting my paraffin heater, I began rummaging under the sink until I had dug out what I was looking for: an old jisves, a small, long-handled metal pot, wide at the base, tapering in at the top. I also found a small cup and accompanying saucer. I filled the pot with water and stirred in two heaped teaspoons of the coffee. Now I searched through the cupboards, looking for a bag of sugar, but none presented itself. I sighed. Some preferred their coffee sweet, others medium. I would have to settle for plain. Sketos.

I heated the pot on the stove, waiting for a creamy froth to form. Slowly the froth rolled in from the sides and began to rise. I removed the pot from the heat and poured its dark brown contents into the cup. I sat in the solitary chair, before my manually operated Singer, and stared at my surroundings.

I looked down at the old machine itself. It doubled as my dining table and was just like the Singer I had in the old days. I looked over to the metal-framed bed with the over-soft mattress, covered by a grey blanket. The wardrobe whose doors wouldn't shut properly. The big old radio, with a wire coat hanger for an aerial, on top of a mahogany chest of drawers with handles that didn't match.

I'd lived in this room for years. But when I took my first sip of coffee, all at once I was transported to another place and time. Home.

3

The coffee-shop   *O gafenes*

The army jeep roared into the outskirts of the village, leaving a billowing cloud of red dust in its wake. A captain of the British army, perched on the passenger seat, looked at the charmingly threadbare one-storey houses and breathed in deeply. His nostrils filled with a potent mixture of rural smells: of burning wood and baking bread, of chickens and donkeys, of citrus fruit and rudimentary sanitation.

The journey to the village, from the army base in town, was always a treat for the captain. From the road, at certain points, one could catch a glimpse of the Mediterranean Sea in the distance. On a sunny winter's day like today the views were truly breathtaking.

God, how the captain loved this place.

This was the fifties, and the mixed village, with its Muslim and Christian neighbourhoods, wasn't the safest place for an excursion, but the captain had always thrived on living a little dangerously. Such visits enabled valuable reconnaissance work to be carried out. And besides, he enjoyed good relations with some of the locals.

The radio was tuned to a Greek station, and a song came on which the captain recognised. It had been introduced to him by his friend Vasos, owner of the village coffee-shop. Vasos had explained that the song repeated the line 'I love you' in several different languages, including English. The captain instructed his driver to turn up the volume, and the bemused driver did so. Now the captain began tapping his lap in time to the music and waited for an English 'I love you'. When it came the captain smiled.

Villagers, outside in the mild weather, observed the approaching vehicle. Motor cars of any description, let alone those carrying British soldiers, were still enough of a rarity in these parts to attract attention, especially ones blaring out Greek music.

The jeep had slowed down as it ventured further into the village to avoid the debris littering the roadside: rusty old ploughs, battered cans and piles of wood and bricks. Women, in colourful dresses and headscarves, interrupted their chores and waved. A few children had formed a line along the roadside and were saluting. The captain smiled and saluted back. He regretted not having any children of his own. Still, what could he expect? People always said he was married to the army.

The captain could see that his driver was pleasantly surprised by the warm welcome. Williams had only recently been posted to the island, now that the troubles had escalated, and was expecting the locals to be far less hospitable.

The captain rubbed his moustache. 'You've a lot to learn about this place, Williams,' he observed.

At that moment a boy on crutches, in his early teens, stumbled into the road a few yards ahead of the jeep. Still preoccupied by the saluting children, Williams didn't appear to have noticed the boy.

Williams was jolted into action by the captain, who grabbed his shoulder and yelled, 'Watch out, man!'

The jeep screeched to a halt just in front of the boy, who now stared back at the jeep and the red-haired soldiers in it, his eyes filled with horror. Then the boy lowered his head in shame and hobbled as quickly as he could across the road. The captain sighed with relief before instructing his driver to move on. A flustered Williams did so, having turned off the radio.

As the jeep ventured on through the village, beyond the Muslim neighbourhood, Williams could sense the atmosphere changing. He noticed that many of the whitewashed walls had been defaced with blue painted letters, repeating a single Greek slogan.

'Enosis, Williams,' explained the captain.

Williams had heard of this word. He knew it meant union with Greece. He knew that's why he and many other young soldiers had been shipped in. To prevent enosis.

As the jeep passed, three young children who had been playing by the roadside were swept up by a woman and pulled into a house. Two old men who had been playing backgammon in a front yard offered defiant stares. One cleared his throat conspicuously and spat loudly onto the dusty red earth.

The captain could see that Williams had become agitated. He put a reassuring hand on the driver's shoulder.

'Welcome to Cyprus,' declared the captain with a knowing smile.

Old man Haji-Markos was sitting on a chair under a big carob tree, wheezing quietly to himself. He was outside the village coffee-shop, a place now run by Vasos, his eldest son. With a hand-rolled cigarette in one hand to coat his lungs and lighten his head, worry beads in the other to count his blessings, this was how Haji-Markos whiled away most days.

He'd earned the prefix 'Haji' after making a pilgrimage to the Holy Land, that other troubled part of the world. A God-fearing man, Haji-Markos was disappointed that his son's convictions lay elsewhere, but he knew Vasos's heart remained in the right place. His son was a compassionate man. His son was a communist.

As always Haji-Markos was wearing his vraga, a pair of baggy old breeches which dangled over the edge of his seat. Once jet black, the breeches were now tinged a ruddy grey, like everything old in the village. Haji-Markos's younger grandchildren found his breeches a source of amusement, and would often tease him with a famous old song.

Haji-Markos smiled as he recounted the first verse.

O! With forty yards of cotton cloth, with forty yards of cotton cloth,
They made, they made, they made a pair of breeches.
O! The crotch it dangled very long, the crotch it dangled very long,
And swept, and swept, and swept the lower reaches.

Haji-Markos could not fathom why grown men these days were so willing, for the sake of fashion, for the sake of being more 'European', to suffocate their loins in these newfangled men's tights they called trousers. To Haji-Markos you weren't a real man unless you were a vragas, a man who wore his breeches with pride.

The old man smiled. He was as content as any old man of Cyprus could be. A lifetime of struggle was behind him. And, though the scars of battle were deeply etched on his face, each line and each wrinkle were testaments to his triumph. Haji-Markos could raise an open palm to life and signal an unequivocal, 'There! I conquered you.'

He had fed and sheltered his seven surviving children, and ensured that they had grown up and produced children of their own. Now he had earned the right to enjoy the autumn years of his existence, filling each day with the joys only grandchildren can bring. And, during the quiet hours, he could occupy himself with memories. Haji-Markos preferred to look back. The past was a country he understood and felt comfortable in. Not like the present.

The modern ways made no sense. As well as men's fashion, everything else was changing, and changes were happening more and more quickly. Changes that, to the old man's mind, were mostly for the worse.

Haji-Markos puffed on his cigarette.

Yes, life had always been a struggle. For Haji-Markos as for all the people of the village. But it had been an uncomplicated existence and, in the main, a happy one. Decisions were made for you. While you were expected to act like an adult from the moment you were old enough to contribute, you were treated like a child until both your parents were dead.

In the meantime they would match you with an appropriate girl from an appropriate family. Your father would pass on land, property and wisdom. Foolishness too. And God would bless you with children of your own, to continue the struggle.

And beyond the suffocating restrictions of family were the suffocating restrictions of the Englezi. And before them it had been the Ottoman Turks. And before them, Haji-Markos knew, it had been the Venetians. And before the Venetians it had been the Crusaders. Haji-Markos knew because when you ran a coffee-shop, you got to know things. All the world's knowledge. All the world's wrongs. And before the Crusaders it had been the Byzantines. And before them the Romans. And before them the Macedonians. And before them the Persians. And before them the Assyrians. And before them the Egyptians. And before them the Achaeans and the Mycenaeans, and also the Phoenicians.

It had always been so in Cyprus, jewel of the Mediterranean. All who came had left their mark, on the island and on the people.

Haji-Markos had been told by his father about the last years of Ottoman rule. Like the others before them, the Turks had exploited Cyprus in their time. Then, as now, the people had to find ways to get by as best they could. To endure.

As a way of avoiding persecution and the heavy tax burden imposed by the Ottomans, some of the peasant folk had felt obliged to declare themselves Muslim. Such people were referred to as Linobambaji, after a cloth woven with linen on one side and cotton on the other, to reflect the two sides of their faith and identity.

Haji-Markos pursed his lips and shook his head. He remembered a time when there wasn't a cigarette paper between Orthodox Christian and Muslim. They worked together, played together, sang and danced together, celebrated each other's weddings, mourned each other's deaths. And why not? They shared the same space, spoke the same vernacular. As did the other people of Cyprus. Maronites, Armenians and Latins. Cypriots all.

It was a time that passed.

How things had changed. Encouraged by the Englezi, the Muslims were opening their own schools, cutting themselves off, declaring themselves 'Turkish'. And why not? When the Orthodox Christian majority were declaring themselves 'Greek'.

Few Muslims now came to the coffee-shop.

Old man Haji-Markos took another long drag of his cigarette and prayed that he might be spared the sight of too many more changes. At that moment he heard the familiar sound of an approaching engine. The captain must be coming. Haji-Markos had made up his mind that, despite his white arse and earth-coloured hair, this Englezos was a decent sort. Always respectful, warm and good-humoured, he was more like a Cypriot. Vasos and the captain had become good friends, and though others in the village disapproved and threatened to boycott the communist's coffee-shop, the old man stood up to them.

'The captain's goodwill is a blessing and won't be rejected here,' he declared, with the confidence of a man who'd beaten life. 'And if you don't like it, you can always take your hatred elsewhere and drink at the coffee-shop of the Turk,' he added, knowing they wouldn't.

The army jeep rolled up outside the coffee-shop and a beaming captain, accompanied as always these days by a nervous escort, waved a friendly greeting. Haji-Markos put a cupped hand to his mouth and angled his head in the direction of the coffee-shop door. He screamed as loud as his smoke-ravaged lungs would allow.

'Vaso! The captain has come.'

The old man now raised himself from his chair, and his breeches flopped between his legs. He leant against his cane and offered a leathery hand. The captain was a tall, lanky man and had to stoop a little to reach it. The pair shook hands affectionately but, beyond the smiles, the 'hellos' and the 'how-are-yous', both knew further communication was impossible.

Haji-Markos could only gesture to the two soldiers to sit at a table of their choice before returning to his chair, to his tobacco and to his memories.

The soldiers sat opposite each other. Williams faced the square. His eyes darted first down the road, back towards the Muslim neighbourhood, then up the road, towards the church.

'A fine spot, wouldn't you say, Williams?' ventured the captain, seemingly oblivious to any threat of danger. Williams remained silent and felt for the revolver in the holster by his lap. The captain grimaced, aware of what Williams was doing.

'Don't think that'll save us,' advised the captain. Then he pointed up the road. 'See that flag, flying from the pole outside the church?'

Williams observed the blue and white cloth flapping in the light breeze with its nine stripes and a cross in the top left corner. 'The Greek flag, sir,' he nodded with feigned interest.

'That's right. Any idea what those nine stripes stand for?' enquired the captain.

Williams shrugged. He had no idea and didn't really care.

'Let's see if I can remember it,' continued the captain, closing an eye and staring skyward. 'E-lef-the-ri-a i tha-na-dos,' he declared finally, counting out each of the nine syllables on the fingers of both hands. 'Vasos, the coffee-shop owner, told me. It was the battle-cry of the Greeks during their war of independence against the Turks.'

Williams waited for the captain's inevitable translation. When it came the escort's unease increased.

'Liberty or death,' the captain announced with deliberate gravity.

The captain now turned his gaze sharply beyond Williams, towards the door of the coffee-shop, eager for Vasos to appear. His superior's sudden movement made Williams panic, and he launched himself from his chair, which toppled over. He turned clumsily and, as he did so, tugged at a seemingly stuck revolver which, after a slight struggle, came free. All Williams faced however was Haji-Markos, looking a little perplexed at having a gun pointed at him. Embarrassed, Williams turned back towards the captain, who was now glaring at him.

'Settle down, Williams! The old man's trying to sleep.'

Williams's face reddened. 'Please, sir, let's head back. It can't be safe for us here.'

'One has to be prepared to relinquish an element of safety, soldier, if one is to occupy a foreign land,' said the captain curtly. 'Put that gun away and sit down.'

Williams hesitated, so the captain explained that an order had just been given. Williams lifted the chair back up and followed orders. There was still no sign of Vasos.

'You know, there's another thing Vasos taught me,' continued the captain, in a more placatory tone. 'A local saying. "Don't bother the snake and it won't bite you." We could learn from that.' Williams shrugged. 'Where are you from, soldier?'

'Lancing, sir. A small seaside town in Sussex, near Worthing,' replied Williams proudly.

The captain raised his eyebrows. 'Really? I know Lancing well. It's not far from my home town. Hove. Peaceful places. Peaceful people,' he ventured, and Williams nodded. 'And the brass band plays Tiddly-um-pum-pum, eh?'

A calmer Williams nodded with a boyish grin. He was familiar with such scenes.

'Now, how would you feel if foreign invaders with guns were to come along and ruin it all?' the captain continued.

Williams was indignant. 'With respect, sir, we're in Cyprus, not Sussex. This place is full of terrorists,' he observed.

The captain laughed dryly. 'The only terrorist I see is you. Ah, here he comes at last!'

The aproned coffee-shop owner had emerged from his shop with a broad smile. Vasos was a huge round man with a thick curled moustache. Unlike many middle-aged locals, he still had a generous mop of dark hair on his head.

'Captain! I am so happy to see you. I think maybe you forget us,' he enthused.

The captain rose from his seat. Two hands clasped each other firmly, one red and bare, the other olive and covered in black hairs down to the fingers. The two men shook hands, like Englezi. Then the two men embraced, like Cypriots.

'Forget? How could I forget your fabulous coffee, Vasos?' hinted the captain with a wink, before retaking his seat. 'A coffee I've been anticipating for quite some time now,' he added with a smile, pointing to his watch.

Vasos smiled back, squeezing the captain's shoulder affectionately, 'I make you one now. Extra special, extra sweet for the captain,' he assured before turning to Williams. 'You like one too, sir?'

Williams glanced at the captain for approval to refuse. The captain shrugged.

'Er, just a glass of water for me thanks,' requested Williams. Then he turned to the captain. 'No offence, sir, but I'm told that stuff's poisonous and tastes like mud.'

'Mud?' boomed Vasos as though mortally offended. 'Poisonous?' he added incredulously, clenching a fist and shaking it at Williams.

Williams shifted uncomfortably in his seat, but Vasos's frown disappeared. Now he laughed heartily, slapping the bemused soldier on the back.

'Poisoning customers is not good for business, sir,' he explained before disappearing inside the coffee-shop, muttering under his breath in a language foreign to Williams, 'although some deserve to be poisoned.'

Not long afterwards Vasos returned with two small cups of coffee in their saucers and three tall glasses of water. He sat down with the soldiers, opposite the captain.

'Your health,' declared Vasos, offering a coffee to the captain, who enthusiastically accepted. He breathed in the strong aroma before taking a noisy slurp, the way he'd observed Vasos do. Vasos too slurped expertly, but more loudly. Williams took a few gulps of water from his glass.

'Wonderful as ever, Vasos,' declared the captain, licking his lips. 'And worth the wait.'

The two friends slurped some more. Williams shook his head.

The captain eventually spoke. 'I do hope my visit won't cause problems for you, Vasos.'

'Problems? No. This is a peaceful village, captain. Never problems here. We all get on just fine. Greeks, Turks, Lefts, Rights,' lied Vasos.

'And the British?' pursued the captain. 'Aren't we just foreigners that have outstayed our welcome?'

'No such word as foreigner in our language, captain. Only guest. Xenos. And, so long as people behave with honour, they are always our guests.'

The captain nodded, then his eyes briefly met those of Williams.

'And if people don't behave with honour?' asked the captain, addressing the coffee-shop owner.

Vasos reflected for a while before answering. 'We have another word. Varvaros.' He gave a wry smile. 'And barbarians usually get what barbarians deserve, I think.'

The captain nodded. Williams frowned.

'Things are getting trickier, Vasos. I'm not sure when I'll be able to visit again,' explained the captain with genuine regret.

Vasos shook a finger at the captain. 'But you must come tonight, captain. I personally invite you to our village festival. There is singing and dancing, eating and drinking. We have plenty good times.'

The captain looked unsure.

'But you must come,' insisted Vasos. 'As my guest, captain. My guest of *honour!*'

The captain turned to his escort. 'Can I refuse such an invitation, Williams? When we should be doing all we can to improve relations with the locals?'

Williams shrugged.

Vasos grabbed the captain's hand. 'Of course, it's much better you come out of uniform,' Vasos advised. The captain nodded.

'And another of course,' added the coffee-shop owner, now turning his eyes towards Williams, 'you be much, much safer without a bodyguard.'

Mihalis sat at the big table in the courtyard behind his house. It was a mild evening for the time of year, and he was enjoying the last hour of daylight. He wouldn't be marvelling at the deep red sun setting in a cloudless sky over the village roof-tops, however, because it did so regularly.

Although middle-aged and with a lined face, Mihalis was still a fine figure of a man. How could he not be when he toiled for hours and days and years in the fields? His muscular frame filled his chair completely and his huge dark brown moustache made him look distinguished as well as strong. The sleeves of his white shirt were rolled up to reveal solid hairy forearms. He had lit himself a hand-rolled cigarette and was drawing on it before blowing clouds of smoke into the still air. The sound of violins, singing, laughing and whistling could now be heard in the distance. The festival had begun.

Mihalis grimaced. He knew his wife Irini would try and persuade him to take a stroll with her later, around the village square. After all, it had been their elder son Andonis who had retrieved the cross from the sea earlier that day. Mihalis hadn't gone along for that, and knew he wouldn't be attending the festival either. He wasn't in the right frame of mind to participate in such social occasions. He would instruct their younger son, Marios, to accompany Irini.

Mihalis knew tonight's celebrations couldn't disguise the tense atmosphere that had descended over the village in recent times. The radio, the newspapers, word from the town, talk in his friend Vasos's coffee-shop, as well as the increasingly intolerant attitude of the Englezi, were hardening people's hearts. So Mihalis now sought to avoid situations where confrontation might arise. He knew it could mean trouble for himself, his wife and two sons, and the extended family that he had vowed to protect. He knew he couldn't stop

25

himself from questioning the views of some, and from making his own feelings known.

So, recently, though he missed the debates, Mihalis had taken to spending evenings at home, with Irini, Marios and the ever-present widow Xenu, wife of his late best friend. Mihalis accepted the responsibility he had for Xenu and her family. The widow had two sons, Yannis, who Mihalis had baptised, and Nigos. And also a daughter, Stella.

There sat the widow, opposite Mihalis. A small hunched woman, dressed, as custom dictated, totally in black. She was working on some embroidery. Marios, a more delicate version of his elder brother, was at the table too. He was mulling over a tattered old Bible, lent to him by the village priest. As a child, Marios had suffered serious illness, from which his body had recovered. But not his soul.

The winter festival was a time for looking forward to the year ahead, and so Mihalis was playing dihi, a Cypriot form of patience. Mihalis against the cards. It was a challenge he now preferred to backgammon in the coffee-shop against a fellow villager.

Before each game Mihalis would set a question for the cards. Will the crops be fruitful? Will my sons marry and live happily? Will I grow to an old age? Will harmony return to the village? Will Cyprus be free?

He had just finished another game, just received another disappointing answer. He tutted, lifted his head skyward and then took another frustrated drag at his cigarette.

The widow sighed supportively. 'No luck again, Mihali?'

'None, Xenu,' replied Mihalis, stroking the top of his head. In his younger days it had been covered by thick dark brown hair. Now only a few greying strands remained. Mihalis's balding head comforted him. It was a reminder that the future would soon be in the hands of another generation. It was a future to which they were welcome.

Mihalis shuffled the cards for another run, but once again dihi seemed to be against him, and he huffed. Marios glanced with sympathy at his father.

'We must put our faith in God, baba. Not cards,' he offered, pointing at the Bible in his hand.

'May the cats fart on you!' scoffed Mihalis, shuffling the deck for yet another game. 'Let me tell you something, Mario. You won't ever find a wife in that book. You should be out having fun with the other youths of the village, not sitting here with us old ones, washing your brain with ancient stories.'

But there was no malice in Mihalis's voice. He knew his younger son was too thoughtful, too pure of heart to be out having what others called fun.

Now Irini arrived with a tray filled with chunks of juicy honeydew melon and slices of tasty hallumin. Mihalis admired his wife. She was still shapely and comparatively well preserved for a woman of her age. Perhaps it was due to Irini only carrying three children. After Andonis and Marios, she'd had a third son, who had died after only a few months. Irini had always wanted more children, but somehow it had never happened. Mihalis was secretly relieved that they had managed to avoid bringing another mouth into the world, especially in view of the responsibility he had assumed for Xenu and her family.

Irini placed the tray on the table and sat down herself. Mihalis observed Marios, Irini and Xenu make their crosses before all four helped themselves to the morsels of food. Mihalis chomped into a slice of honeydew melon. It was cool, fresh and sweet. He nibbled at the hallumin. Salty, dry and hard. The contrasting flavours and textures complemented each other perfectly.

'I'm worried about my Nigos,' declared the widow between mouthfuls. 'His brain's taken wind. That cousin of his, Bambos, is a bad influence. I wish he and his friends would keep away. Stay in their own village.'

Irini rolled her eyes skyward. She had so often endured such moaning.

'Your younger son's a wild one,' agreed Mihalis, not looking up from his new game. The cards, for once, were performing well. 'Just like his father was, God rest his soul.'

'That's what worries me,' sighed the widow. She put her hand to her cheek and rocked her head slowly, recalling her husband's early death. The others round the table shared her thoughts, and for a moment there was silence.

'Compare Nigos with his brother Yannis,' continued the widow. 'Such a good son. Hard-working in the fields left by his father. But Nigos? He hardly lifts a finger to help. It'll take gods and demons to put him on the straight road.'

'Nigos isn't so bad,' countered Mihalis. 'He has a lot of spirit. Unlike Marios here, who's too timid to face the world.'

Marios looked up from his Bible and smiled at his father. 'I must have taken after you then, baba!' he said.

'Leave Marios alone,' insisted Irini, reaching across to her son and pulling affectionately at his cheek. 'Each child brings its own fortune, Mihali. We should accept that and love each of them for what they are.'

Marios nodded and smiled knowingly. 'And not impose your will on us,' he added, addressing both the widow and his father.

Irini turned to Xenu. 'Nigos is still young, Xenu. Slowly his mind will set. You put him, and yourself, under too much pressure. Now that Yannis is betrothed everything's fine for him. He's devoted to Martha. Nigos will settle down too when the time's right.'

The widow sighed deeply. 'Perhaps that's true, Irini,' she agreed, helping herself to another slice of hallumin. 'But I can't help but worry about my children. My Stella's another one. She's growing into a woman and bringing me a thousand and thirty troubles. I try and teach her the trade of a seamstress, but she's got no patience. All she wants is to have a good time. She really lacks a father's influence. I've got to find her a husband, and soon.'

Marios looked up again. If anyone could stand in the way of him devoting his life totally to God it was the widow's daughter. But Marios knew they had other plans for Stella.

'Stella's also far too young, Xenu,' cautioned Irini, sensing what might be coming next. 'There's plenty of time before she's ripe enough to make someone a good wife.'

'But who'll want her?' beseeched the widow. 'Stella and those friends of hers. They're so, what can I tell you? Girls are changing so much these days. It's for weeping. We've got to act soon, or who knows what might befall us? We need to talk seriously, Mihali. Andonis is becoming a fine tailor. It's time he had a woman's love.'

With his eyes still on the cards, Mihalis lifted a finger.

'Don't force it, Xenu. These things must be allowed to happen naturally,' he warned, before laying down more cards. 'Andonis will make it clear when he's ready.'

'But he's such a handsome young man,' persisted the widow. Her face displayed grave concern. 'I'm just scared that his eyes might stray. That another might tempt him. Do you think eventually he'll see sense and realise what's best for him?'

For the first time this evening Mihalis was able to put all his cards on the table. He took a triumphant drag at his cigarette, raised his head and smiled at the widow.

'I'm sure of it,' he declared.

4
The pub   *I biraria*

I sipped every last drop of coffee from the cup. Now all that remained was the dark brown sediment at the bottom. For a moment I thought to turn the cup over into its saucer, as once Vasos's wife would have done, to examine the patterns for some glimpse of what was to come. I smiled as I recalled Mrs Anjela's superstitious ways. Then I imagined her grief, and my smile disappeared. What use was knowing the future?

After an instant meal of Supernoodles I put on my coat and scarf again and took off down Muswell Hill. It was still raining. I leant into a sweeping wind. I tended not to go out much in the evenings, especially when the weather was like this. I'd got into the habit of staying in and listening to the radio until sleep. Music, sport, drama, the shipping forecast. Anything to keep my mind from straying.

But earlier I'd accepted Dave's invitation to go out for a drink. He lived not far away in Crouch End, so it was easy enough for us to meet up. I was happy to oblige him every now and then. I knew how much he appreciated the opportunity to escape the demands of his wife for a few hours.

Dave was already in the pub when I arrived, sitting at a table near the juke-box. His cheeks were rosy, and there was a half-drunk pint of beer before him. Others were in the pub, mostly middle-aged locals, many of whom I vaguely recognised. They appeared vaguely to return the compliment.

'Who loves ya, baby?' Dave said by way of greeting.

Dave was quick to gulp down his remaining beer before handing me his glass for a refill. I went to the bar to order another pint of warm bitter for him and half a pint of cold lager for me. Getting served took a while, and I was reminded of Vasos's coffee-shop.

After I'd sat down opposite Dave, I took out my rolling tobacco. Dave frowned and offered me a cigarette from his packet. 'Have one your mate Mr Marlboro prepared earlier. Made from pure tobacco. No funny Jamaican stuff.'

I lifted my head and eyebrows to indicate refusal.

'I prefer mine tailor-made,' I declared wryly, and Dave laughed louder than my comment warranted. I sensed one or two disapproving glances from around the pub as I lit my do-it-yourself cigarette and took a deep drag. Dave drank his beer.

'Dave, there's something you ought to know,' I announced with gravity, which made him put his glass down. His expectant look gave way to one of surprise when I added, 'I'm quitting.'

'Why? What's happened?'

'I asked for a pay rise. I was refused,' I explained, before taking another drag of my cigarette. I could tell from Dave's expression that he wanted more details, but I didn't feel there was anything further to add.

Dave shook his head. 'But you can't go, Tony. We're such good partners. Me and the Bubble.'

'But we're not equal partners. You and the Bubble.'

Dave seemed genuinely saddened, and I in turn was touched.

'Will you tell Osborne I won't be coming in?'

Dave nodded, and said he understood, before adding that it really was a great shame. We sat in silence for a few moments, drinking and smoking. It was Dave who spoke next.

'Tony, I hope you don't mind, but someone might be joining us later.' He looked sheepish. I frowned and found myself remembering an old saying, about one woman being owed you by God. A foolish saying.

'Oh Dave,' I groaned.

Dave was unperturbed, 'Come on, mate. You could do with cheering up. She's a cousin of mine. Lovely girl. Lives nearby.'

I took a long and troubled drag of my cigarette. Such a trick could never have been played at the coffee-shop. That was strictly a male domain.

'I thought it would be nice for Ruth to get out a bit,' he added. 'Meet new people. She lost her husband a while back, and what with her daughter growing up and doing her own thing, she gets a bit lonely. You know how it is.'

I nodded. Now I felt as Dave was intending me to feel. Guilty.

'I'm sorry, Dave. I'm sure your cousin's a nice person. But you know I'm not interested in all that,' I pointed out, before nervously taking another sip of my lager.

We sat in silence again while I was lost in my thoughts and Dave seemed to be gathering his. Finally, he gave me his look of sympathy and confusion.

'Tony. I've been meaning to ask you this for a while, and I want you to be completely honest with me,' he ventured.

Now he paused, looking for any clues my eyes might reveal. All at once I understood what he was driving at. I shook my head with amusement.

'You may think I'm strange, coo-chi-coo. But don't worry, I'm not that way inclined.' Dave's cheeks grew rosier, and I couldn't help but smile.

❋　❋　❋

When Ruth arrived it was I who spotted her first. It had to be her, unaccompanied at the door, shaking an umbrella. An elegant, not unattractive woman with flowing chestnut hair, looking round in search of a familiar face. She was wearing a distinctive long brown coat with furry cuffs and lapels. I hoped it was Ruth.

Dave noticed I was observing someone and glanced in her direction. He smiled in recognition.

'Ruth!' he called, and I felt my heart beat a little faster as she waved back with a warm smile, making her way over to us across the now busy pub. Dave stretched out a leg to pull an empty stool towards the table.

'This is my mate *Tony*,' he announced, unconsciously adopting a fake foreign accent to pronounce my name, which embarrassed me. 'He's unattached,' he added, which embarrassed me further.

Ruth appeared surprised by my presence, though not unpleasantly so. She tucked her wind-swept hair behind an ear to reveal intriguing grey-green eyes, which now levelled with mine. I felt butterflies in my stomach. I felt uncomfortable.

'I'm pleased to meet you,' I found myself saying, in my best English, getting up from my stool and offering Ruth my hand. I noted how soft and pale her hand was. A little cold too.

'Likewise,' replied Ruth. She released her grip to take off her coat, revealing a well-proportioned figure in a pale blue blouse.

We exchanged knowing smiles as we sat down.

'I'll get the drinks in,' offered Dave, brushing aside my plea to do so and getting up. I turned to Ruth and shrugged helplessly. She laughed, shook her head at the departing Dave, and came to the rescue.

'Goodness, what a day. Those kids really take it out of you,' she complained, and noticed my puzzled expression. 'Didn't Dave tell you? I work in a youth club some evenings. At the Muswell Hill Centre. Do you know it?'

I nodded. The Muswell Hill Centre was only a few minutes' walk away from where I lived, tucked away behind the shops on the other side of the Broadway. I often wondered what happened down there.

'You teach?' I enquired.

'Music,' she replied, and my interest was further aroused. 'I'm trying to set up this performing youth group. But the teenagers can be a real handful sometimes. Don't you have any children?' she enquired.

I was troubled by her question. To make matters worse, my mischievous colleague had gone over to the juke-box and selected a popular soul ballad. The lyrics entreated me to feel brand new, but now all of a sudden I felt old. I shook a lowered head.

Ruth continued, 'I've got a daughter. She's in the sixth form and getting on with her own life. The work at the club helps keep me busy.' Then she added with a suggestive smile, 'And young!'

I smiled back and nodded.

'And it's more rewarding than working in the music shop. I do that during the day. To make ends meet. Still, enough about me. What about Dave's mate *Tony*?'

I looked at her without answering. I didn't feel there was anything worthwhile to say.

'Where are you from?' she pressed.

'Camden Town, at first. But now I live up in Muswell Hill,' I replied, aware that this was not the answer she was looking for.

Ruth laughed. 'No, silly. Where originally? I mean, you're not English are you?'

I found myself rubbing the bristles on my chin self-consciously. I wished I'd made the effort to shave before coming out.

'Oh dear. I should have warned you, Ruth,' interjected Dave, overhearing her as he returned from the bar with a round of drinks. 'He doesn't like to talk about that.'

Ruth accepted her glass of gin and tonic and took a sip. 'I'm not after Tony's life story, Dave. I just wanted to place him. Spanish? Italian? How about Greek? There's quite a few living round here now.'

'Careful, Ruth,' warned Dave, wagging a finger at his cousin. 'He's touchy about people calling him Greek.'

'Turkish then,' Ruth suggested. Dave winced.

'OK, I wish I hadn't asked,' she said with resignation. All three of us sipped our drinks in an awkward silence. I knew I had to be the one to break it.

'I'm Cypriot,' I said, and then felt obliged to add, 'I was born in a village in Cyprus. I came to England when I was a young man. I've not been back.'

'I see,' she ventured, in a way which suggested she didn't really see at all. How could she see? She looked at me expectantly.

'I'm sorry, Ruth. There's nothing more to say.'

Ruth now looked at me with compassion.

'I'm the one who should apologise,' she corrected. 'Where you're heading's more important than where you're from. It's what I tell the kids.'

I gave Ruth an approving smile.

'You should smile more, Tony. It lights up your face,' she suggested and I felt myself blush. The butterflies were returning.

I wanted to know more about Ruth's work and she seemed delighted to tell me.

'They come from so many different backgrounds. English, Irish, Caribbean, Indian. One or two Greek kids too, I think,' she enthused proudly, 'Or do I mean Cypriot?'

'It can't be easy, trying to control so many different teenagers,' I noted.

'It's not about control, Tony. It's about showing them the right way. You just need to be on their level. Use their language.'

I rolled out my lower lip and nodded.

She made a point of inviting me to the Muswell Hill Centre one evening, and I found myself accepting. We arranged a time. Dave thought this amusing.

'I should warn you, Ruth, Tony doesn't like to go out much, so don't be surprised if he doesn't show,' he told her, giving me a wink.

'Now why would Tony do that? Surely he's not the sort of bloke to let a woman down,' she suggested, addressing me more than her cousin.

✳ ✳ ✳

In bed that night I reflected on what had turned out to be an eventful day. It had been a long time since I'd experienced so many different emotions. Frustration for not getting the pay rise I'd asked for. Unease at the talk of my troubled homeland. Sadness at the news of Vasos's death. Determination to pay my respects at his funeral. Empathy, perhaps even attraction, towards Ruth.

I added surprise to the list. In myself, that I was still able to have such feelings.

Thoughts of Ruth remained with me as I approached sleep. That night I dreamt of a girl I once knew.

5

The festival · *Do banairin*

Erden had settled comfortably in his favourite spot. He was propped against an old, old olive tree at the top of a hill. A baby goat, hardy and lean, was sprawled on his lap, sleeping peacefully. Breathing in and out, the goat generated a soothing warmth to go with its reassuring heartbeat. The rest of Erden's flock were around their goatherd chomping at shrubs and wild grass, bleating their apparent contentment. Goats were such dependable creatures, thought Erden, so unconditionally devoted. He drew strength from that devotion. Humans, by contrast, were selfish and unreliable.

From this high vantage point Erden had a panoramic view of the whole village, stretched out before him, less than half a mile away. It was a familiar site. Home. To the left, Erden could make out the bell tower of the church of Saint Varnavas the Apostle; to the right, the minaret of the small village mosque. And, dotted around them, the whitewashed houses belonging to devoted followers of either religion, as well as the more numerous not-so-devoted followers. From Erden's point of view all the houses looked the same. It was only when you got closer that you sensed things weren't as they should be. Erden didn't like getting too close. It was safer and more peaceful up here against the olive tree.

However, on this particular day, as the light began to fade, the developing differences in the village appeared to have been set aside. A concoction of lively sounds carried through the evening air and up to Erden's appreciative ear. Below, on the main road into the village, the goatherd could see people from other villages approaching. The festival had begun, and all were coming to share in the harmony. All except Erden.

Erden leant back, until his head rested against the bark of the olive tree. He recalled that some time ago he'd used his knife to carve two names into it, his own and that of a local girl. A rare beauty, now in full bloom. She was slender, with a rich complexion, straight brown hair and striking green eyes. How Erden longed for her. He glanced down and could still make out the now fading letters of her name.

F-U-N-D-A.

Some years ago Erden had rescued her younger brother Zeki after the boy had fallen from a tree. If it hadn't been for Erden carrying him to the village's Christian doctor the boy might have died. In the event, Zeki's leg had been damaged beyond repair. But at least Zeki had lived, and for that people had Erden to thank. Funda had Erden to thank. And she did so by always showing kindness to the goatherd. More kindness than some of the others showed.

Erden smiled. How wonderful Funda was. How she enjoyed getting attention. No doubt she'd be singing tonight. She was a born performer with the voice of an angel. Erden knew some of the bolder boys of the village were now showing a keen interest. And it wasn't just the Muslims who were attracted to her. How could a poor, simple goatherd compete? Some of these young men had well-paid jobs, in administration, in construction, in the auxiliary police. It was surely only a matter of time before one lucky young man's family would make Funda's father the right proposition, only a matter of time before Erden's heart would be broken for good.

✳ ✳ ✳

Andonis returned from inside the now crowded coffee-shop with a tray containing two small cups of thick coffee and two tall glasses of water. He saw that Nigos had sat at a table near the door with a backgammon set in front of him. Andonis frowned and gestured to his friend to join him at another free table with a clear view of the square, the focus of this evening's festivities. Nigos raised his hands to indicate his reluctance to move; but after a moment he went over and sat opposite Andonis, bringing with him the backgammon set, and sighing deeply. Andonis sat facing the square, now thronging with people. The usual sellers were offering the people a variety of delicacies. Shamishin, melomagarona and sticks of sujukos.

Small crowds had gathered around numerous performers. Two older men squared up for a traditional chatisman, a battle of wits through poetry and music. Each clever riposte was greeted with hoots and laughter from the audience, which Andonis noticed included Nigos's brother Yannis and his betrothed Martha, though in truth the pair appeared more interested in each other than in the chatisman. Yannis looked for any excuse to touch Martha: to wipe a blemish from her cheek, to remove a loose thread from her blouse. She was happy to oblige him.

A group of younger men performed acrobatic dances to whistles and clapping from a different audience, which Andonis noticed included Nigos's sister Stella. She was with her friends, and they were clicking their fingers and taking up provocative poses. Stella was a petite, pretty girl, with long dark hair and a distinctive mole on her cheek which always drew Andonis's eyes.

35

Andonis was aware that Stella had an admirer, a largish boy called Lugas from a neighbouring village. Lugas was innocently flirting with her this evening. Andonis was happy for Stella, though he knew, in truth, she would rather have been flirting with him.

At the far side of the square a Garagiozis show was under way, delighting a crowd of children.

People who passed by the coffee-shop acknowledged young Andonis, the tailor, as the man who'd retrieved the cross from the sea earlier that day. As was customary, they congratulated him and wished him long life. With a proud smile the tailor thanked them, shaking hands and revelling in his moment of glory. He noticed, however, that Nigos was becoming increasingly irritated.

After the pair had finally been left alone, Nigos took out some tobacco and started rolling himself a cigarette. He offered the tobacco and papers to Andonis, who declined. Nigos huffed and ran a hand through his unruly black hair.

'What's wrong, Nigo?' asked Andonis, looking at his friend with concern. Nigos's frown didn't suit his chiselled features.

'Nothing,' lied Nigos, lighting his cigarette and blowing smoke into the tailor's face.

'Yes, I know your "nothing". Those hunched shoulders, the knotted brow, the invisible lower lip. Why is "nothing" having this effect on you?' asked Andonis affectionately. Today the tailor could solve any problem.

'I just don't think it's right, Andoni,' Nigos explained, gesturing to the crowds in the square. 'People singing and dancing and laughing. Not the way things are.'

'Would you rather they cried instead of laughed?'

'Until we're free, what's there to laugh about?'

Andonis smiled mischievously. 'Let's rejoice, Nigo. For isn't today the day the Lord was baptised in the River Jordan?'

Nigos scoffed. 'Since when did you believe in all that nonsense the priest chants?'

'It makes my mamma and my brother happy. And look at all the people, Nigo. It makes them happy. Why can't we be happy too?'

'You don't have to live with what I have to live with.'

Andonis sighed. 'Come on. Let it go a while. Let yourself go a while,' he urged, tapping his friend fondly on the shoulder. Nigos looked at Andonis, and though Nigos's mouth gave way to a smile, his frown remained.

'You're just jealous that your friend's the brave hero tonight,' teased Andonis.

'Brave enough to take me on at tavlin, then?' challenged Nigos, opening up the backgammon set.

Andonis indicated his reluctance to play by raising his eyebrows and lifting his chin. Nigos could not disguise his disappointment, but his friend ignored it. Andonis was too preoccupied with the scene in the square, and in particular with the young Muslim woman who had just arrived, accompanied by a boy hobbling on a pair of wooden crutches.

The girl wore a long red skirt down to her ankles and a white, long-sleeved blouse. She had full red lips and straight brown hair mostly hidden by a white headscarf. Andonis's heart pumped. She had been there at the shore earlier that day when he'd dived into the sea. She had been there afterwards to kiss him on either cheek and to wish him a long life. In better times his father used to get his beard shaved and his hair cut at her father's barber's shop. In better times his father and hers had been friends.

The girl's voice was famous in the village. She was always at such public gatherings, singing to raise extra money for her family so that they might secure a better future for her crippled brother.

The girl bent down and laid a small wooden box on the ground before her. Then, without fear or embarrassment, she broke into song, accompanied after a moment by the boy, who blew inexpertly into a harmonica with the broadest of smiles. The exquisite voice of the sister more than compensated for the musical clumsiness of the brother and soon a large audience had gathered. The pair were performing a traditional folk song, popular at weddings, to the delight of the people, the majority of whom clapped along, reminded of better times.

My sweet and slender basil, my marjoram so fair,
You're the one who'll cause me to leave my mother's care.

Andonis was entranced. The song was one his late paternal grandmother Maria always used to sing, in the sweet Cypriot vernacular, adopted as her own. A song which, so the story went, Andonis's grandfather had used to win Maria's heart and bring her to the island.

'What are you looking at, Andoni?' sneered Nigos, turning his head to observe the performance. Then he glanced back at his friend and shook his head. Nigos took a long and loud slurp of his coffee, which annoyed Andonis.

'Be quiet, Nigo. I'm listening,' implored Andonis, not taking his eyes off the performance. 'Doesn't she sing beautifully?'

'What?' cried Nigos with disdain. Nigos raised a hand and clicked his fingers in front of his friend's face. 'Are you all right, man? Wake up! Leave the Turkish girl to beg, and let's play tavlin.'

Andonis pushed his friend's hand aside to clear his view. The girl had now finished her song and people were dropping coins into the box. She took her brother's hand and directed applause towards him. The pair smiled and bowed.

'Better shoes from home, even if they're tattered,' observed Nigos, quoting an old proverb.

'She *is* from home!' declared the tailor.

Nigos shook his head. Both young men continued to observe the girl.

'Look at those eyes, look at those lips,' said Andonis. 'Tell me she's not the most beautiful girl in the whole village.'

'For goodness sake, Andoni. Stop playing games,' cautioned Nigos. 'Some people might not appreciate them.'

Nigos was unsure whether he was more concerned about people or his own sister, Stella. He dragged at his cigarette self-consciously.

Andonis picked up his cup, slurped down the remaining coffee, and gave a satisfied gasp before wiping his lips with the back of his hand. Then he looked at Nigos, and his eyes narrowed. Nigos looked hurt when Andonis rose from his chair.

'What about our game of tavlin?' Nigos enquired.

'I'm through playing games,' announced Andonis, though as much to himself as to his friend.

He picked up his glass of water, took a gulp from it, then made his way over to where the Muslim girl was now preparing to entertain the crowd with another song. The people gathered there acknowledged the fine young man who'd retrieved the cross from the sea with nods and smiles and pats on the back.

Andonis's eyes met those of the Muslim girl for a brief moment, and he smiled his glowing smile. She couldn't help but offer a hint of a smile in return. True, the girl smiled at everyone. The more Funda smiled, the more coins for the box. But Andonis felt he knew this smile. It seemed to be reserved for him.

Andonis nudged Funda's brother and pointed to the instrument in the boy's hands. The boy understood and handed over the harmonica. Andonis nodded his thanks, ruffled the boy's hair with affection, and placed the harmonica to his lips.

Funda had begun singing the famous breeches song, and Andonis now accompanied her. He played expertly, and the people began to clap in time to the music with even more enthusiasm than before. Funda looked at Andonis while she sang and gave him a nod of approval. Andonis nodded back.

O! With forty yards of cotton cloth, with forty yards of cotton cloth,
They made, they made, they made a pair of breeches.
O! The crotch it dangled very long, the crotch it dangled very long,
And swept, and swept, and swept the lower reaches.

Now playing with only one hand, Andonis contorted himself so that he could roll his trousers up to his knees with the other hand. Then he loosened his belt, pulling his shirt out and allowing his trousers to drop so they appeared baggy around the crotch – like a pair of breeches. Andonis was now dancing round and round as he played. And as he did so his trousers fell further for an amused and delighted crowd. People were whistling their approval.

The poor old pair of breeches, which sweep the lower reaches.
And who will take them for you, down to the lake to wash them?
And who is going to lay them to dry out in the hot sun?
And where's the able woman who'll iron out the creases?
And who will fold them for you, your long and dangly breeches?

Andonis looked over towards the coffee-shop and waved to his sulking friend. Nigos shook his head in disbelief.

O! Instead of marrying a man, instead of marrying a man
Who is, who is, who is in trousers striding.
O! Prefer to wed a breeches man, prefer to wed a breeches man,
Though he, though he, though he can't earn a farthing.

Funda and Andonis had finished their performance to applause, cheers and bravos. Andonis grabbed Funda's hand and offered her to the audience.

She took her bow before offering Andonis in turn. More and more coins were being thrown into the box and onto the ground.

The tailor fumbled inside his pockets looking for coins of his own, but all he could find was a brass thimble, one given to him by his late grandmother Maria. He pulled it out and looked at it a moment before presenting it to the Muslim girl. Funda blushed and looked across to her brother for approval. The crippled boy smiled, and so she accepted the tailor's offering.

'Thank you, sir,' she said graciously.

'The best a humble tailor can offer, I'm afraid,' he replied.

'What wind has blown to bring you here?' she whispered coyly, as if to herself as much as to Andonis.

'The one that led to you,' replied the tailor with a smile which made Funda go weak. She looked at Andonis with warmth and a hint of trepidation.

Meanwhile the crowd was beginning to disperse. Not quite all the people had approved of Andonis's antics. Andonis had noted that one man in particular, a powerful man of the village, had tutted loudly. And Stella had not been impressed either. Nor of course had Nigos.

Funda's attention was diverted by a gasp from her brother. The boy was looking up at a tall and lanky red-haired figure who had just thrown a ten-shilling note into the box. Funda rushed over to her brother and smothered him in a hug. Then she gave the man a polite smile of gratitude before crouching to collect the large number of coins which had missed the box. Her brother joined her.

Andonis looked at the man. He was clearly an Englezos, in his forties and with a bushy moustache not unlike that of Andonis's father – except this one was the colour of earth. Then Andonis recognised the man. He'd seen him once or twice, at Mr Vasos's coffee-shop, in a soldier's uniform.

'You're too generous, sir,' Andonis observed, addressing the Englezos in perfect English and with perfect English irony. The man raised a pair of earth-coloured eyebrows in surprise.

'Your English is most impressive,' he acknowledged in a manner which Andonis recognised as innocently patronising. The Englezos's steel blue eyes pierced Andonis's.

'Better, I expect, than your command of my language,' replied Andonis proudly. 'I was good at school, sir.'

The Englezos nodded.

'I must tell you how much I enjoyed your performance. You and the Turkish girl work well together. It's nice to see,' he declared.

'Our people have worked well together for a long time, sir. It's only when outsiders come and…' Andonis checked himself. How could an Englezos even begin to understand?

'Well I, at least, am one outsider who appreciates the harmony I've witnessed this evening,' continued the Englezos, maintaining his dignified manner.

Andonis felt ashamed, and lowered his head. 'Thank you, sir,' he found himself saying apologetically, almost deferentially.

The Englezos nodded and disappeared into the crowd.

✳ ✳ ✳

Ghlioris poured water from a large metal jar into the bowl on the chest of drawers opposite the marital bed. The water had been standing all night and was the same temperature as the room. He stood, completely naked, before a large mirror that rested on the table. How round, saggy and hairy he was becoming. Ghlioris recalled the lithesome young son of Irini, plunging into the sea earlier that week. How proud that splendid woman had been of her son. Ghlioris wished that he was young again.

Slowly and with grace, his right hand, with two fingers and thumb gathered, rose up to his forehead, swooped down to his stomach, swayed across to his right breast and then to his left. Then, punctuated by Ghlioris's murmured prayers, it rose, swooped and swayed again. And then once more, as Ghlioris completed his crossing ritual.

Now Ghlioris cupped his hands and drew water to his face. He washed the sleep from his eyes and took in the familiar sounds and smells of an early Sunday morning from the open bedroom window. The cockerel chorus was already under way and Ghlioris's wife, still asleep on the bed, joined in with loud snores. As her lungs filled with each breath, the bed's metal frame creaked rhythmically.

Ghlioris knew that, like his wife, most villagers would be enjoying a lie-in this morning. Then they would all enjoy a family breakfast of bread, olives and hallumin. Most of the Christians at least would then ready themselves for church. Ghlioris sighed. Sunday family rituals weren't part of his experience. He needed to be up and out, preparing for a greater ritual for his wider family.

But Ghlioris would not go hungry this morning. He would help himself to something when he got to the church of Saint Varnavas the Apostle. There was always plenty of andidhoron, small pieces of bread that the villagers had already prepared for today's memorial services. Ghlioris was never short of andidhoron. Nor of Gumandaria, the sweet red wine for the baptisms, the betrothals and the weddings. Bottles and bottles had collected in the cupboards of the ieron, the sacred room, the holy of holies, which was out of bounds to his congregation.

Ghlioris saw the wine as a necessary perk of the job. Fortified and fortifying. To wash down the andidhoron. To wet his tongue and lubricate his larynx. The divine-tasting wine, the sweet-smelling incense and the specks of dim light from the candles would take possession of his senses. Working together they would enable Ghlioris to commune with God.

Without doubt the wine was a blessing. Despite his years as the village priest, Ghlioris was still prone to nerves, still open to doubts. Such feelings had to be checked. Ghlioris had to appear strong for the faithful, so that they might remain so. Thankfully, much of the archaic Greek Ghlioris chanted in church was incomprehensible, so the odd slip-up usually went unnoticed.

But it wasn't just the bread and the wine the people brought. Those who could afford it, and those who could not, were obliged to show appreciation for church services. A shilling was now the universally acknowledged rate. And as his wife was a close friend of Yoda, the village gossip, it was a rate people stuck to religiously, for fear others might learn of their lack of appreciation.

And then there was always the church box. Under Ghlioris's watchful and approving black eyes, good Christians would throw in at least a ghrosin coin before kissing his hand and escaping the demands of their church for another week.

How Ghlioris's wife delighted each Sunday evening when her husband brought the takings home for her to count. It was important for a priest's wife to keep an eye on church finances. There were many costs to consider. It was an old building in need of constant repair. New icons, oil for the lamps and other church expenses too numerous to mention had to be paid for. And these things weren't cheap, as there was only one supplier. After all, as the congregation was reminded by Ghlioris each and every Sunday, there was only one faith.

Yes, donations had to go a long way, so Ghlioris thanked the Lord for all the additional services he was obliged to offer his flock. A new home, a new piece of farmland, even, on odd occasions, a new donkey, might need his blessing, his incense smoke and a few well-aimed splashes from his bottle of holy water. And the villagers would kiss the priest's hand and once again show their appreciation to a degree deemed by one, and accepted by all, as appropriate.

Ghlioris had rinsed his long, slightly greying beard, and was wiping it dry with a towel. Then he put on his black cassock and carefully positioned his high black hat on top of his head. Now he was formally on duty.

'Good morning, Baba-Ghliori,' murmured his wife sleepily but provocatively from the bed. She admired his reflection through the mirror. 'My All-Holy Virgin! How becoming my husband looks in his priestly attire. Come to me, my Lord. I'm in need of your blessing.'

'Enough, woman. Have respect for the clothing I wear in God's service,' chastised Baba-Ghlioris dismissively, still inspecting himself. He noticed his wife's reflection, as she wiped her eyes clean and fluttered those black lashes at him.

'I must go,' he insisted. 'I'm already late for God's work.'

'Oh, but how fine you look in your vestments. Surely there's time to administer to your wife before you administer to your flock.'

Baba-Ghlioris winked at his wife through the mirror. If any man could look fetching in a priest's hat it was he. But Baba-Ghlioris was on duty.

'Hush woman, in case you're struck down by a thunderbolt for such heresy. Fornication can be considered a sin unless it's for the begetting of children. And at the last count we'd produced four young demons that take after you. Do not tempt the Lord your God for he'll surely bless us with a fifth.'

But his wife had swung back the sheets and was now clambering down the bed towards him. Before Baba-Ghlioris had time to protect himself he could feel his wife's hands reach for him.

'Get thee behind me, Satan,' warned the priest, turning away, but his voice was already faltering. An image of Irini suddenly entered his mind again, and with it came a feeling of guilt. Ghlioris removed his hat and turned towards his tormentor.

✳ ✳ ✳

That same Sunday morning Irini arrived at the well on the outskirts of the village. Irini was a religious woman, but not so devout as to neglect her earthly duties even on the Lord's day.

She came here most mornings with her large clay jug, in which she would collect enough water for the day. It was a fair walk and a tiring routine, made bearable only by the fact that a visit to the well invariably turned into a social event.

Despite always arriving early, to avoid having to queue too long, Irini was guaranteed an encounter with one or two other women of the village on the same errand. It was an opportunity for conversation.

This morning Irini was particularly pleased to see Yoda already at the well and pulling at the rope to fetch her first bucketful of water. Yoda was a large, gregarious woman, and always a rich source of local news.

Receiving Yoda's gossip was generally a pleasurable experience for any woman, but there was a price to pay. For if you enjoyed Yoda's services you too were expected to feed her with your own morsels of information, for future consumption by others. You also, of course, risked becoming a character in one of her stories.

'Good morning, Mrs Irini,' declared Yoda with a nod, and Irini noticed a mischievous glint in the woman's eyes which could only mean one thing. Another juicy morsel to share.

'I'm so glad our paths have crossed today, Mrs Irini.'

'Me too, Mrs Yoda. I hope you and your husband are in good health.'

'We're well, thank you.'

'And your daughter, Anna.'

'She's well, thank you.'

'And your two boys…' Irini's voice trailed off. Their names wouldn't come to her.

'They're well. Getting up to their usual mischief, as boys do. They're a blessing from God and help keep me young,' responded Yoda. There was a large age gap between her daughter and two young sons. In between, Yoda had suffered several miscarriages.

'And may I congratulate you, Mrs Irini, on your son Andonis,' continued Yoda, 'for his role in the celebrations the other day. You must have been really proud.'

'Thank you, Mrs Yoda,' nodded Irini. 'When he reclaimed the cross from the sea, I have to admit, it was one of the happiest moments of my life.'

'Indeed. And I'm sure all the single girls in the village will have noticed how strong and how handsome he's becoming. You'll no doubt be expecting to receive propositions from a number of families keen to have him as a son-in-law.'

As Irini listened she started to turn the handle to lower the bucket towards the water.

Yoda continued. 'Do you have any matrimonial plans for Andonis at present?' she enquired with mischief. 'Some believe you intend for him to be betrothed to Stella, the widow's daughter.'

Irini hesitated. Perhaps Yoda had been made aware of a particular family's interest in Andonis and was testing whether it was appropriate to pursue the matter on their behalf.

'We've not really discussed this directly with him, Mrs Yoda. Andonis is still young. I think his mind has yet to set fully,' replied Irini.

Yoda closed one eye and nodded.

'Perhaps you're right, Mrs Irini. Perhaps you're right,' she agreed. 'Judging by the other night's performance, it does appear your youngster still has a lot to learn.' Her tone, though still agreeable, was also slightly patronising. The term 'youngster' in particular troubled Irini.

Irini stopped turning the handle and gave Yoda a frown. 'What do you mean, Mrs Yoda? What happened the other night?' she demanded.

'Ah, but you must know,' declared Yoda with a wry smile. 'The whole village has been talking about it. A fine gesture, I don't doubt. But,' Yoda sighed, shook her head from side to side and raised her hands, 'what can you do? There are those who'll read more into it.'

'I'm sorry, Mrs Yoda. I don't know what you're talking about,' countered Irini defensively. 'What exactly is my son supposed to have done?'

'Why? Didn't he tell you?' admonished Yoda, and now Irini knew she had fallen into the woman's trap. Irini realised she should have claimed full knowledge and approval of her son's actions. A family had always to appear united or have others drive it apart.

'Your son was performing with that Funda, the Turkish girl, in the square. A big crowd gathered. They threw lots of money for the girl and her crippled brother. By all accounts Andonis was a star act, a real Garagiozis.' Yoda revelled in the last word, by which she meant a clowning puppet. 'But people can't help but wonder, Mrs Irini. Perhaps Andonis has feelings for this girl? You understand, I'm only concerned for the boy's reputation. You know what people are like. Little things can be misconstrued. Before you know it, you have a scandal on your hands. And none of us want that.'

Irini was stung. For many years she had enjoyed Yoda's tales at the expense of others. Today it was her family's turn to provide the amusement.

'I can't tell you how much I appreciate you talking to me about this, Mrs Yoda,' declared Irini with deliberately over-emphasised gratitude.

'What are friends for?' said Yoda haughtily.

'It makes me laugh how foolish people can be, to read such nonsense into my son's no doubt well-intentioned act,' mused Irini. 'He likes to help people. He's always been kind to those in need.'

'Too kind, perhaps, for his own good, Mrs Irini,' ventured Yoda with raised eyebrows.

'But surely you can never be too kind, Mrs Yoda. Your concern for my son, bringing this matter to my attention, with no thought of gain for yourself – surely that shows that good deeds are a reward in themselves?'

Yoda nodded. She had never had the opportunity to discover how astute Mihalis's wife could be. Yoda picked up her jug full of water and raised a parting hand.

'Of course, you're right, Mrs Irini. A fine young man, your Andonis. One day he'll make someone a fine husband. Good day to you.'

Later that day, in church, people glanced at Irini and whispered. Some also glanced at Stella.

6
The dress factory   *Do fustanadigon*

As I'd quit, I didn't go into work the next day. Instead I made the effort to call one of those numbers advertised in the community newspaper to see whether I could make a living elsewhere.

That afternoon I found myself entering a factory off Green Lanes, near the Harringay greyhound stadium. I came in from the rain. Row upon row of sewing machines were before me, each with its own woman hunched over it. I was reminded of how, during harvest time in the old days, groups of women like this might go out into the fields together, pulling vegetables from the red earth. Then, it seemed, all they did was stoop and gather, chatter and joke, laugh and sing. Now they sat and sewed, gossiped and blamed, argued and complained. Meanwhile the rain pitter-pattered on the corrugated iron roof above them.

One of the women looked up at me with suspicion before turning to her neighbour to announce my arrival. The neighbour did likewise, and so it continued until the knowledge of the wet stranger's presence had swept through the factory. Then the woman nearest to me spoke.

'Are you looking for the boss?' she asked in the Cypriot vernacular. I nodded, and she gestured with a nod to an office at the back of the factory. I smiled a thanks and left the women to their work.

The door of the office was open. Inside I saw the back of a round man sprawled in an undersized swivel chair behind a desk. He was completely bald on the top of his head, but had generous tufts of greying hair everywhere else, including the back of his neck and in his ears. Not noticing me, he continued shouting in English into the telephone receiver lodged between his left shoulder and ear. His accent was heavy. Each time he pronounced an 'h' it reminded me of my father clearing his throat in the mornings.

'He's off today?' he bawled. 'But I need to speak to him now, darlink. Tell you what. You just give me his number at home.'

He swung round and reached for a pen on his desk. As he did so he acknowledged my presence with a raised finger. He appeared to be in his fifties.

'What you mean, you can't? Do you know how many years I been doin' business with him?'

He beckoned me to sit down in the empty chair in front of his desk.

'Listen, my darlink. My orders pay your flippin' wages so you just give me that number, oright?'

He began jotting on a pad. As he did so he glanced up at me with black eyes and gave a triumphant wink.

'No, don't you worry, my darlink. Just leave him to me, oright?'

He slammed the phone down and looked at me again, studying my features.

'Women!' he exclaimed, changing to the Cypriot vernacular. He raised his thick black eyebrows which, while contrasting with what was left of the hair on his head, mirrored an equally thick black moustache.

'Let them sew,' he continued, gesturing to his staff through the open door. 'Let them cook, clean and the rest. But never let them get in the way of important business. Am I right?'

I shrugged. I didn't feel in a position to comment, but hoped he might interpret my gesture as one of resigned agreement. I thought of Ruth and imagined what she might make of such a man. The factory boss nodded and gave me a warm smile.

'So, what can I do for you, Mr...?'

'Tony,' I interjected, turning to English. 'I've come about the tailor's job.' I offered my hand across the desk, which he grabbed and shook firmly.

'Andonis,' he corrected, reverting to the Cypriot vernacular and emphasising the stress on the last syllable. His face contorted as though straining to recollect. 'You've come about a job, you say? What job?'

'The one advertised in the paper,' I explained a little hesitantly in his preferred language. 'I rang this morning and was told to come and see the boss.'

'The job. In the paper,' repeated the factory boss absent-mindedly. Then his face lit up with amusement. 'They still running those ads? I suppose they must be, they keep sending me the bills!' He winked at me, then stroked his moustache for a moment. 'Still, you've got to do your bit. Support the paper. Support the community.'

'I'm sorry, sir. Do you mean there's no work here?' I was unable to disguise my disappointment.

'Work? Sure, there's plenty of work. If you've got the appetite.'

'For a tailor?' I asked.

He began counting on his fingers. 'Tailor, cutter, presser, fixer. Cleaner-upper. Bit of machining if we need. Only thing you won't have to do is make the coffee. I let one of the women do that,' he declared with yet another wink. He offered me a cigarette from a packet of Rothmans on his desk, which I declined. He lit one for himself, and after he'd breathed out his first lungful of smoke asked me where I was from.

I saw this as my chance to impress the factory boss. 'I've been working in the alterations department of a gentlemen's outfitters in the West End. I'm a master tailor.' I spoke in English.

The man huffed impatiently. He spoke in the Cypriot vernacular. 'No, my son. What's your village?'

I shrugged and gave in to his choice of language. 'Is this relevant to whether I get the job?'

The thick eyebrows and moustache drew nearer.

'What's the matter with you? I ask where you're from and you ask if it's relevant? Is your homeland relevant? Your people? Your family?' he fumed.

I felt I had no option but to reveal the name of my village. He gave me a strange look. I resolved not to upset either of us further, and got up from my chair.

'I'm sorry for wasting your time, sir,' I murmured. He shook his finger at me before pointing at the vacated chair.

'Sit down, my son, sit down. Let me take a closer look at you.' I did as I was told and he scrutinised my face. 'You know what? If you're from there then I do believe I know you. One moment. Yes. I do believe you're Mihalis's boy.' He reached across his desk and pinched my cheek. 'I knew your father.'

I searched my memory and tried to place him but couldn't. My father used to know many people from many villages.

'I'm a cousin of Xenu, the one who moved to your village to marry…' His voice trailed off and there was a momentary look of sadness in his eyes. 'For sure. I recognise Mihalis in your face. You know, I haven't seen your father since I left Cyprus all those years ago. How is he?'

I felt more uncomfortable than ever. I was reminded why I'd tried to stay away from this close-knit community, where everybody seemed to know everybody else, where everybody seemed to be related to everybody else. I was unable to answer his question. Nor was I willing to answer those that would inevitably follow. I could do no more than shrug once again.

The factory boss turned his open palms upwards. 'But I don't understand. Tell me, is he – and your mother – over here now?' he enquired. I hesitated a moment longer, but knew I had no choice but to reply to the best of my knowledge.

'I believe they're still in Cyprus.'

'You believe?' challenged the factory boss.

'Forgive me, sir. It's been many years since I last saw any of my family. I left the village under difficult circumstances. It's something I'd rather not talk about. Please don't ask me to,' I explained, and folded my arms tightly to indicate that this really had to be the end of the matter.

The factory boss sighed a deep, deep sigh. I could see that he wished to pursue the matter, but also that he realised this was not an option. He rubbed his moustache and observed his morose staff through the open door.

'What has become of us, Andoni? What has become of us?'

I lowered my head and remained silent. The factory boss nodded.

'I remember your babas being the best of men,' he offered with affection.

At that moment the phone on his desk began to ring. He raised a hand which I took to indicate that our meeting was over, so I rose again from my chair. Then he picked up the phone, told the caller to wait a moment and looked up at me.

'You want work, my son?' he asked. 'I can give you work. And lots of it.'

My mouth smiled but my eyes couldn't. I left the factory boss to his business.

As I made my way back out through the whirring I heard a woman's voice call out. A voice I'd not heard for many years, but which I instantly recognised.

'Andoni? Is it really you?'

I turned to face the woman, and as my eyes fell upon her, sitting there at her machine, I felt a shudder through my entire body.

'My God, it *is* you. I thought so when I saw you earlier,' she added.

It was Stella. The widow's daughter. Our Stella, with that unmistakable mole on her cheek. I was saddened to see her face now marked by the years. Her once rich black hair was flecked with grey. Her sunken brown eyes were fixed upon mine, daring to glimmer with hope. I had to look away in an effort to compose myself.

Then I looked back at her blankly, to convey that she was sadly mistaken, that I was no longer the man she thought I was.

'Andoni. I can't believe it. After all these years.'

She stood up, and her face now glowed with a joy that made the years fall away. Then, with her colleagues looking on in bemusement, she launched herself towards me and engulfed me with her embrace. She kissed each of my cheeks in turn. I couldn't help but wrap my arms around her. I looked over her shoulder and gave an embarrassed smile as the factory women looked away, pretending to busy themselves with their work.

'Stella,' I announced uncomfortably, endeavouring to release myself from her grasp. 'Let me look at you.'

I stared into those loving eyes of hers and found I could smile without effort. As I did so, her eyes began to flood and her bottom lip quivered. She took out a handkerchief from under her sleeve and blew her nose.

'You're late, Andoni.'

I attempted to speak, but no words emerged. The factory boss came out of his office and shook a finger at me.

'Hey, Andoni! When I said I wanted a worker with appetite, I didn't mean in that way. Keep your hands off my girls. Can't you see how busy they are?' I was relieved that his tone sounded more amused than angry.

Stella withdrew and took her place back at her machine. Her face was flushed red with shame. I nodded an apology to the factory boss and turned to go.

Stella called out. 'You'll wait for me, Andoni? I finish at six.'

I raised my hand ambiguously. I found Ruth entering my mind once more. After all, Ruth didn't think I was the sort of bloke to let a woman down.

Stella continued. 'Please, Andoni. Don't disappear. Not like before.'

I nodded. Stella was right. I'd disappeared in the land of the Englezi, from whom we'd all sought to be free.

7
The kiss   *Do filin*

The captain had served in north Africa during the war, and later took part in the invasion of Italy. He was proud of the role he had played in overcoming the Nazis. He'd known what his country was fighting for then. Not like Palestine. Not like now.

He'd been in Cyprus for some time, stationed at the army's base at the busy port town. As well as intelligence work, he found himself becoming embroiled in all aspects of logistics and administration, including arranging the delivery of food, uniforms, equipment and weaponry to British outposts throughout the island and beyond. Demands for supplies were growing, and the captain was beginning to drown in a sea of paperwork. He found himself working all hours, even on Sundays, as today.

The withdrawal of forces from Egypt meant that Cyprus was now Britain's new Middle East headquarters. The island's increased strategic importance coincided with the birth of a dangerous new underground movement, EOKA (or 'Eoga' as the locals seemed to say, if ever they did), the National Organisation of Cypriot Combatants. EOKA was dedicated to the expulsion of the British and the eventual union of Cyprus with Greece, a country considered by the island's Orthodox Christian majority to be the motherland.

Led by Colonel George Grivas, a war veteran and officer of the Greek army, EOKA had the backing of Makarios, the island's archbishop. Privately the captain didn't share British indignation that a Christian spiritual leader could support EOKA methods. It wasn't the first time in history that acts of terror had been committed in the name of God. The captain was certain it wouldn't be the last.

He knew that what in truth disturbed the British far more was how EOKA had so successfully managed to whip up the island's previously manageable Christian population into a state of near frenzy. The influence of this small band of what the British press had termed 'thugs' now extended into every coffee-shop, every schoolyard, every church. In just a few short months Grivas had been elevated to messianic status, while anyone British was now the enemy.

It all made perfect sense to a man who felt duty-bound to understand all he could of the world. Unlike most other British army personnel stationed on the island, the captain had gone out of his way to make contact with the locals. He'd come to know a handful well enough to consider them friends.

He'd been welcomed into their rustic homes, shared their simple but delicious food. He'd drunk their pungent, grainy coffee and their coarse home-made wine. He'd even been delighted and honoured to try their ghligon, the syrup-soaked fruit preserve only ever offered to special guests. He'd attended their religious festivals, listened to their poignant stories, laughed at their crude jokes, danced to their evocative music. He'd come to share their intense love of life.

Yet these were friends whose graciousness could only be motivated by an extraordinary pride, with wives whose exaggerated obedience betrayed an unwavering resilience. And with children whose ingratiating deference masked an unshakable defiance.

And now, suddenly, Grivas had dared to say 'enough is enough' and challenged his people to believe in themselves. He'd called on them all to stand up to the foreign soldier who represented century upon century of suffocation. Not that the British were the worst, by any means. The captain realised that. But by any means the Cypriots were now determined that the British would be the last.

Back home the British government had acted swiftly, and appointed a new governor to Cyprus. A military man. He had proclaimed a state of emergency.

The captain feared the worst. The death penalty had been extended to offences other than murder, including the planting of explosives and the use of firearms. Those caught in possession of such weapons were sentenced to life imprisonment. Other oppressive emergency regulations were also being enforced, including a curfew and the collective punishment of youths under eighteen.

Sat at his desk, the captain gave what he recognised as the deep sigh of a Cypriot. There were reams of paper awaiting his attention. As an officer, he saw a great number of army reports and plans, which were piling up in front of him. He read and shook his head. Try as he might he couldn't see a dignified way out for Britain in the circumstances. Nevertheless there was a job to be done. The captain put on his cap and rose to his feet.

※ ※ ※

'Mr Tailor. Sew me up good or my mother will kill me,' called Nigos from under the vine outside the window of the bedroom shared by Andonis and Marios. Nigos sat astride a bicycle. His comment was a reference to an old joke about a girl of ill-repute who was for ever 'recovering' her virginity with the help of a skilful tailor.

Andonis was roused from his sleep, opened his eyes and smiled. He turned and saw that his brother's bed was empty. Marios was up already, performing errands for the priest in church, as he did every Sunday morning.

After a few moments, a yawning Andonis appeared at the front door, pushing out his own bicycle and carrying two fishing rods.

Nigos and Andonis set off on the short journey to the coast, along roads barely more than dirt tracks and across open country. They headed for a secluded rocky cove where they knew the fishing would be good.

They cycled alongside each other in silence. Each was waiting for the other to initiate a conversation. They hadn't spoken since the night of the festival. They'd been through such rituals many times during the course of their friendship, with a variety of causes. As usual it was Nigos who was eventually to break the silence.

'That was some performance you and the Turkish girl put on the other night,' he mumbled.

Andonis tutted. 'Nigo. My good friend. I see no point in us having this conversation.'

Nigos would not be discouraged. 'Sometimes I wonder about you, Andoni. Seriously I do. And in front of the whole village.'

Andonis increased his speed, moving ahead of Nigos. 'I didn't see anyone complaining. In fact people enjoyed our show so much they gave more money,' he called back.

Exasperated, Nigos had to pedal harder to keep up. 'You just don't see it, do you? The shame you've brought on us,' he puffed.

'Shame? Since when was it so shameful to help a poor crippled boy and his sister?'

Nigos laughed ironically. 'We're the cripples, Andoni. And they're the ones who cripple us. And what do you do? Sing for the Turk, dance for the Turk, kiss the arse of the Turk.'

Andonis frowned. He'd learnt from his grandmother Maria that it was wrong to regard the island's Muslim minority as Turks – that implied they didn't really belong. And all who, like Maria, loved Cyprus deserved to belong. Andonis raised his voice as well as his speed.

'You're just jealous, Nigo. Maybe you fancy Funda yourself. Or maybe you can't take it that I might be more interested in her than in your own sister.'

'Fuck you, Andoni,' cursed Nigos and struggled to catch up once more. 'I'd as much go with that Turk, or any Turk, as I'd dangle my hand in a pit of snakes. When I need a whore I'll go to the town and buy one. An Engleza, so I can fuck her till she breaks, like her country's doing to mine.'

Andonis slowed down and allowed Nigos to catch up. 'You're nothing but an ignorant, foul-mouthed peasant.'

Nigos was unrelenting, however, and kept pedalling. When he was a few yards ahead, he turned.

'And as for you and my sister? I'd rather dangle my own dick in that pit of snakes than let a pimp like you into my family,' he called between breaths, and as he did so lost control of his bicycle, veering off the road and eventually crashing into a bush.

Andonis began to giggle. Quietly at first but then progressively louder, until he had to put his feet on the ground to regain control of his bicycle. Soon he was shrieking with laughter, and Nigos, with only his pride bruised, became infected too. Now both were bent over their handle-bars as though trying to out-laugh each other.

It was then they heard the sound of an approaching jeep. The laughter stopped immediately, and the young men exchanged concerned glances.

'Bastard Englezi soldiers,' cursed Nigos, reversing out of the bush. 'Watch out, Andoni, because I'm not taking any of their shit today.'

If he had been alone Andonis would have remained calm, but he was with Nigos. He knew what his friend was capable of.

'Watch yourself, Nigo, or we'll both end up in jail,' he cautioned.

'Jail?' scoffed Nigos, with what Andonis recognised as exaggerated bravado. 'I'm not scared of jail. I'm not scared of anything!'

'Don't be a fool, Nigo. Let me do the talking,' commanded Andonis. Nigos recognised the gravity of his friend's tone, and understood that he should comply.

The jeep came to a halt in front of them. A tall red-haired officer descended, leaving his driver at the wheel. Andonis recognised the officer, was relieved and smiled.

'Ah, the famous harmonica player,' declared the captain pleasantly, in the only language he knew. 'Good morning to you both. Would you mind telling me what you're doing here?'

'Tell him to go to hell,' hissed Nigos in his own language.

Andonis raised a hand to quieten his friend and addressed the captain in English.

'My friend says, sir, that, as this is his country, he should be entitled to go where he pleases. He wants to know what *you* are doing here,' he said, and offered a wry smile.

'Tell your friend I'm doing my job,' retorted the captain, though he was still in good humour. 'And tell him also that there are parts of it I don't particularly enjoy but that I'll not hesitate to perform if you and he don't cooperate.'

'Please, sir, no threats,' said Andonis, shaking an open palm. 'It affects the high esteem in which my friend holds your Great British Empire. You notice, I hope, our fishing rods. Surely a man of your standing and perception can conclude the obvious? I thought the British forces had good intelligence.'

The captain nodded and smiled. 'Not as good as some, perhaps.'

'Mine's inherited, sir. Our ancestors were the world's greatest thinkers.'

The captain nodded once more, but this time to indicate that the time for flippancy was over.

'This area of the coast has been under observation for some time now. There are reports of weapons smuggling from Greece. We're having to check on anybody passing along this road,' he explained, and there was the merest hint of apology in his tone. 'Now move along,' he instructed with a wave of his hand. 'And make sure you're both home before curfew.'

Andonis shrugged. 'We *are* home, sir. And we know our way around in the dark.'

The captain shook his head. 'Look, young man. Bad things are happening in Cyprus at the moment, so I suggest you take care of yourselves. Endaxi?' he urged.

Andonis raised his eyebrows.

'Endaxi, sir. And you take care also,' he replied with an ironic smile.

The captain turned to leave. Nigos saw this as an opportunity to spit. Before the two young men could resume their journey, the captain called out from the jeep.

'By the way, am I right in saying you're Antony, son of Michael the farmer, friend of Vasos the coffee-shop owner?'

Andonis nodded.

'And am I right in saying you're the village tailor?'

Andonis smiled and called back. 'The best in the district. I guarantee!'

'No doubt you'll accept the custom of an Englishman?' enquired the captain. 'Or, should I say, an Englezos?'

'A man has to eat, after all,' replied Andonis.

The Englezos nodded, and signalled to his driver to start up. The jeep disappeared in a cloud of red dust.

Andonis raised a hand to wave the Englezos goodbye.

'Fuck him and fuck all of them,' fumed Nigos, clearing phlegm from his throat and spitting once more.

'He doesn't strike me as a bad man,' mused Andonis.

'He's an Englezos!' yelled Nigos.

'Come on, Nigo. Your father wouldn't have approved of this. He was a man of principle, God rest his soul,' cautioned Andonis, surprised at himself for invoking Nigos's dead father. Nigos was also thrown by the reference, and took a moment to gather his thoughts.

'Don't insult my blessed father's memory, Andoni,' he said finally. 'His principles are what got him killed. And it's the Englezi who are responsible.'

They resumed their journey, slowly and in silence. Painful memories overwhelmed them both.

Nigos's father and Andonis's father had been close friends, inseparable from childhood. Both had become members of the leftist movement. Some years before, the two men had been at the church of a nearby village, celebrating a national holiday with a group of comrades. Vasos, then as now passionate about his politics, was with them too. After the church service, the group marched through the village for a meeting at the local coffee-shop. They never got there. Some young Muslim policemen under British command stopped them at a bridge and insisted that permission was needed to cross it. Outraged at having their freedom of movement restricted, the group protested forcefully, led by Nigos's father. The inexperienced policemen felt foolish and intimidated. In panic one of them opened fire and shot Nigos's father dead. Mihalis might have been shot too had Vasos not restrained him.

The British authorities expressed regret at the behaviour of their police force and promised to bring to justice those responsible. There was an enquiry, but no report was published and the episode was forgotten.

But Nigos would never forget.

※ ※ ※

Baba-Ghlioris retreated into the ieron, as the last of the faithful were ushered out of the church of Saint Varnavas the Apostle by Marios. The priest thanked God for the valuable support which Mihalis's younger son now provided. The young man gave up a good part of his Sunday to volunteer his services. And, during the week, the farmer's boy would run errands for Baba-Ghlioris. He'd mend a broken pew, rebind an old Bible, trim the wild grass and shrubs growing in the graveyard. In return the priest was happy to impart his knowledge of the scriptures and his understanding of the Orthodox faith to a willing and hungry student.

Marios's connection with the Church was now so strong that some villagers were quite happy to approach him when they needed spiritual guidance. Indeed, there were those who preferred to seek the counsel of young Marios instead of their priest, for they struggled sometimes to make sense of Baba-Ghlioris when the wine was talking.

From the ieron, Baba-Ghlioris could hear that Marios was gathering the spent candles in the church. It had been a long and tiring day, with a betrothal and two baptisms. The priest had poured out the contents of his soul and replenished the people's hearts with the love of God. Now Baba-Ghlioris was completely drained and in need of some replenishing of his own.

And it was God's will that Baba-Ghlioris's eyes strayed towards the cupboard in the ieron. And it was God's will that the cupboard door was ajar and that inside were over a dozen bottles of Gumandaria, their corks stained red from the wine.

'Mario?' called Baba-Ghlioris. 'What are you doing out there?'

'I was about to refill the oil lamps, father.'

'Before you do so, my son, would you go outside and clean up any bits of bread that the people may have dropped. You know how stray crumbs attract the rats.'

'Of course, father,' agreed Marios obediently, and Baba-Ghlioris listened for the young man's retreating footsteps and for the church door to creak open and then shut.

And Baba-Ghlioris did reach into the cupboard and did pull out one of the bottles of Gumandaria. And Baba-Ghlioris did prise off the cork, careful not to let it crumble into the bottle. And Baba-Ghlioris did close his eyes and did lift the bottle to his nose to breathe in the pungent aroma of civilization's earliest named wine. And Baba-Ghlioris did put the bottle to his lips and did remember, at the last moment, to remove the priest's hat from his head.

And Ghlioris the man communed with God.

'Every man at the beginning doth set forth good wine,' he declared between gulps. 'And when men have well drunk, then that which is worse. But Thou hast kept the good wine until now.'

Ghlioris could feel his face glowing with praise for the Lord. Ghlioris replaced the cork in the bottle, the bottle in the cupboard, and the priest's hat on his head. Now Baba-Ghlioris withdrew from the ieron and made his way out of the church.

Outside, Marios was on his knees sweeping up with a small brush. The priest placed a hand on the young man's head.

'Mario. I'm tired. I must go home and lie down. Will you finish tidying up inside for me?'

Marios nodded, and took the priest's hand to kiss it.

'Of course, father,' he said and gave Baba-Ghlioris a look of concern. The priest didn't look at all well.

On Baba-Ghlioris's short walk home he would, of course, pass his old friend Vasos's coffee-shop. The priest had resolved not to stop. He'd drunk enough, and Vasos was bound to notice. It was just the excuse that wily communist needed to have another dig at the Church.

However, as the priest drew nearer, he noticed Mihalis sitting alone at a table outside. The farmer was munching the basadembon seeds which Vasos sometimes put out in saucers for his customers. The priest was pleased to see the farmer. It had been a while since Mihalis had shown his face in the coffee-shop. Marios's father was a man with whom Baba-Ghlioris had always enjoyed a lively exchange of views.

On arriving at Mihalis's table the priest squeezed the farmer's shoulder with affection but also to steady himself.

'But surely my eyes deceive me,' slurred the priest. 'Has God seen fit to bless us with your presence once more?' He remembered to offer his right hand, and Mihalis dutifully stooped to kiss it. The priest stroked the farmer's thinning hair.

'Praise God, it *is* you. We all feared that perhaps you'd been held hostage in the fields by those famous potatoes of yours.'

The priest called into the coffee-shop. 'Hey, Vaso, a drink for your priest! We must make merry and be glad. For behold, our brother is alive again. Was lost, and is found.'

He pulled a chair from under the table and plonked himself opposite an amused Mihalis. Mihalis scrutinised the priest's bleary eyes as both men crunched a few seeds between their teeth.

'Father, I'm really honoured that my absence has been felt. Let me explain. Increasingly of late I find myself preferring my own company. I'm tired of all the confused conversations one always seems to hear in public places,' confessed the farmer.

He gestured to Baba-Ghlioris to draw closer. The priest leant forward and Mihalis, whispering in the priest's ear, continued.

'Between you and me, father, there are many in the village who can't control their mouths. Neither what pours in nor what pours out.'

Were it possible, the priest's face would have glowed even more. Recomposing himself, Baba-Ghlioris nodded gravely, patted Mihalis on the shoulder and whispered, 'Rest assured, I'll pray for them all.'

Then he turned towards the coffee-shop door again and yelled.

'Vaso? Put some wind in your breeches! A man could die of thirst out here!' He looked back at the farmer. 'So, Mihali, now that the prodigal son has returned, might we also expect to hear his prayers in the church?'

Mihalis raised his chin and eyebrows. 'Marios has prayers enough for us all.'

'That son of yours is indeed a gift from God,' agreed the priest.

'For you perhaps, father, but not for his family. His devotion to the Church makes him forget his duties. A monk's of no use to me, nor to my famous potatoes,' huffed Mihalis.

The priest pointed a finger. 'Mihali, why trouble the boy with the earth when his mind's in heaven? Your son's been chosen to serve God. Your heart should be filled with joy.'

Mihalis grimaced. 'My heart would fill with joy, father, if I knew my son would one day produce loving grandchildren for me to spoil in my old age.'

Baba-Ghlioris nodded. A mere priest could marry and have children, as he had done, but Baba-Ghlioris had higher hopes for Mihalis's boy. Marios had even greater faith, even greater self-control. Marios could live solely with God's love. He could achieve a higher office.

'You have more than one son,' observed the priest. 'So long as you ensure that your elder, at least, marries, and marries wisely, your prayers will be answered.'

Mihalis nodded with resignation before releasing a huge sigh.

'Andonis needs a father's guidance,' advised the priest.

At that moment a beaming Vasos emerged with a tray containing a glass of uzon, two cups of coffee and three glasses of water.

'Ah, at last. Here he is. Our friend Comrade Stalin,' announced the priest with a broad smile before offering his hand. Vasos bent down to kiss it while at the same time laying the tray on the table.

'The kiss of Judas,' announced the priest haughtily, pulling back his hand. 'Woe unto thee, hypocrite. Thou payest tithe of mint and anise and cumin, and hast omitted the weightier matter of faith.'

The priest splashed some water into his uzon which turned a cloudy white.

'And why should identifying with the struggle of the workers prevent me from honouring our village's most valued priest?' enquired Vasos, pulling up another chair and sitting opposite the village's only priest. He turned and gave Mihalis a wink.

'Because you pursue an ideology which claims religion is merely the narcotic of the people,' replied the priest, lifting his glass and filling his nostrils with aniseed, which made him shudder slightly.

Vasos shrugged. 'Baba-Ghliori, I know you to be a true believer in the teachings of Christ,' he stated before slurping at his coffee.

'Vaso, I don't wear this black hat for amusement,' declared the priest before removing it and taking his first sip of uzon.

'Then surely our ideologies have much in common,' continued Vasos with a smile. 'For Christ said, 'Blessed are the poor, the meek, the hungry,' which would make him the very first proponent of communist doctrine,' said the coffee-shop owner, and wiped his moustache with satisfaction.

Ghlioris slapped the table. The cups and glasses on it rattled. 'Demon. Foul and evil spirit. I charge thee, thou shalt come out of him,' he commanded. 'Christ said that the greatest commandment of all was to love God with all thy heart and with all thy soul, with all thy mind and with all thy strength. Square that with communist doctrine, Vaso!'

'I'll be happy too,' retorted Vasos, now slapping the table himself. 'Once you've squared Christian doctrine with our Church's obsession with power and wealth, greed and hatred.'

Both men huffed. The priest turned to his uzon, Vasos to his coffee.

'Enough, boys,' instructed Mihalis calmly before taking a quiet sip of his coffee. 'You know, Vaso, there is much in communist teachings with which I've always sympathised. But I also realise that to ignore a man's spirit is a grave error. For it's in the nature of man that if he neglects to nourish his soul, he will instead satiate his mind and his body with earthly endeavours and pleasures. And he'll do so in the only way he knows. By exploiting his fellow man. That's why communism is doomed.'

'Well said, Mihali,' agreed the priest. 'I can see where your Marios gets his depth of thinking from. Create a material world, devoid of God, Vaso, and you create hell on earth. Of that we can be sure.'

'But that's not to say you priests have all the answers, father,' cautioned Mihalis.

Ghlioris, seeing that his profession was now under scrutiny, put on his hat and put in his defence.

'We priests devote our lives to God. Through our self-sacrifice we help others to understand His love for them and to express their love for Him. Surely there can be no greater calling for a man. And there can be no mortal worthy of greater respect than such a true messenger of God.'

Mihalis remained unmoved. 'Father, it's not the robes that make the priest but the priest the robes. While humanity extends its knowledge, the Church stands still. Traditional belief systems are challenged by new science, new discoveries, new ideas, but you priests refuse to move forward, as nearly two thousand years ago Christ moved the scriptures forward. A religion that fails to accommodate a rapidly changing world is also surely doomed.'

Baba-Ghlioris searched his mind for a quote from the New Testament as an appropriate retort, but none presented itself. So he took off his hat and raised his glass to his lips.

Mihalis continued. 'Father. You know there's no greater power in the world than the potential for love within and between us. Some call this energy "Theos", others call it "Allah". Enough energy for all, but we can't see it. So instead we fight for each other's energy. We against the British, Muslim against Christian, left against right, priest against coffee-shop owner. Perhaps, one day, in more enlightened times, people will realise that this needless struggle is the source of all evil in the world.'

Ghlioris scratched his head. Was it the uzon that was making his head spin, or was Mihalis talking in riddles?

It was Vasos who spoke next. 'All I know is that we workers must take control to move thinking forward. For the good of all the people, not just the few. We must rid our land of the parasitic imperialists who milk it dry, as they do on the mainland and in Turkey too. Revolution. Like Russia. We must free ourselves from oppressors and from a Church which stands in the way of true enlightenment. No offence, father.'

'None taken, Vaso. How can I be offended by a man possessed? I'm merely saddened to witness it.'

Mihalis shook his head and addressed Vasos. 'But who'll lead this revolution, Vaso? What manner of man shall stand on top of this new utopia, where religion has been toppled but the need for worship remains? And how shall this man command his people's obedience when all are supposedly created equal? How, if not by elevating himself to godlike status, giving his people what they crave and what they fear? Like Stalin. Like Lenin before him. Like Christ himself. No, Vaso. Until such time as the sheep are ready to think for themselves, perhaps they're better off with the devil they know.' Mihalis nodded at their priest. Vasos smiled and shook his head.

Ghlioris glared at them both.

'Heretics, the pair of you!' he cried, before putting on his hat once more to compose himself. 'Next you'll be advocating that we give up the struggle for freedom against the Englezi devils. Even though it's the sacred duty of every Greek of Cyprus to fight for unity with the motherland. And even though it's what every Greek wants.'

Baba-Ghlioris was dismayed to see the uncertainty in the faces of both his village friends.

'Come on, Vaso. It was your leftists that proposed we have the vote on enosis. And ninety-five per cent of our compatriots said yes to joining with Greece.'

'That's only because the Church dominated proceedings,' interjected Mihalis. 'Whatever our genuine beliefs, we were pressured into signing the petition or risk being seen as traitors.'

The priest lifted his glass and contemplated the cloudy liquid within.

'But you're not really a traitor, are you, Mihali?' he enquired with concern.

Now Vasos interceded. 'All that Mihalis is saying, father, is that our struggle is against the imperialists. Insisting on enosis simply alienates our non-Christian comrades.'

'And you would rather throw your lot in with the infidel than with your fellow Orthodox Greeks? It's what you'd expect from an unbeliever, I suppose.' The priest turned to the farmer. 'What do you say, Mihali?' he demanded.

'You must understand, father. We have a just claim against the Englezi. We want them as friends, not as masters. So we challenge them, because they deny us our freedom. But never forget that our Muslim neighbours have as much right to live on this land as Christians. And the Muslims want us as friends, not as masters. Take care. Know that it is our pursuit of enosis that will leave our people cut and bleeding, that will one day leave our island cut and bleeding.'

Forgetting to remove his hat, the priest emptied the contents of his glass in one gulp. The uzon burnt his throat, and he coughed and spluttered.

'Take care so that God takes care of you, Mihali,' he gasped, finally, and there was alarm in his bloodshot eyes. 'You're a fine man with two fine sons. I beg you, keep such thoughts in check. And keep your elder son's infatuation in check. For no good can come of either.'

✳ ✳ ✳

It was nearly dark when Andonis returned home carrying half a dozen fish. He was sleepy after a whole day out in the open air, and wanted to get straight to bed, avoiding any contact with his parents. He couldn't be bothered to answer his mother's inane questions about his day.

As Andonis wheeled his bicycle through the front yard he was surprised to see his father, sitting on a chair under the vine, holding a burning candle. Mihalis stood up and beckoned to his son to accompany him into the workshop.

No bigger than a shed, and positioned outside Mihalis's house, under a huge carob tree, the workshop was once the home of Andonis's late grandmother Maria. After her death, it had become Andonis's retreat. His tailor's workshop. Here he could escape the family, the village and the tensions. It was as Maria had willed.

Andonis thought his father's request a little strange, and because it was strange he thought it best not to object. Once they were inside, Mihalis looked up at a black and white photograph of Maria which Andonis had hung on the wall near the workshop's long mirror. The farmer studied his mother's pale face and delicate Macedonian features in the half-light. He turned to his son and smiled. Somehow they hadn't communicated much in recent years. But now there was so much that needed to be said. Mihalis stooped and stroked the fish Andonis was carrying, breathing in their fresh salty aroma.

'Well done, my son. We'll eat well tomorrow,' he announced. Then he glanced back at his mother's photograph. The candle flickered, animating her image and bringing her smile alive.

'You know. I'd never noticed before that you put the picture of your yaya up there, amongst all her icons. Look. She seems to belong, God rest her soul,' noted Mihalis with pride.

Andonis nodded. 'She was a good woman, baba. As precious to me as any saint.'

Mihalis nodded. 'I feel I could stay here for hours, Andoni. By your sewing machine. Amongst your cloth and thread. With your lists and measurements. All neat and tidy. You've made a splendid space for yourself. So serene and quiet. Better than a church.'

Andonis frowned. He'd never heard his father speak in this way.

'What's come over you, baba?' he asked.

Mihalis stared at Andonis's manually operated Singer.

'Do you know what your yaya said to me when you were still a small boy? She told me that your destiny was not in the fields. She told me the world was changing and you needed a trade that could open a different path for you. I told her it was impossible. That I needed help to make ends meet. God would provide, she said. And look. He has provided. Learning came easily to you, at school and then in your trade. You've done well, Andoni. A well-carved stone always has its place. And now her little home has become your workshop.'

'It'll always be yaya's home, baba. She always looks after me here. Ensuring my work goes well. Helping me do the right thing.'

Mihalis nodded. 'I sense her guiding hand even now. Wanting to protect you from harm.'

Andonis shrugged. Mihalis let out a deep sigh.

'Tongues are wagging, my son.'

Andonis nodded. Now he knew what this was about. 'Well, let them wag, baba. If people's lives are so dull that they need to invent stories for entertainment then that's their problem, not mine.'

'You know it's not as simple as that.'

'Perhaps not for you, baba, but for me it is. Just because the rest of the world's gone mad that doesn't mean I have to. I've nothing to be ashamed of. In fact, you should be proud of me. I'm sure yaya would be proud,' insisted Andonis. He noticed his grandmother's photograph was slightly crooked, and reached up to straighten it.

'We're living through difficult times, Andoni,' cautioned his father. 'We must think before we act. What you did on the night of the festival was no doubt a well-intentioned gesture and I'm sure most in the village would agree. But it appears some may have misinterpreted your actions. They imagine you might have feelings for this girl.'

Andonis thought of Funda. Indeed he'd thought of little else since that night. He remembered her sweet smile and the fact that she'd accepted his prized possession, the brass thimble his grandmother had once given him.

'And what if I did, baba?' challenged Andonis.

'Well? Do you?' pressed Mihalis. He looked deep into his son's eyes, afraid of what they might reveal.

'Funda's a beautiful girl, that I won't deny. And, that night, I felt an urge to play a tune with her. But now, now that Nigos and you and half the village seem to disapprove, well, I can't help but wonder. What if I did have feelings for this girl? And she for me? What would be so wrong with that?'

Mihalis shook his head and gave his son a stern look. 'Stop it, Andoni. You know that could never be.'

'Why? I don't understand you, baba. You're the one who's always taught me that the Christians and the Muslims of Cyprus are brothers. That it's outside forces that want to divide us and our island for their own gain. Well, I see no outside forces standing in the way of Funda and me. All I see are my own people, my own family, objecting to the merest hint of an attraction between us. It's ironic that the only person who's openly declared approval is an Englezos.'

Mihalis raised his eyebrows. 'An Englezos?' he enquired with incredulity.

'That's right, an Englezos. Mr Vasos's friend. The captain. A good man who can appreciate a good thing when he sees it.'

'A good man? Perhaps. But I'm concerned for your safety and your future,' explained Mihalis. 'You were right earlier when you said the world had gone mad. But we all have to live in it. You, your brother, your mother and I. And what of Funda, her parents and their crippled son? Don't you think the barber has enough problems without his daughter getting mixed up with a Christian?'

'Me a Christian?' scoffed Andonis. 'Do me a favour, baba. I have as much faith in our Church as you do.'

'You can't deny what you are, Andoni. And what she is. It's too dangerous. Now is not the time to embark on a relationship that can never be. Never, ever.'

Andonis sighed and patted his father on the shoulder. 'You don't know how much you disappoint me, baba. You'd compromise all your ideals for the sake of an easy life.'

Mihalis was hurt, and stared into his candle for comfort. 'That's not fair, Andoni. When you were a young boy I saw police shoot my best friend. He gave his life for what we both believed in. And what good did it do? Nothing. I knew from then that the only thing that mattered in life was life itself and the safety of my family.'

'And not just your family. But the widow's family also?' suggested Andonis.

'Her husband took his last breath in my arms, Andoni. I vowed that I'd do everything I could to support his wife and children.'

'And that vow now also includes making me the widow's son-in-law?'

Mihalis hesitated. The subject had never been discussed directly with Andonis before.

'I won't deny that we sometimes talk about what a good match you and Stella might make,' he confessed finally.

'You and the widow have been planning my future. But you never thought to ask what I might want.'

'It's what parents do, Andoni. We have experience of life. In such matters we usually know best.' Experience also told Mihalis that his son would disapprove of his assertion.

'Listen to yourself, baba,' scoffed Andonis. 'It's what the Englezi and the other foreign powers say about Cyprus. They know best. So they control our lives and make plans for our future, without even consulting us. The trouble is, what's best for them isn't what's best for us. And what's best for you and the widow isn't what's best for me. Nor Stella.'

'Your life is yours. You and Stella will have the final say.' But Andonis recognised that there was little conviction in his father's voice.

'What "say"? When the whole village knows what you intend for us and rumours fly if I so much as look at another girl. No, baba, you give me no choice. Like Cyprus has no choice but to accept the fate that others impose,' fumed Andonis, dropping the fish onto the floor.

Mihalis sighed heavily, carefully picking up and brushing down each fish with his hand.

'You might not think it's fair, Andoni, but it's life. And we must get through it as best we can. You're my son. Your happiness is all I could ever want. When you're older, with children of your own, I hope you'll understand. I hope you'll see things differently.'

'Maybe, but for the moment I'm still young and I've yet to lose those ideals you and yaya instilled within me. I still believe liberty is a prize worth fighting for, baba. Worth dying for if necessary.'

Tears were now welling up in his father's eyes. 'We've always tried to teach you right from wrong,' he whispered.

'That's why I am the way I am,' explained Andonis, turning to leave. 'Don't try and change me now.'

'Your mamma has boiled fasolia. She left you some on the stove,' offered Mihalis, in a more placatory tone. The farmer knew how much Andonis loved his mother's haricot beans.

Andonis left his father in the workshop with the fish. 'I'm not hungry,' said the tailor dismissively.

✳ ✳ ✳

Andonis awoke at dawn as he now did on particular mornings. His brother Marios was already up as usual, no doubt doing God's work. Andonis washed, shaved, dressed, and wet and combed his hair. Now he stationed himself at his bedroom window and looked onto the main road to observe the female early risers passing by with their clay jugs on their way to the village well.

He'd worked out the days that Funda fetched the water. Today was one. He waited, but could barely contain his excitement, and had to keep getting up to check his reflection in the small mirror on the wall.

When he first discerned Funda's sweet voice, Andonis felt his heart jump almost into his throat. Funda had taken to singing when nearing the home of the tailor, and he in turn had taken to reciprocating by accompanying her song with his new harmonica.

Off she set, Miss Yeragina,
To the well to fetch cold water.

And then Funda came into view, and she walked with such grace. She glanced over towards the window where she knew the tailor would be waiting for her and smiled.

Drun-drun, drun-drun-drun-drun.
As her bracelets rattle on.

As she passed directly in front of the house, the tailor removed the harmonica from his lips and blew Funda a kiss. And today, for the first time, Funda too put her hand to her lips and kissed them ever so lightly. Andonis thought that an angel was welcoming him to heaven.

Then, as quickly as she had appeared, she was gone and her song faded. But on this morning Andonis wanted more. He dropped the harmonica onto his bed and rushed out into the back yard, where his mother was already up, throwing grain to the chickens and congratulating them for being so beautiful.

'Good morning, mamma,' enthused Andonis, hugging his mother from behind, which made her jump. Then he planted a slobbery kiss on the back of her neck, which made her grimace.

'Get away from here, Andoni. Can't you see I'm busy?' she admonished, but Irini was heartened to see this unexpected display of affection.

'Indeed I can, mamma. And that's why I'm up. I want to relieve you of one of your chores.'

Mother gave son a dubious look.

'And why would you want to do that?' she probed.

'Is a son's devotion to his mother not reason enough?'

Irini rolled out her lower lip and shut one eye to indicate that she was impressed, though not entirely convinced, by her son's apparent new-found sense of duty.

'Fine. How about helping me with some washing? Or, I'm lighting the oven today, how about helping me mix some dough so we can make bread? If you do, I'll give you blessings from my twenty nails!'

Andonis nodded and then went to pick up the large clay jug by the back door. He poured out the last few drops of stale water, which splashed onto the ground and disturbed the chickens.

'Before we can do the washing or make bread we're missing one vital ingredient, mamma,' he exclaimed with a mischievous grin.

Irini was sure now that her son was up to something. She knew that fetching water from the well was a woman's job. The jug therefore gave her son an excuse to be somewhere he wouldn't normally be, an excuse perhaps to see someone he wouldn't normally see.

Momentarily Irini thought to challenge Andonis, make him come clean. But she realised this would lower her son's spirits, and she didn't want that. Besides, she knew her husband had already said what had needed to be said.

'Fine. Fetch the water. But make sure that's all you fetch!' she advised, and her advice came with a smile.

Andonis gave his mother a wink before turning on his heels and rushing off in pursuit of the girl he adored.

Funda and Andonis had played together when they were little. Muslim and Christian children often did in those days. Indeed, wise people, like Andonis's late grandmother Maria, encouraged it.

But then, as the children grew older and the girls developed curves and the boys developed dark fluff on their upper lip, playing together had become less appropriate. And there were other differences emerging which made contact difficult. Differences which had broken Maria's heart.

On the day of the old woman's funeral, the village had stood united again. In grief. Funda and Andonis watched as the coffin was lowered into the red earth outside the village church. The Muslim girl had reached out for the Christian boy's hand for comfort. It was then that the newly ordained Baba-Ghlioris had bustled through with his bottles of olive oil and holy water to pour into the open grave, causing Funda to release her grip on Mrs Maria's grandson. The pair had exchanged glances as the priest spoke loftily about resurrection…

By the time Andonis neared Funda, she was only a few hundred feet from the well. Andonis could make out in the distance that a handful of women were already there. Andonis pulled out his harmonica and began playing the same tune as before. Funda heard it and her heart filled with a great joy. Then with a terrible fear.

Funda stopped in her tracks and turned to face the tailor. The pair exchanged glances.

'Please, Andoni, you'll get us both into trouble. What are you doing here?' she admonished, then began to step forward once more. Andonis pursued, keeping a few paces back. He was near enough to admire her shapely contours, but far enough so that others might not notice that the two were walking together.

'I'm here to collect something I know I can't live without, Funda,' called Andonis.

Funda smiled but didn't dare look back. 'And what would that be, Mr Tailor?'

'Something I thirst for, Funda. Something to moisten my parched lips.'

They were now getting closer to the well, and though the women there did not appear to have noticed their approach, Funda knew they soon would. As much as she wanted to turn and glance at his handsome face, she resisted. She had to be the one to resist.

'Stop it, Andoni. Please. If you're not careful, news of this will be all over the village,' she warned and slowed her pace, forcing Andonis to do the same.

'Let it, Funda. Let me climb to the top of the mosque's minaret and shout out for all to hear. Funda and I had an encounter!'

'Hush, Andoni. You may be prepared to risk everything, but I have my reputation to think of.'

'Then come with me where we can't be seen. I have something important to share with you,' urged Andonis. He reached out, grabbed Funda round the waist and pulled her from the main road. Given how close they were to the well, Funda felt she had no option but to comply. She convinced herself it was the safest thing to do.

The pair were now hidden from view in a lemon grove.

'We're away from prying eyes here,' assured Andonis with a smile. He put his jug down on the ground. Then he took Funda's jug from her and placed it next to his.

'There's nothing for anyone to see. Please give me back my jug, Andoni, and let me get on with my chores.'

'Not till I can claim for real that kiss you almost blew me earlier,' he demanded. 'Then you can collect your water and I, after an appropriate period, can collect mine.' He leant forward until his cheek pressed against Funda's mouth. Funda's lips remained unmoved, though how she wanted them to respond.

'Fine,' cautioned Andonis. 'Then the kiss I blew you. Here it comes.' And before Funda could make even a show of resistance he turned his head and planted a kiss full on her lips.

'Are you quite done now, Mr Tailor?' she enquired, as though addressing an errant child. But inside she tingled. Inside she wanted more. The tailor nodded sheepishly.

'Will I see you again?' he enquired.

'I have water to fetch,' replied Funda. 'No doubt, every now and then, you'll have a similar need.'

Andonis gave Funda one of his smiles, which made her tingle again.

He nodded and licked his lips. 'I'll always have need of water,' he assured her.

8
The namesake   *O sinonomados*

I observed the water trickling off the dress factory's corrugated roof as I waited outside, drawing smoke from a rolled cigarette. Thankfully, the rain had almost stopped. Stella emerged from the factory a few minutes after six.

She was overjoyed to see me waiting for her, and hugged me again. Then she grabbed my arm and led me along the road.

'Where are you taking me?' I asked, offering token resistance.

'Home,' she replied, hitting my arm like a mother chastising her uncooperative child. 'Don't argue. I live near.'

As we walked she shook her head. 'It's been so long, Andoni. Why didn't you get in touch? How could you forget us?'

'I never forgot. But it was impossible for me to contact anybody from the village. Not after what happened.'

Stella nodded. 'And how about your Englezos friend? You know, he was asking after you some time ago. Did you ever get to see him?'

I stared at her blankly, trying to conceal the torrent of emotion which now swept through me. The captain. I'd let him down. I'd let everybody down. After a short walk, past the greyhound stadium, north along Green Lanes and up a side road, Stella steered me into the small front garden of a terraced house.

She opened the front door and ushered me inside. We were greeted by loud English pop music from an upstairs radio. I found the music not unpleasant, but it seemed to irritate Stella. As she took my coat I was struck by a stale concoction of smells: of cigarettes and of cooking, of unwashed clothes and of cat. In the hall, up against the wall, was a Chopper bicycle with wheels caked in mud.

'Come in, come in,' she beckoned, hurrying me through into the back room. The carpet was in need of vacuuming. There were unwashed cups on the coffee table. Stella removed a crumpled magazine on the sofa to offer me a seat. She looked ashamed.

'Sorry about the mess. It's that son of mine. What with work, I just don't have enough time to clean up after him.' She left me sitting on the sofa, returned to the hall, and called up the staircase.

'Nigo! Nick! Turn that awful racket off and come down. An uncle's come to see us.' She turned to me and explained that Nick was her son.

I smiled. 'You called him after…'

'Oh yes. And the rogue lives up to the name.'

A moment later the music stopped and a teenaged boy entered the room, head bowed and with hands in pockets. He had long, unruly hair and dark fluff on his upper lip which made him appear older than his unsure poise suggested.

'He even looks like that crazy brother of mine, God rest his soul,' added Stella, giving the boy's cheek a squeeze which I could tell annoyed him. 'Say hello to uncle Andonis, Nigo.'

The boy looked down at me with a frown. I stood up and offered my hand. He shook it limply.

'So how old are you then, son?' I enquired, retaking my seat. Nick looked down at me for a moment but ignored my question and turned to his mother.

'What's for dinner? I'm starving,' he enquired in English.

His mother replied in the Cypriot vernacular, 'I've soaked some fasolia.'

Nick tutted. 'I hate beans,' he declared, and I was saddened. Then he left the room. We heard him run back up the stairs.

'What can I do with that boy?' sighed Stella, sitting down next to me. I smiled and remembered her brother. Without a father's guidance and discipline, he too had been a difficult one.

'Are you bringing him up alone?' I enquired, and for a brief moment couldn't help but think of Ruth.

Stella scoffed. 'I may as well be. His father works late. He hardly lifts a finger to help. Still. What can I do?'

She glared at me. I lowered my head and stroked a furrowed brow.

Stella grabbed my hand and continued, 'I don't see a ring on your finger. After all this time, you never married?'

I shook my head.

'You know what?' she declared. 'Somehow that doesn't surprise me.' She tutted and rocked her head with her other hand. 'My All-Holy Virgin, Andoni! What evil spell did that Turkish witch cast over you? Over all of us?'

I shook a lowered head. 'Please, Stella. Let's just leave it, shall we?'

'That's right, Andoni. Run away. Avoid facing the truth.'

I slapped the sofa. 'That's enough. You and I were never meant to be. It has nothing to do with...' I hesitated. 'With her.'

Stella nodded and her eyes filled with regret. She began to sob, and so I took her hand and stroked it. I continued more soothingly. 'Come on, Stella. You must be strong. You have a fine son who needs a mother's love.'

Stella stared into my eyes. 'I'm crying for you, you fool. You deserved more. So much more!' she yelled.

We sat in silence for a moment. Then Nick re-emerged. He looked at me disapprovingly. There was anger and defiance in his eyes.

'Why have you made my mother cry?' he demanded, clenching his fist.

'Hush, Nigo. I'm all right,' intervened Stella, but Nick was not convinced.

'Who does he think he is? Coming here and upsetting you like this,' he countered, pointing at me. I was impressed, and also amused, by the young man's bravado. I stood up and squared up to him with a smile. I was a few inches taller and with a larger frame, but young Nick was in no way intimidated, and pushed his chest out at me.

'Don't worry, son, everything's OK,' I advised warmly, in English, and put a reassuring hand on his shoulder. 'Your mother and I were brought up together. In the village in Cyprus. Like brother and sister. It's the shock of seeing me again that's made her cry.'

Nick appeared to calm down a little, and then a look of realisation came over his face. 'I've heard about you. You were really close with my uncle. The one they named me after. Mum says you were with him when...' He paused.

'He'd have been proud to have you as a nephew,' I said, patting his shoulder.

Nick nodded. 'What was my uncle like?'

'Proud. Loyal. Fearless,' I enthused, before turning to Stella for help.

'Reckless. You forgot reckless,' she added, a grin now on her tear-stained face.

Nick gave a proud smile. 'I take after my uncle Nigo, don't I?' he announced.

I smiled back and nodded. Then I had to look away. I didn't want Nick to see the sadness in my eyes.

❊ ❊ ❊

Stella insisted that I stay and eat with them. I helped her tidy up the back room before we laid the table in the front room. Unlike the rest of the house this room was better presented, though I surmised through lack of use rather than out of any particular care. I could see it was Stella's special room, the one reserved for important guests and occasions. There were photographs, of Stella in a wedding dress and a stout man who seemed familiar, and of Nick as a boy, with cropped hair and short trousers.

When we sat down at the table to eat, Nick refused to join us, and a tired look of frustration emerged on Stella's face. The boy announced that he was going out, and as he turned to leave Stella called after him. She rose from the table and went into the hall, where she dug out a handbag from the cupboard underneath the stairs. I saw her drop a few coins into his outstretched palm.

'Go to Andrikos and buy yourself some fish and chips or something,' she instructed. Nick accepted the money with a nod and was gone. I gave Stella a look of disapproval as she joined me back at the table.

'I'm too soft on him, I know,' she admitted. 'But I'm his mamma. I'm meant to indulge my child. His father's to blame.'

'So where is his father?' I enquired.

'At work, I expect,' she replied with a hint of uncertainty. 'He's a waiter, in a restaurant in Holloway. Zorba's. Do you know it?'

I nodded. I knew of it, as I knew of so many other unimaginatively named Cypriot-owned restaurants which had opened in north London over the years.

'Zorba's,' I repeated.

'Don't get me wrong,' she continued. 'My Lugas isn't a bad man but he's weak. He works long hours and his pay isn't good. He won't stand up for himself, and he's too much of a coward to start off on his own, like other men. And so we struggle. And it gets him down.' She paused a moment. 'And he drinks too much whisky. He drinks to forget.'

I shrugged. 'Some men do,' I noted, although I seldom did.

'And he's gambling more and more. They play cards most nights, after the restaurant shuts. Sometimes he doesn't get home until morning. It's got to the point where he's handing most of his wages straight back to his bosses.'

I shook my head and tutted.

Stella continued, 'When I complain, and sometimes even when I don't, he…' She grabbed her hair with both her hands. A cold anger welled up inside me, but I took care to disguise it from Stella. 'But why am I telling you this? It's not your concern,' she announced, trying to recompose herself.

'He shouldn't hit you,' I stated.

Stella glared at me. 'Don't tell me what my husband should and shouldn't do,' she yelled. 'You have no right. I'm not the little girl you and my brothers used to look out for. I'm all grown up now. I look after myself. Understand?'

I nodded. 'I'm sorry, Stella. It's because I care.'

'So you say,' she countered, waving the back of her hand at me. 'Well, I've learnt to live without your care.'

'You must give me permission to talk to your husband,' I demanded. 'He must be made to see sense.'

Stella's face filled with fear. 'No please, Andoni. He's a good man. Honestly he is. It's my fault. I nag him too much. I lash him with my tongue. A man can only take so much.'

'And I can take no more,' I declared, slamming the table with my hand. Stella knew not to respond.

We dropped the subject of her husband. I learnt that Stella's mother and her brother Yannis were still living in the village. Yannis and Martha now had three children and had moved into my parent's house. Stella kept in touch with them every now and then, by letter or by phone, but she'd never been back.

'The village has changed so much. Yannis tells me of the troubles. It's awful. They've built barricades between us and the Turks. I can understand why you've wanted to keep clear of it all, Andoni. But really, it's time you made the effort to get in touch. Your mamma's living in your old workshop now, like your yaya Mrs Maria used to.'

I wanted the thoughts Stella was conjuring up in my head to go away so was relieved when she got up suddenly and left the room. She returned from the kitchen a moment later and handed me a scrap of paper with what I took to be an international telephone number on it.

She pointed to her telephone, on a low table by the door. 'Why don't we call the village? They'll fetch your mamma.'

Stella reached down for the receiver. 'No. Please, Stella. I can't.' I was aware that I was shaking.

'But think of your poor mamma, Andoni.'

'I am thinking of her. Why open old wounds? There's been enough pain.'

Stella raised both her hands.

'She's all alone, Andoni. Marios has devoted his life to God. He might be a bishop now. He's rarely seen in the village. Your mamma at least has a right to know that her other son is alive and well.'

I shook my head. I didn't dare ask after my father. Since Stella had not mentioned him I dreaded the answer.

'Promise me you won't tell them you've seen me, Stella,' I implored, and tears rolled down my cheeks to show how vital it was that she comply with my request.

Stella sat down, grabbed my wet cheeks and pulled my face towards hers until our noses touched. Her eyes burned into mine and she looked deep within me.

'Where's Andonis?' she growled, and within the fearful man staring back at her, a roused consciousness was twitching. 'Bring him back,' she demanded.

I played with my food in silence.

'Why won't you eat?' she enquired. I thought of my father. I remembered how much he loved my mother's cooking. As much as I did.

'I'm sorry, Stella. I'm not hungry.'

9
The fishing boat   *I psarobulla*

Winter gave way to spring. And with the temperature, tensions in Cyprus continued to rise. The British had exiled Archbishop Makarios, to the Seychelles, in an attempt to defuse the tension.

Meanwhile Andonis and Funda continued to snatch forbidden moments as often as they could. Their love blossomed. The early morning kisses they exchanged grew more passionate as the belief grew stronger that nothing could stand between them.

Mihalis had questioned his wife as to why Andonis had suddenly become keen to fetch water, but Irini had made excuses: their elder son was maturing into a sensitive young man happy to share his mother's heavy burdens. Though unconvinced, Mihalis had no desire to pursue the matter, and Irini was relieved.

Early one morning, to the accompaniment of his father's snores in the next room, Andonis washed and shaved and combed his hair. Having put on a fresh white shirt, he rushed to the back yard and reached out for his mother's jug. Andonis was dismayed to see it already replenished with fresh water. He ran an agitated hand through his hair.

'I've been already,' explained the solemn voice of his mother. Andonis looked round the back door to see her, sitting outside, by the lemon tree, with a tray of green lentils on her lap. She was picking through them one by one, weeding out any tiny stones.

'I was up with the first cockerel and thought I'd save you the effort,' she added.

Andonis was unable to disguise his agitation. Irini beckoned him over to sit in the empty chair next to her. Resigned, Andonis did so.

'Really, you shouldn't have,' he declared. 'You know I don't mind fetching the water.'

Irini looked up and nodded. 'I know,' she said with a sigh. Andonis sighed back. Irini looked down again at her lentils.

'We're having mujendra tonight,' she explained. 'And we must safeguard your father's teeth!'

Andonis picked up one of the stones from the tray. He screwed up his face as he imagined the pain it would cause if crunched inadvertently.

'I take a lot of care, Andoni. I wouldn't want your father to come to harm,' added Irini, still picking through the lentils. 'After all these years, I still love him, you know. As much as the day we were married.'

'After the trembling heart, the breathlessness and the flushed cheeks – after the animal urges diminish, what remains is real love, Andoni.'

Andonis thought of Funda and nodded.

'I'm a fortunate woman,' continued Irini. 'For when I fell for your father, it wasn't only for his firm body, strong limbs and rich hair. I fell for his principles. His honesty. His integrity. The things that will always be with him.'

Irini kept picking through the lentils.

'Of course, our relationship has evolved. The years demand it and motherhood changes a woman's perspective. But I've always wanted to protect my man of principle from the harm those principles might bring,' she continued. 'And I always will.'

Irini had picked out another stone, and now rubbed it between her fingers a moment before letting it drop to the ground.

'What are you saying, mamma?' asked Andonis.

'If she loved you, Andoni, really loved you, wouldn't she want to protect you? Wouldn't she want to put an end to this dangerous game you're playing?'

Andonis stared at the jug full of water that stood in the way of Funda's lips.

'Would anything have stopped you and your man of principle from being together?' he asked.

Irini sighed but did not speak. She knew the answer was nothing.

'If you loved your son, mamma, really loved him, you'd let him go.'

With eyes watering, mother poured the water from the jug onto the dry ground around the lemon tree. With eyes watering, son now stooped to kiss her.

Andonis grabbed the empty jug and was gone.

✳ ✳ ✳

It was a warm Sunday morning. The liturgy was over. Marios had a cloth in his hand and was wiping the icons in the church. He had reached the icon of Saint Varnavas the Apostle, and looked deeply into the apostle's light brown eyes in search of guidance. He whispered a prayer for his brother. And then one for his homeland.

Baba-Ghlioris emerged from the ieron having disappeared behind the screen some moments earlier. He did so more and more of late, noted Marios, and would always return with eyes glazed and with feet unsteady. Marios hoped this might be the effect of intense prayer. Perhaps for their country's archbishop. Marios gave his priest a sympathetic look.

'Are you well, father?' he asked. 'You look so troubled. I'd be happy to assist, if only you'd share your thoughts with me.'

Baba-Ghlioris reached out to pat Marios on the shoulder, but ended up leaning on his student for support.

'You're my rock, Mario. And in you lie my greatest hopes.' He paused, rubbed his beard a moment, and then continued. 'And there is indeed something troubling me that perhaps I should share with you now.'

Baba-Ghlioris released his grip on Marios and manoeuvred himself into the nearest pew, beckoning his student to sit by him. Marios did as instructed.

'Your babas and I have discussed your future, Mario. I explained that you're not cut out for a life in the fields. And there's nothing more you can learn from this tired old priest in this tired old church. I believe the time would now be right for you to take the next step along the path that God, in all His wisdom, has set for you.'

Marios nodded gravely. He had prayed for such a moment. 'Spiritually, all that I am I owe to you, father.'

'God planted the seed within you, my son. All I've done is enjoy the spectacle of its early growth,' corrected the priest. 'I would dearly, dearly wish to recommend that you be accepted at the monastery of Jikos. There's so much for you to learn there.'

Marios's face filled with joy. Jikos. It was where his beatitude, Magarios himself, had begun his ministry.

'Father. It's what I've always dreamt of. Your influence would go a long way to enable me to embark on a life serving our Holy Orthodox Church. And I've so much to give, father. I'm so happy. And so grateful.'

The priest sighed. 'As I said, Mario. I would wish to recommend you to Jikos, but as things are at the moment I'm afraid I may not be able to.'

Marios lowered his head. 'What have I done, father? What cause have you to question my devotion to Christ? Tell me and I'll do everything I can to remove your doubts.'

'Mario, Mario,' murmured the priest soothingly. 'You've done nothing wrong. It's your brother's behaviour that concerns me. I'm worried that his indelicate actions might affect your reputation.'

Marios knew what his priest meant.

'Andonis is a fine man, father. He'd do nothing to harm his family. This infatuation will pass. I'm sure of it.'

'You must understand, my son. There's a lot at stake. We both know what some people are like, with their loose tongues and wagging fingers. Think of the scandal if things with your brother were allowed to get out of hand. Andonis takes after your father, Mario. He's headstrong. I'm worried this might become more than a passing fancy. It might turn into a futile point of principle for Andonis, regardless of the consequences. And I've invested too many hopes in someone I love as much as my own flesh and blood to see them all come to nothing.'

Marios was moved, and stooped to kiss the priest's hand. 'Oh, father. What can be done?'

The priest lowered his head. 'Perhaps only the intervention of Saint Varnavas the Apostle himself can save us now,' he mumbled.

Marios nodded. He knew of Saint Varnavas the Apostle's interventions, or as those less religious termed them his curses. Some years ago, to the horror of Baba-Ghlioris and other Christians of the village, the Englezi had appointed a Muslim as the village policeman. He was allocated a house in the middle of the Christian neighbourhood.

Within the week, after the Muslim had moved in with his family and all their possessions, he was begging the Englezi to have him transferred, and transfer him they did. The following Sunday the church was full of grateful Christians giving thanks to their apostle. They believed he had miraculously intervened to make the Muslim and his masters see sense. Those less devout had other theories as to why the Muslim had fled.

'I'll pray to Saint Varnavas the Apostle that this madness that's taken over my brother passes as quickly as possible. Don't you see, father? God's testing my faith. I must pray and pray until Andonis is delivered from temptation. Pray until my eyes are red and my feet unsteady.'

'Mine also,' agreed the priest, rising from the pew and making his way back to the ieron. 'And don't worry, my son, I'm certain that one day soon Saint Varnavas the Apostle will answer our prayers.'

⁂ ⁂ ⁂

The few people who owned motor vehicles in the village rarely washed them. There wasn't the water to spare. And besides, washing was futile against a relentless dust which would soon turn the machine a ruddy grey.

Property is theft, thought Nigos, leaning against the small ruddy grey van which was the property of Mr Vasos. It was what Nigos's late, blessed father always used to say. It's what the party taught. Nigos was too young and too petulant to care for communist ideology. Still, it was a phrase that had stuck in his mind. And, as he stood outside the coffee-shop, before Mrs Anjela, Vasos's rotund and pleasant wife, pleading with her to let him have the van's keys for the day, it was a phrase he now repeated with a cheeky smile.

Anjela grinned and examined Nigos with maternal affection. What a handsome young man the widow's boy was becoming. Muscular, full of fun and bravado, with that wild black mane of his. She shrugged.

'You're putting both my feet in one shoe, Nigo. It's not up to me. But the master will be awake soon. Come back later and ask him yourself.'

Anjela folded her arms with finality. She knew what her husband's response would be.

'Come on, Mrs Anjela,' pleaded Nigos. 'By the time Mr Vasos wakes up, much of the day will have passed. Your husband's a fine man, one who'll always stand up for the rights of the poor and downtrodden. Surely he wouldn't want to deny my blessed father's children the use of this fine vehicle. On a day when it would otherwise just sit here under the sun gathering more dust.'

Nigos used his finger to draw a hammer and sickle in the thin layer of dust covering the van's bonnet. Anjela slapped his hand and pushed Nigos away, placing herself between him and her husband's property.

'You're determined to make trouble for me, you rogue,' chastised Anjela. 'What do you want it for, anyway?'

Nigos rubbed his slapped hand tenderly. He looked wistfully at the communist's wife.

'I'd really like to take my brother and sister to the beach, along from the old monastery. It would so fill our poor widowed mother's heart with joy to see her children escape for some recreation on God's day. Please let us borrow it, Mrs Anjela. I beg you.'

Anjela closed one eye and rubbed the fine black hairs on her chin.

'I wish I could, Nigo. I really do.' Then she appeared to make a decision and turned purposefully towards the coffee-shop. 'Stay here. I'll wake him now and see what he says.'

'No! Don't do that, Mrs Anjela,' implored Nigos with desperation. He knew the couple well enough to be aware that wife rarely got the better of husband, particularly when the husband was roused from what, due to Vasos's intense relationship with caffeine, was a rare and much-needed sleep.

'Mr Vasos works hard all week. I'll not have his rest interrupted, even for the sake of three poor orphans. Don't worry. I'll go back and tell Stella and Yannis that it's not possible to lie on the soft golden sand or to feel the cooling sea breeze against our faces, nor the soothing salt water on our skin,' said Nigos woefully.

He raised a palm to his temple and shook his head.

'We can spend another sad day, mourning the death of our brave father. The man who lived by and died for the principles your husband so passionately believes in.'

The woman stopped in her tracks and, with her back still to Nigos, gave out a deep sigh.

'All right, enough. May the devil take you, you can have the van!' she huffed, before waddling off into the coffee-shop to return moments later with the keys. 'I can't believe I'm doing this.'

She passed the keys to an overjoyed Nigos, who kissed her hand repeatedly. The woman wagged a finger at him.

'Now you take good care of it, you hear me? If I see so much as a tiny scratch that wasn't there before, I'll get my husband to grind you all up and serve orphan-flavoured coffee in the shop next week.'

Nigos nodded, opened the van door, jumped up into the driver's seat and wound down the window.

'Mrs Anjela, be sure to thank Mr Vasos for this wonderful gesture. You're truly blessed with the most generous of husbands.'

'Put wind in your breeches! Just get going before he wakes up,' urged the woman.

Nigos blew Mrs Anjela a final kiss and crunched the van into gear. He drove off noisily, and Anjela grabbed her head, frantic that her husband might be roused before she had prepared a good enough explanation for the van's disappearance for the day.

❋ ❋ ❋

Nigos drove inexpertly, staying in the low gears more than was necessary. It wasn't merely bad driving, but to draw attention to his latest triumph. As he passed villagers, he honked the van's horn. They waved back, amazed at how Nigos had contrived to commandeer the coffee-shop owner's prized possession.

Driving past the church, Nigos saw Marios sweeping the steps. Nigos pulled up outside the gates.

'Mario!' he called, revving the engine. 'What say you take a break from God's work and join us for an afternoon by the sea? The day will be sweet, medium or plain, depending on your taste.'

Marios smiled. 'I don't think so, Nigo. I've got some reading to do.'

Baba-Ghlioris had heard the van from inside the church, and now emerged unsteadily.

'Nonsense, Mario,' he slurred. 'Go to the sea, my son. Go to the sea. For was it not at the Sea of Galilee that the fishermen, Andreas and Bedros, found Christ and became fishers of men?'

Marios was reluctant to leave his priest in this unsteady condition. But the priest pushed him forward.

'Please go, with God's blessing,' he urged.

Marios nodded and bent down to kiss the priest's hand. Next stop for Nigos was home, to pick up his brother and sister. Stella was overjoyed and jumped in the back of the van, but Yannis refused to join them. He said he preferred to spend the day with his beloved Martha, who would be helping their mother and Irini prepare the evening meal. Nigos raised his eyebrows and wished his brother a pleasant day. Next stop, Mihalis's house, to pick up the tailor.

❋ ❋ ❋

The clear sea lapped against the golden sand. Four young people sat in a line on this otherwise deserted beach, a few feet from the water. Nigos was busy removing his shirt and trousers, getting ready for a swim. Marios sat next to him, enjoying the rhythmical sound of waves brushing against the shore, feeling the warm sunshine on his brow. He marvelled at the glory of God.

Andonis, next to his brother, had taken out his harmonica and had started playing a tune. Stella, next to Andonis, was now singing along. Her voice, though not as sweet and perfect as the one Andonis adored, was not unpleasant.

A fishing boat takes to the water,
Out from the shore, out from the shore.

A fishing boat takes to the water,
From the little isle of Hydra,
And it's sponges that she's after,
Out from the shore, out from the shore.

When her singing was done, Stella spoke.

'That fishing boat must have been really precious for someone to go to the trouble of writing a song about her. Like he was writing about a woman.'

Nigos smirked. 'Perhaps the songwriter wanted to find out how fishy she was inside!'

Stella's mouth dropped. 'What are you saying, you animal? You have such a filthy mouth!' she rebuked.

'So would he!' retorted Nigos, and screamed with laughter before springing up and running into the water.

Stella turned to Andonis, who was staring out to sea. 'Do you have your eye on any fishing boats, Andoni?'

Andonis blushed, and Marios retreated from his reverie so as to hear his brother's response. Andonis turned to Stella and admired the mole on her cheek. He reached out and played with her long black hair. Then he turned to look at Marios, in an attempt to deflect attention.

'Doesn't every young man?' he replied, a little uncomfortably. Then Andonis rose to his feet and began removing his shirt.

'I don't think your brother does, Andoni,' remarked Stella, looking up and admiring the tufts of hair on the tailor's masculine chest. His body aroused feelings within Stella, feelings which Andonis could see in her eyes. He dropped his trousers, shrugged and fled into the sea to join Nigos. The two friends started playing headers with a small leather ball they'd brought with them.

Stella sighed and nudged at Marios. He turned towards her, and she recognised the longing in his eyes. She'd seen such longing before, and though she could not return it the longing comforted her.

'Is your heart so full of love for God, Mario, that it can't find room for another?' she enquired coquettishly.

Marios sighed. The sun, sea and sand had their effect on him. He turned to Stella. If any girl could capture a part of his heart…

'I am a man,' he declared. 'I have feelings like any other. But my feelings for God are so much stronger. I believe my life will be more fulfilled in His exclusive service. A priest may take a wife, but not a bishop or archbishop.'

'You have such high ambitions. But let's just imagine,' she suggested, unconsciously fluttering her eyelashes. 'Imagine that a girl you admired told you she loved you and loved also your devotion to God. That she wanted you this way.'

Marios's heart leapt. 'Such a woman would be hard to find these days. A life serving God is full of hardship. Material comforts aren't a priority. It wouldn't be fair on her or on any children which God might grant.'

'But God would provide, wouldn't He? All that she and the children needed, if not all that they desired.'

'That's true,' nodded Marios.

'And if a woman accepted that fate in order to occupy a small corner of a heart otherwise devoted to God, then wouldn't you give her that small corner?'

Marios peered deeply and lovingly into Stella's eyes. 'If God were to bless me with such a woman, one prepared to make that sacrifice, then I would see it as His will, and would gladly sacrifice any higher aspirations I might have to serve Him.'

Stella nodded. She reached over and pecked Marios on the cheek.

'I wish you well in whatever God chooses for you, Mario,' she said.

Marios nodded back and smiled.

'I wish you the same, Stella,' he replied, and returned a kiss to her forehead.

And Marios turned from Stella and devoted all his attentions to the sun and the sky and the sea, marvelling once more at the wonder that was God's creation. Stella rose and told Marios she was going for a walk along the beach.

Still playing in the sea, Nigos observed his sister get up. 'Where do you think you're going, Stella?' he called.

'For a walk?' she asked rhetorically.

'On your own? Get back here!' demanded Nigos, raising his hands as though the very idea of his sister going anywhere alone was preposterous.

'I'm a single girl, Nigo,' she replied defiantly.

Nigos turned to the tailor. 'Andoni, why don't you go with her?' he prompted.

Andonis frowned. 'Why me? She's your sister.'

'Because you've won at headers,' exclaimed Nigos. Andonis nodded. He supposed it was a just reward. 'Besides,' urged Nigos. 'It's clear right now she'd prefer your company to that of her own flesh and blood.'

Andonis nodded once more before leaving Nigos in the sea.

'Wait, Stella. Wait for your chaperon,' he called as he jogged to catch her up.

Stella turned but continued walking. 'I don't need a chaperon, Andoni. In case you hadn't noticed, I'm not a little girl any more,' she rebuffed with a frown too forceful to be genuine.

'I had noticed, Stella,' conceded Andonis, having now caught up with her. 'In case you hadn't noticed, I'm not a little boy.'

Stella nodded and smiled. They carried on walking for a moment without exchange while Stella built up courage to speak.

'So, since we're no longer children then, can we talk openly as adults?' she enquired nervously.

'We can but try,' suggested an equally nervous Andonis.

Stella turned to him.

'Are you in love with the Turkish girl?'

Andonis was shocked by Stella's openness, and hesitated.

'Why do you ask?' he stalled. 'Would you rather I was in love with you?'

Stella stopped walking, sighed and looked out to sea. Andonis did likewise.

'I'm not sure what I want any more, Andoni,' she said eventually.

Then Stella made her way back along the beach, back to Marios and her brother, leaving Andonis's mind out at sea.

❋ ❋ ❋

'Come on. Time to play.'

A hot and increasingly bothered Nigos had had quite enough of lying on the beach. A subdued Stella had wandered off with Marios to visit the Venetian monastery in the tiny fishing village, and so Nigos was left with Andonis, dozing next to him. Nigos nudged his friend lightly. How could he just fall asleep like a lazy dog when Nigos had plans? And with a contented face, despite having earlier upset Nigos's sister. Nigos nudged once again, this time with more force. Disturbed, Andonis groaned and opened one eye.

'Get up,' pressed Nigos, now pulling at Andonis's limp arm. Andonis was having none of it. He frowned and pulled it back.

'Come on, Nigo. Why can't you sit quietly? It's such a peaceful place. Let me sleep.'

Nigos frowned. Without him, Andonis wouldn't be in this peaceful place.

'You can sleep later. Tonight. When you're in your bed,' retorted Nigos. He poked a finger hard into the flesh of Andonis's upper arm. 'Let's do something!'

Andonis ignored him. Nigos huffed. Then he stood and deliberately kicked sand onto Andonis's chest. Andonis opened the same weary eye and spied the unwanted sand. He shook his head with irritation, but knew better than to react. Instead, to his friend's displeasure, he turned slowly on his side to let the sand drop away. Andonis, now with his back to Nigos, bit at the air a few times to announce his intended return to sleep.

But Nigos wasn't finished. He cleared his chest and his throat and his larynx and spat out a huge globule of green mucus. It landed a few feet from an unmoved Andonis. Near where it fell Nigos noticed a large shell, half-buried in the sand. He paced over and bent down to pick it up. He carried the shell into the sea with a broad grin. Andonis was vaguely aware that his friend was up to something. But his mind was trained to switch off at such times. And switch off it did.

Nigos meanwhile was a man with a mission. He had filled the shell with water and was now creeping back to where Andonis lay. Nigos hesitated for a brief moment before pouring cool sea water over the side of Andonis's face. Andonis shuddered briefly but remained still. He waited for the taste of salt water to penetrate his lips. For the wetness to soak his hair. And for his temper to simmer.

Nigos had already taken precautionary measures, stepping back a safe distance. He chuckled quietly to himself.

'You've pulled out both the rope and the post,' declared Andonis, and now launched himself head first towards his friend's legs in an attempt to bring him down. But Nigos knew what was coming and simply manoeuvred backwards to avoid the attack. Andonis fell empty-handed into the sand and growled. He leapt to his feet and gave chase. Nigos turned on his heels and fled along the shoreline.

Nigos's tongue rubbed the bristles on his upper lip with satisfaction. He'd finally got his way.

'Bravo, Andoni,' he called back to his friend. 'So good to see you up and about. And don't forget your harmonica!'

'I'll give you harmonica!' screamed Andonis in hot pursuit, face partly caked with sand. He grabbed the instrument, until now tucked in his shorts, and threw it at the fleeing Nigos. It shot inches over his head and landed a few yards further along the beach. Nigos bent down to scoop it up as he ran past.

'Thank you so much. But I think you play it better than me!' panted Nigos, still running at full pace. He puffed breathlessly and tunelessly into and out of the harmonica.

Two young men darted along the deserted golden beach near the monastery. One laughed. One cursed.

Nigos had now reached a rotting old rowing boat, tied to a rock. One end was half immersed in the sea, covered in algae and molluscs. Exhausted, Nigos jumped in and lay down, expecting, at any moment, an angry Andonis to bundle in on top of him.

Nigos waited, still breathing through the harmonica. Andonis halted when he reached the boat to consider his next move. He bent forward and grabbed his thighs to catch his breath. A moment later, he was untying the rotting rope and pushing the boat out to sea.

A voice started singing from inside the boat.

A fishing boat takes to the water,
Out from the shore, out from the shore.

Then Nigos blew into the harmonica to punctuate his words.

'That's right. A fishing boat sets out. Carrying you with it. Next stop Egypt!' declared Andonis. Andonis was now hanging on to the boat, which was being carried out to sea by the waves. Nigos had sat up, and started rowing with the two rotting oars from inside the boat.

'Get in, Andoni,' he called.

Andonis struggled to pull himself into the boat. He clambered over Nigos, twisting his friend's ear vengefully as he did so. Andonis leant over the front of the boat and read the faded name painted crudely on it. *Eleftheria.* Liberty.

'It must have been sitting on the beach for years. I wonder who it belongs to,' said Andonis.

'Probably some poor fisherman long since passed away, God rest his soul,' mused Nigos with a grin. 'With lazy, good-for-nothing sons who refused to inherit his work.'

He stopped rowing for a moment to wipe the harmonica dry against the bare skin of his chest. He returned it to Andonis.

'Come on. Time to play.'

Andonis put the harmonica to his lips and commenced a traditional tune. Nigos nodded recognition and began to sing along. Andonis played expertly. Nigos sang inexpertly. It was hard to row and sing, especially if you were skilled at neither.

Girl from Limassol, girl from Limassol,
Girl from Limassol, she's an angel-fashioned doll.
I'm not looking for a castle, I'm not interested in wealth.
She should spare me any hassle, and just love me for myself.

The boat zigzagged clumsily along the shoreline. After they had been floating a while, singing and joking, it was Nigos who first spied a dozen or so men on the beach. Some were lying in the sun, others were playing football with a heavy brown leather ball. Their backs and chests were hairless, and more red than brown. Their khaki shorts and heavy black boots confirmed what the Cypriots had surmised already. Soldiers. Englezi.

One such soldier, not as young as the rest and lying on a towel, turned his attention from the game being played before him to the approaching boat in the sea. He raised the pair of binoculars which hung round his neck and focused on the two young Cypriots. He recognised them.

'Shitty Englezi soldiers,' cursed Nigos, and spat overboard.

'It's their Sunday as much as ours. Let them enjoy themselves,' cautioned Andonis.

'That's it, Andoni,' growled Nigos. 'So reasonable. So civilised. Let the barbarians enjoy our sunshine, our beaches, our island. After all, it's theirs as much as ours!'

Nigos now screamed, 'Fuck them all!'

Andonis was dismayed to see his friend react with such intolerance when no good could come of it. 'Calm down, Nigo. They're not troubling anyone.'

'They are! They're troubling me!' Nigos now stood up in the boat and, struggling to maintain his balance, he called out to the men on the beach. 'Bastards! Asprogoli! Go back to your cold country!'

The soldiers on the beach could just make out that a foolish young local in a boat was screaming something at them in his native tongue. They were amused. Only the older soldier, with the aid of binoculars, was able to note the anger in the cursing Cypriot's eyes. He was saddened but not surprised to see such venom directed at him and his men.

'Save your breath, Nigo. They can hardly hear you, let alone understand you,' advised Andonis.

'Well, let's get a little closer then,' suggested Nigos, who had now pointed the boat shorewards. 'We need to show them what they're up against.'

'Don't you think we could do with a few more ships if we're planning to retake the island?'

'Don't be such a coward, Andoni. It's our duty as patriots to offer the Englezi even passive resistance. Can you play the national anthem?'

Andonis deliberated. 'I didn't think we had a national anthem.'

Nigos was annoyed. 'Don't act the fool, Andoni. We have enough problems with the Turks without foolishness from our own people.'

Nigos filled his lungs and began to sing at the top off his voice.

I can see you in the sword-blade striking terror all around.

'Play it!'

Andonis smiled. It was amusing to see his friend so animated. He began playing his harmonica.

I can see you in the figure moving swiftly over ground.
From the sacred bones extracted of the Greeks through history,
And with courage rediscovered, we salute you, Liberty.

The boat was now only thirty or so feet from the beach. The tall soldier heard the tune being played on the boat. He recognised it and smiled.

And with courage rediscovered, we salute you, Liberty.

Nigos now stopped singing the words of the Greek national anthem. He stood up again, and the boat wobbled. Steadying himself by holding onto Andonis, Nigos cupped a hand round his mouth to direct his voice. Now he constructed lyrics of his own, using a language with which the soldiers were more familiar.

English-English, English-English, English-English, fuck-off-home!

The amusement of the soldiers on the beach turned to outrage. The more senior figure stood up and tried to calm his men, but they were in no mood for compromise. They pulled off their boots and socks and threw themselves into the sea in pursuit of the boat. Nigos was quick to turn it round and seek safety in deeper waters.

'Bye bye!' called Nigos, and Andonis took out his harmonica and played a familiar tune for the flapping soldiers.

The figure on the beach smiled. His men were congratulating themselves for seeing off an attack from this rotting Cypriot fishing boat. The captain, for it was he, sang along to the young tailor's tune under his breath.

Rule Britannia, Britannia rule the waves.
Britons never, never, never shall be slaves.

It was later that same Sunday. Hazy sunlight streamed through the open door of Andonis's workshop, catching the tiny dust particles floating in the air. Outside, in the back yard, Irini, the widow, Stella and Martha were laying the table in preparation for the evening meal. Inside, the workshop light flickered off Andonis's needle as he worked it in and out of navy-blue cloth. He was adjusting a jacket, which Yannis was trying on. It was part of the new suit which Andonis had been making in his spare time for Yannis's wedding in the summer.

'Let's be done with it, Andoni,' demanded an increasingly impatient Yannis. Bent over before him, the tailor was blocking Yannis's view of himself in the long mirror.

'Keep still, Yanni. Don't rush me,' advised the tailor, before leaning forward to break the thread with his teeth. 'OK, that'll do for now.'

Andonis moved out of the way to allow Yannis to admire his reflection. Yannis turned first to the left, then to the right, looking over each shoulder in turn, while Andonis observed with a proud smile.

'This suit's going to be so fine. You're a genius. Thank you so much,' enthused Yannis.

'I'm the one who should thank *you*,' corrected Andonis modestly. 'When the village sees such a fine groom they'll all be wanting a suit from Andonis the tailor.'

Yannis gestured to the window with his head. 'But the next suit ought to be for yourself, Andoni. For your own betrothal to our Stella.'

Andonis sighed and shook his head. 'Yanni. I love you as I love your mother and brother. And sister too! But please don't presume to make plans for my future.'

Yannis was not offended. He knew Andonis too well.

'You're just a little unsure of yourself. I understand. It was like that for Martha and me. Until things are out in the open it's a delicate matter.'

Delicate indeed, thought Andonis.

At that moment Mihalis appeared at the workshop door and entered.

'Let me take a look at you,' he instructed, grabbing his godson by the shoulders. Mihalis was visibly moved, and shook his head from side to side. 'No, my friend! The image. The image of your father, may God rest his soul.' He kissed Yannis on both cheeks. 'He would have been so proud,' he added. 'You must go and show your mamma and godmother and then get changed. Dinner will be ready soon.'

'OK, godfather,' nodded Yannis obediently and left the room, observing his movements in the mirror.

Mihalis breathed in deeply as if about to speak, but then checked himself and instead exhaled heavily. Andonis flushed. Father and son had not had a free conversation since the night, some time before, that Mihalis had confronted Andonis about Funda. The tailor was now busying himself putting his needle and thread into a small wooden box. Mihalis reached over into the box and picked out the needle.

'I want to talk to you,' he said, rolling the needle in his fingers. Andonis refused to make eye contact with his father.

'Son, you know how disappointed I was with you not wanting to follow me into the fields,' observed Mihalis.

Andonis huffed. 'Baba. We've been through this so many times. I've chosen a different life.'

'I know, I know. And I made it hard for you.' The older man hesitated. 'But seeing Yannis today, dressed so fine, makes me so proud. So very proud. That suit will make him into a man.' Mihalis's cheeks glowed red.

'He'll make a fine groom,' agreed the tailor.

'And you've become a fine tailor,' added the farmer. 'Your yaya was so right to support you. What I'm trying to say is that it's you I'm proud of, my son. Of the man you're becoming.'

Mihalis handed the needle over to the tailor. 'And whatever you wish for, I'll support you. All I ask is that you take care.'

'Thank you, baba,' said Andonis accepting the needle. 'This means a lot to me.'

The family of Mihalis and the family of the widow, including Martha, were seated around the table in the courtyard. The women had prepared an array of dishes. There were luganiga. There was rizin pelafin. There were bamies.

There was dashin. There were fried potatoes from Mihalis's fields, salad, and Irini's home-made bread.

There was also Gumandaria, to which Nigos in particular had been helping himself as they waited for Yannis to change out of his suit so they could all eat.

Yannis returned and took his seat next to Martha. Nigos, already rosy-cheeked from wine and an empty stomach, sat on his other side.

'How fine your devoted Yannis is, Martha. Fit for a blushing bride,' declared Nigos provocatively. Martha did indeed blush. 'I can see why you can't wait to redden your sheets.'

The widow could see the irritation in her elder son's face. 'Hush, Nigo,' she implored.

Irini didn't have to see the anger in her husband's eyes to grab his arm and prevent him from reacting. Nigos hushed.

The group turned its attention to the meal. They ate and chatted. Mihalis poured everyone more wine, and they toasted to the future health and happiness of Yannis and Martha. In the distance they could hear a female voice singing. It was an exquisite voice, and it was now Andonis's turn to blush. It had been a number of days since he'd last seen his love. Stella blushed too, and hated herself for it.

'It's the Turkish girl,' announced Nigos mischievously, dropping fried potatoes into his mouth with his hand. Everyone round the table knew who he meant. 'I wonder why she's so happy this evening,' he added.

Andonis smiled. Funda always sang. Whether happy or sad, she sang.

'Maybe our Andonis knows,' hinted Nigos. Andonis glared at his friend. Stella glared at them both.

Unperturbed, Nigos turned to the widow. 'You know what, mamma? If it wasn't for these Turkish dogs and their Englezi masters you'd be able to show your children a great deal more love. Instead we've no inheritance even from the sun, and can only eat properly at another family's table!'

'Please, Nigo! No more talk like this,' fumed Mihalis, banging his hand against the table.

'That's the trouble with us Cypriots, isn't it, Mr Mihali?' taunted Nigos, shaking a fried potato at the farmer. 'We're all too scared to stand up and say the truth. Well, I'm not, and no one's going to stop me.'

Mihalis launched himself out of his seat.

'Truth, Nigo. What truth?' he fumed. Irini pulled at her husband's arm so that he might sit back down, but he would not.

Nigos also rose from his seat and squared up to the farmer from across the table.

'The truth about these Turks,' he said. 'They're the excuse the Englezi need to keep us from our mother.'

Mihalis sighed heavily. 'Our mother?' he repeated bitterly. 'It's what the teachers and the priests tell us, isn't it? Our mother Greece. But do you know what the Greeks call us?'

'Brothers,' suggested Nigos confidently.

'Bastard Cypriots,' corrected Mihalis, pointing a finger accusingly at Nigos. 'And if that's what we are, then what would that make our mother?'

10

The fish fryer   *O fishadis*

After I'd left Stella's house, rather than use public transport I decided to walk the mile up Green Lanes to Turnpike Lane, where I could catch a bus home. The fresh air and walk through Harringay would help clear my head, and might also give me time to consider what was to be done about Stella's husband Lugas.

Although it was late, I noted that one or two shops still had their lights on, though without being open for business. Blinds were up, and behind them, I knew, men smoked, drank whisky and lost money to each other. Men like Lugas.

I knew this part of town was known as Little Cyprus, and I noticed that many of the shop signs were written in Greek or in Turkish, or in both languages. I imagined what it would be like during the day, when old ladies dressed in black would fill their bags with imported fruit and vegetables from the greengrocer, when bleach-blonde women would buy their spoilt dark-haired children syrup-soaked pastries from the bakery, when grey-haired or bald-headed men would be content to sit and watch the world go by through coffee-shop windows.

It was not something I wanted to experience.

I could see that a shop some fifty yards ahead was still very much open for business. Its bright lights stood out like a beacon, and the distinctive smell of fried fish and chips now filled the air. I slowed my pace as I drew nearer. Fish and chips. The English national dish. I smiled and thought of Ruth.

The door of the shop was open, and I could now make out the voice of a man with a heavy Cypriot accent gently teasing a customer who, from his slurred responses, must have rolled in from one of the local pubs.

'No, Andy. Just a steak pie, pleashe.'

'You sure you don't want a bottle of brandy to wash it down with, Albert? Only me don't reckons you drunk enough tonight.'

'Just pie.'

'Just pie,' repeated the cheery Cypriot voice. A moment later the customer made his way out into the street, his mouth already full of meat and pastry. The voice called out after him.

'Mind when you is crossing them wet roads, Albert. I wouldn't want my bestest customer getting run over by a flippin' bus!'

As Albert stumbled past me, I heard him mutter the words 'stupid Bubble' under his breath.

As I hadn't managed to eat at Stella's, the thought of being kept company on my journey by some warm chips from this warm place suddenly appealed to me. My rumbling stomach agreed.

I entered the fish and chip shop. The chubby, bald-headed man grinning at me from behind the counter seemed familiar. Somehow I knew he felt the same. It was clear we were around the same age. I resolved not to search my mind to place him, in case the memory I found was a bad one.

'Yes sir, my friend,' he said warmly. I was a little surprised to hear that he spoke to me in English. I surmised that this was out of deference to my status as a paying customer.

'Just a bag of chips,' I said with an apologetic smile.

'Just a bag o' chips,' he repeated. 'You sure I can't tempt you with some of my good quality cods or haddocks? Guaranteed flippin' fresh. I catch them myself this mornink, in my fishing boat!' he declared with a wink. There was a twinkle in his big black eyes which I'd definitely seen before.

I raised my eyebrows and shook my head. 'No thanks. I'm not that hungry.'

'OK, boss. Just a bag o' chips.' He scooped a generous helping of oily chips from the deep fat fryer and into a greaseproof bag. Then, with my approval, he sprinkled them with salt and vinegar.

'Cyprus potatoes these, my friend. Only the bestest for my customers.'

I gave a deep sigh. They could have been pulled from the red soil in the fields round my village. The big eyes of the fish fryer were filled with compassion.

'Only a woman can cause a man to drain his lungs with such sadness, me reckons,' he noted with a knowing smile.

I found myself nodding absent-mindedly. He wrapped the chips up in layers of white paper before pushing them across the counter to me. I placed the appropriate coins down in exchange.

'Your friendly fish fryer Andrikos may not have an education, but he got the experience of life. So take it from me, sometimes you just got to swallow your pride and say sumink nice,' he offered.

'You think so?' I enquired, carried away for a moment by his certainty.

'Sure,' he continued, pleased that I was willing to hear his counsel. 'Oh-my-darlink-I-love-you-so-flippin'-much-I-can't-live-without-you. That type o' stuff. Then see if everythink won't be oright!'

Then, unexpectedly, he began to sing a familiar old Greek song. His surprisingly exquisite voice evoked a sweet sorrow within me.

I've told you this so many times, my only love,
And many more I'll tell you so.
Now hear me say that I love you, my only love,
In all the tongues there are to know.
S' aghabo elliniga, io d' amo idaliga,
Ze vuz em frantseziga, ai lav yu engleziga,
Yo de amo ispaniga, ge bortoghaleziga,
Yahabibi arabiga, tse-tsa-ko gineziga.

I smiled, nodded and raised my hand to indicate I'd heard enough.

'I don't suppose Andrikos knows how to say "I love you" in Turkish,' I enquired as I picked up my bag of chips and felt their heat through the paper.

The fish fryer looked down and began collecting the coins from the counter. I was concerned that my question had offended him. But after a moment he looked back up at me with those big eyes.

'Me reckons we've all forgotten, my friend.'

I left the warmth of the shop, and returned to the cold night.

11
The dance *O horos*

It was a warm spring night. The sun had long since bid a crimson farewell, but its influence refused to vanish. A sultry, southern breeze was to blame, wafting across the Mediterranean and carrying with it traces of the Sahara.

Normal sleep was impossible for Andonis on nights like these. He'd drift from one troubled dreamlike state to the next, interrupted by long periods of consciousness in which he would toss and turn and curse. And wish even a nightmare might come to rescue him from this sweat-drenched reality. For the moment, Andonis found himself semi-conscious once more, so could direct his thoughts. He directed them to Funda.

She, a beautiful hen, and he, a fine cockerel, were living with their fluffy little chick in an idyllic chicken coop with fresh straw and an endless supply of grain. Anyone could see they were made for each other. They were the same species of bird. Clucked the same cluck. But the joy in the coop was to be short-lived. Who should arrive but the sly fox from stories told to Andonis in his childhood. It wasn't long before the fox had clambered over the low fence to stand before the terrified birds. Andonis had wrapped Funda and their little chick under his protective wing, and gave them both a goodbye peck as the fox pounced.

Andonis forced himself awake. But the sounds of panicked clucking and flapping feathers persisted. It took a moment for Andonis to understand what was happening. He kicked at his sweat-soaked sheet, leapt out of bed and rushed into the back yard.

'Black devil! Get out of there, you filthy beast!'

Andonis was screaming at a real fox helping itself to real chickens from the coop. The disturbed animal made his escape into the twilight. Andonis caught a glimpse of a lifeless chicken dangling from its mouth. Andonis ventured into the coop to assess the damage. Another chicken lay badly savaged on the floor, but the remainder appeared unharmed.

By this time the rest of the family had been roused. Andonis was amused to see his father, still half-asleep, ambling out in baggy long-johns. His mother, in flowing white night dress, followed, clasping her hands together and praying skyward to the All-Holy Virgin. She was comforted by Marios, in shorts and vest, and with gold cross hanging from his neck.

'That's it, Irini. We're getting a dog,' insisted Mihalis, shaking a finger at his hysterical wife. He turned towards his elder son. 'So? What have we lost?'

Andonis raised a hand to calm his father. 'It could have been worse, baba. I think I scared her off in time. She took one though.' Then Andonis prodded a toe at the wounded hen on the ground, which twitched helplessly. 'And look. This one's finished.'

Mihalis turned to his wife. 'You'll agree, I trust, that this poor creature can lay no more eggs and produce no more chicks.'

Andonis exchanged a knowing smile with his father. Irini's faint-heartedness when it came to killing their domestic fowl for food was a long-standing family joke. She slapped her cheek and shook her head. Tears were pouring down her face.

'My God, what have we done to deserve such retribution?'

'Hush, woman!' commanded her husband, bending over to scoop up the bird in both hands. Then, without hesitation, he snapped its neck. Irini gasped and grabbed Marios for support.

'At least we'll have the chance to eat a little meat again,' declared Mihalis. He offered the bird to his sniffling wife, who recoiled in horror behind her younger son.

※ ※ ※

The widow and Irini sat outside under the shade of the veranda at the back of the house, peeling tomatoes and laying them on a large sheet out in the sun to make purée. The pungent smell of over-ripe fruit filled the air, and tens of flies buzzed around to take advantage. The widow was being poor company. As usual she was complaining about her children, even Yannis, who, according to Xenu, was now neglecting her and spending too much time with Martha. Irini had switched off a while ago, and simply grunted agreement whenever the widow paused for breath.

Xenu's monologue was interrupted by the sound of an approaching engine. It was the distinctive clanking of Vasos's old van. It came to a halt at the front of the house. The women peered through the house and its open front door to see Mihalis jump out of the van holding a leash. At the end of it, following the farmer out of the van, dropped an Alsatian puppy.

'The old fool's really gone and done it!' declared Irini with dismay. The widow couldn't contain her amusement, her own troubles suddenly forgotten, as Irini tutted her disapproval.

'As if there weren't enough mouths to feed,' noted the widow by way of solidarity.

Mihalis waved Vasos off, and then dog and man trotted through the house towards the women. The beast yapped with excitement, and Mihalis mimicked with apparently greater excitement. Irini looked first at her husband, then at the dog. She saw the same gormless expression.

'Woman, meet your new son,' beamed Mihalis, picking the animal up and presenting it to his wife. Irini was quick to push the dog away with her forearm.

'Get that animal away from me,' she reproached, but failed to disguise her interest. 'And don't you dare let it off that leash while we're making purée.'

Mihalis pretended to be offended. 'So this is the thanks I get for presenting you with another boy?'

For a moment husband and wife recalled the death in infancy of their third child. For a moment they felt each other's pain.

'I have two clean boys already, thank you,' said Irini, but could not stop herself taking a closer look at the animal in her husband's arms.

'But this one won't disappear into the Church. Nor run off with a Turk,' rejoined Mihalis with a smirk, and immediately wished he could take back his words. Irini was not amused.

'Get out of here, you Garagiozi!' she fumed, and turned her aggression onto the tomatoes she was slicing.

The widow intervened. 'You just hush with your nonsense, Mihali, and let me have a closer look at him,' she instructed, getting up and wiping her hands on her apron. Irini gave a look of disapproval as the widow began stroking and tickling the dog, which yelped with glee.

'Mashhalla, mashhalla. What a beautiful boy you are,' she cooed.

Irini tutted. 'Ah! Mind you wash your hands before you touch any more tomatoes.'

Mihalis frowned. 'Do stop your moaning, woman. He's completely clean. He's a fine dog. And tomorrow the vet in the town is going to…' he hesitated. 'Well, all I can say is, don't expect grandchildren!'

Now Mihalis pulled up a chair and sat down, putting the dog on the ground. He and the widow continued to play with the animal. Irini's curiosity was now aroused.

'You mean, they're going chop it off?' she enquired.

'You just peel your tomatoes and don't worry about it,' said Mihalis. 'His cucumber will still be there. They just remove the pips!'

'That's so cruel,' exclaimed Irini, suddenly unable to use her knife on the juicy red fruit in her hands. 'Poor thing. Let me see.' They opened the dog's hind legs, and all three humans were taken aback with what the little beast had to offer.

'I've never seen anything like it!' ventured the widow, rocking her head with her hand.

Irini and Mihalis looked at each other and couldn't prevent themselves sniggering.

The widow was embarrassed. 'Well, I mean, not since my husband passed away, God rest his soul.'

Irini and Mihalis sniggered once more, but this time both guiltily.

'So what's his name, Mihali?' enquired Irini, no longer able to feign lack of interest.

'I was hoping his mamma would christen him,' replied Mihalis with a wink.

'So you want me to name this creature?' enquired Irini with mock gravity.

Mihalis nodded and panted like a dog, his tongue hanging from his mouth and his hands dangling like paws in front of his chest.

'And you want me to take him into my home and feed him and care for him. And shower him with love and affection. And clean all his important places?'

Mihalis nodded, and the widow giggled nervously.

'I'm not sure there's enough room in my heart for another. But if a husband commands, then it's a wife's duty to obey,' declared Irini with a show of solemnity, patting the dog's head. She strained to have another look at the puppy's private parts. This time she rolled out her lower lip and nodded her approval to the widow.

'And as for his name? Such good looks, such a *huge* presence. There can only be one name for him. Eros.'

'Eros?' repeated her husband with surprise.

'After the biggest hero of them all. Eros Flynn, the Hollywood film star!'

Andonis was working late in his workshop, as he often did. He was thinking of Funda, as he always did. He'd not managed to engineer an opportunity to see her for some time. It was nearly dark outside, and two oil lamps generated enough light to enable him to continue pulling confidently at his needle and thread. Whatever other reputation Andonis was developing, his reputation as a tailor of quality guaranteed him a steady flow of work. Andonis knew that Nigos would be expecting him in the coffee-shop soon, but Nigos could wait.

When Andonis heard a knock on his door, he expected it to be his friend, come to fetch him.

'Come in. The door is open,' called Andonis, still hunched over his work. 'Can't live without me, eh?'

The door opened and Andonis was completely taken aback to see, not Nigos, but the form of a young woman, her head covered with a shawl. Once inside she removed the shawl and shook her long brown hair free.

'With you, without you, life would be difficult,' she replied.

'Funda! What are you doing here?' Andonis said, having risen from his chair. He suddenly felt like a host with nothing to offer an unexpected but important guest.

'I saw the light on and, as no one was around to fuel rumours, I thought to pay you a visit. But I'll go if you think it's best.'

'No. Please stay. It's wonderful that you came.'

They kissed.

'Where else is a girl to go when she's in need of a fine tailor?' enquired Funda with a smile. Andonis's heart began to pound.

'So this is now the workshop of Andonis the tailor,' she declared, looking around the room and noticing the icons on the wall. Her eyes fixed briefly upon the photograph of Andonis's grandmother, Mrs Maria.

'I'm at your service, Funda. What can I do for you?'

'It's my brother Zeki. He seems down these days. I've been thinking, Andoni. I'd like to order a stylish new shirt for his birthday, to help lift his spirits. I still have that ten-shilling note the Englezos gave us at the festival. I can think of no better way to spend it than on the tailor who helped raise it. Will you do it for Zeki, Mr Tailor?'

Andonis was moved with compassion and pride. 'It'll be my pleasure, though I wouldn't dream of relieving you of the Englezos's offering. Your brother may suffer the misfortune of a bad leg, but he's blessed with the love of a remarkable sister.'

'Thank you, Mr Tailor. But I assure you, Zeki fully deserves his family's love. He has a beautiful heart and is a constant source of joy,' she said.

Andonis's mind was already racing over the material and style of the shirt. 'Zeki must come here, so I can measure him and see his taste.'

'Mr Tailor, he mustn't,' warned Funda, shaking an open palm at Andonis. 'It's to be our surprise. You decide. I have every confidence in your taste. And as for his size? Aside from the obvious differences, I should think he's the same sort of build as his sister.'

'Then perhaps I should measure you,' suggested Andonis, and he noticed he was breathing more heavily. 'And I can use my imagination to make adjustments.'

Funda looked unsure. 'If you honestly think it's important for the cut of the shirt.' Now she too was breathing more heavily.

Andonis took on a professional tone. 'Oh vital, vital. I'll need something to go on,' he explained with a grin.

The tailor picked up his tape-measure from the table. He placed a hand on Funda's shoulder and turned her around so he could measure her from behind. He put one end to her neck and pulled the other to the small of her back.

'I remember this room from when I was a little girl. I used to love coming here sometimes with the other children to visit your grandmother, God rest her soul.'

'They were good days,' said Andonis.

'She used to tell us stories, and taught me the old songs. She encouraged me to sing, you know. She said I had a gift.'

'I remember,' said Andonis, remembering also the old woman's gift to him, that he in turn had gifted to Funda.

'Do you still have the thimble I gave you, Funda?' he asked as he pulled away, having noted a measurement.

'I won't let it go, Andoni,' she replied. Now Andonis instructed Funda to raise an arm so he could take another important measurement between armpit and waist.

'Perhaps I ought to bolt the door. I don't want anyone to disturb us, or I may get my figures wrong,' whispered Andonis.

Funda was in a daze. She nodded, and the tailor bolted the door. Now she turned to face him. With shaking hands, Andonis passed the tape-measure around Funda to measure her waist. His face was practically touching hers, and he could feel her warm breath on the back of his neck. Having taken the reading, Andonis withdrew and began scribbling on a piece of paper. He knew Zeki's waist wouldn't be this narrow.

Now, a little tentatively at first, Andonis wrapped the tape-measure around Funda's bust and pulled. Funda gasped. She closed her eyes and her lips parted. Andonis could contain himself no further. He pushed his mouth against hers and they kissed passionately. Andonis let the tape-measure fall to the floor, and cupped both of Funda's breasts with his hands.

'My parents don't approve of this,' whispered Andonis.

'Nor mine. They say you're a Christian. And that Christians and Muslims can't be together.'

'Our parents are wrong, Funda. I love you.' Andonis leant across to the oil lamp nearest him and blew it out.

'I love you too, Andoni.' Funda blew out the second lamp, which was nearest to her.

It was now dark in the tailor's workshop as the two young bodies entwined. They clung together in the dark silence.

But they were interrupted by a loud banging on the door.

'Andoni? Are you in there?' called an aggrieved voice outside. Andonis immediately recognised it as belonging to Nigos. Funda froze and her face filled with panic. She reached for her shawl. The door banged again.

'Stay still, Funda,' whispered Andonis. 'It's only my friend Nigos. He'll be gone soon.'

'He's not here, Nigo. Come on, let's go,' said another voice which Andonis recognised as that of Yannis on a rare night out without his Martha. After a few moments the Christian and the Muslim could hear footsteps withdraw. They heard Nigos speak again, his voice more distant this time.

'We should try the neighbourhood of the Turk. Maybe he's gone to visit his whore,' he said, and both brothers laughed.

Andonis and Funda stood in silence for a few moments, avoiding each others' eyes. Funda wrapped her shawl round her head, while Andonis went over to unbolt the door.

Without another word, or even a glance exchanged, Funda pushed open the door and disappeared into the warm night. Andonis sat back on his chair and stared at his grandmother's photograph in the half light.

⁂ ⁂ ⁂

Andonis arrived at the coffee-shop and approached Nigos and Yannis, who were at a table outside playing backgammon and drinking coffee. Sitting with them was their cousin Bambos. Andonis was annoyed to see him there. The tailor had little time for Bambos. There was a ruthless streak in this big man which disturbed Andonis. There were rumours that Bambos had connections with Eoga.

The coffee-shop radio could be heard in the background. As always it was tuned to Athens. A male announcer spoke the Greek of another land.

Andonis raised his hand in greeting. 'Sorry I'm late, boys. I've been a little busy.'

'Yes, we passed by the shop earlier, didn't we, Yanni?' declared Nigos, not lifting his head from the game. He was smoking a rolled cigarette. 'We could see how busy you were.'

Yannis laughed. Andonis felt his cheeks glow red. Surely they weren't aware of Funda's visit. The tailor reached down and grabbed the dice to prevent the game from continuing.

'What are you implying, Nigo?' he demanded.

Nigos raised his head and gave Andonis a confused look.

'What's got into you, you madman? I'm not implying anything. All I'm saying is there was no one at the shop, so if you were busy, you weren't busy there,' explained Nigos, opening his hand and gesturing for the dice to be returned. Andonis was relieved.

'Now stop acting like my mother, Nigo. Since when did I need your permission to drop my water?' asked Andonis with a relieved grin. He gave up the dice, grabbed Nigos's cigarette from his mouth, and took a long drag.

'Since your mind took air over the cripple's sister, perhaps?' suggested Bambos coldly. Andonis raised his eyes to heaven. He was dismayed that Bambos too was now aware of his relationship with Funda. Andonis blew smoke and raised his hands in exasperation.

'Don't take it the wrong way, Andoni,' interjected Yannis. 'It's only because we're worried about you.'

'So now I have two, three, four mothers,' announced Andonis counting the three young men at the table. At that moment the radio inside the coffee-shop was turned up.

'Hush now, Andoni,' instructed Bambos. Andonis sat down and shook his head. The young men stared into space as they listened to the radio broadcast from Greece.

'With the overwhelming support of the Greek Cypriot people the guerrilla movement Eoga continues to wage a fierce armed struggle against the British authorities in Cyprus, with acts of sabotage in the districts of all the major towns. Many thousands of pounds worth of damage has been inflicted on British property.'

There was a discernible delight in the radio announcer's voice, and the men inside the coffee-shop murmured their approval.

'But it's not enough for the Englezi. They deserve more!' shouted Bambos.

'News from London: Britain is to invite representatives of the Greek and Turkish governments to a conference to discuss political and defence questions affecting the eastern Mediterranean, including Cyprus. A spokesman for the exiled Cypriot leader, his beatitude Archbishop Magarios, has warned that the people of Cyprus could never accept any decisions which did not accord with their rights and aspirations, even if those decisions were endorsed by Greece.'

The voices from inside the coffee-shop rose again.

'Shit and double shit. What are they talking about? What the Greeks want is what we want. Enosis and only enosis,' fumed Nigos. Bambos nodded his approval, and Nigos smiled proudly. Andonis tensed the left side of his mouth and shook his head from side to side. The news continued.

'The British authorities have announced that further measures are to be introduced to combat the Eoga threat. Road-blocks and house-to-house searches are to be intensified, and the British government is to pass a special bill enabling its forces on the island to arrest and detain anybody suspected of participating in Eoga activities. Responding to this announcement, a spokesman for Archbishop Magarios has warned that any moves to restrict the freedom of the people of Cyprus would only serve to increase hostilities.'

Expressions of concern carried from inside the coffee-shop.

'If the Englezi hit us we'll hit them back. Only much harder!' declared Bambos, slamming a clenched fist against the table, which made the backgammon pieces and coffee cups jump.

'Eoga leader, Colonel Ghrivas, has issued a statement declaring that the Eoga movement is not anti-Turkish. He warns against attacking or antagonising the island's Muslim minority, adding that the Turks of Cyprus must be assured that the struggle is not against them but against British imperialism. Eoga's feelings towards the Muslim population are friendly, and the movement expects Turkish cooperation for the cause of national freedom and social justice.'

'You can expect cooperation, colonel, but you won't get it!' scoffed Nigos.

The announcer moved on to other news, and the radio was turned down. The murmurs inside the coffee-shop had now turned into heated debate.

'Ghrivas is right. The Englezi need to learn their lesson. But attacking Muslims? What good will that do?' said Andonis.

Nigos tutted. 'All that nonsense with the Turkish girl is affecting your judgement, Andoni,' he replied.

Bambos interjected. 'The colonel is a clever man, Andoni. He doesn't give a damn about the Turks, but he knows not to wage war on two fronts. His message is simple. Once we've rid the island of the Englezi, then it'll be the turn of the Turks.'

Nigos looked admiringly at his older cousin and nodded. Andonis shook his head.

'No, Bambo. Justice is on our side in the struggle against the Englezi. And justice will triumph in the end. But the Turkish question is different. Any conflict with them would be madness.'

Yannis gave the tailor a questioning look. 'Why should there be conflict, Andoni? Once the Englezi are out of the way, and stop stirring it, the Turks will sit quietly,' he said.

Bambos laughed. 'Don't be soft, Yanni. This village is too soft! Do you think for one minute these infidels will agree to join with Greece? Sooner or later we're going to have to deal with them as well.'

Andonis shook his head. 'But they've lived here for generations. Cyprus is as much their home as it is ours,' he said.

Bambos ignored him. 'And no doubt we'll have to deal with the Turk-loving communists too!' he added, taking an aggressive slurp of coffee.

'Cyprus is Greek, Andoni. It always has been and always will be. If our Turks can accept that and accept Greek rule, perhaps they can stay,' offered Yannis, adopting a more placatory tone.

'I don't think they'll accept that, Yanni,' warned his younger brother. 'They should be given boats and some money to start a new life. Then Andonis can bid his beloved Turkish girl farewell from the harbour. After all, her beloved Turkey's only forty miles away.'

Now Andonis laughed. 'You're all living in a fantasy world. Do you honestly expect our Muslims simply to get up and go? Leave their homes, their livelihoods, their villages. Leave their Christian friends and the only life they know?'

'They'll have no choice, Andoni,' said Bambos smugly. In his village the Turks had been driven out long ago. His village wasn't soft.

'Oh, but they will, Bambo,' responded Andonis. 'Like your cousin says, their beloved Turkey's only forty miles away.'

Bambos shook his head and got up from the table. 'I've had enough of this treacherous rubbish,' he seethed and went inside to join the older men.

❋ ❋ ❋

It was now after midnight, and Andonis and Nigos were the last remaining customers at the coffee-shop. Yannis had left them already, as Martha had insisted that he be home with his mother before dark. Bambos had returned to his village. The friends were smoking. An ashtray full of cigarette butts lay between them on the table, as did a number of cups of coffee, with sediment caked dry at the bottom. There was also a collection of glasses of water.

Vasos, who had been cleaning up inside while humming along to music from Athens, now emerged. On seeing the young men outside, he folded his arms and raised his head with a tut.

'Still here? After curfew?' he admonished, but with affection.

'Curfew?' retorted Nigos and spat at the ground. 'That's what I think about your Englezos friend's curfew.'

Vasos nodded. 'You're a fearless man, Nigo. I pray it won't be your undoing,' he warned.

'Communists have no business with prayer, Mr Vaso. My blessed father taught me that,' retorted Nigos. Andonis could see the look of hurt in the coffee-shop owner's eyes.

'Don't worry, Mr Vaso,' said the tailor. 'I'll take care of Nigos.'

Vasos grabbed Andonis's shoulder and peered into the tailor's eyes. 'And of yourself also,' he advised. The tailor blushed.

Nigos waved an arm at the coffee-shop owner. 'Away with you, Mr Vaso. Why not do us the favour of fetching two more cups of coffee? While we still have the ghrosha to pay you.'

Vasos nodded and went back inside, to his water, his ground beans, his jisves and his radio.

Nigos turned to his friend. 'It's good to have a close friend, don't you think, Andoni?' he probed.

Andonis considered his friend's invitation and, knowing a positive response was required, nodded.

Nigos continued, 'I mean, we've both got our brothers, but, well, it's not the same, is it?'

'The love of God gets between me and mine,' offered Andonis with a sigh.

'The love of a woman gets between me and mine,' returned Nigos, and his eyes narrowed slightly.

Andonis nodded again, aware that Nigos was also alluding to the tailor's own romantic pursuits.

Nigos continued. 'But you wouldn't let that interfere with the bond between us, would you, Andoni?'

Andonis remained silent, but thought of Funda and how she must be feeling right now. He sighed. A heavy dance came on the radio. Recognising it, Andonis called inside and requested a little more noise. The coffee-shop owner complied, disturbing some dogs hidden somewhere in the shadows of the village square. They gave a few disapproving but lazy barks.

'Come on, Nigo. Let's dance!' beckoned Andonis, launching himself from his chair.

Nigos was a little taken aback, and frowned. He recalled the last time he'd seen Andonis dance. 'What's got into you?'

'Shut up and get up,' demanded Andonis, before raising his arms and clicking his fingers.

He turned and hopped and skipped. He kicked his leg into the air and slapped his foot. Nigos, meanwhile, had knelt on one knee and was now clapping his hands in time to the music.

'Obas!' Nigos called when appropriate. Andonis closed his eyes, squatted, and brushed the ground with an outstretched hand before rising up once more.

Now, with one hand behind his back, the other helping him to balance in front, he swung a leg over Nigos's head. When next Andonis squatted, Nigos was quick to place a glass of water onto the tailor's crown. Andonis appeared oblivious to the glass, and the dance continued. Each spontaneous movement now merged into one coordinated whole until Andonis's entire being was perfectly expressed through a body in control of itself.

Vasos emerged from within the coffee-shop carrying a tray with two more cups of coffee and two more glasses of water. He looked admiringly at the athletic young tailor.

Andonis's face reflected his higher state of consciousness. Beads of sweat were sprouting on his forehead, and the ground accepted drops of water, sometimes fresh, sometimes salty. But the glass remained on his head.

'Come on, Andoni,' encouraged Nigos. More frenzied grew the dance. Wilder grew the spins, more animated the hand movements, more aggressive the jumps and kicks. But more steady grew the head. And the glass remained. And so it continued. On and on, until Nigos could take it no more. He reached for the glass on Andonis's head to break the spell. Andonis stopped still as Nigos drank the glass dry.

Now the roles were reversed. Andonis wiped his brow with his palm before crouching down and clapping his hands. Nigos took over the dance, slowly at first but with similarly increasing energy, both external and within. Andonis reciprocated his friend's gesture with the glass, and encouragement.

And Nigos was now a man possessed. His jumps and kicks grew more violent, his movements more reckless. But still the glass remained on his head. And Nigos was taken over by the dance, and Nigos was the dance. And like a whirlwind he rushed and flipped and spun. Until he was out of control. Until he had lost his head.

Until the glass had fallen to the floor, smashing into small pieces.

The coffee-shop owner sighed and went inside in search of a broom.

12
The funeral *I gidhia*

I stood before the iron gates of the All Saints Orthodox church in Camden Town. It was a cloudy day, as usual, but thankfully there was no rain. From out here little distinguished this from any other Christian place of worship in London. Hunched, sombre people slowly manoeuvred around me, on past the imposing pillars, through the main doors and into the darkness. Short women in long coats, some silent, some sobbing, supported by dark-suited men, mostly grey, some bald.

I hesitated outside the gates. There would be other people here from the village. As well as Christians, perhaps one or two Muslims. All good people. But I had no desire to be recognised by any of them. I caught a glimpse of an older, withered Mrs Anjela and her daughter Eleni as they hovered into the church. Clothes black, faces white. The pain of Vasos's loved ones enveloped me. Thoughts of Dave's widowed cousin came to the rescue. After all, hadn't Ruth shown there could still be life after death?

I waited a moment, then lifted the lapels of my coat, lowered my head and followed the other mourners, leaving the sights, sounds and smells of the city. Inside, the candles, the icons and the incense took control of my senses. And the years rolled back. I rarely and reluctantly went to church in the old days. Like my father, I'd never cared much for organised religion. My views hadn't changed. Still, now at least, there was no denying the imprint those early experiences had had on my subconscious. All at once that familiar feeling of reverence tinged with resentment returned. I thought of my younger brother.

At the front of the church, before the steps leading to the ieron, they'd laid out the coffin of Vasos. Coffee-shop owner. Friend of my father. Communist. A man who had rationalised God out of his life but who, like me and others, could never fully free himself from the awe ingrained so deeply within him. No doubt the fear of the unknowable had remained to the end until, here and now, he would be welcomed back into the true faith. His sins forgiven.

Avoiding eye contact with the other people greeting each other inside the church, I dropped some coins in a tray and lit a candle in memory of Vasos. As I did so, an older man's hand reached across, taking the flame from my candle to light his own. Even in this half light I could tell immediately his skin was paler than my own. I couldn't help but look up into the man's face, and found myself staring into familiar blue eyes. I was overwhelmed, and felt myself becoming unsteady. His hand reached out and grabbed my shoulder. I went to speak, but found no words. Instead I shook my head in disbelief. He put a finger to his mouth before beckoning me to follow him. The funeral service was about to begin.

We found a space at the back of the church, away from the other mourners, and with no further exchange stood in silence to remember Vasos.

When the priest emerged from the ieron, I recognised him immediately. Baba-Ghlioris. The village priest. His face was older, his beard whiter, his paunch wider, his cheeks redder. He began to chant.

On and on went the liturgy. The meaning of his words was as much beyond me as it was beyond the man next to me, and, I suspected, the majority of the congregation. But I realised, as I'd never realised before, that this was not a time for comprehension, but for connection. For through the priest's voice, through his chanting and his song, we were at one with the earliest of Christians, going through the same rituals and emotions as they had when invoking the name of their Saviour to deliver them from unbearable pain and suffering.

At the end of the service, Baba-Ghlioris raised a hand to the congregation before turning his back on us and disappearing into the ieron. I found this odd. It would have been more customary for him to have instructed everyone to take their seats once more, before inviting someone to say a few words in memory of the life of the deceased.

We all remained standing, and an uncomfortable silence descended over the church, interrupted now and again by a cough or a woman's sniffle. I looked at the man next to me, and he shrugged. It was a good few minutes before, to everyone's relief, the priest re-emerged, his eyes now bloodshot.

He hovered unsteadily forward and leant against the coffin for support. At last he raised and lowered his hands to indicate that he wanted us all to be seated. Baba-Ghlioris waited for the congregation to settle. When silence came, he lowered his head, took a deep breath, and began to speak, his voice quivering. His language was no longer archaic Greek but the Cypriot vernacular.

'I should like to take a few moments now to talk about the man we all knew and loved. Our dearly departed Vasos, who leaves behind a loving wife, family and many, many friends.'

Baba-Ghlioris looked up and stared into the faces of the people gathered before him. At one point I was certain that his eyes looked directly into mine. Fearful that he might recognise me, I covered my face with my hands, blotting sodden eyelashes.

Baba-Ghlioris continued, 'And forgive me, I wish to speak of Vasos not in my role as a priest.' He removed the tall black hat from his head and placed it carefully onto the coffin. A few women gasped at what they clearly perceived to be an improper act, but Ghlioris was undeterred. 'But as a friend. For he and I were the very best of friends.'

Ghlioris's face now changed. It looked more composed, like a huge weight had been lifted from his mind.

'We were from the same village, he and I. The same village as many here in the church today. How he loved our village. But it was that love which forced him to flee and, like many compatriots, including myself, to seek a new home in England. He could no longer stand by and see his country torn apart. Not a man of conviction like Vasos. And so he left for the sake of his sanity.

'In the old days I would often visit my friend Vasos, at the village coffee-shop, on a Sunday afternoon. After a tiring day of church services I'd enjoy a cup of his divine and reviving beverage. Indeed, on the odd occasion, we might enjoy a glass of something even more divine, even more reviving.'

The priest looked up, and there was a twinkle in his eyes, as though happy for us to know what he knew we knew.

'We would while away the hours together, discussing many things which concerned us, and many which did not. And always we'd end up on the ultimate question. Of life and its meaning. I had my views, the views of a dedicated priest, that we should look no further than God for answers. That only through Him could we find real meaning. Our Vasos, of course, had a somewhat different perspective. He believed he was capable of finding answers for himself, through love for his fellow man, through equality for the poor and the downtrodden. Vasos claimed he didn't need a divine presence in his life.

'I would chastise him for his lack of faith in the Lord, and he would return the compliment for my lack of faith in humanity. And always, after both our tongues had sprouted hairs from overuse, we'd end up agreeing to disagree. For, after all, we both wanted the same thing: a better world. Only our methods were at odds.

'Needless to say, Vasos was not a regular churchgoer. His excuse was that he couldn't get used to seeing me as the village priest. He thought it strange that the teachings of our Orthodox faith should be delivered by a man with whom he'd played, fought, laughed and cried as a boy. I understood, and I believe God forgave, as He always forgives.

'And as Vasos generally refused to visit me at my place of work, so I would seek him out in his. The coffee-shop of his father and of his father's father. And Vasos was always there to help an old friend in need of a more spiritual sustenance than coffee-shop offerings could supply. On such occasions Vasos would take the role of teacher, with words of comfort if I was distressed, encouragement if I was weak, and wisdom if I was in doubt. For while a priest may not doubt, sometimes a friend does.'

Ghlioris paused and took a deep breath.

'And Vasos was to carry on helping his old friend when we left our homeland for an uncertain future. I needed him often here in England.'

Ghlioris fought hard to contain the tears, as did the man next to me. He recognised few words, yet appeared to understand everything.

'And so today, of all days, as I say goodbye to my oldest and dearest friend, I feel an emptiness I know can never be filled. As he embarks on a journey I can't yet contemplate, and enters a realm I don't dare imagine, I find myself needing his friendship, now more than ever, to help me through these difficult times.'

Ghlioris paused again to gather more strength.

'You left this world before me, my Vaso. I know the years changed you. Though you would never admit it, I know they brought you ever closer to God. For, like all of us, you needed the hope of something more to this earthly existence which so diverts us from our true destiny. And now, you at least are certain of that destiny.'

Ghlioris looked up and saw the tears streaming down all our faces. We needed our priest to be strong. He bent down and picked his hat up from the coffin, placing it carefully on his head.

'You rarely came to church in the village, Vaso, but you've done so today. In this foreign land miles and miles away. I knew you'd come one day. And for once you have need of me, not as a friend but as a priest. And as your priest I know for sure that your spirit is here by my side, comforting me, guiding me, giving me strength as you used to. For I know that it is only our faith in God that can grant us eternal life.'

He raised a hand and smiled.

'Goodbye, Vaso, goodbye my friend. May you find peace. And may your village and your homeland find it also.'

The people now stood up, wiped the tears from their eyes, and shuffled forward. They formed a queue to pay their respects at the coffin before going up to kiss the icons of the saints and then over to commiserate with Vasos's widow. I couldn't face them.

Vasos was dead, and I thought of my own father. I gestured to the man next to me that I had to leave. He nodded and followed me out of the church.

13
The repartee *Do chatisman*

'Dead, sir!' screamed Irini, addressing the village muhtaris as he sipped coffee in his village shop. 'My poor little ones. Dead.'

The farmer's wife had just stormed in, carrying a battered chicken. Some weeks had passed since Irini's last chicken tragedy. This time a man not a fox was to blame. This time she wanted justice. She laid the dead bird on the counter, also used as a coffee table and a desk.

'See what that bastard bus-driver Simos has done. And two more lie flattened in the road!'

The muhtaris tutted loudly.

Every village in Cyprus had a muhtaris, a supposedly learned man accepted by his peers as the local authority. If a villager had a land dispute with his neighbour, the muhtaris might just be asked to settle it. If a donkey had shat in someone's back yard, the muhtaris might just be asked to instruct the beast's owner to clear up the mess. If a barber accidentally cut a man's chin while shaving him, the muhtaris might just be asked to arrange for appropriate compensation. The muhtaris's decision was final.

Muhtaris was not a paid position. However, someone favoured by a particular decision knew that it was in everyone's best interests to reward the muhtaris, to encourage a repeat of such wisdom in future judgements. Conversely, someone not favoured by a particular decision knew that a forfeit should be paid to him, to demonstrate remorse and to ensure one's misdemeanour would not prejudice future judgements.

Win or lose, the tariff system was a little complicated for most villagers, so the muhtaris used his indisputable judgement to assist them. His palm remained open until the right level of consideration had dropped into it. The muhtaris was a wise man indeed. Just the threat of involving his unquestionable logic ensured that the majority of disputes were settled privately and amicably between the villagers concerned.

Of course, that didn't mean the muhtaris didn't have a role to play. His position gave him immense power and influence to guide the villagers, or the Christian villagers at least.

Brave indeed was the man who questioned the authority of the muhtaris, or who went against his wishes.

The muhtaris of Andonis's village was a substantial, educated man with dark olive skin and heavy features. He had a bulbous nose and hairy nostrils. He was bald, but compensated by growing a large and intimidating moustache.

He had a small shop near the village square which was also his office. He sold a range of items such as stamps, stationery, cigarettes, olive oil, macaroni and wine. People in need would drop in for provisions, decisions and directions.

Consistent with his high status, the muhtaris had adopted what he perceived to be a loftier way of talking. He spoke like a Galamaras, a Greek from the mainland. Galamaras actually meant pen-pusher, someone educated, like a teacher, lawyer or civil servant. Only such people needed such Greek.

For 'and', the muhtaris would say 'ge' instead of 'je'. For 'dog', he would say 'skilos' instead of 'shhillos'. For 'bed', he would say 'grevadi' instead of 'garkola'. For 'chicken', he would say 'godobulo' instead of 'ornitha'. For 'lemon', he would say 'lemoni' instead of 'oxinon'. The muhtaris referred to himself in the plural, and he used the supposedly respectful plural form of you, a mainland Greek affectation copied from the French.

Thus the declarations of the muhtaris, uttered to all intents and purposes in an unfamiliar tongue, were often beyond the average villager, who could only listen with awe and acquiescence.

On this particular afternoon, the muhtaris had been sipping a cup of coffee in his shop. Sketos. He always had his coffee plain. And he always had it alone. He refused to drink at the coffee-shop of the communist, and suggested that others also refuse. But this was one suggestion of the muhtaris with which they could not comply. There was no better coffee than the coffee offered by Vasos, and the only alternative was the Muslim coffee-shop.

'What are you going to do about my chickens?' fumed the farmer's wife.

This was not usually the way to address the muhtaris, but Irini was one of the few villagers not intimidated by him. They were cousins, and as children had played intimate games of discovery, as cousins sometimes do, given the opportunity. It was an opportunity for which Irini was grateful, as she knew that, beneath it all, the mighty muhtaris was a more modest man.

For his part the muhtaris was pleased to see the farmer's wife. That Mihalis was a lucky man. Unlike most Cypriot women of her age, Irini had retained some of her former beauty. And Irini was kin, so whatever the dispute the muhtaris would find in her favour. He stood up, took his cousin's hand and steered her into a seat, before sitting back down opposite her. He glanced at Irini's breasts before fixing onto her eyes and stroking his big black whiskers.

'So, Irini. Suppose we establish exactly what transpired,' he declared officiously, opening a large book on the table and beginning to scrawl with a large elaborate fountain pen.

'That man and his bus are a menace. I let the chickens out for some exercise. They may have strayed a little beyond the yard. Well chickens do, don't they? Who should come hurtling past but that crazy Simos. And, I swear, he made no attempt to swerve to avoid them!'

'You're saying that Mr Simos deliberately ran over three of your chickens?' enquired the muhtaris gravely.

Irini nodded. 'Either he's a madman or he's a blind man, sir. Either way, he shouldn't be driving a bus. Only God knows how many eggs these three fine birds might have laid for my family.'

'Aside from your chickens, would you say there was any other damage?'

'I'm damaged, sir,' insisted Irini, clasping her forehead. 'The shock of seeing my little ones flattened by that barbarian. My nerves have turned to water.'

The muhtaris nodded solemnly. 'And you're saying that Mr Simos didn't stop after this...this incident?'

'Stop? Don't make fun of me. He drove past as if nothing had happened. I was shouting and screaming after the bus. But the bastard kept on going. May he go to the devil!'

'So, what is it you want by way of compensation?' enquired the muhtaris.

Irini was offended. 'Nothing can replace my beautiful chickens, and I want nothing from that imbecile. But he needs to be taught a lesson. I say ban him from driving for a month. No, six months. And make sure that while he's banned he goes and gets his eyes examined.'

The muhtaris called out to his son, a teenaged boy who appeared from a door at the back of the shop. The boy was instructed to pop out and fetch the bus-driver.

'You may go now, cousin. We'll deal with the matter from here,' instructed the muhtaris.

'But I want to see him punished,' insisted Irini. However, the muhtaris had already got up, and was now ushering her out.

'All in good time, cousin. All in good time,' he advised.

At that moment a coy Simos entered the shop. He was a tall, skinny man in his thirties. He had light brown hair and blue-green eyes, unusual for someone from the village. His skin was a few shades lighter than that of the muhtaris. Simos grinned proudly, revealing a gold tooth.

'Aren't you ashamed of yourself? No wonder you're still a bachelor. Who'd have you?' screamed Irini, shaking her fist at the bus-driver as she passed him. 'Just you wait until I tell your cousin, Yoda. The whole village will know what a cruel murderer you are!'

'That's quite enough, Irini,' insisted the muhtaris, pushing her on her way. 'Thank you for bringing this matter to our attention.'

The muhtaris now grabbed the bus-driver by the collar and pulled him towards him. Meanwhile Simos had reached out for a few bottles of wine, and put them on the counter. He showed no sign of being concerned by the accusations levelled against him.

'Mrs Irini believes you to be mad or blind or both. And we must say we're inclined to concur. What have you to say by way of explanation?' demanded the muhtaris, sitting back in his chair.

Simos laughed. 'I'm innocent, sir. Honest I am. It's all Mr Mihalis's idea. He knew his wife would come to you. He told me to invite you along, by way of gratitude for your…what were his words? Your irrefutable wisdom!'

'We're most confused,' said the muhtaris, rubbing his whiskers. 'Mr Mihalis told you to invite us along? Where?'

'Why, to dinner on Sunday, of course!' declared the bus-driver with a knowing smile. He put some coins on the counter in payment for the wine.

The muhtaris was not amused. He launched himself from his chair and grabbed the bus-driver by the ear.

'Are you making fun of us?' he fumed.

'No, sir. I wouldn't dare,' squeaked an alarmed Simos. 'Let me explain. Mr Mihalis asked me to mow down a few chickens. Mrs Irini's too soft-hearted to butcher them herself. So you see, with our help, Mr Mihalis gets to eat a bit of flesh on the Lord's day. And so do we!'

The muhtaris loosened his grip. 'So this was all agreed beforehand? To kill three of Mrs Irini's chickens?'

'Two, sir. But I thought I'd catch one extra, seeing as an appetite as big as yours might be joining us at the table,' replied Simos.

The muhtaris let go of Simos and shook his head gravely. 'You and our clever friend the farmer play disrespectful games. Mrs Irini is expecting a judgement from us. What exactly are we supposed to tell her?'

Simos picked up the bottles of wine and made his way to the door, giving the muhtaris a final flash of his gold tooth.

'Please don't ask me, sir. I'm just a poor bus-driver. See you on Sunday.'

❊　❊　❊

That Sunday, the muhtaris, the bus-driver and the farmer sat in the courtyard of the farmer's house. Three guilty men, drinking wine and smoking.

A dutiful Irini had served them a tasty Sunday meal of chicken tavas.

But there had been no disguising Irini's resentment towards her husband and his guests. She had thrown their cutlery at them. She had slammed their plates onto the table. She had plucked a lemon from the tree above them and purposely dropped it into her husband's lap, making him jump. She had neglected to put salt and pepper onto the table, knowing no one would dare complain. She had also saved the best bits of meat for her sons, both of whom cared little for the pompous muhtaris, and had made themselves scarce in Andonis's workshop.

The colourful bunch of wild flowers which Simos had been instructed to bring by way of compensation could not placate Irini. Nor could the bar of English chocolate from the muhtaris, nor even the affectionate slap on the behind from her husband. These three men had conspired to make a fool of Irini, and they in turn had to be made to suffer.

The men were pathetic. They had thanked and thanked Irini for all her efforts, complimented her on how delicious the food she'd prepared looked and smelt. Irini remained silent, and having served the men and uttered a contemptuous 'good appetite', disappeared into the house to undertake some unnecessary chores. She would sigh loudly every now and then to remind those outside that they had not yet served their penance.

Even Eros, who since his arrival had taken to following Irini wherever she went, was letting her down. The animal had settled outside, a little distance from the other selfish males, intoxicated by the smell of meat and awaiting the inevitable scraps.

The men had turned to the heavy red wine for comfort, and by the time the meal was done were onto the third bottle. It took Mihalis finally to dare break the silence as he raised his glass.

'Boys, I propose a toast. To my lovely wife Irini,' he announced before lowering his voice to add, 'and her excellent chickens.'

The men clinked their glasses, and also the empty bottles on the table before gulping down the wine.

'And also to Simos, his bus and his excellent eyesight,' added the muhtaris. 'May he use it to find a good wife soon, if God permits!'

They clinked glasses and gulped some more.

'And to our most wise muhtaris,' added Simos, 'and his magnificent judgements.'

They clinked glasses and gulped until their glasses were drained. Then they smiled at each other and, encouraged by drink, their smiles gave way to laughter, though it was a little self-conscious at first, for fear the wrath of Irini be roused once more.

Further fuelled by the alcohol, Mihalis and the muhtaris were soon debating the troubles. Simos was out of his depth when these two great heads of the village got together, so he had brought along his violin for protection. If ever things got too heated he would begin to play, and invite the two of them to settle their differences with a chatisman. Both had a reputation in the village as skilled improvisers of insult, irony and nonsense.

The muhtaris was speaking in his affected Greek. Mihalis was more comfortable with the Cypriot vernacular, which was after all closer to the language of Homer.

'The Englezi must be made to see that they cannot deny the people of Cyprus their true identity,' boomed the muhtaris. Even he used the vernacular to describe the occupying imperialists; they deserved no respect.

Mihalis viewed the muhtaris's Levantine features with a mixture of affection and contempt. Why was it that those amongst his people who shouted loudest for being Greek looked the most Middle Eastern?

'And what is our true identity?' posed Mihalis in a tone that was deliberately provocative. The muhtaris shook his head in dismay that the issue was even open for discussion.

Simos flashed his golden tooth. 'Not Englezi, for sure!' he declared, desperate to inject some harmony into the proceedings. 'They have no right to govern us.'

'Indeed,' encouraged the muhtaris. 'We don't belong to the Englezi, as we never belonged to any of the other barbarians that ruled before them.'

'Don't get me wrong, though. I bear the Englezi no grudges,' offered the bus-driver. 'It's sad that we find ourselves in conflict with them. I fought alongside Englezi soldiers in the war.' Simos liked to remind people of this fact, and did so at every opportunity. 'They were as brave as any Greek, and together we freed Crete. Give me the Englezi ahead of the Italians or the Germans any day!'

Mihalis nodded. 'There is much about the Englezi to be admired. They are, by and large, an honourable, decent race. Courteous, fair-minded…'

'As sly as foxes,' added the muhtaris, to which Mihalis had to nod in agreement. The muhtaris continued, 'The Englezi will always favour the underdog. And in Cyprus that means the Turk.' He uttered the word with undisguised contempt.

'Perhaps,' mused Mihalis, 'but the misguided nationalism which is now sweeping across Cyprus makes the Turk vulnerable and in need of protection.'

'But in protecting the infidel the Englezi deny us the right to express our true identity,' countered the muhtaris.

'But I ask you again, sir,' insisted Mihalis. 'What is our identity? To whom does an island belong that has seen so many peoples, ideas, religions and cultures pass through?'

The muhtaris's face screwed up. 'Greece of course!' he announced, put out that he'd been forced to state the obvious. 'Our connection goes back thousands of years when the ancient Mycenaeans colonised the island, followed by the Achaeans, Macedonians and then the Byzantines. The cultural seeds of Cyprus were planted way back then, making her what she is, making us what we are today.'

'These aren't the only seeds. Cyprus was inhabited before the Greeks,' countered Mihalis. 'And our island's history is rich and complex. The blood flowing through our veins is impossible to trace, with a procession of races within it. From the west came the Greeks, yes, but also the Romans, the Crusaders and the Venetians. From the east the Phoenicians, the Persians and the Turks.'

'Others may have passed through, but out of all that confusion the spirit of Greece still shines through. Perfectly recognisable to all who care to open their eyes to see!' The muhtaris's dark features grew passionate, and he stared at Mihalis accusingly. 'Why deny it, Mihali? You, whose mother was Macedonian!'

'I don't deny it. And I am proud that our distant ancestors were, above all, great thinkers. I hope I have inherited some of that ancient wisdom. It's a shame that others who claim to share this honourable past seem not to have done so.'

The muhtaris was incensed. He was not used to being questioned, even mocked, so eloquently.

'What do you mean by that?' fumed the muhtaris, standing up and looking down accusingly at Mihalis.

Mihalis refused to be intimidated. He raised himself, and also, he knew, the stakes. He was taller and broader in the shoulders than the muhtaris, who was now visibly nervous at the prospect of losing face in front of the bus-driver.

'Think, sir. Think,' the farmer implored. 'Whichever history we choose to construct for ourselves, we must all work together to construct a single future. A future in which all Cypriots, *all* Cypriots, have an equal stake. Otherwise…' Mihalis hesitated.

'Otherwise?' prompted the muhtaris, regaining some of his composure.

'Otherwise we fall into the trap the sly fox has laid for us. A trap that will cut us in two,' said Mihalis sombrely.

The muhtaris sneered. 'You speak with passion, Mihali, but you fail to convince. You know what? You're as spineless as that communist coffee-shop owner and his wishy-washy drunken friend the priest.'

The farmer lifted his hands in exasperation. 'My friend, I beg you. Where are we heading if we undo the ties of friendship which have bound our people together for centuries? Where will we be if we allow extremists and outsiders to destroy the harmony on this small island? How much more pain must we go through before we realise that all this tension, all this anger, all this hatred must end, for ever?'

The tension, anger and hatred of which Mihalis spoke was evident in the eyes of the muhtaris.

'It will stop with enosis and only enosis,' he screamed.

Mihalis grimaced. 'Enosis? We're going to make a hole in the water, and nothing else! You know, someone said to me recently that the trouble with us Cypriots is that we're too afraid to say the truth. Well here's my truth, and mark my words. Not even the nail of my little finger would I give for union with Greece.'

The face of the muhtaris turned purple. 'You're after truth, you stupid farmer? Well here's the truth of the muhtaris. There is no room for your dangerous treachery in the struggle ahead. So you watch yourself, sir, and watch also your elder son. Or the power of the muhtaris will not be able to protect you.'

Mihalis sighed deeply. The muhtaris did likewise. The two men had reached an impasse. A difference of ideology that rational argument would not overcome.

Simos knew it was time to play his violin. Irini, who had been sitting in her bedroom working on some embroidery and trying to shut out the men's disturbing quarrel, now began to listen.

The two champions squared up to one another for their improvised onslaught of words. All expression now focused on their mouths. One would open, the other would respond. The repartee was instantaneous, keeping pace with the unrelenting rhythm of Simos's violin.

Irini followed each verse carefully, and giggled quietly to herself.

The farmer:
  Tonight we'll take a stroll, my friend, a little to and fro.
  But let's establish, from the start, to where our path will go.
The muhtaris:
  Take the open road, my friend, and leave the path aside.
  For you are but a donkey and on your back I'll ride.

The farmer:

> *When we were younger men, my friend, I'm sure you will recall,*
> *We'd always have a scuffle and you would always fall.*

The muhtaris:

> *Then you'll recall for certain, the last time I beat you.*
> *To this day, I'll wager, your sides are black and blue.*

The farmer:

> *The things I did to you, my friend, why do you fail to mention?*
> *Why, to this day, you're still in need of medical attention.*

The muhtaris:

> *I used to knock your senses out, up where we threshed the wheat,*
> *And you would go to bed at night and wet your mamma's sheet.*

The farmer:

> *I'm going to tell it how it is, your mamma had a fit.*
> *I may have wet my bed at night but yours was full of shit.*

The muhtaris:

> *You dare to lock your horns with me, get ready then to die.*
> *Go back now to your family and wave them all goodbye.*

The farmer:

> *Come now, let's be friends once more, the fighting now must cease.*
> *Together you and I, my friend, should always work for peace.*

Irini smiled at the mention of peace, the meaning of her name.

The exchange over, Mihalis and the muhtaris embraced, as was customary. Simos's forehead was dripping with sweat from his vigorous playing. He was pleased to see the adversaries put aside their differences, at least for now, and gave a golden smile of approval. A moment later, Irini emerged from the house with a tray covered with grapes, figs and slices of watermelon.

Mihalis and the muhtaris retook their seats, Simos refilled their glasses with wine, and the two champions toasted each other's health. Then, as each helped himself to a different type of fruit, each gave the other an uneasy look. The muhtaris and the farmer knew things between them would be changed for ever.

14
The truth   *I alithkia*

Outside the church, the mystical fervour conjured by the priest within was instantly swept away by the sharp London air. I looked up at the gathering dark clouds.

'Looks like a storm's brewing,' remarked the man who'd followed me out. I turned to him and nodded. I noticed how the years had lined his face. Much of the hair on his head and in his bushy moustache was white. He seemed, in return, to be acknowledging the changes time had inflicted on me. He seemed saddened by what he saw. He put his hand on my shoulder.

'It's good to see you again, Tony,' he announced with authority.

I felt myself blush, and squeezed his bony arm with affection. 'Likewise, captain.'

He smiled. I sensed he must have risen in rank but seemed happy for me to call him captain, for old times' sake.

At his suggestion we started making our way towards Camden High Street to find a café where we could exchange contact details. He asked where I'd been all this time. I told him nowhere but London, admitting I'd never been back to the village. He shook his head, saying he'd asked everywhere after me among the Cypriot community. I explained that I'd kept myself to myself. He chastised me for making no effort to get in touch.

I felt guilty, but could see little point explaining myself further. Instead I diverted attention to him. I learnt he had a flat overlooking the sea in a south-coast resort called Hove. He invited me to visit him one day soon, as there was something important he needed to give me. I was uncertain.

At the café we ordered two instant coffees and carried our cups to a table by the window. We sat opposite one another, our coffee before us. His was white, mine black.

'Not how Vasos used to make it,' observed the captain sombrely, looking down into his cup.

'No one could make coffee like Vasos,' I agreed, looking down into mine.

The captain tried adding some sugar from a shaker on the table, but it was clogged. He tutted and took a tentative sip regardless. I could scarcely bring myself to do so.

'What would he make of coffee like this?' he mused.

I rubbed my stubbly chin and tried to recall. 'He'd say it was a good thing, if you were in a hurry.'

We observed the pedestrians outside, rushing to escape the imminent downpour.

'Vasos was never one to hurry,' noted the captain. I nodded pensively, looking up into the sky.

The captain took another sip.

'So tell me, Tony, what have you been doing with yourself?'

'Not much. Plying my trade. I've been a master tailor in Regent Street.'

'Really?' he enthused. 'Well done. I knew you'd make a success of your life here.'

'I've survived, captain. How about you? What do you do in Hove?'

The captain thought for a moment.

'I keep myself occupied,' he said eventually. 'It's good to be by the sea. You'd like it.'

I shrugged.

'Did you never marry, Tony?'

I gripped my cup in its saucer and felt its warmth. I shook my head and returned the question. He laughed.

'You know me. Married to the British army. Best relationship a man could have. Loyalty. Stability. Security. Together we took on the world.'

'Sounds ideal,' I agreed, then couldn't resist adding with a smile, 'if world domination is what you both desire.'

He shook his head. 'They prepare you for everything in the army. Except how to retire.'

There was a distant flash of lightning in the sky.

'Your life loses its meaning. Everything you fought for, everything you believed in, becomes an illusion. Gone for ever,' I suggested.

A faint rumbling of thunder followed.

'You put it well, Tony.'

'I've felt like that ever since I came to this country,' I admitted.

The captain took another sip of his coffee. 'You don't know how much it saddens me to hear that. England was to be your escape. Your chance for freedom. A new life, away from all the madness. Instead, it seems you've become a…' He searched for an appropriate word.

'Prisoner?' I offered. 'It's what I deserve.'

'And you mean to tell me that, in all this time, you've never wanted to go back to the village. To see what's happened?'

I shook my head.

'But your mother. Surely you've kept in touch?'

'I've caused her enough suffering.'

There was another flash in the sky, more intense than the last.

The captain lowered his head. 'Then you don't even know.'

The thunder that followed made me shudder.

'Really, captain, whatever it is, I prefer not to know,' I urged, raising a hand.

'But you can't keep avoiding the truth.'

Our attention was momentarily diverted by more flashing, followed soon after by more booming. The heavens were about to open.

'You've served your penance, Tony. It's time for release.'

I could tell he was gathering difficult thoughts, and before he could speak I'd put my hands to my ears.

'Don't do this to me, captain. Please.'

The captain reached for my hands and gently pulled them down to the table. His steel blue eyes pierced mine and I had to look away. I lost myself in the blackness of my coffee.

'After your disappearance,' he began.

I could make out my distorted reflection.

'He really lost it, you know,' he added.

I could see someone old.

'They couldn't control him, Tony. They feared what he might do.'

Someone familiar.

'You have to know, Tony. They killed him. They killed your...'

'Baba!' I cried. The coffee rippled. The reflection was lost. I buried my face in my hands.

'That's right, Tony. Let yourself go. Let it all come out,' urged the captain.

It began to pour.

'And the Turkish girl...' he tried to continue, but this time I grabbed his hands and stared back at him.

'I beg you, captain. No more truth!'

The captain nodded and fell silent.

15
The barber   *O barperis*

Funda did what her father told her. Like a good little girl. He'd instructed her to sweep up all the hair from the barber's shop floor, and so she did as she was told. She knew she had to do it after the last of Nuretin's customers had departed. She did so every evening. But always she'd wait for her father's command. Only singing in public did the barber's little girl do without his express say-so. Everyone knew, as Mrs Maria had known, that her voice was too beautiful to be contained. It evoked happier times. And the money collected had always been permission enough.

Funda looked down at all the different tufts of hair collected by her broom. Different textures. Different colours. Some coarse. Some greasy. Some jet black, others dark brown. Some flecked with grey, others milky white. She thought of Andonis's rich and perfect mane, imagined her fingers passing through it and felt herself tingle.

How she adored Mrs Maria's grown-up grandson. A man who, with the old woman's encouragement, now had his own trade and with it his own mind. The young tailor had courted Funda in front of the whole village. Serenaded her with his harmonica. He'd shown them all what magic could come from his lips. And then he'd shown her a different magic. He'd lifted an open palm at all the gossiping women at the well. From right under their noses he'd swept her away in his strong arms and, with a kiss, dared the little girl to grow up. He'd infused her with such passion that the emerging woman had even dared seek him out at the workshop. To brush against those rugged cheeks once more, to feel his warm breath against her face, to bask in his masculinity. To kiss and caress him. Now she even dared imagine making love to him, here in the barber's shop. She tingled again.

But would she still tingle when his hair had thinned and lost its colour? Could she know for sure? Funda imagined how she might feel if Andonis was banished from the village, for loving her, for being a traitor. A cold shiver passed through her. She felt for the reassuring presence of a small lump in the pocket of her skirt, and as she did so the fear subsided. She knew she loved the tailor. Now and for all time.

Funda pulled out the brass thimble, stared at it a moment and smiled. Then she passed her finger through it as though it were a wedding ring. It was more precious to her for not being gold. More symbolic for not having been blessed inside a mosque or a church. It made her a woman who knew no fear. She knew it was time to stand up to her father.

※ ※ ※

Nuretin slapped the table. 'You go too far, Funda,' he insisted, and pursed his lips.

Being angry didn't suit Nuretin. He was a small, dapper man with a black pencil moustache, the sort designed to accentuate a cheeky smile rather than act as a second furrowed brow. He ran his hand through a full head of greying hair. It was slicked back with cream, the way many of his customers requested theirs. He sat there, at the table, in the room behind the barber's shop. Facing him were Funda, her brother Zeki and their mother Leila. Now Nuretin wagged a finger at all three.

'No daughter of mine is going to the town to train as a hairdresser. There are jobs for you here, Funda, helping me in the shop. Helping your mother at home.'

Funda folded her arms and sighed. 'You know as well as I do that the shop isn't making enough to support us properly, father. Not since so many Christians stopped coming.'

This time Nuretin clenched his fist and punched the table repeatedly. 'You leave that to me, you hear? That's my business. My responsibility.'

Funda turned to her mother, who hid behind the white headscarf that she and all Muslim women of her generation wore. Funda reached over and pulled the material away from Leila's face.

'Can't you say something?' she implored. Leila shrugged.

'Please, Funda. We have so many problems to overcome,' pleaded Leila meekly. 'Your brother, the troubles. Don't bring your father more pain.'

Zeki shuffled in his seat, and his sister could sense his unease. Zeki didn't like to be seen as a problem.

Funda addressed her father. 'This is a family. We're all responsible for its well-being. You, me, mother, Zeki. We all have a contribution to make. I am able to work and I want to work. Why won't you give me a chance? Why won't you give this family a chance?' she demanded.

Her father glared at her.

'It's not right, I tell you, for a girl like you to be working in the town,' he declared. 'Just as it's not right for a girl like you to be performing those old songs to Greeks, like some poor beggar.'

Funda's mouth dropped. Her father had never objected to her singing before; had never referred to her audience as Greeks before.

'But it's right that we cut ourselves off? That we forget the past and fear the future?'

'Why do you always question me?' demanded Nuretin. 'Is it because I never thought it right to discipline my daughter?'

Zeki shifted in his seat once more. Despite his disability, he had not enjoyed the same immunity from a beating as his sister. Leila sensed her husband was near breaking point. She stroked her daughter's arm.

'The bad times will pass, Funda. You'll see,' she urged, but Funda's frown showed that she was far from convinced.

Nuretin turned to his wife and put his finger to his lips. Then he turned to Funda.

'Funda, listen to me,' he commanded. 'You're still young. There's more that we must teach you. But I think it's right for you to know that there have already been a number of good Muslim families, of substance and of standing, that have approached me, on behalf of their sons. Your future...our future is secure. So long as your reputation is maintained and your honour protected. So long as you behave yourself and do the right thing.'

Funda's eyes flashed with realisation. She shook her head.

'No more teaching's necessary, father. You've explained it all now. You won't let your daughter express herself, you won't let her make an honest living. It might open her eyes and free her spirit. It might ruin your plans to turn her into...' She hesitated a moment but then resolved to say what she had to say: 'Into a rich man's toy!'

Without warning, Nuretin swung out and struck Funda across the head with the back of his hand.

'Not her face, not her face,' cried a panic-stricken Leila, grabbing her husband's arm to restrain him. But the anger was not yet gone from Nuretin's eyes. He shook loose and rose from the table.

Zeki lifted a crutch to block his father from getting round it.

'Don't you dare touch her,' declared Zeki forcefully.

No one was more surprised by the cripple's actions than the cripple himself. The threat of violence against his sister had brought him to life. Jolted in turn by his son's intervention, Nuretin regained some of his composure and sat back in his chair.

Still in shock, Funda rubbed her cheek, feeling the warmth of the blood rushing to it. The unthinkable had indeed just happened. Zeki put an arm round his sister, who only now burst into tears.

'See what you make me do, Funda?' exclaimed a shaking Nuretin. 'With all your nonsense! Why can't you see it from my point of view? I have to do what's best for my family under difficult circumstances. Here we are, blessed with a daughter of rare beauty. And with a son who's…' His voice trailed away.

It was Zeki's turn to slap the table.

'Go on, father, say it! Crippled. Less of a man than you. Blessed with a beautiful daughter and cursed with a cripple, whose only function is to be provided for, cared for and pitied.'

'That's not what I meant,' mumbled Nuretin, and looked down, unable to meet his son's eyes.

'Isn't it? Don't you pity the cripple then, father? Look at me!' implored Zeki, but Nuretin was unable to. 'Look at me!'

Their eyes met and Zeki continued. 'After all, how can a cripple possibly cut hair properly? Or shave beards properly? Or learn any trade properly? Go on, pity me. You ought to. After all, the rest of the village, including the Christians, pity me. They pity the cripple's father.'

Nuretin shook his head, shocked and saddened by his son's frankness.

'That's enough, Zeki. I do my best. For you and for your sister. There's no reason for anybody to pity us.'

'I may be a cripple but I'm not dumb and I'm not deaf, father. I hear what people say about me. I'm back here, remember. Out of view. Sitting on that chair all day, pulling the rope for your fan. I know how patronising the villagers can be to their barber. Poor old Nuretin, who tries so hard to earn enough money, to feed his family, to secure some kind of future for that poor boy. Too bad, they think. We must all make a point of getting our hair cut as often as we can afford. We could wait a week but the cripple's father needs the money. It's what they all think, isn't it, father?'

Silence.

'Isn't it?'

Nuretin couldn't bring himself to reply, couldn't bring himself to face what he knew to be true.

'And you don't like it, do you, father?' continued Zeki. 'Because you're a proud man. You don't want people's charity. It demeans you. Makes you less of a man. So know how it feels, father. Know how I feel.'

The tears rolled down the cheeks of Nuretin. Leila thought to speak, but was inhibited by years of being told to be quiet. Funda also remained silent, but Zeki was not finished.

'And now that I've opened up, father, there's something else you should know. Your imperfect son has urges. Oh yes. All his equipment works. But who'd want to be with him? He can't walk, he can't dance, he takes an age just to get into bed. What woman would marry the cripple or bear his children and his name? So you have to compensate for your inadequate son by smothering your precious daughter. You inhibit her talent. You restrict her freedom. You seal her fate. You turn her into a cripple too!'

Funda nodded approval and encouragement. She was the only one who ever approved of Zeki, the only one who ever encouraged him. Zeki turned to her.

'Don't ever stop singing, Funda,' he urged. 'Those old songs help me forget about my crutches. They remind me of better times. They make me feel whole again.'

✳ ✳ ✳

Andonis looked up from the shirt he was making. Zeki's shirt. His eyes adjusted to the sunlight now streaming through the open door of his workshop. It took him a few moments to make out to whom the silhouette of the tall man standing before him belonged.

'Er, welcome, captain,' he said with surprise, beckoning the British officer to come inside. The Cypriot felt a little self-conscious. He hadn't been expecting visitors today, and so had bothered neither to shave nor even to wash his armpits.

'It's good to see you again, after all this time, young man,' announced the captain with a warm smile, and stepped in. Earlier the captain had arrived in the village alone and unannounced, in his army jeep and in his army uniform. He'd been told at the coffee-shop where to find the village tailor.

'It's good to see you too, sir. I think,' ventured Andonis. 'Though most of the village may not agree.'

'I had no choice but to come. Where else is someone in need of fine craftsmanship to go?' enquired the captain, which made Andonis smile.

'Don't worry, captain. People will understand. Sure, there are those who'd prefer I slit your throat. But I've been taught that killing your customers is no way to make a living,' said Andonis with a grin, which the captain returned, happy to tolerate the young local's affectionate impertinence.

'You've been taught well, Tony. It's a good philosophy. May I call you Tony?'

Andonis shrugged.

'So, how's that attractive Turkish girlfriend of yours, the barber's daughter?'

Andonis shrugged once more.

The captain nodded. 'I see. Forbidden love, eh? Shame. You two would make a fine couple.' There was genuine regret in his tone. 'Still, if there's anything I can do…'

'Thanks, but no thanks,' said Andonis. The captain frowned.

'Tony, why do you people resent us so? Why this need to fight? Take away the cap, the khaki shirt and shorts, and we're the same as you. Men trying to do their best during troubled times.'

Andonis shook his head.

'It's not the same, captain. We're fighting for freedom. You're fighting to prevent it.'

The captain shook his head in turn. He realised this was one conflict that might never be resolved.

'Enough!' he announced. 'I'm here as a paying customer, not a soldier. I've been invited to my nephew's wedding in England later this year, and I need a new suit. Are you a tailor or a terrorist?'

Andonis smiled before taking out a notebook and a tape measure from his box on the sewing machine.

'Let's measure you up, then, sir.'

The captain raised his arms as instructed. As Andonis went about his work, the captain scrutinised the small icons of various saints on the wall of the workshop. Among them he noticed a picture of an elegant and proud old lady.

'Who's that woman?' he enquired.

Andonis followed the direction of the captain's gaze.

'My grandmother, sir,' explained the tailor proudly. He began writing down a series of numbers in the notebook.

'She seems very fair, for a Greek,' noted the captain.

'You mean for a Cypriot. But you see she wasn't born in Cyprus. She was from Macedonia in northern Greece. There are many fair Macedonians.'

'So how did she end up here?'

'She moved to Alexandria with her family and met my grandfather, who used to go over there sometimes on fishing trips. They fell in love and he brought her back to the village, where they were married,' explained Andonis. 'They're both dead now, God rest their souls.'

The tailor was now kneeling down in front of the captain to take his inside leg measurements.

'Macedonia via Alexandria, eh?' mused the captain. 'Well, well, Tony, I wouldn't be surprised if you were a descendant of the great Alexander himself.'

'If I had Alexander's blood wouldn't I be an EOKA warrior, fighting to free my country from foreign oppression?' ventured Andonis, pushing the long metal end of his tape-measure up into the captain's crotch, making him jump.

'EOKA? They're not warriors,' said the captain dismissively. 'They're cowards. Bombing soldiers and their families while they sleep. Alexander wasn't a coward. He was a brave leader. Perhaps the greatest soldier the world's ever known.'

Andonis took his pencil and wrote some more numbers in his notebook.

'I know who Alexander was, captain. He united Greece and went on to claim the ancient world as his empire – just like you British have tried to do with the modern one.'

'Indeed,' agreed the captain. 'Greek and British. Ancient and modern. Great empires. Great civilisations.'

'So why are you here, sir? The people of Cyprus were civilised already.'

The captain scrunched up his face. 'You civilised? You don't even know how to shave!'

After the two men had discussed and agreed on the suit's style, cloth and colour, Andonis wrote one last figure on a blank page of his notebook, before tearing it out and handing it to the captain.

The captain looked at the number, raised his eyebrows in mock surprise, then gave the tailor a warm smile.

'Tony, if I didn't know you to be such a fine tailor, I'd have you thrown in jail and beaten for extortion,' he said with a smirk.

'Sir, if I didn't know you to be such a generous customer, I'd plant a bomb under your bed,' replied the tailor.

The captain took out his wallet from a back pocket, and put a five-shilling note into Andonis's hand as down-payment. Andonis's eyes lit up.

'Thank you, sir.'

'And I've more work for you. That's if you're interested,' suggested the slightly hesitant captain.

'Why wouldn't I be interested? I'm not afraid of work, sir,' declared the eager tailor.

'Not even army work? Finishing off uniforms?' enquired the captain. 'I mean, won't your people object?'

Andonis rubbed the long bristles on his chin.

'It's not the uniforms they object too, captain. Just the men inside them,' he explained.

'Is that so?' said the captain, breathing an ironic sigh of relief. 'Come and see me at the army base in town a week from today. I'll show you what needs to be done, and we'll agree an appropriate fee.'

Andonis nodded. 'I'll do that,' he said.

The captain pointed to the money in the tailor's hand.

'You can afford to go and get that shave now,' he instructed, and left the tailor to his measurements.

❋ ❋ ❋

Shortly after the captain's departure, and after washing his armpits thoroughly, Andonis emerged from the workshop and braved the heat. He headed towards the square, and then ventured further into the neighbourhood where the Muslims lived.

It was a walk he used to enjoy often when he was younger, but since the troubles a walk he now rarely took. Andonis passed familiar shops he no longer frequented, scrutinising each one in turn, recognising familiar details with affection. The butcher's, the cobbler's, the baker's. The smell of sickly-sweet pastries evoked myriad happy childhood memories. The people he passed appeared pleased to see the young tailor, though none spoke to him.

His pace slowed, and his heart pumped as he reached the barber's shop. Funda lived there. At the back. Andonis looked up, and for the first time took note of the old wooden sign, dangling above his head, at right angles to the shop-front. Two words were written on it, one Greek, one Turkish. Barber. Below was a crude drawing of a pair of scissors. A barber's trademark, but also a tailor's.

Andonis entered. The Englezos had instructed him to get a shave, so here he was. And while the barber lathered the tailor's face the tailor would express his undying love for the barber's daughter. And as the barber's sharp blade scraped the tailor's cheeks, the tailor would ask for the barber's daughter's hand. And, if the barber refused, then the tailor would offer his throat and beg the barber to finish the job.

But inside he was not greeted by Nuretin, but by Funda herself, who addressed the surprised but delighted Andonis as she would any other of her father's customers.

'Good day, Mr Andoni. Are you well, Mr Andoni?' she asked with surprise and delight. And with a touch of trepidation too.

Funda's voice was like a song, lifting and lowering as the words glided out of a smiling mouth. It was a song Andonis knew well, and he sang along as though they were performing a smiling duet.

Very well, Miss Funda. And you?
Thank you, very well.
And your family?
They are all well, thank you. And yours?
They too are well, thank you.

Above their heads the big canvas fan began swinging to and fro as it always did when a customer entered.

Their song over, Funda gave the tailor a frown before glancing up at the swinging fan. Then she glanced back at him, to indicate that their conversation could be heard. She lowered her voice barely above a whisper and spoke.

'What are you doing here, Andoni?' she demanded.

The tailor glanced up at the fan and pointed to his cheek, as though requesting a kiss. Funda shook her head.

'Where else is a man to go when he needs a close shave?' he replied with a grin, seeing no reason to lower his own voice. 'So where is our barperis?'

'He's gone to the town to buy provisions,' replied the barber's daughter out loud. Andonis gave Funda a knowing smile to indicate how grateful he was for this opportunity to catch a few moments alone with the object of his desires. He was disappointed that Funda did not return his smile, but instead glanced back up at the swinging fan.

The tailor turned to go. 'I'll come back another time then,' he sulked.

'He won't be long, Mr Andoni. Please stay. We could do with the work. Business is slow. What with all the troubles, some men are now less inclined to concern themselves with how they look. Please stay, sir. We get so few Christian customers these days,' pleaded Funda, then added with feeling, 'It would be a shame to lose you.'

Andonis looked longingly at Funda and, lowering his voice, said, 'You'll never lose me, Funda. Between you and me, I'm not much of a Christian.'

Funda nodded. 'Nor I much of a Muslim,' she whispered.

The tailor raised his voice. 'I can only give you my custom on one condition,' he declared.

'And what's that, sir?' enquired the barber's daughter.

The tailor spoke louder than was necessary. 'Well, I'm in a bit of hurry, you see. Is it possible you could shave me yourself?'

Funda glared at Andonis, and then bit her lip in an attempt to contain a growing smile. The fan stopped.

'Oh, but I couldn't, Mr Andoni,' declared the barber's daughter. 'It wouldn't be right. My father would disapprove.' The fan refused to resume.

'Even if it meant turning away a valued customer?' asked the tailor out loud.

Funda frowned. 'I'd never turn you away,' she whispered.

'So you can shave me?' called out the tailor, and looked up at the fan, which began to swing again as though by way of approval.

'It appears I've no choice,' replied the barber's daughter, offering Andonis a seat in one of the two barber's chairs.

Funda wrapped a white towel round Andonis's neck. Though clean, the towel nevertheless had a discernible tinge of pink from the many dusty faces with which it had come into contact over the years.

In silence, Funda began delicately caressing Andonis's rough cheeks with a brush, until his face was bathed in soft white foam. Delicate fingertips now caressed his chin. As Funda leant over Andonis, his nostrils filled with the smell of soap. It was the same soap he used, that the whole village used, yet on her it had a sweet and unique fragrance all its own. Like lemon blossom. Now she took the blade that had been soaking in a cup of water. Nervously, and with great care, she began scraping the bristles from his face.

Mindful not to move his jaw and interfere with her work, Andonis whispered, 'I want you, Funda.'

Funda wagged a finger at Andonis. 'Yes, it's getting too hot, Mr Andoni,' replied the barber's daughter out loud.

'I want to devour your breasts this very minute, Funda,' whispered Andonis.

Funda grimaced. 'I'm sure your father's melons will be the tastiest and sweetest yet,' declared the barber's daughter.

'I want to wrap my naked body round yours and love you,' whispered Andonis.

Funda raised her eyebrows. 'No doubt the seeds will soon be sewn,' returned the barber's daughter.

Andonis grabbed Funda's hand with the blade. A dollop of foam specked with tiny black bristles fell to the floor.

'What would your father say to me if he were standing here now, Funda?' whispered Andonis.

'He'd tell you to get out of his daughter's life,' whispered Funda. 'And what would you reply?' she continued.

Andonis let go. 'I'd tell him to put his blade to my throat and take mine,' he whispered.

The barber's daughter shook her head, finished her work, and gently wiped Andonis's cheeks dry with a wet flannel. They were as smooth as silk. She stepped back, smiled flirtatiously, and admired her work. And there was a yearning in her eyes.

'You do look wonderful, Mr Andoni,' said the barber's daughter proudly and loudly, holding a mirror to the tailor's face. 'A fine job, even if I say so myself.'

At that moment the two young Cypriots were jolted with shock and fear. Nuretin had burst through the door, carrying a big brown paper bag. He glared disapprovingly at the scene before him.

The fan stopped. The blade slipped from Funda's hand and struck the floor. Andonis stood up from the barber's chair and smiled a nervous greeting. Nuretin ignored the tailor and addressed his daughter.

'Funda,' he commanded. 'Go and make me some coffee.'

Funda frowned. 'Leave us!' implored the barber, handing her the bag. 'I need to speak with Mr Andonis.'

'Your conversation may concern me too,' insisted Funda.

Andonis gave her a look to convey that he wished her to do her father's bidding. She shook her head, but did as she was told. The barber gestured to the tailor that he should retake his seat. Andonis did so, and Nuretin sat next to him in the other barber's chair.

'Why have you come here?' he asked.

'Please, Mr Nuretin. I must talk to you about Funda.'

'Your visit's ill-judged,' cautioned the barber. 'Many believe a mutual attraction has developed between you and my daughter. I laugh. I tell them such ideas are fanciful, dangerous even. But the rumours persist and cause my family, and no doubt yours too, a great deal of embarrassment. A great deal of distress.'

Andonis bowed his head. 'I'm sorry, sir. That wasn't my intention.'

'And now I find you here in my shop and I start to wonder. Perhaps you enjoy the attention. Perhaps you enjoy the danger. But I don't, and my daughter doesn't. So I ask you to go from here and to leave her alone. Please. This nonsense must stop now. For only trouble can come of it.'

'I can't stop, Mr Nuretin,' declared Andonis. 'I came here today because I love Funda. I want your permission so that we may marry.'

Nuretin shook his head and there was exasperation and dismay in his eyes. 'Do you know what you're saying?'

'I'm in love with your daughter and I believe she's in love with me. That's all I need to know.'

Nuretin shook his head. 'Love? Love is on shit, Andoni, and heaven help whoever falls,' he said. 'I should be angry that you choose to insult me in this way. But you're so young and naïve, I can't be angry. I pity you. And if my daughter feels the same way about a Christian then I pity her too.'

'I'm no more a Christian than your daughter is a Muslim. Why label us? It's what the Englezi do to divide us. To control our land and our lives. I'm a Cypriot. Your daughter's a Cypriot. I believe we belong to each other. As Cyprus belongs to us both.'

'You romantic fool. Have you explained how you feel to your parents? What did they have to say?'

'The same as you. That you should be in your home and we should be in ours. But we've only one home, Mr Nuretin, and we've lived together here for generations. In peace. Why not in love?'

Nuretin laughed. 'All sensible people want peace, my son. Tension, fighting and death are no good to any man. But there are extremists who think differently. They insist on hate.'

'But once we've rid the island of the Englezi we'll be free to live together. Free from outside interference.'

Nuretin lowered his voice. 'Son, there are people not far from this shop who believe this island is merely an extension of the Anatolian peninsula, on loan to the Englezi. So if we rid Cyprus of the Englezi they believe it should be handed back to its rightful owner.'

'Is that what you believe, Mr Nuretin?'

'It's what our youth is being brainwashed to believe. They're on a collision course with your Christian friends who believe in enosis with Greece.'

'But what do you believe?' pressed Andonis.

'What I believe is irrelevant. There are powerful forces in control of the destiny of this island. To try and resist such forces is to court disaster.'

'I love Funda.'

'Love her from a distance. For her sake. For your sake. For my sake,' urged Nuretin, pulling Andonis from his chair and ushering him out of his shop. 'For your father's sake,' he added, before closing the door.

Andonis remained outside for a moment, staring at the pair of scissors on the old wooden sign above his head, his eyes watering.

16
The Englishwoman   *I Engleza*

I stood outside the Muswell Hill Centre, looking up at the sign above the entrance. I thought of the Turkish girl. I thought of my father. Since the truth had been confirmed I'd done little else.

It was a pleasant evening, still light and warm. Perhaps spring had finally arrived.

I rang the bell and saw Ruth approaching through the glass of the door. She looked a little flustered, but no less attractive than how I remembered. I could feel my heart pumping as she pushed the door open and greeted me with a relieved smile.

'You're late,' she observed testily. I nodded. 'I thought you might not come,' she added.

I shook my head. 'I'm not the sort of bloke to let a woman down,' I assured, making the effort to smile. She smiled back.

'Better late than never, I suppose,' she ventured, grabbing my hand to lead me inside. 'Welcome to the Muswell Hill Centre.' She presented me to an empty hall. 'Shame you've missed all the kids. Apart from Ravi, that is.'

Now she pointed over to a teenaged boy, slumped in a chair by the door, wearing an oversized Parka jacket with the hood up. At the mention of his name the boy pulled back his hood to reveal sombre black eyes and a complexion a little darker than mine.

'We're waiting for Ravi's dad. He works late,' explained Ruth. Ravi fidgeted uncomfortably. I offered him my hand and he seemed surprised at my gesture.

'Come on, Ravi,' encouraged Ruth. 'Say hello to Tony.'

Avoiding eye contact, the boy reached up and shook my hand loosely.

'What's that you've got there?' I asked, noticing the silver harmonica in his other hand. He shrugged.

'Play Tony that tune we've been working on,' suggested Ruth.

'All right then,' muttered Ravi reluctantly, though I could tell he was pleased to have Ruth's attention. He half-smiled before putting the harmonica to his lips.

I recognised Ravi's tune immediately. It was being played a lot on the radio: a duet by Donny and Marie Osmond about a forbidden love between a boy and a girl from different sides of a mountain. Ruth started singing along. She had a pleasant voice. When Ravi had finished, I applauded. I caught Ruth's approving eye. She was applauding too.

'You play well, Ravi,' I remarked encouragingly.

'Not really,' he insisted, but I could tell he was pleased with the praise. Ruth was pleased too.

'Do you play?' she asked. Ravi looked up at me for the first time.

I shook my head. 'I used to. A long time ago.'

Ravi began to wipe the harmonica on his Parka. 'Will you play us something then?'

I hesitated and looked to Ruth for guidance. None came. She seemed happy merely to observe.

'Go on,' he asked, offering me the instrument. I took it, examined it a moment, then put it to my lips.

I began to play. Cautiously at first, but with each true note my confidence increased. I hadn't forgotten how to play. On and on I went until my hands, lips and tongue were working together perfectly. I was consumed. I shut my eyes and felt myself transported to another world. There were crowds, happy faces, clapping hands. And all at once, singing along, was the voice of an angel.

When I had finished, I was met with applause from Ruth and Ravi.

'Wow. That was really good,' he enthused.

'What tune was that, Tony?' asked Ruth.

'It's an old song. From a different world,' I replied before passing the harmonica back to Ravi, who wiped it on his Parka once more.

'Sounds like a world worth knowing,' she hinted. Before I could think of an appropriate response, Ravi was tugging at my sleeve.

'Can I ask you something, Tony?' he enquired with a cheeky grin.

'Ask away, young man,' I declared, and smiled proudly at Ruth. Ravi beckoned me closer, and I stooped.

'Are you Ruth's boyfriend?' he whispered, before giggling nervously.

There was an awkward silence before the youth worker came to the rescue.

'Tony's a friend, Ravi,' she said. Then she squeezed the boy's cheek with affection. Despite his light-brown skin, I could see he was blushing. I knew I was blushing too.

Soon after, Ravi's father arrived. He was darker than his son. He looked tired and distracted. He apologised to Ruth for being late, and was quick to usher the boy out. Ruth pulled the door shut behind them, and turned to me with a sigh.

'Ravi's become a bit of a handful since his parents' separation,' she explained. She seemed troubled, which troubled me. 'I think the outside pressures were too much in the end. What with her being English and him being Asian.'

I stroked a furrowed brow.

'Ravi tells me they still love each other. God knows what knowing that does to the boy.'

'It makes him passionate about his music,' I suggested. 'Which, I suppose, is where you come in.'

She nodded. 'I suppose you're right,' she said.

We emerged from the centre. She locked up and turned to me with an expectant smile.

'Hungry?' I suggested. She shrugged. 'How about a coffee, then?' I offered. She nodded. I knew a café nearby that would still be open. As we walked, we talked.

'Dave wanted me to let you know that your job's still there if you want it,' she said. 'He says they're all missing you.'

I smiled.

'Oh, and he also mentioned that someone called Osborne might be willing to talk. Whatever that means.'

My smile grew broader, but I shook my head.

We arrived at the café and I bought us both a coffee. We found a quiet table and sat opposite each other.

She sipped hers, but I could scarcely bring myself to sip mine.

'What's the matter, Tony?'

'Forgive me, Ruth. I had some bad news.'

She looked at me expectantly.

'I lost my father.'

She grabbed both my hands across the table, and I was grateful for the comfort the touch of those soft, feminine fingers brought me.

'Oh Tony, I'm so sorry. You should have told me earlier. How old was he?'

'He'd have been in his forties when it happened,' I replied, conscious of how strange this might sound. I could tell Ruth had been preparing to be caring and consoling, but was now too confused.

'What do you mean?' she asked.

'I only found out recently,' I said. 'I've been away from home a long time.'

I could tell she wanted more details, but I had none to give. We sat there in silence stroking each other's hands. I avoided eye contact.

'None of this makes any sense,' she said eventually, withdrawing her hands. I nodded.

'I'm sorry, Ruth. Perhaps I should go,' I suggested, shifting in my chair.

'Please don't,' she urged, staring at me intently. 'My husband was around your father's age when I lost him. Two years ago, to cancer. One day he was alive and well, the next he was ill and dying. And then he was gone. That didn't make any sense either. When people go before their time, how can it make sense?'

With sorrow and regret, my eyes filled.

'It's really hard when you love someone and there's no bringing them back. No putting things right,' she added.

I felt for those gentle fingers once more and took comfort from the fact that now it was I doing the comforting.

'Have you never been married, Tony?' she asked. I looked down into my coffee and shook my head. Soon after I offered to walk her home. She nodded and told me her house was on a turning off Fortis Green.

'If I told you something, do you promise you won't take it the wrong way?' she asked as we walked.

'You can tell me anything you like, Ruth.'

She hesitated a moment before speaking.

'It's just that…you're not like other…'

'Foreigners?' I suggested.

She nodded. 'I mean, the Greeks – sorry Cypriots – I've come across seem too preoccupied with work and money and material things,' she explained.

I nodded. 'They came over with wide eyes and empty bellies. They're used to working hard, but for someone else. Now, here in England, they can work for themselves. And for a better future for their children.'

'I see,' she remarked. 'So is that why you're different? No children?'

I shrugged. 'Another generation or two, then perhaps we'll see what these foreigners can really achieve,' I mused.

Ruth smiled. 'I think you're capable already.'

'Me capable?'

'Thoughtful. Intelligent. Creative…Good-looking!' she suggested with a smile, and I felt myself blush. 'I mean, you speak English better than many people born here. And Dave's told me what a good tailor you are. And what about the way you play the harmonica? You're capable, Tony. Maybe you just need to realise how much you have to offer.'

I checked my step and turned to her.

'But my people have already created songs and stories and poetry full of beauty and meaning. It's just that no one's ever taken the trouble to listen.'

'Or perhaps no one's ever really taken the trouble to share them,' corrected Ruth. 'Because I'm sure there are many who'd want to listen.'

When we reached her home, Ruth invited me in for coffee. I knew it wouldn't be right, and I sensed she knew too, so I joked that we'd already had some.

'Will we see each other again, Tony?' she asked.

'I'd like that, Ruth,' I replied, and she smiled before leaning forward to kiss me on the cheek. I thought to reciprocate but found myself strangely frozen. I could see she was a little put out. I went to speak, but she'd already turned her back on me and retreated inside, shutting the door behind her.

'Ya su,' I found myself saying through the closed door.

✳ ✳ ✳

A few days later I stood waiting on the Broadway for a bus that would take me to where Stella had explained her husband worked. There were things that needed to be put right, and I felt ready to make a start.

17

The bus   *Do leoforion*

The dusty old bus was parked in the village square waiting for passengers. It should have set off at seven-thirty in the morning, bound for the town. But, as always, it would be late. It was already a quarter to eight, and commuting villagers were only now emerging from their homes and making their way to the square. They came from down the road as well as up, Muslims as well as Christians. These were people without either enough acres or enough stomach to make their living in the fields. Younger people. Those with jobs in the town. Civil servants, labourers, cleaners, shop workers.

Recently the Muslim passengers had taken to arriving a little earlier than usual. They would take up seats at the rear of the bus, away from the Christians, who would now all squeeze in at the front a few minutes later. The bus-driver Simos didn't agree with what some Christians of the village were now openly suggesting in the coffee-shop. That the bus was getting too crowded, that seats should be reserved for Christians, that Muslims should organise their own transportation.

'My customers can bow to Allah, to God, or even to Satan for all I care. So long as they hand over their shilling, they'll always be welcome on my bus,' Simos would declare in the coffee-shop, and old man Haji-Markos would nod in agreement.

The sun was blazing and casting long shadows across the square. Simos, in the dark glasses which he always wore for driving, was leaning up against his livelihood, enjoying his first cigarette of the day. One knee was bent, and his foot rested on the front wheel near the bus door. As today was his name day, the day of Saint Simon the Apostle, he had a big bag of lukumia which he was presenting to each of his passengers on their arrival. Both Muslim and Christian passengers accepted a lukumin with a smile and a wish that he have a long life. Simos thanked them, before relieving them of their fares and allowing them to climb aboard.

The bus was now practically full, and the bus-driver was about to get on himself when he saw the young tailor approaching. An intrigued Simos waited for Andonis to draw nearer before flashing his gold tooth.

'Good morning, Andoni. So we're going into town?' he enquired, bowing his head with mock reverence.

'Yes, sir. I have some business to discuss,' replied the tailor, immediately on the defensive.

'Business, eh?' probed the driver.

The tailor nodded. 'That's right, Mr Simo. I have a new customer.'

The bus-driver offered a knowing smile. 'Andonis has a new customer. In town. Well, bravo. And this new customer will recommend Andonis to all his friends, and they in turn to all their friends. And before long, Andonis will be the richest, most famous tailor in the whole of Cyprus. No doubt.'

'No doubt,' agreed the tailor, and reached down to pick at some old chicken feathers still lodged underneath the wheel arch of the bus.

'I only wish I had as much faith in your skills as a driver as you have in my skills as a tailor,' he remarked.

The bus-driver smiled his golden smile. 'In ten years I've never lost a passenger,' he declared proudly.

'Thanks only to God!' said Andonis, looking up to heaven. 'By the way, Mr Simo. My mamma sends her best curses.'

Simos looked down and took an embarrassed drag of his cigarette.

'So, who's this new customer, Andoni? Is he rich? I know all the rich families in town. I've been to their houses. They have servants and eat meat every day.'

The tailor shook his head. 'It's an Englezos. The captain.'

'You're working for the captain? Well, bravo again, Andoni,' declared Simos, patting the tailor's shoulder.

'Yes, and for the army,' explained Andonis. 'Finishing off uniforms. Tiresome work, but no doubt lots of it. And well paid, hopefully.'

Simos considered for a moment whether to show disapproval, in the way that his cousin Yoda or, more importantly, the muhtaris might show disapproval. However, it was not in Simos's nature to discourage such entrepreneurial endeavour, so instead he patted the tailor on the shoulder once more.

'Good for you. Be sure to make as much out of the Englezi as you can. And then a bit more,' he urged with a wink.

'I will,' nodded Andonis, returning the wink.

'Oh, and Andoni, I wouldn't go telling people your business. Someone with a big appetite may find it difficult to digest,' advised the bus-driver with genuine concern.

'My business is none of his,' proclaimed Andonis defiantly.

'Correct. And if he doesn't know, it won't be,' urged the bus-driver, offering Andonis a lukumin.

Andonis took one and nodded his thanks. 'May you live, Mr Simo,' he said, then added with a cheeky grin. 'And may we find you the right woman before you're too old!'

'Likewise,' replied the bus-driver, matching his grin.

Now Andonis took out a shilling, but Simos gestured for the tailor to put his money away. He pointed to the feathers by his foot.

'Your mamma's chicken paid the other time,' he advised.

Simos threw away the last of his cigarette, and both men now boarded the bus. It was then that Andonis's face reddened and his heart began to pound. For there, towards the back of the bus, sat Funda.

Simos now slapped Andonis on the backside and whispered into his ear, 'Have a safe journey.'

In a trance Andonis made his way slowly along the bus, passing Christian after Christian, each of whom smiled and nodded a greeting which, one by one, Andonis returned. Eventually he reached Funda. She was sitting among the other Muslims, by a window. The seat next to her was free. She looked up, smiled nervously and nodded a greeting of her own. She looked unsure. She looked ravishing. Smart and well groomed, in a pretty flowery dress and with her hair uncovered and tied in a bun. She even wore lipstick and a touch of rouge on her cheeks.

'Is this space taken?' enquired Andonis politely, pointing to the empty seat.

'It's there to be filled, I suppose,' she replied, turning away from Andonis and gazing out of the window.

Andonis looked up and down the bus. Both Muslims and Christians tried their best not to stare. A few whispered. Andonis hesitated for a moment, then took his place next to Funda. The two remained silent. Simos turned on the ignition, and the engine spluttered into action.

The passengers now began chatting to one another, or else observed the passing sun-drenched fields of their homeland. Peasants and wives and donkeys already at work. Andonis was desperate to talk to Funda, but with her still looking away found it difficult.

'So, you think it's wise to fill the space?' enquired Funda, her voice no louder than a whisper. As much as she wanted to face the man she loved, she kept her head turned away.

'There's no law preventing it,' whispered Andonis in return, staring at her rich brown hair.

'None written,' whispered Funda with regret. 'But people will disapprove. People will talk.'

'Only cutting their tongues out will prevent that,' whispered Andonis. Funda's bun nodded.

'And now, don't you worry, they'll have even more to say…So you're going into town?' she whispered.

'And on to hell too, if that's where you're headed,' whispered Andonis.

The bun shook its disapproval. 'I'm only going as far as the town today. I start my apprenticeship as a hairdresser. Two days a week. I'm learning a trade so I can earn my own money.'

'Your father must be proud,' whispered Andonis.

'Proud?' Funda scoffed a little too loudly, then remembered to lower her voice. 'I don't think so, Andoni. My father's so stubborn. He says only sluts work in the town.' She paused then added, 'Perhaps he's right.'

'Parents have old ideas,' whispered Andonis.

'Old ideas won't put bread on the table,' whispered Funda. Then she turned to face Andonis for the first time. His heart raced. 'And please, Andoni. Don't get any ideas about happening to be on the bus each time I travel. It's too public. It's not safe.'

Andonis nodded, and looked around at the other Muslim passengers. He could sense their disapproval. Funda tugged at Andonis's sleeve, and he turned back to her.

She whispered a demand: 'Tell me what my father said to you.'

Her beautiful green eyes burned into his until he could take it no more. He turned away and stared down into his lap.

He sighed before whispering, 'He said that I should love you from a distance. What did he say to you?'

'That I should forget you. That with time the feeling would pass,' whispered Funda.

Andonis was filled with a thirst that only Funda's face could satisfy. He turned to her, but was disappointed that there seemed to be no warmth in Funda's eyes to reciprocate that in his. Only sorrow.

At that moment the bus came to an abrupt halt. All the passengers gasped and were jolted out of their seats. At the front, Simos was cursing and waving his arms.

'Have you gone completely mad?' he screamed.

Andonis rose from his seat, and through the front window saw a young man trembling in the middle of the road. It was Erden the goatherd. He was carrying a baby goat in his arms. Now he tried to make his way up onto the bus.

'Please, Mr Simo. Forgive me,' he pleaded.

'You're not bringing that thing on,' declared Simos, getting up from his seat and pushing Erden off.

'But my little Yasmin is sick, Mr Simo. Very sick. I must take her to town to see the vet or she'll die.' The small goat bleated pathetically.

'What if Yasmin is sick on my bus?' enquired the bus-driver. 'Or worse still, what if Yasmin shits herself?'

The Christians at the front of the bus began to voice their disapproval.

Someone called out, 'Let the Turk go on foot. This bus is for humans, not filthy animals.'

The goatherd looked at the bus-driver with imploring eyes.

'Any mess I clean up, sir. I promise,' assured Erden. 'But please take me to town. I couldn't bear it if Yasmin were to die.'

'I really don't know,' pondered Simos. He took off his dark glasses to get a closer look at the animal. It looked clean enough. He stroked his chin a moment before opening his palm.

'A shilling for you,' he announced. 'And another for the goat.'

Erden's mouth dropped a moment, but then he nodded and pushed past Simos's outstretched arm.

'I can't pay you now, Mr Simo. I'll need what little money I have for the vet. But tomorrow I'll bring you cheese. I'll bring you yogurt.'

'Two shillings, please. Today. Or you and Yasmin can go to the devil,' insisted the bus-driver.

The Christians murmured their approval, and both Funda and Andonis could see that Erden was getting more and more agitated.

'Please, Mr Simo,' pleaded the goatherd, now dropping to his knees, though mindful not to jolt the beast in his arms. 'I beg you. Don't let Yasmin die.'

At this point Funda slapped both her cheeks. Andonis launched himself from his seat and marched to the front of the bus. To incredulous Christian stares, he took two shillings from his pocket.

'Let him on, Mr Simo,' he instructed. The bus-driver looked up at Andonis, shook his head, then shrugged and took the money.

'Thank you, sir. Thank you,' said Erden, bowing before Andonis.

'And tomorrow, Yasmin will be well,' assured Andonis, stroking the sick goat affectionately. 'And you'll bring my mamma cheese and yogurt.'

'For sure, sir. Plenty of each,' agreed the goatherd.

Andonis smiled and beckoned Erden and his goat forward, past the stares of stunned Christians and embarrassed Muslims. Only a pair of eyes at the back, beautiful green eyes which Erden knew and loved, showed any compassion. And one other pair, big and black.

And as a relieved Erden shifted slowly forward, with Andonis behind him, a young man with a powerful voice suddenly broke into a popular song of the time and completely drowned out the disapproving murmurs from the other passengers.

I've told you this so many times, my only love,
And many more I'll tell you so.
Now hear me say that I love you, my only love,
In all the tongues there are to know.
S' aghabo elliniga, io d' amo idaliga,
Ze vuz em frantseziga, ai lav yu engleziga,
Yo de amo ispaniga, ge bortoghaleziga,
Yahabibi arabiga, tse-tsa-ko gineziga.
S' aghabo, ih libe dih.
How else can I make it clear?
I love only you, my dear.
S' aghabo, ya vaz liubliu.
I love only you, my dear.
How else can I make it clear?

The passengers were entranced by the voice, and had fallen silent to listen to the words. The mood on the bus was transformed. The singer was a chubby man, with prematurely thinning hair and a distinctive twinkle in his eyes. Andonis, who had never noticed this man before in the village, gave him a nod of thanks.

When Erden and Andonis had reached the back of the bus, the tailor tapped the goatherd on the shoulder.

'Take my place,' he offered. Erden sat next to Funda and settled the goat on his lap.

18
The waiter   *Do garsonin*

It was a moonlit night. I was on an almost empty bus, as it made its way down towards Archway tube station. Beyond that was Holloway, where Stella had told me Lugas worked. Zorba's restaurant.

I thought of Stella. I realised how fond I still was of her. If things had been different she and I might never have ended up in England. She and I might have stayed in the village, raising a family together. She and I might even have been happy. Stella deserved to be happy.

The only other passengers on board were a pair of young men on the seat directly in front of me who talked loudly at each other. I could discern the smell of beer on their breath, and assumed they were on their way home after a few drinks at the pub. One of them pointed out of the window as we approached the high bridge that stretched majestically across Archway Road. I overheard him refer to it as 'suicide bridge'. It was a landmark I'd never noticed before, but its name now filled me with dread. I couldn't help myself staring morbidly.

※　※　※

As I approached Zorba's, a pungent smell of meat scorching on hot charcoal evoked in me visions of the outdoors on a dozen Easter Sundays. My father would always barbecue a small lamb, and I remembered what a special treat it was to eat so well.

Once inside the restaurant I could see that there were only three other customers. They were at a table together, and having already finished their meal were enjoying a cigarette as they settled their bill.

I sat down at a table away from them, nearer to the window, and lit a rolled cigarette of my own. While I waited to be served, I looked up and appreciated the painted plates hanging on the wall, depicting old men wearing baggy breeches, old women dressed in black, village wells, whitewashed houses and laden donkeys.

Before long, a stout waiter appeared through the door at the back of the restaurant. He looked vaguely familiar. He wore a black waistcoat not quite big enough to contain a stomach bulging through a plain white shirt. I could see the bothered look on his face as he shuffled towards me. He ran his hand through his grey hair before speaking to me in the Cypriot vernacular.

'I'm sorry, sir,' he said, 'but it's a little late. We'll be shutting now, once these people leave.' He gestured to the three smokers.

'Come on, my friend,' I pleaded, 'I'm so hungry. Are there no pieces of meat already cooked back there you can offer me?'

The waiter sighed. 'Forgive me, sir. I really don't think my chef can help us. It's been a long day.'

'But you can make an exception for a compatriot, surely? Tell me, does a Lugas work here?'

The waiter rubbed his chin and looked at me closely. I could see there was now a flicker of recognition in his eyes.

'Do I know you, sir?' he asked.

'Ah, so *you* are Lugas?' I enquired with a hint of a smile and offered him my hand. I shook firmly like I used to as a younger man. 'I'm Andonis, from your wife's village. Stella said I would find you here. Surely Stella's mentioned me to you.'

Lugas raised his eyebrows, smiled and nodded rapidly. 'Oh yes, Mr Andoni. She has. Often. She feared you might be dead.'

'I may well be soon if I don't have something to eat, eh?' I hinted with a wink.

He raised his hand. 'Leave it to me.'

Before returning to the kitchen, he took payment from the other customers and helped them on with their coats. Now I was left alone in the restaurant. From behind the door at the back, I could hear the voices of perhaps two other men speaking with Lugas. I could just make out their mentioning of a game, and also, from Lugas, an assurance that he would try not to be too long.

Soon after, Lugas reappeared with a tray, on it a plate of suvlagia and some salad and rizin pelafin. Also four smaller plates, one with bita, one with black olives, one with slices of lemon, one with dashin. He placed the plates before me on the table.

'Good appetite, Mr Andoni. And what will you drink?'

I licked my lips. 'I'll only drink something if you'll join me.'

Lugas smiled. 'OK, then.'

I squeezed lemon juice onto the cooked meat, and with delight inhaled the resulting steam. 'Stella tells me you're fond of whisky. Why not fix us both a glass?'

'OK, then,' he declared once more, and went over to the bar. Meanwhile I picked up a succulent cube of charred lamb from my plate and savoured a taste I had almost forgotten.

Lugas returned with two tumblers generously filled with golden liquid. He sat down opposite me, clinked his tumbler against mine, and began to sip. He could see I was enjoying my meal, and watched me eat in silence. When I was done I wiped my mouth carefully with a napkin before taking a sip of whisky. It burned my throat a moment, but soon after filled me with its calming influence.

'You know which country makes this stuff?' I enquired, looking him directly in the eye and pointing to the contents of my glass. I could see he was confused as he looked down and stared blankly into his own glass. Eventually he shrugged.

'It's the Englezi, isn't it?' he replied, although without certainty.

'The Englezi,' I repeated dismissively. 'Make Scotch?'

'Englezi. Skochezi. They're all the same, aren't they?' he ventured.

'All the same, eh?'

Lugas shifted uncomfortably in his chair before helping himself to another gulp of his drink.

'What are you trying to say, Mr Andoni? Why treat me like a fool?'

'Because I believe you're behaving like one, my friend.' I took another sip of my drink, as did he. Then I followed up with another question. 'So, you don't know Skochezi from Englezi. Do you know what you are at least?'

'I know what I am. I'm a Gibreos,' he proudly declared his Cypriot identity. I could see he was getting annoyed. 'Why, what are you?'

I dismissed his question with a flick of the hand. 'OK, let's put it another way.'

This time I asked the same question in English and asked him to reply in English.

'Greek,' he announced with incredulity. I returned to the Cypriot vernacular.

'So in our language you're a Cypriot and in theirs you're a Greek.'

He stared into his whisky again and shrugged.

I shook my head. 'Sounds like you're a little confused, my friend. Too much whisky perhaps?'

Lugas tapped the table repeatedly. 'Hang on a minute. What is this? You turn up after we close, demanding food, and I, out of respect for your friendship with my wife, do all I can to show you hospitality. I bring you food…'

I raised my finger to interrupt. 'Which was delicious by the way.'

He ignored me. 'I bring you food and drink, and all you do is mock me!' he huffed, and then folded his arms as though to shield himself from me.

'Calm down, Luga, and listen to me. I'm here because I want to help you, OK?'

Lugas scoffed. 'He wants to help me, his lordship.'

'That's right. What can you tell me about Scotland?'

'Look, I've never been and I wouldn't want to. I expect it's even harsher there than it is here, though hopefully with fewer insane Cypriots like you.'

'Harsher?' I pressed.

'Yes, harsher. Colder, wetter, darker.'

'So if you were a Skochezos you'd need to create a potent drink like whisky to take your mind off things. Off the cold. Off the dark.'

'Hmm. I'll drink to that! To the Skochezi and their whisky,' declared Lugas, and clinked my glass once more before emptying the contents of his. 'Now, come on. What's this all about?'

'It saddens me to see a compatriot so attached to a foreign habit,' I mused, looking into my own glass with disdain, though feeling a little hypocritical. I myself had succumbed to other habits.

'Drinking isn't foreign to us, sir. Our ancestors gave the world wine!' he retorted.

'To enhance life. To help make it more delicious. Not like this…this burning drink of the devil. Designed to make us forget life. To forget who we are!'

'Well, when you're here, my friend, you do as they do,' shrugged Lugas. He tried to take another sip from his glass, but I reached over the table and held his arm.

'Even if it makes you stupid like they are?'

Lugas shook free of me and got up.

'That's it. I've had enough of your insults,' he fumed. 'Please leave now. No wonder my wife's so difficult. Must be the village you both come from.' He reached down and finished the contents of his glass. I rose to my feet and gave Lugas a look of such violent intent that he began to shake.

'Sit down,' I commanded, placing my hand on his shoulder and pushing him down as I retook my own seat.

'What has Stella told you about me?' I asked.

'She…she mentions you often. And your brother Marios. And your mother and late father. She speaks as though you were all one family.'

'Did she tell you why I disappeared?'

'She's never fully explained it. I don't think she knows herself. I understand you and her brother were involved in some unpleasant Eoga business and that's why he…'

'He has a name, sir. Nigos, God rest his soul. You called your own son after him. Now let me tell you something that nobody knows. I made a promise to Nigos. An important promise, to look out for his sister.'

Lugas shut his eyes for a moment as though trying to block my presence.

'My God. Forgive me. I really need a drink,' he said, reaching across the table for my glass. I grabbed his hand. Then I reached across and grabbed his face, so that he could not look away from me.

'I'm a man from your wife's past, Luga,' I said. 'And that's where I belong, along with too much pain and suffering. Any contact between us only serves to bring it all back. For her and for me.'

'I…I understand,' stuttered Lugas, his head trembling with fear. I held it steady.

'But I need to be certain that you'll stop gambling with your son's future. Certain that you'll stop forgetting who you are. Do we understand each other?'

'I…I think so.'

'You think so? Well maybe the drink of the Skochezi is still clouding your mind, so let me try and make things clear. You're looking at a man cut off from his past and without a future. No wife, no family. I'm a free spirit, Luga, unlike you. I can do anything I choose. *Anything*. And you know what? It wouldn't really matter.'

I released my grip. Now back in possession of his face, he covered it with his hands. I rose from my seat and threw a few pound notes on the table. A dazed Lugas remained slumped in his chair. As I walked past him I put a hand on his shoulder.

'Stella deserves better,' I murmured.

He looked up at me. His eyes were filled with guilt. As were mine.

'I do love her, you know,' he assured me. 'I've always loved her.'

I smiled my approval and raised a farewell hand.

'Don't ever forget that,' I urged.

As I stood waiting for a late bus to take me back up to Muswell Hill I looked up into the unusually clear night sky and marvelled at the beautiful full moon.

19
The moon   *Do fengarin*

Andonis was sitting at his window waiting in vain. It was dawn on a Sunday morning. In a few hours the church bells would ring and Christian villagers would prepare for the week's most important ritual. Before then, however, women would be fetching water.

It had been some days since the incident on the bus, some days since Andonis had last seen Funda. He missed her more than ever.

Only her mother ever passed by to fetch water now. Yesterday morning Andonis had been tempted to approach Mrs Leila to ask after her daughter's health. Yesterday he'd thought better of it. But today, when Andonis saw that Leila was standing in for Funda yet again, he knew he had to act, or risk going insane.

After Leila had passed, Andonis waited a few moments, to put a suitable distance between her and the house. Then he rushed out in pursuit.

'Good morning, Mrs Leila,' called Andonis, catching her up.

The Muslim woman stopped and turned. She had to pull her white headscarf away from her face to see who it was, though in truth she had guessed. Her heart beat a little faster. There he was. The son of Mihalis the farmer; grandson of the late Mrs Maria. Leila had learnt, though not from Funda, about the incident on the bus, about how the young tailor had helped the goatherd. It was a gesture that had been much appreciated by the Muslims. Andonis was an honourable man, like his father. And handsome too.

Leila and Andonis had never had much occasion to speak before. Such interaction had seldom been necessary. And, since the troubles, such interaction had become inappropriate. She bowed her head a moment then faced ahead and continued onwards.

'Please,' implored Andonis, now coming up alongside Leila. She turned to him with pitying eyes. He looked so desperate, so full of pathos, that it would have been inhuman for her not to be moved, but she continued onwards.

Andonis asked, 'Doesn't your daughter collect water for your family any more, Mrs Leila?'

Leila lifted her chin and eyebrows. 'Why should this concern you, sir?'

'Forgive me, Mrs Leila,' said Andonis. 'I know that in better times my father and your husband had an understanding. A friendship. Good people are hard to find. Is Mr Nuretin well?'

The woman shrugged. 'Under the circumstances, he's well. Thank you for asking. And your father. Is he well?' she reciprocated.

'He's well,' replied Andonis. 'And your son, Zeki. Is he well?'

'As well as can be expected,' offered Leila, and Andonis nodded with compassion. Then she added politely, 'And your mother and brother? Are they well?'

Andonis shrugged. 'They survive, Mrs Leila. We all survive somehow.' Andonis hesitated a moment before continuing, 'And your daughter, Funda. Is she well?'

Now the Muslim woman stopped. Andonis did likewise. She looked down and sighed. If only things were different. Then she turned to the young tailor once more, and spied him with one eye closed.

'All will be well with my daughter, Andoni, if you leave her in peace,' she advised before continuing onwards. Leila had made it clear to Andonis from her departing words that she wanted him to pursue no longer. Her expression had made it clear how sorry she was.

✳ ✳ ✳

Stella was wearing a smart pink dress which hugged her body. Her long black hair was tied in a ponytail with a white bow. Her hair bounced off her upper back as she strolled arm in arm with her mother, towards the village square. A few steps ahead of them was Yannis and his betrothed Martha. The church was in the opposite direction, but they always took this walk around the village square on a Sunday morning before doubling back on themselves in time for the liturgy.

Other villagers were also responding to the call of the bells, and were on similar excursions. For most young women of the village, this was the highlight of the week. An excuse to scrub thoroughly their tender young bodies with plenty of soap and water, to wash and brush their rich hair, to put on their best outfits and pointed shoes. To use, even, a bit of lipstick and rouge, though not too much, lest their mothers disapproved; lest they be thought too coquettish.

On Sunday it was permissible for a young woman to display how she was blooming, and to do so with the priest's blessing. Indeed it was his blessing that made it all possible. And all the fresh flowers of young womanhood would gather together in the square like a huge bouquet. They'd kiss each other's soft cheeks, mindful always to wipe away any red marks, and would wonder how a young man's clean-shaven face might feel against their ripening lips.

And outside the coffee-shop, young men of the village, and some not so young, would flock like birds in a tree. Sitting with their knees apart, in white shirts and with jet black, slicked-back hair, they'd smoke, sip coffee, look, admire and imagine. And, when not catching up on much-needed sleep, Vasos would have his radio on, playing the latest tunes from Athens, and the girls would perform their provocative greetings in time to the music.

The girls wear ribbons, pure and white in their hair,
And the boys stop and stare, those who're up for the show.
But I'm not bothered and I'm not taking part,
For the girl in my heart isn't one that they know.

But the young men whose cheeks the girls most wished they could be kissing wouldn't be at the coffee-shop. They were too cool to be up and about this early, too cool to take part in such old-fashioned charades. Too cool for church. Some of the girls, though they'd never admit it to one another, were a little resentful of their absence, but what could be done? The young women of the village weren't as free as the young men, and had to make the most of what few pleasures they were allowed.

Today at the coffee-shop were a number of young men from neighbouring villages. The travelling cinema was coming later. A white sheet would be pegged to the carob trees in the square to act as a screen. The men had come for what they knew would result in another chance to see, and maybe even meet, the girls of the village, who would be out a second time, again in their Sunday best.

Approaching the coffee-shop, Stella noticed that her cousin Bambos was there with a group of what her mother always termed bad boys. Stella knew they had access to a car. This made it easy for Bambos and friends to get to wherever there were opportunities for mischief. And the travelling cinema would no doubt present such opportunities.

Stella lowered her head when she realised another boy she knew from another village was also at the coffee-shop. A boy called Lugas. He'd flirted with her once or twice before. Stella had been reliably informed that Lugas admired her. He wasn't bad looking, though perhaps a little overweight and also, by all accounts, somewhat immature. Young Stella was nevertheless flattered, intrigued and no less self-conscious that this boy or any other should desire her. But she was mindful not to give Lugas any signals that she might in any way be interested. After all, Lugas wasn't the boy she'd always desired. He wasn't the boy she'd always felt there'd been no choice but to desire. Still, it was nice to have options.

Stella was disappointed, though not surprised, that Andonis wasn't waiting to see her at the coffee-shop. He was never there. Andonis's family was only ever represented on a Sunday morning by his mother Irini. And Marios of course.

The widow could sense her daughter's dismay, and gently squeezed her arm. Stella knew that the squeeze was meant to reassure her that Andonis's inappropriate preoccupation with the Muslim girl would pass, but this did not comfort Stella. Yes, one day, perhaps, Andonis might come to his senses. But Stella feared that Andonis's heart would never be hers.

'Look, Stella. It's Eleni and Anna,' announced the widow, keen to lighten her daughter's mood. Two young women of the village were waving to Stella from the square.

'Go and join them!' instructed the widow, releasing her grip on her daughter. 'I'll be OK with Yannis and Martha.'

Stella smiled at her mother and fluttered off to join her friends. The three girls performed their kissing ritual.

'Good morning, Stella,' said Anna with a smile to show off her healthy teeth. 'You look lovely today. I'm so glad you're still making an effort.' Anna was Yoda's daughter, and she had inherited both her mother's full body and sharp tongue.

'Some of us try,' retorted Stella, accentuating her narrow waist by putting a hand to it and looking mockingly at the larger girl's ill-fitting dress.

Anna was visibly hurt. 'I didn't mean anything by that. It's just that...'

'We've been hearing about Andonis, Stella,' interrupted Eleni, having raised a graceful and slender hand to quieten Anna. 'And what happened on the bus. I hope you're not too troubled by his actions.' Eleni was Vasos's daughter and she had inherited her father's compassion.

'And why should I be troubled?' huffed Stella, folding her arms to lift and support her shapely breasts. 'I'm not his keeper. Andonis and I aren't betrothed. He can do what he pleases.'

But the sombre look in Stella's eyes conveyed to her friends that she was indeed troubled.

'But it's such a shame,' said Anna. 'Andonis is so handsome. If I were you I'd be upset to know his affections lay with another. Particularly one so inappropriate.'

'Stop it, Anna,' insisted Eleni, wagging a polished red fingernail at the larger girl before turning again to Stella. 'Don't worry, Stella. Andonis is still young and full of bravado. In time he'll see what's right.'

Stella gave Eleni a dubious look. Eleni nodded towards Anna and continued, 'If others aren't allowed to interfere, then you and he can still be happy together one day, I'm certain.'

Stella shook her head. There was defiance in her eyes.

'You may be certain, Eleni, but perhaps I'm not,' she ventured. 'You know, Andonis isn't the only handsome man in the district.'

Anna looked bemused, and casually cast her eye across the motley collection of men sitting outside the coffee-shop, all of whom avoided eye contact with her.

'You've got your sights on someone else, Stella?' she enquired nosily. 'Who? And why haven't you mentioned him? I'm older than you by two months. My need's greater than yours,' she declared.

'Hush, Anna,' instructed Eleni, before turning to the widow's daughter. 'Don't be silly, Stella. Surely you're destined for Andonis. There are few, if any, in the village to compare. Especially now so many of our best men are leaving for the town or for England.'

'And, of course, it doesn't help that so many of the bachelors that remain are Turks!' observed Anna.

'While the rest are ugly or stupid,' added Eleni.

'Or fat!' added Anna. Stella and Eleni giggled, but Anna pretended not to see the irony.

Stella announced, 'There are other men, girls. I have it on good authority that those from our neighbouring villages are fine. And good Christians too!' There was a look of mischief in Stella's eyes.

Stella's two friends nodded. They knew some of these men were here today at the coffee-shop.

'She wants a husband and she wants him now,' mused Eleni, repeating an old Cypriot expression.

'Perhaps I'll ask my mamma for permission to come to the travelling cinema this evening. To help take my mind off things,' mused Stella, and gave Eleni a wink.

Eleni nodded. 'I don't doubt the change of atmosphere will do you good, Stella. Of course, I'll have to ask my mamma for permission to come with you. With all these strange young men around it would be unwise not to have a trustworthy chaperone,' she observed.

Anna nodded. 'And me too, me too. To protect you both. From yourselves!'

❋ ❋ ❋

Andonis had made himself scarce – creating needless chores in his workshop. It was a Sunday morning ritual, a way of avoiding church.

Saddened by his earlier exchange with Mrs Leila, he took comfort in his harmonica. He tried teaching himself that song he'd heard on the bus. The one about love. As he was more or less perfecting the tune, he heard loud voices from outside. Innocent voices, but ones nevertheless filled with hate. He recognised them as belonging to Yoda's young sons.

Emerging into bright sunlight, Andonis spied the two boys marching up and down the road outside his father's house. Each held a stick against his shoulder. On seeing the tailor the boys stood to attention and saluted. Andonis smiled before adopting a serious expression and saluting back.

'What are you doing, boys?' he enquired.

'We're brave Eoga warriors,' replied one defiantly.

'Protecting the village,' added the other.

'Who from?' enquired Andonis, knowing full well the answer.

'The Englezi of course!' declared one with a sneer. 'Those who exploit us and our homeland. They're not welcome here.'

'Death to the Englezi!' chanted the other, shaking his stick at Andonis. The tailor rubbed his chin. The sons of the village gossip had evidently been well briefed on his recent business activities.

'And the Turks too,' sneered one. 'The dogs of the Englezi. Spies, cheats, traitors all!'

'Death to the Turks!' chanted the other, shaking his stick at Andonis. The tailor rubbed his chin once more. Evidently they had also been well briefed on his recent romantic activities.

This time Andonis reached out and snatched the stick.

'Hey, that's my gun, Mr Andoni,' protested the boy.

'You don't mind if I have a go, do you?' asked Andonis, ruffling the youngster's hair with affection.

Now Andonis began pacing up and down, stick against shoulder. The brothers gave him a curious look. They knew the tailor was too old to be playing soldiers. Nevertheless they were glad of the attention. Despite his recent indiscretions, they still looked up to him.

'What are you doing, Mr Andoni?' asked one boy.

'Can't I protect the village too?' asked Andonis. Then he stopped and beckoned the boys closer to him. His face filled with exaggerated fear. 'After all, I know of an even bigger threat,' he added ominously.

The boys glanced at each other. Surely the tailor was teasing them.

'What threat, Mr Andoni?' they enquired in unison.

'Lies,' he proclaimed, now shaking the stick at them.

'Lies?' they both repeated, unconvinced.

'The most dangerous enemy there is. Creeping up on us, taking control of our minds. Filling our hearts with hate. Making us do wicked things,' declared Andonis. 'In some extreme cases, leading us even to kill.'

The boys glanced at each other. The tailor looked too serious to be teasing them. Andonis smiled.

'Death to lies!' he chanted, shaking the stick at them.

'What lies, Mr Andoni?' asked one of the boys.

Andonis put a finger to his lips. He glanced up the road, then down it, his eyes darting in all directions.

'There are some who believe,' began Andonis, his voice lowered almost to a whisper, 'that lies are already among us.'

The boys gulped.

'They come disguised. Wrapped in flags, hidden away in old myths and anthems. No one's immune, boys. No one. Mothers, fathers, sisters, brothers. Teachers. Priests. All can spread lies without realising the terrible consequences.' The boys looked fearful. 'And only the young can save us.'

'What do we do, Mr Andoni?' asked one of the boys.

Andonis reached into his shirt pocket and took out his harmonica.

'Let me play you a song,' he offered. He began the tune he'd been learning. The one about love. The notes came easily. The boys recognised it and began to click their fingers and sing along. The threat of the Englezi and the Turks was forgotten. Now there were only smiles and happiness. When Andonis had finished, the boys applauded. Andonis bowed.

'You must trust nothing but the goodness in your own hearts,' he instructed, returning the stick to its owner before saluting.

The boys saluted back, and began marching again. Andonis turned towards his workshop.

'Death to the Englezi liars,' called one of Yoda's sons.

'And their lying Turkish dogs,' added the other.

Andonis grimaced. Clearly a lot more work would be needed on the young.

※ ※ ※

Private Bartlett was tiring. The relentless heat and the alcohol in his bloodstream didn't help. He became aware of the regular clicking of the front wheel of the bicycle and of his throbbing head, heavy rhythmic breathing and sweat-dripping forehead.

He'd cycled a few miles already, and the novelty had long since worn off. The evening provided myriad exotic but somehow threatening sounds and smells. Night was falling, and with it grew his sense of unease. He looked up and was grateful for the stunning full moon.

At least he was now on a slight downward gradient which offered a momentary respite from pedalling. The air on his face was helping both to cool and to sober him. Bartlett shut his eyes and imagined. How he wished he could keep going like this, on and on, released from this island furnace and home to mild, green, pleasant England.

He needed to be back at barracks, in the town, before it got too late. By that time the effects of the drink should have worn off. Enough, at least, so that Bartlett could handle any questions he might face.

The bicycle was not his. It had been borrowed. Bartlett would request permission to return it to where he'd found it at the earliest opportunity, of course. He'd endeavour to explain to its owner that the bicycle had been commandeered to defuse a potentially dangerous situation. The owner would understand. And if not, well, that was too bad. Bartlett, representing Her Majesty's armed forces, would know he had done the honourable thing. These locals needed lessons in how to be grateful.

It was fortunate that Bartlett had come across the bicycle. The rest of the blokes were intent on seeing the film, but the atmosphere had become tense in the village and Bartlett had felt compelled to get away.

As a change from the town, the blokes had grabbed a taxi to one of the local villages. They'd heard a travelling cinema was doing the rounds. The James Dean film *Rebel Without a Cause* was playing.

After enjoying a few drinks in a local, none-too-religious Muslim coffee-shop, where they'd been made to feel welcome, the off-duty servicemen made their way down the main road towards the square where the film was being shown. They happened to pass three unaccompanied local girls. Bartlett had noticed that the girls were in high spirits, carrying themselves the way young single girls do the world over. Buoyed by drink, some of the blokes had wolf-whistled, and Bartlett had even taken the arm of the pretty one with a mole on her cheek, and enquired whether she might like to join him in the back row.

A harmless gesture, a compliment even. In general Bartlett didn't find the dark, olive-skinned women of Cyprus that attractive. Far from being flattered the girls appeared terrified. The one he'd touched screamed, her plump friend kicked and pinched him. Within seconds, a group of people had gathered, mainly young and angry-looking local men. The girls kept gesturing at Bartlett.

Although no one dared openly challenge the servicemen, it became apparent that, at the very least, Bartlett's presence in the village was no longer welcome. British servicemen were under strict orders not to provoke the locals, and the locals wanted to show that Bartlett had done just that.

The point made, the crowd was slowly breaking up. The rest of the blokes, having long since learnt to accept Cypriot resentment, had remained calm, and resolved to continue their evening's recreation. But Bartlett knew that was no longer an option for him. He indicated to his friends that he would be leaving and, after convincing them he could take care of himself, brushed his way through the last of the dispersing locals. He marched a short distance along the main road, in the opposite direction to the square, and then down one of the side turnings. Feeling the danger had now passed, Bartlett sighed with relief and leant against a wall to consider his next move. He'd wait for the film to start and everyone to settle before making his way back to the Muslim coffee-shop. There Bartlett would get someone to call for a taxi.

It was then he had noticed an old bicycle propped up against the wall opposite him. Who did it belong to? A Greek or a Turk? It didn't matter. They wanted him to leave? Fine. He looked around to make sure no one would see, and as a final act of defiance to the people of this Godforsaken village, got on.

That had been a while ago. Soon he'd be back in town. A quick wash and safely in his bunk.

Now Bartlett could just make out the bleating of a herd of goats on the hill up ahead, but this was soon drowned out by the humming of a car engine from behind. The noise was increasing rapidly.

Without glancing back, Bartlett steered himself to the edge of the road to allow the vehicle to pass. He realised that his own transport was without lights.

The car came directly alongside Bartlett. Slowing down to his speed, it was now veering dangerously close. Bartlett turned towards it, and noticed two young men inside. He struggled to keep his nerve and his balance. He cursed at the car. The young man on the passenger side leant out of the window. Bartlett glared at the man, who smiled back with disdain.

Bartlett pedalled more aggressively, pulling away from the now crawling car. If these fucking Bubbles wanted to wind him up, it was working.

The car accelerated and drew up alongside him once again. Bartlett was finding it more difficult to manoeuvre the fast-moving bicycle on the rough surface. He heard a throat clear. A second later, a globule of spit hit him straight in his ear. Sickened and outraged, he lost his concentration. The bicycle wobbled out of control, and he fell off awkwardly, landing in the dust.

Disorientated, a little bruised, but not badly hurt, he began wiping the gunge from his ear with his sleeve. Sick, sick bastards, he thought.

Only then did Bartlett become aware that the car had stopped a few yards further ahead. Two men paced towards him, faces visible in the moonlight. Faces full of hate. Bartlett sensed what was coming.

He glanced up at the full moon and a flood of adrenaline washed through him. He rose quickly, ready to face the strangers. But his resolve was shortlived. The mixture of shock, fear and alcohol clouded his thinking. He was now aware once more of his throbbing head, heavy rhythmic breathing and sweat-dripping forehead. Bartlett shut his eyes and imagined he was home.

❊ ❊ ❊

'Have you gone totally mad?'

'Totally. Mad for your love, Funda.'

Andonis stood there in the moonlight, by Funda's bedroom window, at the back of the barber's shop, exchanging frantic whispers with her. It was the early hours of the morning, and the whole village was asleep. Some villagers were snoring loudly, within earshot.

Earlier that night Andonis had sat at his Singer. He was working on the captain's new suit. A dozing Eros kept him company in the workshop. The suit was the excuse the tailor needed to avoid going out and facing the commotion in the village caused by the travelling cinema.

Andonis addressed the dog. 'Anyway, who needs James Dean when I've got a much bigger star here with me? What say you, Mr Flynn?'

Nigos had turned up and tried to persuade the tailor to go along to see the film, but the tailor refused to take part in the sad charade: unbetrothed men and unbetrothed women eyeing each other up. No different from Sunday mornings, except with a Hollywood movie taking the place of an ancient liturgy as the excuse.

Nigos made the point that at least the movie would have subtitles. Andonis laughed and pointed out that he was able to get by without subtitles, and get by even better without Hollywood.

When Nigos had left, Andonis wondered whether Funda would be allowed out that evening. Perhaps she'd been waiting for such an opportunity to see Andonis. If so, perhaps she'd be disappointed if he didn't show up. Or perhaps she'd be relieved. After all, she'd said that public encounters between them were no longer advisable. Maybe that's why she was no longer fetching the water. Maybe she even resented him now, after his exchange with her mother. Andonis looked down at the young dog.

'What am I going to do, Ero?'

The animal's eyes opened, and ears shifted at having his name called.

'You wouldn't understand,' continued Andonis. 'Not now they've removed your pips.'

Andonis smiled, the animal nodded off once more.

A few hours later the film was over. The young men and women of the village were now safely in their beds, heads respectively filled with thoughts of Natalie Wood and James Dean. But Andonis had remained, alone in his workshop. And his head was still filled with thoughts of Funda. He knew he had to see her. He blew out the oil-lamp and made his way into the night. He passed the square and ventured into the Muslim neighbourhood.

And now here he was, having tapped at what he had fortuitously guessed was her window. Saying her name, over and over, until she had been roused from sleep.

'What are you doing here?' hissed Funda. She was in a long flowing nightdress through which Andonis could clearly make out shapes that had previously existed only in his imagination. As she approached the window he was struck by how innocently beautiful she looked in the moonlight. How beautiful and how panic-stricken.

'I said, what are you doing here?' she repeated to a man whose jaw muscles had momentarily stopped functioning.

'Er, defying the curfew of the Englezi?' suggested Andonis. Funda couldn't believe the tailor's fearlessness.

'Never mind the Englezi, if my father catches you here, he'll cut your throat for sure,' she warned, and Andonis knew this was no exaggeration.

'I've nothing to fear from your father,' whispered Andonis with a smile, then nodded towards the next window. 'Not with a snore as loud as that. It'll take gods and demons to wake him!'

'He sleeps the sleep of the just,' she admitted. 'Though I can't think why, the way he treats me and Zeki sometimes. He wouldn't even let us go to see the film tonight.'

'Your father's always been a good man,' corrected Andonis. 'Only difficult circumstances lead him to be the way he is. But don't worry, I wasn't there either, Funda. I thought it safer for us not to be seen together. Like we mustn't be seen at the well. Like we mustn't be seen on the bus,' said Andonis with a smile.

Funda couldn't help but smile back. How much more she loved Andonis for what he had done that day on the bus.

'That's why I'm here now instead,' he added.

'And you call this safe?' she demanded. 'I love you so much, but it's the middle of the night. Please, Andoni. You must go home.'

Andonis shook his head and reached for her hand. His face turned serious. 'I love you too, Funda,' he declared before stooping to kiss her soft fingers.

'If you loved me, Mr Tailor, you'd take more care,' she warned, pulling her hand from his lips.

'I care for you more than anything else in the world.'

'Please, Andoni. You don't know the trouble you're causing me. Talking to my mother this morning. And now this!'

'Forgive me, Funda. I mean no harm. I haven't seen you for so long. I feared something was wrong.'

'Something *is* wrong. This is wrong. You and me. It's all wrong,' she insisted, but there was no conviction in her voice. Only helplessness.

Andonis put his hands to his ears. 'No, don't say that. Everyone else says that. Not you too.'

Andonis's expression was that of a desperate little boy. Funda reached out through the window and embraced Andonis, rubbing the back of his head to comfort him.

He continued, 'It's never wrong when two people need each other. Where would the world be without love?'

Andonis pulled Funda closer to him, and she felt his warm breath on her neck. Funda's maternal instincts started giving way to others more appropriate to her age.

'We should stop dreaming, Andoni. Both of us. Before it turns into a nightmare.'

'What are you telling me?'

'We can't go on like this.'

Then their lips touched.

'You make me feel so strange, Andoni. It's not safe.'

'When I'm with you I feel so strong. I'm not scared of anything. I can do anything.'

'Can you make the troubles go away?'

'Have faith in our love and who knows? Maybe I can, Funda.'

'Make them all go away, Andoni.'

Funda clambered out of the window and was enveloped by Andonis's arms. Then slowly she guided him round to the front of the building and through the door of the barber's shop.

※　※　※

Andonis opened the door, but Funda didn't want to let him go. He turned and kissed her. When their lips parted, she stared dreamily through the open door up into the sky.

'Look at the moon, Andoni. It's so beautiful tonight,' she said. But Andonis couldn't take his eyes off Funda.

'You're my moon,' he said.

The moment was interrupted by the faint sound of vehicles in the distance. Then the engines stopped, and voices replaced them. Angry voices. Englezi.

'Go quickly, Andoni, and take care. If they catch you, God knows what they'll do to you,' whispered Funda.

Andonis rubbed Funda's arm to calm her. 'Don't worry, my love. They're too far away. Whatever it is they're after, it isn't me.'

The lovers strained to hear, but the Englezi made no more sound. Only Nuretin's reassuring snores from his room behind the shop interrupted the silence. Funda watched the tailor's figure recede in the moonlight.

20
The palace   *Do baladin*

The morning after my chat with Lugas I was roused from a dreamless sleep by the communal payphone ringing from the downstairs landing. I prised my eyes open and glimpsed the sun's rays streaming through my bedroom's frayed net curtains. The unexpected appearance of bright light filled me with a sense of wellbeing, a sense even of purpose. I heard a knock on my door and the voice of a retired fellow lodger – the call was for me.

Only Dave ever telephoned, so I concluded it must be him, no doubt ringing from work on behalf of Osborne. I put on my dressing gown and went downstairs, wondering what I would say. I didn't enjoy disappointing people.

I picked up the receiver and said, 'Who loves ya, baby?'

'Is that you, Tony?' A woman's voice.

'Ruth!' I declared, with what I recognised as enthusiasm.

'I hope you don't mind me calling. Dave gave me your number. He said you still haven't gone back to work.'

'No, of course I don't mind you calling. It's great to hear from you. But I hope your cousin didn't put you up to this – to try to convince me to go back – because I don't think I can.'

In truth, I was afraid she might be capable of convincing me that I could.

'I understand. And don't worry. That's not why I called,' she said, to my relief. 'I'm not working till later this afternoon. The weather's so nice. I was wondering whether you fancied a walk up to Alexandra Palace?'

'I'd like that.'

'Good.'

Ruth sounded full of zest. She told me she had something important she needed to pick up from the music shop where she worked, but wouldn't elaborate further. She asked whether we could meet at the top of Muswell Hill in an hour, and wanted assurances that I'd be on time. I was happy to give them.

It was an unusually warm and beautifully clear day. I was waiting for Ruth as agreed, and admired her graceful approach. I admired also the cut of her long-sleeved white blouse, flattering to her figure. When Ruth saw me she waved. I waved back. She was carrying a small brown bag.

'This is for you,' she announced with a broad smile, offering me the bag.

'Thank you,' I muttered awkwardly. I'd nothing to offer her in return. Inside was a box containing a small, metal harmonica. I took it out for a closer look. It caught the sunlight.

'I thought it was time you started playing again,' she hinted. I resisted the temptation to put the instrument to my mouth. In truth, I was afraid to.

'That's nice,' was all I could think of to say, returning the harmonica to its box. Ruth seemed disappointed.

'Maybe later,' she said, taking hold of my arm and pulling me along towards the path that led through the park to Alexandra Palace. 'We've got the whole day ahead of us.'

Soon we were facing north London's most famous landmark. I remembered how, not long after arriving in this country, I'd taken a bus up here from Camden Town. I came because I'd been told of the breathtaking views and historic significance. From here the BBC had made the world's first television broadcast. I came also because the name Alexandra had attracted me, as it had many of my compatriots. Somehow we felt a sense of belonging. As though it was a place connected with home.

I'd never been again, despite living only a short walk away.

Ruth and I stood in silence for a few moments, appreciating the panorama. I could make out the Post Office Tower, and a little further along the skyline St Paul's Cathedral. It was a little breezy, and I wondered whether Ruth might be getting a little cold in just her blouse. I at least was wearing a polo-neck jumper. I thought to take it off and offer it to her, but only had a vest on underneath. I put my arm round her. It seemed the right thing to do. I sensed she appreciated my gesture. She snuggled closer to me.

'How's Ravi?' I asked.

'Oh, he's fine. He's been on good form recently, and working really hard. I think your performance inspired him.'

'It's his teacher that's inspiring,' I corrected.

She smiled and squeezed my hand.

'I've been encouraging his dad to make contact with Ravi's mother again,' she said. 'I think there might still be a chance for them. I really do.'

'That's good,' I mused, looking out into the hazy distance where the horizon blurred into the sky.

'Isn't it amazing, Tony, to think there are millions of people out there, like you and me, going through life?'

I shrugged, aware that for far too long I'd not had much of a life.

'You know, being up here brings back memories of a place I used to know,' I said. 'A hill overlooking the whole village with an old olive tree at the top. It's so peaceful. Shepherds and goatherds would spend hours up there with their flocks. And the sound of clanging bells would carry all the way down into the village square…'

It was only then I realised how painful the memories were, and had to close my eyes a moment. Ruth must have sensed my unease. She squeezed my hand again.

'Look, Tony,' she said, gesturing towards a passing young couple with a little girl between them. We began to follow them a while before stopping to sit on a bench.

'Don't you wish you had children?' asked Ruth, clasping my hand. Hers felt soft, smooth and cold.

I took a moment to answer. 'I prefer not to wish.'

'But children bring so much joy and meaning,' she offered. 'I don't know what I'd do without my daughter. Especially now that…' she checked herself and I squeezed her hand. It was warming up in mine. 'Sorry. I can be such a mother sometimes.'

Somehow I sensed what Ruth might say next, but was no less shaken by her request.

'Tell me about *your* mother, Tony.'

I looked into the distance.

'I haven't seen or spoken to her in a long while,' I admitted eventually, and my now clammy hand began to slip from her loosened grip.

'You mean you've not been in touch? Not even now you've learnt about your father?'

I shook my head and Ruth shook hers in turn.

'Don't, Ruth.'

'But what has your mother done to deserve this?' she demanded.

I sighed, but said nothing. I knew the answer was nothing.

Ruth looked out at London. 'What must that poor woman have gone through? What must she still be going through?'

'Please, Ruth. You wouldn't understand what Cypriots have gone through.'

Ruth pulled her hand away from mine.

'Wouldn't I? I lost my husband too, remember. Your mother's a human being, Tony. A poor widow, just like me.' She huffed. 'You know what? I've had it up to here with this ridiculous "Cypriot" thing of yours,' she added, pressing the back of her hand under her chin.

She shifted away from me and folded her arms. I looked out at London. It was only then I realised how alone I was. I also realised I no longer liked being alone. I reached over and put a hand on Ruth's shoulder.

She turned towards me, her eyes full of resolve. 'You're going to write to her, Tony. You're going to tell your mother her son's alive and well.'

A head full of dread shook. Ruth grabbed it and her eyes burned into mine. I glimpsed my mother.

'Do it!' she demanded, and all I could do was nod meekly.

'Good,' said Ruth, and leant over to kiss me gently on the cheek. A mother's kiss. She shifted closer to me and we held hands once more.

'Tony, can I ask you something?'

I hesitated. I wasn't sure I could take any more of her awkward questions.

'What does "ya su" mean?'

I smiled and returned her kiss.

'It means "your health"', I explained. 'It's used for hello and goodbye.'

'Ya su, Tony.'

'Ya su, Ruth.'

We walked arm in arm towards the lake on the other side of Alexandra Palace, where boats were available for hire.

'Come on. Let's go rowing,' I suggested, and she eagerly agreed.

We clambered into a boat and I reached over for the oars, but Ruth pushed me away.

'I'll row. You play,' she instructed, pointing to the brown bag poking out of my pocket.

She struggled to manoeuvre the boat out into the lake. I was a little embarrassed, as I felt rowing was really a man's duty. Then the sleeve of her blouse caught against a loose splinter on the side of the boat. Ruth stopped rowing to examine the tear. She pretended not to be upset.

'I don't suppose you can fix it, Tony?' she asked hopefully.

I instinctively felt for the needle and thread I tended to carry with me, but the tear looked beyond my capabilities. I shook my head with regret.

'Never mind,' she said. 'Who needs a tailor when I've got a musician aboard? Come on. Play me a tune.'

'What shall I play?' I felt like one of Ruth's youngsters at the Muswell Hill Centre.

'Something from home,' she requested, now managing to establish some rhythm to her rowing.

I began to play. And as I played I found myself remembering the last time I was in a rowing boat. And the tune came easily, and I could tell Ruth appreciated it. When I was done, she stopped rowing and clapped.

'What's that called?' she asked, and I knew her interest was genuine.

'Psarobulla,' I replied. 'It means fishing boat.'

Ruth smiled dreamily. 'Oh to be in a "saropoola", floating on a deep blue sea, with the warm sun beating down on us.'

I didn't respond. 'Tell me more about home, Tony.'

I shrugged. 'It's been so long.'

'You must remember.'

I shook my head. 'It's like trying to recall summer in the middle of winter. Trying to remember warmth when, for so long, you've known only cold.'

'Please, Tony,' urged Ruth. 'Or I'll take the harmonica back.'

My mouth smiled but my eyes couldn't.

'I'm not the man I was.'

Ruth had yet to resume her rowing. We drifted slowly towards the island in the centre of the lake as the sunlight danced on the surface of the water. I found myself remembering something which brought a genuine smile to my face. I started playing 'Rule Britannia'.

'Where is that man, Tony?' Ruth asked when I'd done.

'I think he's gone,' I replied with a shrug.

She grabbed both my hands, and her touch filled me with hope. 'But Tony. Winter can't last for ever.'

I stared at the tear in her blouse. 'Can't it?'

She leant forward to kiss me on the lips.

'Can't you feel it, Tony? Summer's coming.'

21
The oath *O orkos*

Summer had started to grip Cyprus. There was much to do in the fields. As well as potatoes, Mihalis grew watermelons, tomatoes, courgettes, aubergines and, of course, gologasin, the sweet potato which Cyprus had made its own.

The farmer sat astride his donkey. Every now and then he tapped its hindquarters to quicken the beast's pace. It was early morning, and Mihalis was on the road out of the village, heading to his fields with Eros trotting alongside. The farmer had started taking the dog along occasionally as company.

Mihalis wore a wide-brimmed straw hat. Andonis had bought it for him on his last visit to town, to protect his father's head from too much exposure to the sun.

The farmer raised his head and eyebrows. He had helped to bring two able pairs of hands into the world, but both had developed lives of their own. One wasted away the hours in prayer, the other preferred sewing garments to watering melons.

'What can be done, Ero?' mused Mihalis. He looked down at the young dog, which looked back up at the farmer, tongue dangling from mouth. Away from the house, from the coffee-shop and the villagers, Mihalis had taken to talking to the animal, really talking, like he once used to talk to his own sons when they were younger and more willing to listen. How Mihalis enjoyed having Eros around. How he valued the dog's unconditional love.

'You see, Ero, we have a perfect bond, you and I. I throw you scraps to eat and sticks to fetch, I provide you with shelter. You in return guard Irini's precious chickens, chase away the rats and bark at strangers. We both show each other loyalty, respect and understanding,' he observed. 'A perfect bond.'

'And when I talk, you listen. You do. You know I know what's right. You know I'd never do anything that wasn't in your best interests,' continued Mihalis.

The dog trotted and panted and wagged its tail.

'And yes, Ero, that includes the removal of your pips.'

The dog barked with excitement.

'Oh yes, yes, yes. I know you're still upset with me for that. But, please understand. I rescued you from a life controlled by urges and by instincts.'

The dog trotted and panted and wagged its tail. Mihalis thought of Andonis.

'Urges that create only problems for us warm-blooded males, whatever the species. We're born, we mate, we provide for the resulting offspring until they're able to provide for themselves. Then we die.'

The dog barked with excitement.

'Oh yes, yes, yes. Without your pips you're more than just an animal, more than just a machine. You're free to love and be loved.'

The dog trotted and panted and wagged its tail.

It was then that Mihalis noticed a stationary army jeep on the road ahead of them with two soldiers inside, wearing red berets. They were observing him, waiting for him.

Mihalis's back stiffened and he began to shake. He'd been stopped by Englezi before.

'Watch out, Ero,' warned Mihalis. 'Look at those cold expressions on those burnt faces. Something terrible must have happened.'

As the farmer and his animals drew nearer to the jeep, Eros, emboldened by the presence of his two-legged protector, happily growled at the soldiers.

'Morning,' said Englezos number one, tipping his beret and descending from the jeep. It was an English greeting which Mihalis recognised and repeated. The soldier beckoned for the nervy farmer to get down from his donkey, and he obliged.

'Where were you last night?' demanded Englezos number one.

'May the devil take you! I don't recognise a word you're saying,' retorted the farmer politely in the Cypriot vernacular.

Englezos number one grabbed the farmer by his shirt and the farmer's hat fell to the ground.

'What have I done to you, my friend?' pleaded Mihalis, though he knew the Englezos would not understand him.

'Leave it, Johnny,' called a calmer Englezos number two from the jeep. Englezos number one looked back at his comrade, nodded and released his grip on the farmer.

'OK, mate. Search time,' instructed Johnny.

'You demon. I told you, I don't understand you,' muttered Mihalis, but with an incongruously pleasant tone. How Mihalis wanted to grab the heads of these two asprogoli and smash them together.

Johnny patted his chest and thighs to illustrate his instruction, and the farmer understood. He raised his arms and allowed the Englezos to do his job.

'You fool. If I had a weapon on me I swear I'd have let you have it by now,' muttered Mihalis with a pleasant smile. He knew his deliberately ambiguous statement would have meant nothing to the Englezos, but a chance to show some defiance nevertheless meant a lot to Mihalis.

Johnny smiled back. His search had proved fruitless. Now he stooped down to pat Eros on the head. The dog growled.

'Good doggy,' enthused Johnny.

'Careful, or he'll bite your hand off,' muttered Mihalis.

Johnny turned back to his comrade in the jeep.

'What do you reckon, Charlie? Shall we take the dog?' he asked, nodding back at Eros.

Charlie shook his head. 'He won't let it go without a fight, Johnny. And he's a big bleeding Bubble.'

Johnny nodded and felt for the revolver in his holster.

'Leave it, Johnny,' warned Charlie. 'There'll be other opportunities. We know he's from the village.'

Johnny nodded and turned his attentions back to the farmer.

'On your way, then,' he instructed with a wave of the hand.

'Go to hell,' muttered Mihalis with a pleasant tone before picking up his hat and getting back onto his donkey.

It was now late morning, and Andonis was in his workshop, making progress on Zeki's shirt. This was without doubt the most enjoyable piece of work he'd ever undertaken. He'd sat at his Singer and sewn each stitch with the tenderest of loving care. Zeki would look so fine.

Andonis glanced down on the table to examine the piece of paper with the shirt's measurements on it. He recalled with a smile how each had been arrived at. Now his mind was replaying last night. He remembered the moon. It all seemed like a beautiful dream. Until it ended to the distant sound of armoured vehicles and angry voices of Englezi. He recalled his fear. That was all too real. He wondered what all the commotion had been about. He knew it was only a matter of time before he would find out, not something he was looking forward to knowing.

At that moment Andonis heard a knock on the door. He recalled the time this had signalled Funda's unexpected arrival. He imagined it might be her again. Coming to check on progress, coming to share another forbidden moment of intimacy. He dismissed the notion. It was broad daylight. Funda could never be so bold. Nevertheless a rush of adrenaline flowed around his body, making his loins twitch. He dreamt it might be her.

Nigos burst in. His face was red and dripping with sweat. Andonis readjusted his mind to this reality. He smiled a greeting but continued his work.

'I've got something to tell you, Andoni,' declared Nigos, between anxious breaths. 'Something important.'

Andonis gave a laugh. He always found Nigos's passionate outbursts amusing.

Nigos frowned. 'This is serious. Put that needle down and listen to me. Please.'

Andonis stopped sewing and leant forward to indicate that Nigos had his undivided attention.

'I have to get away. I'm leaving for the hills,' declared Nigos, and then, more emphatically with a clenched fist, he added, 'I'm joining the struggle.'

Andonis was aghast. 'What are you saying, Nigo?'

'Eoga. I'm taking up arms against the Englezi and against all who stand in the way of freedom. Eoga need all the help they can get.'

Andonis shook his head. 'My All-Holy Virgin. What's brought this on?'

'What's brought this on? Years and years of oppression. Of having our land and the fruits of our labour stolen. Of being looked down on by inferior people who believe they're superior. Of being treated like children, like pieces in a game of tavlin. Of seeing my mother in black, bringing us up on her own.'

Nigos was shaking as he spoke. Andonis nodded, but his face remained blank. He knew there was more to this. Nigos knew he knew.

'The Englezi picked up Bambos this morning,' explained Nigos. 'This very minute he's no doubt being tortured in the town prison.'

Andonis's good humour was gone. He was certain the commotion earlier that morning was connected. He feared the worst.

'My God, what happened to you all last night?' he demanded.

'We were protecting Stella,' insisted Nigos defensively. Andonis raised his hands to indicate his disbelief.

'My sister. Remember?' added Nigos accusingly.

Andonis's mind was racing. He suddenly felt protective of Stella.

'Is she all right?' he asked.

'Don't worry yourself, Andoni. Stella's all right now,' retorted Nigos dismissively. 'But she had a bad time last night. One of your bastard Englezi friends tried it on with her. Me and the boys weren't having it. We chased him out of the village. Then me and Bambos followed him in the car and gave him a good thrashing. But the Englezi found out about Bambos. Some treacherous devil must have recognised the car and snitched on him. And when I find out who...'

Andonis interrupted by raising a hand. 'What were you and Bambos thinking? How many times have you chatted to girls in the square? Boys are boys.'

Nigos was fuming. 'This is my sister we're talking about, Andoni. It just goes to show how little respect you have for Stella. Or for any of our girls.'

'Come on, Nigo. Did this soldier really deserve a beating? What's going on? What are we becoming?'

'Fuck it, Andoni. What are *you* becoming? Whose side are you on?'

'The side of reason, Nigo. I'm concerned about Bambos, but you and he were foolish. No doubt the Englezi will knock him about a bit. Then they'll let him go. He's only getting what he deserves.'

Nigos shook his head. His face was full of fear.

'What if Bambos tells them I was with him? They'll arrest and torture me too. And what if the Englezos dies? Bambos hit the bastard real hard, Andoni. They'll hang us both.'

Andonis was shaking now. 'My God, Nigo. What have you done?'

'What else were we to do? Stand by and let some Englezos harass my sister? Let him run off with my bicycle? Fuck it, Andoni! He had the nerve to steal my bicycle!' Nigos was close to tears.

Andonis shook his head. 'So now you're the outlaw.'

Nigos drew consolation from Andonis's description.

'That's right. I'm the outlaw. The rebel, like James Dean, only *with* a cause! Come with me, Andoni. We could be outlaws together. We could fight the Englezi. Fight for liberty. Like we did that day in the fishing boat. Only with guns now instead of songs!'

Andonis looked at his friend. He was filled with an overwhelming sadness. He shook his head once more.

Nigos's face snarled with contempt.

'I don't believe you're a coward, Andoni. All this dangerous nonsense with the Turkish girl shows you're not. But it also shows you've turned into something else.'

Andonis sighed and turned his attentions back to Zeki's shirt.

'I'm still the same man I've always been,' he countered. 'It's you who've changed. You've turned into a madman.'

Nigos's eyes narrowed. He snatched Andonis's needle.

'You've turned into a traitor,' he declared.

Andonis tried to snatch the needle back, but Nigos dodged his friend's hand. He withdrew a folded sheet of paper from his shirt pocket and gave it to Andonis.

The tailor unfolded the piece of paper and read.

I swear to the holy, just and liberating struggle we are conducting for the freedom of our great island of Cyprus in the following terms:

(a) *I shall obey the orders of my superiors in whatever difficult, arduous or dangerous task they entrust me.*

(b) *I am ready to sacrifice my own life for the sake of the freedom of my homeland.*

(c) *I shall not abandon the struggle unless I am instructed by the leader of the organisation or until our aim has been accomplished.*

(d) *In serving the organisation I shall obey its commands, setting aside all obstacles.*

(e) *I shall not reveal the secrets of the organisation or the pseudonyms of fellow combatants.*

Whoever violates the above terms shall be executed by his superiors. Whoever feels fear, timidity or hesitation need not take this oath.

Andonis passed the piece of paper back to Nigos as though it were a dirty sock. Nigos took it and refolded it carefully.

'You're either with us or against us,' Nigos hissed.

Andonis shook his head. He wasn't with Nigos. Nigos had gone too far. And now he'd changed things for ever.

'Adio then, Andoni,' sighed Nigos, and stormed out of the workshop.

'Adio, Nigo,' whispered Andonis after he had gone. 'And may God help you. May God help us all.'

After a few moments' contemplation, the tailor's attention returned to Zeki's shirt, while his mind inevitably returned to Zeki's sister.

22
The city *I bolis*

I walked Ruth to the youth centre and thanked her for the pleasant day we'd spent together and for her gift. We didn't kiss again. It didn't seem appropriate. Not here. Instead I squeezed her hand and assured her I'd be in touch soon. She smiled.

'And don't forget your mother, Tony,' she advised, before leaving me outside.

I had to stand there a moment to reflect. I felt like knocking on the door and telling Ruth that I'd never forgotten my mother. That she'd remained in my mind. Always. Occupying areas that I'd always feared to venture into fully. She and all the others.

I wanted to, but feared the words would come out wrong. They always came out wrong. I shook my head and turned to go. A letter needed to be written.

Before returning to my lodgings, I popped into a local haberdashery and bought a length of white silk. Now I sat at my Singer and rubbed the smooth material against my rough cheek. I smiled as I remembered how radiant Ruth had looked in her blouse. An amazing woman. There was no denying that.

The warm, cloudless day had given way to a cooler evening. I recalled the clear views from Alexandra Palace and became conscious once more of sharing this huge city with countless others, all getting by.

Many had origins in other parts of the world. People like me, struggling to make a home amongst people like Ruth. And amongst each other. And all at once I was filled with hope. I glimpsed a future when all these different people had come together to share the best each had to offer. A future when this diversity and colour had merged, the whole much deeper and much richer than any of its parts. It was a future I knew I'd almost glimpsed once before. I wondered whether I'd ever live to see it for real.

But today, even, this big, multi-cultural city wasn't a bad place to be. You could lose yourself. Find yourself. Be yourself. Not like in the village, where every move was scrutinised, every life mapped.

And that's when I became angry with myself. I realised I'd done wrong. Here I lived, in a place that offered so much, and yet I'd experienced so little. So many ways of thinking that I'd never allowed myself to come into contact with. So many years of imagining that a warped world view was the only one possible. And I was angry not just for shutting myself off from others, but for shutting myself off from a man I used to know. A man named Andonis. A man capable of dreaming the impossible.

It was then I remembered a wise man Andonis had met, a Cypriot Maronite. A man who'd also shut himself off. But only after he'd experienced all that he needed. Only after he'd established what the world really meant to him and how best to play his part in it.

I recalled how he always had a way to recommune with his true self, whenever the need arose, and in turn recommune with the beauty of a world he'd left behind. A beauty which in a real sense need only ever exist in his own mind.

I threw the silk material onto the bed. That would have to wait. I began to shiver, but not from the cold. I needed inspiration. I needed to find the right words. My body raised itself. My hand felt for an appropriate coin in my trouser pocket, and my legs now carried me down to the payphone at the bottom of the stairs.

My finger dialled a number, and my voice said hello to a West Indian I knew of. A supplier of inspiration.

It was good living in a big, multi-cultural city.

23

The goatherd *O voskos*

It was hard living in a small, divided village. Everyone told you to take care. It's what his mother had been reiterating to Andonis ever since the attack on the British soldier and the disappearance of Nigos. And Andonis's father had sat him down and given him a long lecture. Back and forth went Mihalis, over and over the same ground until Andonis had switched off. They both knew there was only one message. Take care.

His mother continued to say it, whenever Andonis left the house, even if he was only going over to his workshop. According to Irini one could never be too careful now. Marios assured them all that he was praying to God to take care of the family, and that he was putting in extra prayers for his brother, because Andonis needed extra care.

Andonis took extra care. How he longed to see Funda again, but now it really was too dangerous.

British soldiers had come to the village on the days following the attack and made their presence felt. They were in no mood for compromise. They were determined to find all those responsible. They stopped and searched and questioned people at random. Even the women.

Then they rounded up a dozen or so youths, herding them away in armoured trucks. Yannis, as he was related to Bambos, had been amongst the unfortunates, but Andonis had not.

The widow was bedridden with worry for both her missing sons. The whole village was in disarray. Relations had reached a new low, with Muslims no longer prepared to ride on Simos's bus. There were rumours that the soldier who'd been attacked had died of his injuries.

The villagers were so full of fear they couldn't even bring themselves to celebrate the festival of Saint Varnavas the Apostle.

People feared reprisals, feared for the lives of their sons. So people turned to their priest for guidance, and he offered stories from the Bible. They turned to their muhtaris, and he offered hatred. Mothers wept openly in the streets, fathers sat in stern silence in the coffee shop.

One or two younger men not taken by the Englezi left for the hills.

Then, a few weeks later, the armoured trucks returned, and the youths were released. Relief swept through the village like a cooling breeze. The youths had been roughed up, but that didn't matter. They were free. They were home.

Now some of the villagers dared hope that life might return to some kind of normality.

Only Bambos had not been freed. Yannis had brought back news that his cousin was still being tortured. But Bambos was not a son of the village.

✳ ✳ ✳

Funda's mind was changing. It had to change. She was starting to change inside. Before, maybe it was possible to dream of running away with Andonis. To the town, perhaps eventually even to England, where they could start a new life together, far from all the madness. But not now. Of course, if she went to him, the young man of principle would stand by her. Of that she was certain. But it was too dangerous, for both of them. Now there was more to consider.

No, this wasn't a time for principles. Funda had to be practical. She had to be protective. Her love could not be in vain. Happiness would have to be forgone. Life was at stake.

She stared at the tailor's thimble and banished fear. She had to endure.

✳ ✳ ✳

Erden sat at his favourite spot, blowing into his flute. He played a Greek song, the one he'd heard that time on the bus. The music comforted him. He remembered how grateful he had been to the Christian tailor for intervening on his behalf. The very next morning Erden had gone straight round to the house of Mihalis with a dozen chunks of goat's cheese in a sealed glass jar and a clay jug filled to the brim with fresh yogurt. Mrs Irini had tried to refuse him, saying Erden was far too generous, but Erden would not hear of it. He told her it was her son who was the generous one.

Now Erden was surrounded by his extended family of grazing goats. He had a fully recovered and content Yasmin sleeping peacefully on his lap. Would that people were more like goats. Would that their leaders were more like an honest goatherd. For then there would be no problems, could be no hatred or wickedness. Not like that terrible moonlit evening when, down there in the distance, on the road leading to the town, Erden had witnessed a poor man being savagely beaten.

Erden was fearful of the Englezi. Fearful of what was happening in the village and of what further acts of violence might follow. He allowed his thoughts to lose themselves in his tune. And as he played he became aware of a distant voice, humming along. A woman's voice. So sweet and so pure.

Funda? Was he dreaming? He stopped and strained to listen, but could hear nothing. He chastised himself. See what happens when you cut yourself off from everyone? See how your mind starts to dream up company?

Erden resumed his tune, and was surprised to hear the humming return. No. Erden had not been dreaming. He squinted into the distance and could see the figure of a woman, headscarf covering her face, head lowered. He was sure now that this really was Funda. He roused Yasmin from her sleep and placed her carefully on the ground. He rose from under the old olive tree and raced down towards the woman he adored.

He noticed that her headscarf was sodden with tears.

'Funda? What are you doing here? What's happened?'

Funda stared at the goatherd through watery eyes.

'Is that you, Erden?' she enquired, as though unsure.

Erden reached into his pocket and removed a white handkerchief. Framed by soaked lashes, Funda's intense green eyes appeared all the more beautiful to Erden as he began wiping away her tears. Funda could see love in the goatherd's eyes, and drew strength. She took a deep breath and composed herself.

'Oh, Erden. I had to get away from the village. I didn't know where to go. Your music drew me here. It's so calming. You play so well.' She forced a smile.

Erden's heart was filled with both joy and pain. Joy at Funda's compliment, joy at this chance to share a private moment with her. Pain at seeing Funda in such distress, pain at being so close to her yet knowing her mind was so far away.

'Things are getting worse and worse, Erden. The whole village has come down with a terrible sickness.'

Erden nodded. 'I know. I saw what they did to that poor man on that night of the full moon,' he agreed. 'There were angry soldiers everywhere afterwards. And now everyone's become angry.'

Funda shuddered, and Erden suddenly felt protective of her. How he wanted to deliver her from this sickness.

'But what's happened to you, Funda? Why are you crying?' he pressed.

'I can't say, Erden. No one must know. But I must leave this place for ever. Will you help me?' she implored, her eyes full of desperation.

Erden was shaking. With anger at the thought of someone upsetting Funda; with fear at the thought of her going away. Somehow Erden always knew he could bear the idea of another man of the village taking Funda as his wife. For the goatherd would still catch a glimpse of her now and again, still feel close to her, still dream of her. But the idea of Funda leaving, of him never being able to set eyes on her again, that was something Erden could not stand.

'Please tell me what's happened. Whatever it is, I won't tell a soul, and I'll do all I can to help you,' he vowed.

Funda nodded, drawing strength from the goatherd's loyalty.

'Thank you. You make me feel better. Perhaps I should tell you,' she deliberated, though in truth this had been her intention.

For his part, Erden suddenly felt more alive than ever before. Funda needed him as his goats needed him. He took her hand, and led her to the old olive tree.

'Sit here. In the shade,' he instructed, and she did so, leaning against the tree.

Then she saw her name carved on the bark next to that of Erden. He pretended not to notice that she'd spotted his handiwork, though he was pleased she had. Funda smiled a resigned smile. Erden was the best of men. And her instincts told her she had to do what was best.

The goatherd now crouched down before her. His goats clambered around him, but he shooed them away. Funda tried to compose herself. This would be the one and only time she would be recounting her story, and she was nervous, despite the attentiveness of her audience.

'Tell me you won't hate me, Erden,' she pleaded, grabbing the goatherd's hand for reassurance.

'I could never hate you, Funda. Please don't be afraid,' he implored. Funda squeezed his hand and he squeezed back. Kismet had brought Funda to Erden today, and he would not let go.

'Whatever it is, we'll get through this,' he added soothingly. 'Tell me what you have to tell me.'

Funda looked down and began her story. She told Erden about the tailor. About the breeches song. About the romance between them. About everyone's disapproval. About their stolen moments together. About her father's anger. About the episode on the bus. About that fateful night of the full moon, when the tailor had come to her. And now, about her realisation that this love could never be.

She paused and sighed. 'Do you understand, Erden?' she asked.

Erden nodded, and felt both relief and joy sweep through him. Funda had loved another, but had rejected that love and was now turning to him. Funda shook her head.

'You simple goatherd, you don't understand do you?' she admonished. Now Funda pulled herself up and looked down at the still crouching Erden.

'I'm pregnant, Erden,' she announced, and Erden's mouth dropped.

Funda's eyes filled again, and tears streamed down her cheeks. Erden stood up too. He was shaking. He tried to speak, but no words emerged. Funda placed a hand against her forehead.

'I've no one to turn to. How can I tell my father? How can I face the rest of the village? Or the Christians. Or the tailor and his family?'

She grabbed the knife from Erden's belt and was turning the blade towards herself. Erden was quick to react.

'No, Funda,' he commanded, wrestling the knife from hands which offered only token resistance.

'But what else can I do? My life is over,' she cried.

'I won't allow it. I promised I'd help you, and I will. Forget the past. Forget the tailor. Forget everything,' he instructed, replacing the knife under his belt.

'But how, Erden? In a few weeks time I'll have a bump. What then? Then I'll have a baby. A Christian's baby. What then?'

'You'll have a baby that can by mine, Funda,' declared the goatherd, grabbing her hands. 'I love you. I've always loved you. I'll ask your father for your hand. Will you be my wife?'

Funda was drunk with emotion, and had the goatherd not held her she might have fallen to the ground. Slowly she regained her composure. She knew she had to be strong. She knew drastic action was needed, to protect the man she loved. She had to endure so the fruit of their love might endure.

'Yes, Erden. Yes,' she announced, and kissed the goatherd on the cheek. Erden went to embrace her, but Funda pulled away and sat back down under the old olive tree to consider the future. Erden sat next to her.

After a moment's silence, a look of horror appeared on Funda's face, and she turned to the goatherd.

'Erden. There's so much danger,' she warned. 'Tell me. After the night of the attack, did the soldiers come and ask what you witnessed?'

Erden shuddered but said nothing. He knew he had already said enough.

'Be sure never to say anything to anyone,' instructed Funda.

✳ ✳ ✳

By now Andonis should have taken delivery of the big army job promised by the captain, but the increased tensions meant all that had been postponed for the time being. The tensions also meant there was now little demand for the tailor's services in the village. People had more important things to worry about than ordering new clothes.

Of course there was still the captain's suit to work on, but the tailor was in no mood for that. So instead he had kept himself busy, putting the finishing touches to Yannis's wedding suit. The wedding at least would be going ahead as planned; nothing could come between Yannis and Martha. There was also the shirt that Funda had ordered. Andonis hadn't seen Funda since the night of the full moon – everyone had to take care.

It was care, however, that was eventually to drive the tailor from his workshop one afternoon with Zeki's completed shirt folded in a brown bag. It was care that was to propel him towards the coffee-shop of the Muslims.

He was met with disapproving stares and mumblings from some of the regulars there, but no one openly challenged him. After all, he was the son of Mihalis; grandson of the late Mrs Maria. And he had helped the goatherd.

Andonis sat alone at an outside table with a glass of airanin which the Muslim coffee-shop owner had grudgingly served him. He sipped and waited. He was certain Zeki would hobble by soon, on his way home from the mosque's youth club. Here young Muslims were being taught to identify with another country. Just as the young Christians were.

Sure enough, Andonis soon heard the boisterous voices of young people at the entrance to the mosque, signalling that the club was over for the day. Zeki appeared, surrounded by a group of friends, and they all made their way along the road in the direction of the coffee-shop, laughing and joking. They walked slowly so that the boy with crutches could keep up.

As they neared, Andonis looked over to them and smiled, but Zeki looked away.

'Zeki! Please come here. I have something for you,' called Andonis in Turkish. Like most Christians of the village, Andonis had a smattering of the language brought to the island by the Ottomans. Zeki's friends started sniggering, and the boy's face reddened. He shook his head.

'Leave me alone, Mr Andoni,' he implored in Andonis's language. The other youths, realising their crippled friend was distressed, looked dubiously at the tailor. There was an uncomfortable silence.

Andonis reached into his shirt pocket and pulled out his harmonica. He began to play the tune he'd once played for Funda on the night of the festival, all those months ago. The one about the breeches. The youths recognised the tune and started swaying to and fro around Zeki, preventing him from hobbling away as he had wished to do at first. Eventually Zeki too joined in, swinging on his crutches. When Andonis's tune was over all the youths applauded, including Zeki.

'Please, Zeki. Won't you sit with me a while?' suggested Andonis.

Zeki nodded and spoke to his friends in Turkish. They nodded, waved goodbye to the tailor and continued their walk home. Zeki hobbled up to Andonis's table and sat opposite him.

'Can I get you a drink?' offered Andonis, but Zeki shook his head.

'What do you want?' Zeki enquired. His command of the Cypriot vernacular wasn't as good as Funda's. Its use was discouraged at the youth club. 'You make trouble for us, Mr Andoni. You Christians make nothing but trouble.'

Andonis bowed his head and nodded. Then he looked up and smiled.

'Look, Zeki. I've made something for you.' He pushed the paper bag across the table towards Zeki. 'Go on. Open it.'

Zeki hesitated a moment before tearing at the paper. He smiled as he pulled out the white silk shirt.

'For me?' he enquired, pressing the material against his cheek to feel its softness. Andonis nodded.

The boy hobbled to his feet, unfolded the shirt and put it over the one he was wearing. The new shirt was a bit big, but Zeki knew he would grow into it.

'Thank you, Mr Andoni,' enthused a grateful Zeki. He retook his seat.

'Don't thank me,' corrected Andonis. 'Thank your sister. She asked me to make it. Tell me, how is your sister?'

The delight was gone from Zeki's face. A frown replaced it.

'Will you tell her I must see her, Zeki? We must sort things out, once and for all.'

Zeki remained silent. The tailor took a sip of his airanin.

'So you like your new shirt?' Andonis asked eventually.

Zeki nodded. 'It's perfect. Beautiful,' he replied, then continued with a bitterness that took Andonis by surprise. 'All I need now is a matching new leg, and all the girls will fall in love with me.'

Andonis raised his eyebrows. 'Love can be as much of a burden as a crippled leg, Zeki,' he advised. Zeki considered whether he was being patronised, but decided to give the tailor the benefit of the doubt.

'I'd take my chances,' Zeki declared.

Andonis rolled out his lower lip and nodded.

'OK, so you're in love and you know she loves you. But everyone else disapproves, for foolish reasons, which only make you love each other more. What would you do?'

Zeki considered the tailor's question while feeling the sleeve of his new shirt between his fingertips.

'With my new shirt and my new leg, I'd go looking for a few more loves before making my mind up,' he replied. 'Ones more appropriate!'

Andonis raised his head and eyebrows. 'You think it's that easy? To switch your emotions on and off?' he asked.

Now Zeki felt certain he was being patronised. 'Hey, I'm just a stupid cripple. What do I know about love?'

'You know I love your sister.'

'So you say, Mr Andoni. But you're not the only one. The difference is she's my sister, so lust doesn't get in the way of *my* love.'

Andonis was hurt. 'What are you saying to me?'

'I can see what's best for her, whereas maybe you can't. Leave her alone, Mr Andoni. She needs to get used to a life without you.'

'Now you sound like the barber,' said Andonis with a frown.

'Perhaps. But it's still the words of the cripple. You see, Mr Andoni. I wish things were different for you and my sister. Really I do. But we must face reality. Like I have to every day, on these damned crutches.'

He pushed himself up and onto them. Andonis sighed deeply.

'Believe me, you get used to it,' said Zeki, hobbling backwards from the table.

❋ ❋ ❋

Early next morning, when Andonis had gone to his workshop, he noticed a sealed brown envelope pinned to the door. He pulled the envelope down and tore it open. Inside he found a ten-shilling note, together with a short, handwritten letter.

My dear Andoni

Thank you for all you've done for my brother. Thank you for making me a woman. Farewell, my love. I must devote my love to another now.

I'll think of you always.

Funda

Andonis was stunned beyond tears. He stumbled into his workshop, slumped into a chair and read and reread the note. But the words offered no hope.

Some moments later, Marios walked past the open door. Andonis looked up. He called out to ask why Marios wasn't helping their father in the fields.

'For the same reason you're not with him.' There was an uncharacteristic hint of defiance in the younger brother's tone. The tailor picked up his needle and shook it at Marios.

'I'm not with him because *this* is my work now,' Andonis snapped. A look of calm emerged on Marios's face.

'Forgive me, Andoni,' he said. 'I was thoughtless. Please try to understand. I have another calling too. Baba-Ghlioris has entrusted me with some important errands. Now, more than ever, people need the strength and guidance of our Church. Our priest can't cope on his own.'

Andonis rubbed the stubble on his chin a moment before giving an apologetic nod.

'I'm the one who should ask for forgiveness. I'm being selfish. I expect you to do what I'm not willing to do myself. Our father must get by without either of his sons, and you must do God's work. Please. Come and sit with me. I need strength and guidance too.'

Marios sat down, and his brother rolled himself a cigarette. A light breeze swept through the open door of the workshop, bringing with it the intoxicating fragrance of jasmine from a nearby tree. The moving air made it difficult for Andonis to light his cigarette. Marios took the box of matches from his brother, and as he did so the air became still. Marios scraped the match against the rough surface of his chair-leg and reached over to the cigarette dangling from his brother's mouth.

As Andonis blew his first lungful of smoke into the air, the morning breeze returned. Andonis nodded his thanks to his brother. The nicotine rushed through Andonis's bloodstream as thoughts of Funda rushed once more through his mind. Then a steadily growing sound of young singing voices overtook his thoughts.

'Listen to the children, Mario. Where do you think they're going?' enquired Andonis.

'I imagine their teacher's taking them to the little church of Saint Marina,' offered Marios.

Andonis nodded, remembering going on such trips when he and his brother were schoolchildren. The old church of Saint Marina was no more than a mile from the village, off the main road, along a dirt track. The good Christian children would collect flowers on the way to the church. The girls would make necklaces and bracelets, the boys would make wreaths. All would be left as gifts to Saint Marina.

Before entering the crumbling church, the teacher would sit the children down under the shade of some trees and recount the story of Saint Marina. And the children would listen, in awe.

And then the children would be ushered inside the church. They'd cross themselves and their little lungs would fill with the church's cool musty air. They'd step delicately on the floor of straw and caked earth, they'd marvel at the wooden crucifix hanging from the entrance to the ieron. So much history and so much holiness, so close to their own homes.

And the teacher would point at the beautiful but fading icons painted on the walls. Of Saint Marina herself. Of Christ and of the All-Holy Virgin. Of Saint Andreas the Apostle and Saint Varnavas the Apostle. And the teacher would point to where the eyes of the saints should be. He'd show with his pen how they'd been dug out with the sharp and jealous blades of the destructive Ottoman Turks at the time when Cyprus had become enslaved by their evil empire. How could these non-believers damage this most sacred of places? And such wicked acts had been committed by those whose religion was shared by people still living in the village.

And later Andonis and Marios would tell their father about the terrible things that had been done to the icons in the church of Saint Marina, and their father would shake his head and tut, tut, tut. And he would sit his sons down to talk to them.

If the Sultan's soldiers were responsible, he would say, then they had done wrong. However, it was important to put aside such wrongs from the past in order to ensure better things for the future.

And Andonis would nod and sort of understand. But not Marios.

'Do you remember the story of Saint Marina?' asked Andonis.

Marios nodded with a smile.

'Then please, tell it to me once more, Mario.'

Marios, pleasantly surprised that his older brother was taking an interest in matters of faith, obliged.

Ever since Marina was a little girl, she had dreamt of entering the local monastery to devote her life to prayer. But there were no places for women. Marina resolved to crop her hair and disguise herself as a young man so that the abbot might accept her. And accept her he did.

All knew her as Marinos. So full of faith and so calm of spirit was Marinos that, before long, she, now a he, had made a favourable impression on the abbot. The abbot attributed the monk's soft voice to his intense self-discipline and vigilant prayer.

It came to pass that the abbot needed to do some important business on the other side of the island. He chose Marinos to accompany him and the young monk's heart was filled with pride.

It was a long trip, and they had to spend the night at an inn before resuming their journey the next day.

The innkeeper had a daughter who was in love with a young man from a poor family. The innkeeper disapproved of this love.

Now it so happened that the daughter became pregnant. So consumed with rage was the innkeeper that he took out a knife and threatened to kill his daughter's lover. The daughter pleaded with her father not to harm the man she loved. She claimed he was innocent and that the child was fathered by the young monk, who had seduced her on the night he and the abbot had come to stay.

When the child was born, the innkeeper brought it to the monastery and demanded that Marinos take responsibility. Marinos did not deny that the child was his, for fear that the truth about his identity would be revealed. Marinos was banished from the monastery and made a new home for himself and for the child in an abandoned old church. Marinos was utterly devoted to his adopted son, accepting him as a blessing from the Lord.

The years passed, until one day old Marinos passed on to heaven. His adopted son, now married with children of his own, returned to the old church to clean his father's body and prepare it for burial. It was then that the world discovered that the devout Marinos had in fact been Marina all the time.

And the old church where she had lived all those years was renamed after her, and to this day is known as the church of Saint Marina.

'It's a fine old tale,' said Andonis with sadness. But there was also a hint of dismissiveness in his tone.

'Oh, but it's much more than that,' insisted Marios. 'Don't you see? It demonstrates the miracle of God's love. For God's love Marina was prepared to sacrifice her life as a woman. But God in return, in all His love, thought fit to grant the righteous Marina what every woman can't help but wish for. Motherhood.'

Andonis nodded but then frowned. 'But Marina lived a lie, Mario. That doesn't sound very righteous.'

'For the love of God, all is permissible.'

Andonis considered what he would do for the sake of Funda's love. Would he sacrifice everything?

Marios could see that his brother was deeply troubled.

'Put your faith in God, and all will be well,' he insisted.

Andonis smiled and shook his head.

'This God of yours has more than one face. Which one should I choose?'

Marios replied as though addressing a child. 'There's only one God, Andoni. He is the light and He is the way. He is truth and He is love.'

'I don't see much love in the village at the moment. Only confusion, fear and hatred. Maybe we've all got the wrong God.'

Marios shook his head and looked deep into Andonis's eyes. He spoke slowly and with passion.

'It's Satan who places such blasphemous notions in your head. I beg you, don't turn your back on God.'

Now Andonis wrapped his hands around his brother's head and pulled it towards him, kissing Marios hard on the cheek.

'I feel so distant from this fine old religion of ours, Mario.'

'Why?'

'Because I don't see it as the answer to our problems. I see it as the cause.'

'Then I shall pray for you,' stated Marios calmly. 'As I do for all God's lost sheep, that you may one day find salvation.'

'Yes, pray for me, Mario, like you've never prayed before. Cure me from this terrible sickness. The pain cuts through my heart like a knife, and I fear I might never recover.'

Marios lowered his head as though looking for divine guidance. He grabbed his brother's hand and held it tightly.

'Don't be afraid, Andoni. We'll go on a journey together. To a special place where you may find comfort, where Satan's demons may be cast out of you,' he announced. 'We'll go to visit the monastery of Saint Andreas the Apostle.'

24

The journey   *Do daxidhin*

After sending the letter to my mother, time passed uneventfully. I busied myself with the silk and the Singer.

One evening I received another telephone call. I was hoping it might be Ruth, but it wasn't. It was the captain. He asked me why I hadn't called him, and I apologised. He asked me what I'd be doing on Sunday. When I said that I had no plans, he insisted that I should get on a train to visit him in Hove.

I told him that while it would be nice to see him again, I was reluctant as I found long journeys difficult. In truth I was afraid of more truth. But he was most insistent – the change of scene would do me good. He asked when I'd last set eyes on the sea. I replied that I cared not to remember, but that since coming to England I'd spent all my time in London.

He said this saddened him, as he knew the sea to be in my blood. He added that he wanted to help me rediscover my true self – a visit to the coast would help me do that. I said I wasn't sure. He explained patiently that, as he'd already told me on the day of Vasos's funeral, he had something important to give me, and that he was therefore unable to take no for an answer.

I found myself joking that with these coercive powers I could see how the British had established and maintained their huge empire. He laughed and said he was pleased I still displayed a sense of humour – there might still be hope for me. I told him his patronising approach was typical of a power in decline. He responded with details of trains and stations and timetables.

✳ ✳ ✳

On the day of the journey, the alarm woke me at half past seven in the morning, as it used to every weekday when I was still working. A few minutes later, I was at the bus stop at the top of Muswell Hill. It was a pleasant day, warm enough for me to have folded my jacket over my arm and to have rolled up my shirt sleeves. Sometimes, I thought, this country was almost bearable.

The bus dropped me at Turnpike Lane. I noticed that the continental shop along Westbury Avenue was open, so before going into the station I went in to buy the captain a packet of that coffee I knew he liked.

The owner smiled a greeting in his usual unimposing way, though I could tell he was curious to see why I was up this early on a Sunday.

'I'm surprised to see you open today,' I observed, surprised also at myself for making the effort to converse. The shopkeeper seemed a little put out.

'Only mornings,' he explained defensively. He had clearly taken my comment as a criticism for working on the Lord's day. In a sense it had been, and I'd said it because I myself felt guilty for rushing around on a day set aside for rest, contemplation and, for some, prayer.

'We all have to compromise to survive,' I said reassuringly, handing over some money. The shopkeeper nodded before looking directly into my eyes.

'Thank you, sir. You're a good man,' he declared as he wrapped the coffee in a brown bag and presented it to me. I found his comment oddly comforting.

'Thank you,' I replied with a smile. 'So are you.'

I arrived at Victoria Station half an hour later with a weary resignation. Just like the last time I had been here, when the train had brought me from Dover following a long, long journey from my homeland. Weary but resigned to having to start a new existence.

Back then, I knew, the captain had pulled the necessary strings to secure my passage. And now here I was, on another journey. The captain's doing once more.

Pulling the necessary strings.

✳ ✳ ✳

Back then the captain was the last familiar person I'd seen as the boat departed, waving vigorously to me from the shore at the town's port. I had left without fuss, and no family or friends could be there.

The captain's face grew ever more distant as I stood on deck, together with a group of other travellers, to catch a last glimpse of our fading homeland. The other people attempted to ease the pain for themselves by offering words of comfort to their companions.

'It's for the best.'

'We've suffered enough.'

'We must look forward to a new life.'

I mourned alone.

As the shoreline disappeared from view, I fixed my stare downward to observe the edge of the boat cutting through the waves. My lower lip had quivered, my cheeks had tightened, and before long my tears were joining the gallons of salt water which now separated me from all that I had known and loved.

It wasn't a very big boat. Somehow I had expected a huge ocean liner to transport its human cargo from this colonial outpost to the heart of the empire. The *Capidolio* was an Italian boat with a good-humoured Italian crew. They gave their passengers bread and cheese and water, and tried to raise our spirits with singing and crude jokes.

It was a gruelling five-day trip to Marseilles, with stops at Smyrna, Bari and Venice, followed by a two-day train journey across the length of France and a ferry trip over the English Channel. The experience had put me off travelling for good.

I occupied myself by befriending two young sisters. The elder, in her early teens, had her hands full taking care of her little sister of about seven, who was struck down with seasickness; though in truth we all suffered.

The sisters were joining their parents and brother, who were already in London. The elder girl asked me if anyone would be waiting for me in England. When I shook my head she took my hand and squeezed it, assuring me that her family would no doubt be able to help.

I also spent time observing a rather sour, middle-aged lady who spent the entire journey guarding the load she carried: a huge watermelon and a bag of gulluragia.

'I'm bringing them for my son,' she would declare to those who cared to listen, as well as those who cared not to. 'He's doing so well in London, thanks to God. He has a restaurant.'

The rumbling stomachs of the sisters had been cared for by the Italian crew with occasional biscuits. But now that we were travelling by train from Marseilles to Paris, the emptiness grew. Free from seasickness, the younger sister in particular had recovered her appetite, and declared to her elder sister that she was famished. It was a feeling I shared.

'What can I do?' sighed the elder sister turning to me. 'I've nothing to give her.'

I raised my hand to reassure them both, and spied the middle-aged lady. On the seat next to her were her prized melon and bag of gulluragia. She stared blankly out of the window at the green vastness of the French countryside.

'Surely you must be dying to relieve yourself, auntie,' I remarked, calling out to her from where we sat. 'We've all been, but I've not seen you go yet.'

She turned to me and frowned.

'Impossible,' she declared. 'Someone might be tempted to steal the gifts for my son while I'm gone.'

I stood up and went over to her, taking the woman's hand and pulling her gently from her seat.

'Don't worry, auntie. I'll take care of everything.'

As the lady made her way along the carriage towards the toilets I beckoned the children over.

'Come. Let's eat,' I said, pushing the melon to the floor. It shattered into pieces. The children were cautious at first, but knowing how soon the old lady might return, decided to take their chance. Soon they were grabbing at the juicy red morsels and stuffing them into their mouths. I handed out the crispy bread-sticks too, and before long other Cypriots in the carriage had gathered round us like vultures to share in the feast. We all ate ravenously. The melon was the sweetest I'd ever tasted, and as the son of Mihalis the farmer, that was saying something.

'Thank you, sir. You're a good man,' said the sisters between mouthfuls, and everybody present agreed. The woman returned after a few minutes, pulling at her hair and shrieking at me.

'They're for my son! You liar. You cheat. You thieves. They're for my son.'

I raised a hand and frowned at her.

'Hush, you silly woman,' I countered. 'Aren't you ashamed of yourself? Your son has all the food he needs in his restaurant in England, while these children of Cyprus go hungry.'

She huffed and cursed at me some more, but was shouted down by the other vultures. Then, resigned and acknowledging her own need for sustenance, she became a vulture herself.

From Paris we caught another train to Calais. And from Calais another boat, a bigger one this time, with an English crew, who looked at the tired, unwashed and swarthy group of Cypriot travellers with disdain. I realised it was a look I would have to get used to.

I tried practising it myself when looking at the white cliffs of Dover. And again when I saw the English train which was to take us to London. But after I caught the taxi from Victoria Station to the temporary lodgings arranged for me in Camden Town, when we passed Buckingham Palace and the fountains of Trafalgar Square the look was gone.

It was replaced by one of awe.

25

The sage   *O sofos*

Marios had borrowed the coffee-shop van, and the brothers journeyed along dirt roads towards the island's north-east peninsula, which points like a sword towards the belly of Asia Minor. Near the tip is perched the monastery of Saint Andreas the Apostle.

It hadn't been difficult for Marios to persuade Mr Vasos that the van was needed for God's work. Vasos may have been a good communist, but he was also a good friend of the priest and of their father. And friendship was more important than politics.

This wasn't the first time the brothers had made such a pilgrimage. As boys they had travelled with their parents to visit the famous monastery. They had paid homage to the apostle and prayed for a miracle to cure Marios of a terrible illness.

Marios assured Andonis that the apostle would once again respond to their prayers. As they travelled Marios spoke of the wonders of Saint Andreas the Apostle in an effort to focus Andonis's mind on something other than Funda.

Among Christ's first disciples, Andreas was the apostle most revered by the people of Cyprus, more so even than Varnavas. According to legend, Andreas was travelling east by boat for the feast of Passover in Jerusalem. On sailing past the island of Cyprus, it was discovered that the drinking water on board had run dry. Fearful that they would perish from thirst, the sailors turned to Andreas for guidance. He instructed them to land, and assured them that water would be found.

To the sailors' amazement, water in the form of an unlikely spring was indeed found, and their thirst quenched. News of the miracle spread around the island. The people's thirst for enlightenment was similarly quenched as Cyprus was to become the first Roman province to convert to Christianity. A shrine was built near the site of the spring in honour of Saint Andreas the Apostle.

On arriving, the brothers got out of the van and approached the monastery. They stared in awe at the whitewashed building, and beyond at the deep blue sea, which stretched into the distance all around. Each brother, in his own way, marvelled at the beauty of creation.

Marios went down on hands and knees, customary when entering, but Andonis remained upright.

'I'm not sure I can do this,' he pleaded. 'I'm an unbeliever.'

Marios pulled Andonis's hand. 'What are you saying, Andoni? We've come all this way. Saint Andreas the Apostle awaits us. Salvation awaits you.'

Andonis refused to budge.

'Andoni, I beg you. For God's sake,' implored Marios.

Andonis rubbed the bristles on his cheek with his free hand and looked down at his brother. Marios had been there for him. Marios was real. Andonis dropped to his knees. For his brother's sake. As they shuffled into the monastery, Marios was aware that his brother was trembling.

Inside, three women helpers observed Andonis follow his brother's lead as both dutifully crossed themselves. They observed Andonis follow his brother's lead as both ritually kissed all the icons. Then they observed Andonis's impatience while his brother knelt before the icon of Saint Andreas the Apostle, his hands joined in prayer. They observed Andonis pull at his brother's shirt to hurry him out. They observed the look of desperation on Andonis's face.

The women helpers followed the brothers back out into the sunlight, and with sympathetic eyes enquired as to Andonis's wellbeing. Andonis remained silent. He wanted to get away, but his brother felt driven to explain something of Andonis's affliction. While Andonis huffed at having his personal affairs aired, the women listened intently and nodded gravely.

'Yes. We can see your brother has a severe case of the sickness,' said one, as the other two nodded.

'Perhaps Mr Gibros may be willing to offer him a few words of wisdom,' added a second, as the other two nodded.

'He has a strange philosophy that some find comforting,' added the third, as the other two nodded.

There was affection in their eyes as they talked of Mr Gibros. Andonis was intrigued.

'Mr Gibros?' enquired Marios dismissively. It didn't sound as though this man was connected to the Church. Surely he could be of no use. 'Who is this Mr Gibros?'

'A teacher, so he claims. Though perhaps what he is isn't as important,' replied the first woman, as though reading from a book.

'As what he can become. To those who are susceptible,' added the second, as though reading from the same book.

'Another outlook. Helping some to see more clearly,' added the third, aware that she was being enigmatic.

'Those are his words not ours,' added the second, by way of explanation.

'He's a Maronite,' added the first. Marios raised an eyebrow. The Maronites of Cyprus were Levantines originally from the Lebanon. Those Maronites who followed Christ followed the Christ of Rome.

Andonis nodded enthusiastically. He turned to his brother.

'Perhaps we ought to meet this man,' he suggested. Marios rolled his eyes up to heaven. Andonis turned back to the women. 'Do you think Mr Gibros would agree to talk to us?'

'It's his life. The old fool enjoys having visitors. It gives him a chance to recount old stories,' advised the first woman, then all three giggled.

'Do you ever visit him?' asked Andonis innocently. The women appeared a little shocked and no less embarrassed. And then they became defensive.

'An eccentric like Mr Gibros may be a source of comfort to lost sheep, but he's of little consequence to the faithful,' they protested.

Andonis nodded. He was sure now that this Mr Gibros was worth seeing. Before being allowed to take their leave, the brothers were given half a dozen or so fresh figs, which the women had delicately wrapped in a blue napkin.

'Mr Gibros has a sweet tooth,' they explained.

The women gave directions. Before setting off to find the Maronite, the brothers visited the unlikely spring discovered by Saint Andreas the Apostle and stopped a moment to be refreshed by its cool water. For Marios, the spring was a real revelation, confirming that his thirst for true enlightenment might one day be satisfied. For Andonis, the clear, sweet-tasting cascade lapping against his lips reminded him of those snatched moments with Funda on their way to the village well.

When both had had their fill, the brothers headed along a rocky path for an old hut at the edge of a secluded sandy beach.

The man Andonis took to be Gibros was sitting on a wooden bench in front of the hut. He was staring out to sea. He was thin, with dark olive skin, big round eyes, curly black hair, a wild black beard and a huge hooked nose. He looked to be in his early fifties. He was shielded from the sun by a white cloth attached to wooden posts extending from the hut. The cloth fluttered like a sail in the sea breeze. Gibros waved a greeting as he saw the brothers approaching.

'Welcome, my boys. And what have you brought me in that fine blue napkin which I recognise?' he enquired.

'A gift from the women at the monastery,' declared Andonis, presenting the napkin to Gibros, who remained seated. The Maronite grabbed and unfolded it immediately to reveal the purple figs within.

'How wonderful. Delectable figs from those delectable women, may God keep them safe. Some sow and reap, while others eat and bless,' he smiled, offering the figs to the brothers, who both refused. Gibros stuffed a fig whole into his own mouth.

He spoke as he munched, 'They claim they love the Lord up in heaven but what do you think? Perhaps it's me they really worship, down here on earth!'

Marios and Andonis glanced at each other and then back at the Maronite. Both shrugged. Gibros proceeded to devour another fig.

'Perhaps you're right. A mere delusion,' he sighed, but there was still mischief in his eyes.

He beckoned the brothers to sit on the bench with him, shaking hands with each as they did so. Andonis went to speak, but Gibros was quick to get his words in first.

'Can't say I'm not tempted by the old goats though,' he admitted with a smile. 'A cat may age but the claws it had it has!' Then he rolled up the sleeve of his tattered white shirt and presented his bare arm to Marios. 'Feel it.'

Marios hesitated.

'Go on. Feel it!' Gibros commanded, and this time Marios stroked the man's skin.

'See? Flesh! Blood! The juices still flow through me as they do through any man!'

Marios was unimpressed. Gibros stood up, stared out to sea and continued.

'But I've nothing to gain from such liaisons. I learnt all I needed from the female many years ago. And if that wasn't reason enough to avoid her, there's another thing I've had to come to terms with.'

He paused a moment for effect, before adding, 'I've nothing left to teach her.'

Andonis gave Gibros a look to indicate he wasn't quite following. Gibros responded by throwing him a fig which an unprepared Andonis did well to catch. Gibros sat down again and continued.

'Like all foolish young men I thought she alone could give my life meaning. They say one woman's owed to you by God. And so I worked hard to win her heart. And after I'd won it, worked harder still to keep her safe, warm and satiated. And happy too, by presenting her with useless gifts every now and then. In short, I did my damnedest to satisfy all her desires.'

Andonis ate his fig, turned to his brother and smirked. Marios frowned back. He wanted to leave.

'But my desires weren't satisfied. I found myself still thirsting for meaning while she now began to thirst for something else.'

Andonis was a man still thirsting for meaning, and gave an expectant nod. Marios wasn't and didn't.

'I wanted to make sense of this mysterious universe and my place within it. All she wanted was to make babies.'

All three men sitting on the bench sighed for different reasons.

Gibros consumed the last of his figs before continuing, 'Love me like I love you, want me like I want you, for there may come a time when you will want and I will not. No, my boys. A woman has nothing to learn from a man like me that she doesn't believe she knows already. I've no time for such students. And she, may God always look after her, has no time for me.'

Andonis raised his eyebrows. Marios lowered his into a frown.

'And so began my search. Near and far. High and low,' continued the Maronite.

'And did you find what you were looking for?' asked Marios, convinced Gibros hadn't.

'Oh yes,' smiled Gibros. 'I found that it's for the unnecessary things that we sweat and slave and scour the world. And so now I while away the hours, here, near the holy monastery at the very tip of this beautiful island of ours. Seeking harmony with the universal spirit within me. And making time for those who come in search of guidance.'

'Will you make time for us, sir?' asked Andonis. Gibros turned towards Andonis and scrutinised his face. Then he looked back out to sea and gave a deep sigh.

'The question is, are you ready to hear what I have to say? Are you ready to give up your youth?'

Andonis nodded. 'What use is youth when it brings with it such fear and helplessness? Such uncertainty and pain?'

'They say God torments those He loves. You can't avoid this without extinguishing a great deal of what it means to be a mortal creature of God like any other. You want to free yourself from pain? Then you must also relinquish joy.'

Andonis stared out to sea and tried to look where Gibros was looking.

'I've learnt already, sir, that joy is an illusion.'

Gibros boomed with laughter, and nudged Andonis with his shoulder.

'The words of a love-struck fool. It's your childish view of love that's the illusion,' he bellowed. 'When you come to terms with that, you'll learn also that joy and pain are different sides of the same coin. A coin you'll no longer have reason to flip. Make freedom your goal.'

Andonis nudged back.

'Forgive me sir, but my love is all too real. It consumes me. But it's a love that can never run its course. Please help. Help this love-struck fool get through this difficult time. My heart has been drained.'

'My heart has been drained,' mimicked the Maronite with disdain. 'Enough of this. You're making me ill. Free your mind from such transient trivialities. Relinquish to nature and all will be well,' urged Gibros. Then he smiled. 'So, let me guess. She's rich and you're poor.'

Andonis frowned and shook his head. Marios grimaced.

'OK, OK. You're rich and she's poor,' offered Gibros.

Both brothers rolled their eyes skyward. Gibros raised a hand.

'OK, OK. You're both poor and...'

'Now we're getting somewhere,' encouraged Andonis.

'She's a Turk,' intervened Marios, keen to end what he considered to be a pointless charade.

'Ah, now I understand everything,' nodded Gibros. 'And the whole village disapproves. And your families object. And there's lots of tension. But...'

'Well bravo, sir. How did you work all that out?' enquired Marios. His evident sarcasm appeared lost on the Maronite, who ignored him and continued addressing Andonis.

'But you're so love-struck these problems would count for nought if only she were willing to share your dreams. Share your quest for meaning. But how can she? When she's a female; with female weaknesses and female intuitions.'

Andonis nodded and thought of Funda. Marios nodded and thought of Stella.

'You're right, sir. How did you work all that out?' enquired Andonis without sarcasm.

Gibros smiled and swelled with pride. 'Like I said, I spend more time than most thinking, thinking, thinking. You get to understand certain things.'

He patted Andonis on the back.

'And I could tell you more. About your so-called love. About what could and should be. But you're a young man with an open mind, so I cannot. You must acquire knowledge in the natural way. The lid must roll until it finds its pot.'

Then he frowned, and raising his voice addressed Marios.

'You Greeks and Turks. Can't you see you're both the same? Both as bad as each other. Like children. Like cats and dogs. One day you'll learn. Listen to Gibros,' said the man named for Cyprus.

Marios went on the defensive. 'I can't help but wonder, sir, whether you're avoiding giving my brother the advice he needs because you can't. Because all this solitude and self-obsession have cut you off from the real world. Cut you off from love and what it really means.'

In an instant, the face of Gibros was painted with rage.

'Love?' he yelled. 'Let me show you what love can be!'

To the surprise of both brothers, he took out a small bag of dried green leaves and some cigarette papers from his shirt pocket and rolled himself a large and perfect joint.

Marios turned to Andonis and whispered, 'Look at this. The man's a total hashishis!'

Marios tried to get up from the bench, but Gibros pulled him back down. Now Gibros put the joint to his lips and beckoned to Andonis, with thumb springing from fingers, to give him a light. Andonis responded by striking a match. After four long drags, Gibros passed the joint across to Marios who refused it. Gibros shrugged and offered it instead to Andonis, who accepted. Marios tried to intervene, but Andonis pushed his brother away with uncompromising force. Andonis inhaled and his head filled with a new kind of awareness. His mouth pulled on the joint once more, and he began to rock unsteadily. Then he smiled at Gibros and Gibros smiled back.

'Are you inspired? Do you see now?' slurred Gibros, taking the joint back from Andonis and smoking it some more.

Andonis stared out to sea and nodded. He was definitely beginning to see something.

'What you have to understand, my friend, is that in this life there are no straight roads, only clever donkeys,' continued the Maronite.

Marios shook his head and pulled at his brother's sleeve. 'Come on, Andoni. Please. Let's not listen to any more of this nonsense,' he urged, but Andonis was now becoming fully captivated by Gibros's philosophy.

'What do you mean, sir?' Andonis asked.

'Let me tell you a story,' announced Gibros.

Once there was a donkey, a young boy and an old man. And they passed through three villages. At the first village the young boy was on the donkey and the old man was pulling them. The villagers saw the old man, who was sweating, and they said, 'Isn't the young boy ashamed? Having the old man pull them in this heat!'

At the second village the old man was on the donkey and the young boy was pulling them. The villagers saw the young boy, who was sweating, and they said, 'Isn't the old man ashamed? Having the young boy pull them in this heat!'

At the third village the old man and the young boy were carrying the donkey on their shoulders. The villagers saw the donkey, who was resting, and said, 'What a clever donkey!'

'We must go,' insisted Marios.

Though Andonis resisted, the Maronite, with a nod and a wink, encouraged him to acquiesce. Marios had already risen to his feet, and began to walk away. He was praying that his brother would follow. As Andonis got up, Gibros grabbed Andonis's hand and slipped into it the bag of leaves.

'In case you ever need more inspiration,' he advised.

26

The coast   *I baralia*

I boarded the Brighton train and settled in a window seat. I'd overcome my initial reservations about travelling, and was now looking forward to seeing the captain once more. And the sea.

Arriving in Brighton, I was struck by the crisp freshness of the sea air. Though it was as sunny and clear here as it had been in London, it felt a little cooler, and I had to put my jacket back on as I walked along the platform to give up my ticket. And there, beyond the barrier, was the captain. He'd yet to spot me, and his eyes were darting around the station. I laughed at his attire, pale shirt and knee-length khaki shorts. All it took was a glimpse of the sun and the Englezos was dressed for summer. Willing it to come. Then he saw me, and we smiled at each other until I got close enough for us to shake hands.

'Look at you!' I said, regarding him up and down and pinching the material of his shorts as a tailor would. I recalled him wearing similar shorts in the old days when they were part of his uniform.

'All that's missing is your cap, captain,' I teased. The captain nodded with a grin.

'And my revolver to keep unruly peasants like you in order,' he added with a wink.

I grimaced. 'I'm sure the good people of Brighton would object to such a display, especially as they're no doubt already in shock from seeing your bony old knees.'

The captain laughed. Then his face became more serious, and he put his hand on my shoulder.

'I thought you might not come, Tony,' he admitted.

I nodded and looked down to avoid those piercing blue eyes. I was a little hurt, though not wholly surprised, by his lack of faith in me.

We walked south from the station, and arrived at what the captain described as Brighton's famous Clock Tower. We stopped for a moment so I could take in my first clear view of the coast.

The cloudless day made the sea almost blue, though not as blue as the sea I remembered. I noticed all the colourfully decorated shops along West Street, which led down to the seafront. They seemed to offer nothing more than the chance to lose money in penny arcades and fruit machines.

'It's a bit busy and not quite the Mediterranean,' said the captain as I observed. 'But I'm happy to call it home.'

'It seems peaceful enough to me,' I remarked.

'Indeed,' he said, with a knowing smile.

We walked further, down to the beach, and settled at a café on the esplanade for a cold drink.

'So, what do you do down here, captain?' I enquired.

'When the weather's good, like today, I may take tea on the Hove lawns and do the *Times* crossword. Also, I have some friends who run a travel agency near my home. I help them some days, advising holiday-makers on where to go and what to do when they get there. My knowledge of the world comes in handy. You should pay us a visit, Tony. Perhaps I might persuade you to fly away somewhere. Somewhere *really* warm.'

I shook my head dismissively.

'And there's another thing that occupies my time,' continued the captain, and his face reddened a touch. 'I get a lot out of it but you'll probably laugh. I'm involved with the Red Cross. We fund-raise. Street collections, sponsored walks, that sort of thing.'

I did laugh. 'Coming to the rescue, after all those wars you've helped create around the world.'

The captain frowned. 'That's quite enough of that. There are important things you should know,' he said. I shrugged, and he continued. 'The situation in Cyprus. It's getting critical.'

Now he looked at me like a doctor might look at a patient before breaking news of a terminal illness. I remained silent. My lungs filled with sea air, my head filled with a sense of dread.

'How much do you know about what's been going on, Tony?'

'Not a lot,' I conceded. 'I know that since you British gave the island her independence and an unworkable constitution there's been continuing tension.'

The captain nodded. 'Anything else?'

'Not really. The more I hear the more I realise it's best not to. It's like that when you know you're to blame but at the same time you can't put things right.'

'I don't feel that way any more,' advised the captain. 'Perhaps you shouldn't either.'

He suggested we walk to his flat, and we did so in silence, along the seafront, heading west past the pier. The captain bought us both some greasy chips, and we munched as we walked. I was reminded of Andrikos. I much preferred his offerings.

When we reached the lawns, just past a statue of Queen Victoria, the captain announced that we were now in the town of 'Hove actually', and welcomed me to it.

'So explain to me, captain. Is Hove part of Brighton or not? The two seem merged into one.'

'Officially not. There are two town councils, two town halls. Most people never think about it. They just see Hove and Brighton as one place. Brighton. But us Hovians are a funny breed. We believe Hove is a distinguished resort with an identity all its own. When people ask us where we're from, we don't like saying Brighton. So we say "Hove actually". Even our rock says "Hove actually".' He looked embarrassed. 'I expect it sounds silly to an outsider like you.'

I shook my head. 'On the contrary, captain. It makes perfect sense.'

He lived on the top floor of a tall Regency building facing the sea. Only now did I hand over the brown bag from London. He couldn't contain his excitement when he saw what was inside.

'My goodness. I haven't had coffee like this since leaving Cyprus! I'll make us both a cup right now,' he enthused. He wasted no time in ushering me from his hallway into the kitchen, where he grabbed a saucepan and proceeded to prepare coffee in the Cypriot way. The way Vasos must have shown him; like once he'd shown me.

As the captain watched over the stove I wandered into his living room. The window offered a glorious sea view, but I was more interested in the various black and white photographs hanging from the walls. They were of a younger captain I remembered, and other uniformed soldiers. I could tell that a number of photographs, perhaps the majority, were taken in Cyprus. I noted his smile seemed broader in these. One photograph, in particular, caught my attention. It was of a group of bare-chested young soldiers, posing with a football. On a beach I knew.

'The best of times,' noted the captain, returning from the kitchen with a tray, on which were two cups of coffee and two tall glasses of water. I shook my head. He'd used teacups.

'And the worst,' I added, thanking him. I took my first slurp. It was sweet, the way I preferred it. Ghlijis.

'The worst is still to come, Tony.'

I shrugged, and sank into one of two large armchairs. He joined me in the other. I took a long and loud slurp. He did likewise, only louder and for longer. We continued to slurp loudly, in silence.

The coffee appeared to evoke myriad memories within him. I remembered how I'd felt, drinking that same coffee after reading about the death of Vasos.

'Why have you brought me here, captain?' I asked. The captain turned to me and lifted a palm, as though still returning from a pleasant dream and needing a moment to acclimatise. Eventually he smiled.

'Ah yes. I made a promise that I would give you something when I found you. Who'd have thought it would take this long?'

He got up and started rummaging around in a chest of drawers. It took him a few moments to find what he was looking for.

An old brass thimble.

Nothing could have prepared me for this.

He handed it to me and sat back in his armchair. I rubbed the dull metal. My mind was racing uncontrollably.

'What is this?' I asked.

'You're the tailor, aren't you? The finest in the district, you used to say,' replied the captain.

I examined the thimble more closely, as though in it I might see my true reflection.

'Where did you get it?' I asked.

'Come on, Tony. I was there on the night you gave it away, remember?'

Now I found it difficult to utter a coherent string of words in my adopted language.

'You mean? She…'

The captain came to the rescue.

'She gave it to me to pass back to you, if ever our paths crossed. No matter how long it took.'

I shook my head in disbelief. 'I don't understand.'

The captain smiled.

'Don't you? She seemed to think you would. That you'd understand everything.'

'My God, I can't,' I found myself saying. 'What's happening?'

'There are things you need to know, Tony,' continued the captain, and I clasped my ears in an attempt to shut out his words.

'She had a little girl.'

I found myself fighting my instincts, trying to be rational. For a moment I thought of the goatherd…And then I thought of Ruth.

'Why do you tell me these things, captain?'

'You have a right to know.'

'But it does me no good. No good at all. Like when you told me my father died. Did you do it to make me feel better? Because it didn't, captain. It made me feel a lot worse. And now? Now you give me this!' I tried to give the thimble back to him, and it fell into his lap.

'As I said, she asked me to give it to you. It was my duty to do so.' He retrieved the thimble and placed it back into my hand. 'What you do with it now is entirely your business.'

'My business? After so many years? What *can* I do?' I demanded, standing up.

The captain shook his head. 'Well, perhaps you could start by saying thank you.'

His words struck me like a slap across the face. I could feel blood rushing to it. I clenched the thimble so hard the upper rim almost cut into the skin of my palm. I felt no pain. Only deep, deep shame. I reached down and grabbed the captain's bony white hand.

'I'm sorry, captain. I'm grateful. For everything you've ever done for me. You really have been a good friend.'

'I did what I had to do, Tony,' he assured me with a wave of the hand.

'You saved my life,' I said, aware of how dramatic I sounded. 'I'm sure it was against the rules.'

'You were a human being. I was trying to be one too.'

I nodded. 'But it's not your responsibility any more,' I said. 'Let's just let it be. It's over now.'

'I don't think you understand,' he said, and I glared at him. He raised his hand to deflect my objections.

'Listen to me, Tony. This isn't just about the thimble. There are other things you need to know. I'm a retired British army officer, remember? That makes me privy to certain information. And what I don't know I can guess.'

'Meaning?'

'It's not over. This Cyprus thing. There's unfinished business. They're going to partition the island. Slice her in two. And anyone in the way will be sliced with her.'

I stared at the thimble, and he stared too, and while my face remained blank his grew more and more agitated. He grabbed my arm and shook it.

'For God's sake, man, do I have to spell it out?' he screamed. I was shocked. I'd never seen him lose his temper like that before. The captain quickly regained composure and released me, putting his hand on my shoulder.

'She told me she'd always love you, you know. She wanted to protect you. Protect your love.'

I kept staring at the thimble, my face now filled with emotion.

'Funda's daughter,' he continued. 'She's yours, Tony.'

27
The goddess   *I thea*

After the trip to the monastery Andonis was in a calmer mood. Painful thoughts of his lost love had been pushed to the back of his mind. He still loved Funda, of course. Still longed for her. But he now also longed for meaning. Knew that only through the new meaning he'd been offered might he be free from pain.

Marios wanted to be pleased by what he hoped was his brother's improved state of mind, but was finding it difficult. After all, he knew Andonis's transformation was not inspired by his visit to the apostle's monastery but by the unhinged philosophies and dubious practices of a weird Maronite hermit. Marios could only marvel at God's mysterious ways and look forward to a life in His exclusive service.

The tailor decided to throw himself into his work, which meant the captain's suit. The Englezos was due soon for a second fitting, and to deliver the army uniform job. The hours passed, the suit was taking shape, but Andonis could sense his mood changing. The pain was returning. And not just in relation to Funda. When dusk arrived, Andonis realised how much he missed his friend. Loyal, fearless, reckless Nigos. He had often dropped by at around this hour to fetch the tailor and take him to the coffee-shop. But there would be no Nigos at the coffee-shop this evening. And there would be no Funda going to the well tomorrow morning.

All that was over now.

As dusk gave way to night, Andonis felt more and more alone in his workshop. He continued working until eventually the pain and the solitude overwhelmed him. Andonis knew he needed inspiration. He carefully replaced the captain's half-finished suit onto its hanger before feeling for the gift of the Maronite, wrapped in a handkerchief in his trouser pocket.

He consoled himself with the gift. And the gift conjured beautiful visions.

How Andonis loved the perfect image of Funda that arose in his mind. In her name he could put the misguided Nigos and the other outlaws in their place, redirecting all that anger and hatred.

In Funda's name Andonis could see himself joining with all good Cypriots, Orthodox Christians, Muslims, Maronites, Armenians and Latins. He could challenge the Englezi, as once Moses had challenged the Egyptians, to let his people go. And, against the irresistible wisdom inspired by his love for Funda, the mighty rulers of the waves would be rendered powerless. How easy would it then be for Andonis, with Funda at his side, to show his people the way out of the wilderness and into the promised land. And to enter they needed only to open their hearts.

Andonis loved Funda as much as any man had ever loved any woman before. For he knew now that in his love for her was the key to meaning…

✳ ✳ ✳

My darling. You are my goddess of love. All-holy daughter of Uranus, a virgin sent from heaven to bring the gift of life into the world.

Like the most precious of pearls, your love was placed on a shell and gently carried to me by the moist breath of the North Wind. And as the waves broke against the jagged rocks of Cyprus, the foam was fashioned into human form.

And the sea nymphs wrapped you in divine silk. They perfumed you with incense and anointed you with the sacred oil of the gods, to create an effervescent beauty with the power of the ocean.

And upon your head they laid a crown, bejewelled with precious stones. And from the pierced lobes of your ears they suspended ornaments of copper. Round your delicate neck they hung a necklace of pure gold. And round your milky-white hips they placed the embroidered girdle of desire.

Your melodious call entranced all who heard you; your fragrant aroma intoxicated all who breathed you. Your perfect figure captivated all who set eyes on you, and your immaculate flesh beguiled all who touched you. Like the ocean, you beckoned all to come to you. You demanded that all explore you.

And no man could resist your spell. Even the gods themselves wished to possess you. For the love you offered was eternal. But you rejected them all. Like the ocean, you were tempestuous, and sought vengeance against anyone who dared try and conquer you.

And so the maiden of love sought sanctuary. In accordance with ancient rites you sat in the sacred garden waiting for the lonely stranger to claim you. Only he with an open mind, a generous heart and a pure spirit could triumph over those who sought only to control you.

I threw a small offering to you and invoked upon you the name of Afrodhidi, born of the foam. I begged you to share with me your sensuous blessings. We came together like the union of the goddess of fertility with the god of vegetation. You unlocked within me the door to affirmation and self-love, and I in turn released within you the seed of devotion and of honour.

Oh, my goddess of love, let no impediment hinder our path to ecstasy and meaning. Open to me my own true feelings. Spark our beings with the magic of love. Guide our pairing with wisdom, and fill our hearts with tender devotion. Let us dance the love and passion of equals. Radiant, joyous beings, sipping from the cup of eternity.

※ ※ ※

A military truck arrived at the village. It was noisy, and attracted attention. And fear. As it passed through the square, villagers sitting in the coffee-shop speculated nervously on the reason for its presence. The last time the Englezi had come, they'd taken away young men, and with them the spirit of the village. The young men had returned, but the spirit had not.

What would the Englezi take now?

Andonis no longer felt inspired, and after the high of last night's dream came the realisation that Funda's love, and any meaning which came with it, was way beyond reach.

Andonis heard the truck pull up outside his workshop. He made an effort to give the captain's almost finished suit a wipe down with a brush before placing the jacket and trousers on their hanger. Then a subdued Andonis ventured out into the heat to greet the Englezos, who was now descending from the truck. An accompanying soldier had begun unloading box after box of khaki shirts.

'Welcome again to my humble workshop, captain,' said Andonis in a half-hearted effort to be jovial. When he saw the shirts, however, he gave a deep sigh.

'What's the matter, Tony?' pursued the captain with concern.

'You know, captain. The usual problems,' mumbled Andonis. 'Cyprus problems.'

The captain grimaced, and the two made their way inside the workshop.

'Come on. What's put you in this mood?' enquired the captain.

Andonis observed the soldier carrying the first box of shirts into the workshop and frowned.

'Those who bring anger, hatred and division to Cyprus,' he explained.

The captain frowned.

'Oh, I see,' he said. 'All your troubles are the British Empire's fault. You Cypriots really are something. Blame everybody else. Never yourselves.'

Andonis raised a finger. 'Since others make decisions on our behalf. Since others control our destiny, how can we be blamed, captain?'

'No. You're never to blame,' retorted the captain. 'That poor serviceman who was found lying in the road outside the village a while back; none of you are to blame for that either. He must have just accidentally kicked and punched himself to death!'

Andonis turned pale. If the serviceman was dead, Bambos's fate was sealed. And, once they'd caught him, Nigos's too.

'To death?' gulped the tailor.

'That's right, Tony. To death,' confirmed the captain, having taken note of the tailor's reaction. 'We picked up one of the killers. And, you know what? He was a young man, just like you. And before he stands trial he'll tell us the name of his accomplice. Another young man, just like you, no doubt. The ones who are never to blame.'

The captain looked accusingly at the tailor.

'You know what, Tony? If you weren't such a fine tailor I might even suspect you. I trust you have a good alibi for the night in question,' he enquired in a tone that was half serious.

Andonis shrugged. 'Your suit is my alibi, captain. I was working on it until the early hours,' he replied nervously, and thought of Funda. If only he could go back to that night.

The captain gave Andonis a stern look.

'And how about that cheeky, hot-headed friend of yours? Any idea where he was that night? Any idea where he's been since?'

Andonis lowered his head and remained silent. Then he reached over to the nearly finished suit and presented it to the captain.

'I'm your tailor, captain, not your informer.'

The captain admired the suit wistfully for a moment. The way events in Cyprus were unfolding, he might not be getting any leave for a wedding.

'What's wrong with your people, Tony?' he demanded. 'Why do you insist on enosis? You have more freedom under British rule than an Athens government would ever afford you.'

'I know enosis won't work, captain. But with that kind of patronising, I can see why so many of my people are fighting for it.'

The captain nodded. 'Like your missing friend?' he suggested.

Almost imperceptibly, Andonis nodded.

'But not you,' added the captain.

Almost imperceptibly, Andonis now shook it.

The captain nodded, and turned his attentions to the new suit. He tried it on, and Andonis was filled with pride. It fitted perfectly. A few finishing touches and it would be ready for delivery.

※ ※ ※

Andonis sized up the boxes of khaki shirts before him. And there was one smaller box, filled with embroidered army crests for the sleeves and tiny metal insignia for the collars. The tailor picked up a shirt and considered whether he could really do it.

After all, it wasn't a weapon he was being asked to work on, just a harmless item of clothing. Designed to keep the sun off a man's back, to protect his white skin from the foreign furnace into which he'd been dropped. To make him feel part of something, to give him a little more courage, a little more hope as he risked his life in an incomprehensible struggle. Trying to get through troubled times. No different from Andonis. Or Nigos.

Unfortunate young men.

The muhtaris, sitting in his shop, had seen the army truck leave, had been informed soon after where it had stopped and what it had delivered. He had flown into a terrible rage, and marched directly towards the house of Mihalis. One or two villagers at the coffee-shop had been as angry as their muhtaris, and had rushed to march with him, but the muhtaris had turned on them.

'Go back to the communist's coffee, you demons. I've a warning to deliver. All who side against the struggle for liberation will be punished as traitors.'

The muhtaris stormed into the tailor's workshop. He looked at the pile of army shirts with disgust.

'We couldn't believe it so we had to come and see with our own eyes,' announced the muhtaris. Then he looked at the tailor with real venom.

'What are you doing, you filth?' he demanded angrily. 'Have you gone totally mad?'

'I don't know what you mean, sir. Business has been so slow, but there's work here to last me a good while. It would be madness to turn it down,' replied Andonis, riling the muhtaris further. He pointed a threatening finger.

'There are people who won't approve of this. Won't approve at all.'

'People?' countered Andonis. 'Which people are these, sir?'

'Don't play the fool, Andoni. Your friend's cousin is this very minute waiting to be hanged by the Englezi, and here you are in their employ,' he fumed.

'I feel bad for Bambos, sir, but I'm just making a living.'

The muhtaris gestured at the shirts with a contemptuous flick of the head.

'You call that a living, you dog?'

'Forgive me, sir. Perhaps I'm still young and inexperienced in business. Why must politics interfere with honest affairs of trade?' asked Andonis.

'Transforming shirts into the livery of power? Transforming nervous boys into ruthless soldiers, committed to fighting freedom, committed to killing your compatriots? Honest affairs of trade?' demanded the muhtaris.

'I'm a tailor, sir. It's what I was put on this earth to do,' replied Andonis, and as he said the words he became aware that his whole body was trembling.

'You just watch yourself. You hear us?' cautioned the muhtaris, and was gone.

Alone in his workshop Andonis sat down defiantly at his Singer with one of the khaki shirts. Try as he might, however, he couldn't bring himself to start sewing. All he could do was stare at the photograph of his grandmother.

28
The news   *Da nea*

I'd been sitting at my Singer all evening, but hadn't been able to bring myself to start sewing. All I could do was stare at an old thimble my grandmother had once given me. I recalled how she'd done so after witnessing a fierce debate between her son and grandson concerning our conflicting plans for my future.

'Here's your future,' she'd whispered to me when my father's back was turned, slipping the thimble into my hand with a reassuring wink. 'Use it wisely.' How I longed for her guidance now.

I tried without success to imagine a daughter I'd never known. I thought of her mother. And then I thought of another mother with a daughter. A person who might help me make sense of the news I'd had.

I threw on a jacket and headed for the Muswell Hill Centre, hoping Ruth would be working.

I sat on the grass verge across the car park and waited for all the young people to leave. Ravi was among them. His father and a white woman had driven by to pick him up. Ravi looked happier, and waved to me as he got into the car. I smiled and raised a hand. When it was clear all the young people had gone I went over to ring the bell. I was relieved to see Ruth open the door soon after. I could tell she was surprised to see me, though perhaps not pleasantly so.

'Hi Ruth,' I mumbled uncomfortably. I noticed she was wearing a tight red pullover which accentuated her shapely figure.

'Hi Tony,' she replied half-heartedly. 'It's been a while.'

I nodded guiltily. 'How have you been?'

'Getting by, I suppose. And you?'

'Where do I start?'

She raised an eyebrow.

'I know from Dave you've not been back to work,' she noted with a frown. 'And I also know you're not in his good books.'

I rubbed the bristles on my chin and nodded. I'd not been in touch with Dave. In truth, I'd not known what to say.

'But I did what you asked. I wrote to my mother,' I offered with a placatory smile.

She nodded. 'Good. Thank you.'

'No, Ruth. I'm the one who should thank *you*.'

At that moment my eyes strayed down to assess Ruth's bust.

'Do you mind, Tony.'

I could feel myself blushing. 'Please don't take it the wrong way. I was just...'

'You're worse than a teenager!' she rebuked with a knowing smile, now grabbing my arm. 'What am I going to do with you?'

What indeed, I thought as she pulled me inside.

'Was that Ravi's mother I saw, in the car with his dad?' I asked in a bid to divert attention.

She nodded with satisfaction. 'Isn't it wonderful? It looks like they're managing to make a go of it.'

'With your encouragement,' I added, but Ruth raised a hand to brush aside my praise.

'Ruth,' I said with urgency, my eyes now fixed on hers. 'There's something important I must share with you.' She looked apprehensive.

'How about a cup of tea?' she suggested. I nodded, and Ruth led me upstairs to the staff kitchen. She sat me down on a stool by the table before filling a kettle with water and putting it on the stove to boil.

'I'm listening,' she prompted, picking up a couple of teacups from under the sink and putting them on the table. When she'd settled on the stool next to me, I began.

'Do you remember when we were up at Alexandra Palace and you asked whether I wished I had children?' She nodded expectantly. 'Well, it appears I have.'

Ruth stared at me. 'I'm sorry?'

'I'm a father, Ruth.'

She gave me a curious look. 'You're full of surprises, Tony,' she declared, taking an open packet of tea leaves from the table. 'Congratulations. Boy or a girl?'

'Girl,' I replied, somewhat thrown by her flippancy. 'Well, young woman now, I suppose.'

'Oh, and let me guess, you've only just managed to find out.'

I gave a helpless smile. 'That's right.'

'News travels slowly in your family,' she mused, dropping a few spoonfuls of tea into a strainer before resting it on one of the cups. 'So where is she, this daughter of yours?'

'Back in the village, I expect. With…her mother.'

'I see,' said Ruth, picking up the kettle and pouring boiling water slowly through the strainer.

'I'm so confused,' I admitted.

'Me too,' she said, reaching over and pulling out a not-quite-empty bottle of milk from the refrigerator. 'So what happened? Why aren't you with them?'

'It's a little complicated.'

She nodded with resignation before sharing out the insufficient milk equally between the cups.

'It always is,' she mumbled, offering a cup to me. I took my first sip, shuddered and thought of my mother, who would always brew tea in the pot, flavouring it with cloves and sticks of cinnamon.

'We were from different backgrounds, she and I,' I explained.

'Like Ravi's parents,' she suggested with a sigh.

I nodded absent-mindedly, then checked myself.

'So what are you going to do? Will you go back?' she asked.

I observed the steam rising from my cup.

'I don't know. I mean, I don't even know if they're alive. Or if they'd want to see me, after all this time. What do you think I should do, Ruth?'

Ruth shook her head. 'I'm not sure I'm the right person to ask.'

'But I've no one else.'

She shook her head. I could see she was troubled, and I felt a surge of guilt. I put my cup on the table and rose from my stool.

'Perhaps I ought to leave.'

'No, don't,' she said, grabbing my hand to pull me down again. 'You know what? A day doesn't go by without me wishing I could have my daughter's father back.' Then she released my hand. 'But some things just aren't possible.'

I lowered my head and nodded. 'I'm so sorry, Ruth.'

'It's all right, Tony. Really,' she assured, taking another sip of her tea. I did likewise.

'Tell me about life with a daughter,' I asked, and she smiled.

'She keeps me strong. It's bad enough losing her father, without having to worry about her mother falling apart too. I owe it to her to keep busy, to keep my spirits high.'

I nodded.

'Of course she's growing up now, but she still needs to know her mother's OK. That I'll always be there if she needs me. I hope she'll always be there for me too.'

'I know she will,' I assured her. 'You're a wonderful mother. A wonderful person.'

'Enough of that,' she countered. 'I'm nothing special. Just trying to get through difficult times, coping as best I can. I'm being human, Tony. You should try it. You've every reason to now.'

I nodded and felt a surge of happiness.

I asked Ruth if she'd care to have dinner with me that evening, together with her daughter, who I suddenly wanted so much to meet. Ruth rang her from the public payphone at the centre, and we were both pleased when she agreed.

We met Ruth's daughter at the bus stop. She was charming and attractive, as I had known she would be. I felt at ease with both of them. Almost like we were family. On the bus I learnt more about their lives together, and I in turn was able to share a little of what had happened to me in my homeland. They made it easy for me. They seemed to understand.

I took them to a place I knew in Holloway. The waiter greeted us warmly. They in turn were charmed both by him and the atmosphere. The waiter asked how things were with me, and I smiled and told him I was trying to keep busy and my spirits high. I returned his question, and Lugas explained with pride that he was spending more time with his wife and son. I nodded my approval.

Afterwards I walked mother and daughter home from the bus stop. They thanked me for an enjoyable evening, and both gave me an affectionate kiss on the cheek at their door.

✼ ✼ ✼

The following morning I caught the bus to Turnpike Lane, to visit a man I knew could tell me more about what was happening back home. The shopkeeper.

And when he smiled a greeting, I smiled back, and when I made it clear I wanted to have a real conversation, he looked surprised.

'I want to know what they've done to our homeland,' I demanded in the Cypriot vernacular, and he frowned.

'Why blame others, compatriot, when we should look no further than ourselves?'

'What do you mean?' I pressed. 'Gather your thoughts, compatriot, and tell me everything. I've kept away for too long. I'm starved of news. I'm starved of so much.'

As I spoke I began picking items from the shelves at random. Items with which, after all this time, I wanted to be reacquainted. Some gologasin, some sujukos, a bag of gulluragia. I put them on the counter.

'What can I say? The Englezi grudgingly give us independence. Good,' he began. 'The Turks and Christians are to share power. Magarios as president, one of their lot, Kuchuk, as vice-president. Good.'

'Yes, yes. I understand. That's reasonable enough,' I nodded. I grabbed some hallumin, some gubes and some haluvas.

'Yes, but is it reasonable, for example, to have a shared army, sixty per cent Christian, forty per cent Turkish, if Christians are more than eighty per cent of the population and only Christians are obliged to join?' he enquired.

'Who wants to join the army?' I asked, and picked up a packet of Cypriot coffee. I thought of the captain.

'Well, no Turk will. But of course, their politicians can say, "Look. The rules aren't being followed. Our citizens are being treated unfairly." So our lot can say, "OK, we'll change the rules because the balance of power is too high in your favour." And their lot can argue, not without reason, "Look. They want more control to force enosis." Well, we're asking for trouble, don't you think?'

'But is that what our lot still want? Enosis?' I enquired.

'What do you think, my friend?' ventured the shopkeeper knowingly. 'And if you were a Turk, how would you feel?'

I reached inside my pocket and felt for the thimble.

'We ask for trouble, so we get trouble,' he continued. 'Lots of trouble. Between us and them. Between ourselves. Mindless acts of violence? Organised, politically motivated attacks? Who can tell? The effects are what matters. Hundreds of people, hundreds of compatriots, massacred. And thousands more fleeing their villages. Filled with fear and anger.'

I was now shaking with both. I thought of my father. I picked up a packet of haricot beans. I wanted to make fasolia.

'So our lot tear up the constitution, and their lot walk out of government. And our lot say, "Fine, we'll run things alone." Well, we're asking for more trouble, don't you think?'

'So what's happened to our Turks?' I asked, picking up a packet of green lentils. I wanted to make mujendra.

'They reject Christian rule, of course, escape into enclaves, and look to Turkey for protection. Meanwhile, in Greece, a military junta comes to power and is out to grab it in Cyprus too. More violence. More bloodshed. And then Ghrivas comes back to the island, to finish the job he started in the fifties. With, or more likely without, Magarios. But now Ghrivas himself is dead. They buried him upright because he said he couldn't rest until enosis had been achieved. Some enosis we're likely to get!'

'What do you mean? What's happening now?' I demanded.

'What's happening now? For God's sake, my friend. Open your eyes! Read the papers!' he urged.

I looked round for a community newspaper, but he told me he'd sold out soon after they'd been delivered. So hungry were our people for news.

'But this story is bigger than that, my friend. Just look in the papers of the Englezi!'

※　※　※

I was up early the next day. I ate some bread and hallumin for breakfast, and took the short walk along the Broadway and round the corner to the Muswell Hill library.

I made my way to the reference section, sat at a desk, and began to leaf through the day's broadsheets, one by one. Then I asked the librarian for back issues. He disappeared behind the counter for a moment, returning with a large pile of newspapers. He explained that he only kept them for a few weeks, and that his collection might not be entirely complete. I thanked him.

'Are you looking for anything in particular?' he enquired, not I felt in a prying manner but one meant to convey that he was prepared to offer further assistance if he could.

'I suppose I am,' I nodded. 'But don't worry, I'm sure I'll find it.'

He nodded and left me to my research.

I found many references to Cyprus, mainly small news stories tucked away in the international or European sections but also, on occasion, more prominent articles nearer the front, covering Britain's policy and strategic role on the island.

I learnt how Britain had refused to allow America to use its sovereign bases on Cyprus to support the Israeli conflict with Egypt. I learnt of the subsequent frantic efforts to ease the rift between the two western powers through the establishment of a radar installation on the island to enable them both to spy on the Soviet Union. Meanwhile America was gripped by the Watergate scandal and an implicated President Nixon was losing his grip on both power and reality.

I shook my head and tutted loudly, which must have aroused the librarian's interest.

'Found anything of value?' he enquired softly from behind the counter with a look of sympathy. I pursed my lips and shook my head.

I continued my research. I read of how America was trying to safeguard her interests in the eastern Mediterranean by propping up a military dictatorship in the birthplace of democracy. I read of how growing tension between Greece and Turkey over the continuing inter-communal problems in Cyprus, as well as oil exploration rights in the Aegean, was threatening to turn into a full-scale war between the two NATO member states. I read meanwhile of President Makarios's developing relations with the Soviets.

At that moment I noticed that the librarian was hovering over me, so I looked up and raised my eyebrows. He had found more newspapers for me.

'These might be useful,' he offered with a smile which I returned.

I read of warnings from Cyprus that attempts were being made on the life of the president, of how the island's National Guard was now controlled by army officers from Greece. I read of the establishment of the right-wing terror group EOKA B which had resumed the struggle for enosis.

I read and I shuddered, as I realised that the captain and the shopkeeper had been right. This story was no longer merely about an island people not being allowed to live in peace, but one with profound implications for the whole region, if not the world. And the story had a long way to run.

I'd not taken much of an interest in international affairs since coming to England, and of course I'd cut myself off totally from news from Cyprus. I paid what little attention I could muster to domestic issues. Heath and Wilson, Conservative and Labour, right and left, industrial strife, power-cuts, three-day weeks. It was an interest I'd inherited from my father, but it all seemed so irrelevant now. So parochial.

I took the newspapers back to the librarian and told him I was done. He gave me a smile.

'I couldn't help but notice some of the reports you were looking at.'

He paused as though waiting for confirmation from me. None came, so he continued.

'It's just that if you wanted the latest news, you might consider tuning to Radio Moscow or Radio Budapest on long wave. They have a Greek language broadcast late at night. I can get you the frequencies if you wish.'

I nodded to indicate that I did. I was expecting him to look up the information in a reference book, but instead he used the telephone behind the counter. After a short conversation, rounded off with an 'I love you too', he handed me a scrap of paper on which he'd written two radio frequencies.

I found the episode a little puzzling, and my expression must have conveyed as much. The librarian smiled.

'My wife. She's Greek,' he declared proudly. 'From Cyprus,' he continued, innocent of the irony.

'My best wishes to her,' I said warmly, and as I left the librarian to his books I felt for the thimble in my trouser pocket.

On my way back home I managed to get hold of a packet of sugar. I wanted to make myself a proper coffee. Sweet. Ghlijis.

29
The coffee   *O gafes*

Unable to start work on the army shirts, Andonis whiled away the afternoon in his workshop with the last of the gift of the Maronite. Then he decided he needed a cup of coffee, and maybe some advice to go with it. He made his way unsteadily to the village square. It was mid-afternoon, and the coffee-shop was still free of customers. Vasos was there though, sitting outside under the shade of the carob tree, reading a newspaper. And old man Haji-Markos was there next to him, dozing in his chair.

Vasos waved a greeting to the tailor.

'Welcome, Andoni. I hope our finest tailor is well on this finest of days,' he enquired warmly, looking over his paper with a smile.

'I survive, Mr Vaso. Though I'm a little troubled by the attitude of some of our fellow villagers,' replied Andonis.

Vasos put his paper down and gave the tailor a look of solidarity. 'Why so, my son?' he asked.

'They disapprove of my customers,' explained Andonis. Vasos gave a sympathetic nod. Then he raised himself, reached up and pulled down two ripened black pods from a branch of the carob tree. He handed one to the tailor. Both men snapped at their respective pods and sucked at the sickly-sweet syrup as it trickled out. The syrup had never tasted so good to Andonis.

'When I had that problem, you know what my babas did?' offered the coffee-shop owner, nodding over to his sleeping father.

Andonis shook his head.

'He invited those who objected to take their objections elsewhere,' continued Vasos, then added with a wink. 'But you know what, Andoni? They never did.'

Andonis nodded, took comfort from Vasos's words, and smiled.

'Your coffee has a special hold on the people,' declared the tailor. Vasos nodded and gave a deep sigh. Then he grabbed Andonis's arm.

'Come then. Let's make you a cup now, and I'll show you how I keep everyone on my side.'

Vasos led Andonis inside the coffee-shop and through to the kitchen. There he scooped two spoonfuls of ground coffee and two of sugar into a small glass before adding a little water. He stirred vigorously until the mixture had dissolved fully.

'This ensures we get the richest and smoothest of heads,' advised Vasos before half-filling his jisves with water. Now he put the jisves on the stove.

'The trick is to heat your water slowly and add your mixture bit by bit,' explained Vasos. The pot came to the boil, and the coffee-shop owner added his mixture, bit by bit.

'Now for the real trick, Andoni, and for this I must swear you to complete secrecy.'

The tailor smiled and nodded acceptance. Vasos took down a bottle of zivania from a shelf above the stove. Vasos's zivania was home made, as was all zivania, a pure and potent spirit distilled from the pips and skins of grapes. As the mixture rose and rolled in from the sides of the jisves, Vasos winked at Andonis and added some.

'Only a splash mind, to ensure the coffee flavour isn't impaired. Of course, if I'm making a cup for our esteemed priest I always add a little extra!' confessed Vasos. Andonis smiled broadly. It had been a while since he'd done that.

Vasos poured the brown mixture into two tiny cups, and also filled two tall glasses of water. He put them all on a tray, and carried them outside.

The two men sat at the table under the carob tree and slurped together, loudly and with satisfaction. Old man Haji-Markos was still asleep in his chair, and was now snoring.

'I can't imagine life without your coffee,' mused Andonis, turning to Vasos with sad eyes.

Vasos shook a finger at the tailor.

'But there are other coffees, my son. I have it on good authority that in England they make it instantly, pouring boiling water over processed coffee powder which dissolves in the cup. They call it neskafes. A good thing if you're in a hurry, I'd say.'

'But coffee should never be rushed, Mr Vaso. Half the enjoyment is anticipating its arrival. And yours is always worth the wait,' exclaimed Andonis with a wink.

Vasos smiled knowingly before continuing. 'And in Italy they have a coffee called espressos which is not dissimilar to ours but less grainy, and without the troublesome sediment at the bottom.'

'But that's what makes your coffee so wonderful, Mr Vaso,' countered Andonis between sips. 'We savour every last drop of quality, carefully avoiding the unwanted bit at the end. A coffee without sediment is…is like a grape without the pips!'

'That's a good one,' laughed Vasos. 'The Italians have another type of coffee they call gabuchinos, made with creamy milk which is frothed up with steam until it's like the head of a shaken beer.'

'I want a strong drink, sir, not milky air,' insisted Andonis. 'And yours is the best in the world, there's no doubt. That blend of bitter ground coffee and sweet sugar. Perfection itself.'

Vasos revelled in the tailor's praise, but then checked himself and stared into his cup.

'Of course, there are some who insist on coffee that's plain, Andoni. Sketos. Without sugar.'

Andonis nodded. 'Bitter people. Denying themselves the sweet pleasures of life, Mr Vaso. Why, a coffee without sugar is…is like our village without its Muslims!'

Vasos gave Andonis a knowing look.

'Am I right in thinking there's one particularly sweet Muslim without whom our village would be a less pleasurable place?'

Andonis sighed and thought of Funda. 'Aren't all honest Muslims worthy of comradeship?'

'Indeed,' Vasos nodded, 'although I'd urge caution. Our Muslim brothers are a rare breed. Those not of Ottoman stock are converts who turned their back on the Church to avoid taxation and persecution.'

'Meaning?'

'Meaning they're descended from those of us less hampered by convictions. People who in troubled times will do what's necessary to get by, for an easier life. It's not a bad trait, Andoni. I only mention it so that you take care not to put too much trust in someone who may end up letting you down.'

Andonis nodded, and tears welled in his eyes. The coffee-shop owner was a wise man indeed.

'Dear Mr Vaso. What do you think I should do?' implored the tailor.

'It may be best for you to leave this village. Leave this island. Make a new life for yourself away from all this madness. You can always take some coffee with you.'

'But no one makes coffee like you do,' noted Andonis, before draining his cup of any liquid worth consuming.

'My coffee may not be around for ever,' explained Vasos before doing likewise. 'Like the Turk, the communist turned his back on our Church too, remember? But it wasn't for an easier life. And life gets harder and harder for people like me in Cyprus.'

A depressing silence descended over them. Even old man Haji-Markos was now breathing quietly in his sleep. It was the coffee-shop owner who spoke next.

'Shall we have a bit of fun?' he suggested with a mischievous glint in his eye. Andonis merely shrugged. Vasos gestured to the tailor to turn the remains of his cup of coffee upside-down in the saucer. The tailor did so.

'You know what I believe, Andoni?' announced the coffee-shop owner. 'I believe the future's what we want it to be. And that if we all work collectively for the common good, we can't help but get there. My superstitious wife, however, is convinced that our future's in this here sediment. Let's see whether she can point us in the right direction.'

'Fine. Wherever the coffee leads, I'll gladly follow,' declared Andonis, grateful for an opportunity to forget his troubles.

Anjela's coffee-sediment-reading ability was well known amongst the women of the village, who often used her services to speculate over which thin men might be bringing bad news or which fat women might be bringing good news. The menfolk were less inclined to admit an interest. The Church warned that reading coffee sediment was the devil's work, while the leftists warned that fortune-telling was no different from God or Satan, each an equally irrelevant superstition.

Vasos cupped a hand to his mouth and called for his wife. Then he called again, only louder, when she had not emerged immediately. From inside the coffee-shop a woman's voice could be heard.

'All right, I'm coming, sir. I'm coming,' she balled. As Anjela waddled out, she saw the tailor sitting there with her husband.

'Your health, Andoni,' she said with a warm smile.

'Your health, Mrs Anjela,' he replied.

'Come sit with us, woman,' instructed Vasos. 'Andonis wants to know his future, so we need a witch to read what's in his cup.'

Anjela wagged a finger at her husband.

'Don't mock me, Vaso. You know as well as I do that it's a gift,' she admonished, then turned to the tailor. 'I've been reading coffee cups since I was a little girl, and I've never been wrong!' she declared.

Anjela sat next to her husband, who pushed Andonis's upturned cup towards her. She raised it carefully from the saucer, allowing all the loose sediment to fall out before bringing the cup to her face for a closer look. Her eyes became transfixed, and Andonis felt uneasy.

'So? What do you see?' pressed the coffee-shop owner. She shook her head slowly, but her eyes gave nothing away.

'Well, Mrs Anjela?' urged Andonis.

Anjela remained silent.

'Come on, woman,' commanded her husband.

'I see froth, foam,' she said eventually.

Vasos scoffed. Anjela ignored him.

'I see someone leading something, someone away…' She paused before adding, 'He must take care.'

Andonis rolled his eyes upwards. Despite the two men's pleas and protestations, Anjela would say no more.

✳ ✳ ✳

Andonis became conscious. He found himself slumped over a table outside the coffee-shop, nursing a throbbing head.

'God help me,' he slurred, trying to focus on Vasos, who was collecting cups and wiping down tables.

It had been Vasos's idea initially for them both to have a glass of zivania. The coffee-shop owner had seen the effect Anjela's enigmatic reading was having on Andonis, and wanted to help lighten the troubled tailor's mood. But after knocking back his first glass, Andonis insisted he be given another. And then another. Vasos didn't have the heart to refuse him.

Soon after, other men of the village, and some from beyond, had arrived at the coffee-shop, bringing with them news that Bambos had been hanged. Some villagers had glanced disapprovingly at the red-cheeked tailor. One or two had even tried to give him a tongue-lashing for accepting work from the enemy.

By this stage an intoxicated Andonis had told them all to go to the devil, which made them angry. Vasos tried to intervene, and advised Andonis to calm down, but Andonis told him to go to the devil too. At that moment Andonis fell asleep in his chair, and was soon snoring loudly. People couldn't help but laugh, and Vasos was relieved that trouble had been averted.

That was a while ago. Now all Vasos's customers had gone home to their beds, and it was time for a dazed Andonis, who had just opened his eyes, to do likewise.

'Ah, good. You're awake at last,' announced the coffee-shop owner with a smile. 'Come on. Away with you. And don't forget to take care. There's a curfew.'

Andonis nodded and rose unsteadily to his feet. He stumbled out into the square and headed into the night. A few yards from the coffee-shop Andonis sensed that he was being followed. He turned and saw the outline of two men. Who were they? What were they doing out at this hour?

He thought to run, but his legs wouldn't respond.

He took a deep breath before turning to face his pursuers. As he did so a fist immediately crashed into his face. Before Andonis could adjust to the pain, another fist struck his jaw. Instinctively Andonis raised his hands to protect his head from further blows. Then he was struck a third time, in the stomach, making him double up in pain. He was pushed over onto the ground, where he curled up and started groaning in agony.

'Scream out and we'll finish you,' whispered one of the men venomously. Both were now kicking him relentlessly. He felt heavy blows against his shins and into his back. He also took a brutal kick in the forehead, and soon after felt blood trickling into his eye.

When they saw they had drawn blood, the men stopped, and Andonis was relieved. They didn't mean to kill him. Only to warn him.

'Take care,' whispered one of the men.

'The next intervention will be your last,' added the other.

The two men disappeared into the darkness, leaving Andonis bleeding in the dust, with only an orchestra of cicadas for company.

✳ ✳ ✳

The cockerels had jolted Andonis back into consciousness. He sensed that he was out in the open air. He became aware of the hard dusty ground against the side of his face and body. He felt a throbbing in his head and countless bruises all over his body. He sat upright, and now felt nauseous. Soon women would be passing on their way to the well for water. He had to get himself home before anyone saw him.

When Andonis staggered into the bedroom, he roused his brother from sleep. Marios was shocked to see the state of his brother. Andonis's shirt was covered in dust, boot-marks and drops of blood. His forehead was cut.

'My All-Holy Virgin, what happened to you?' cried Marios, though not too loudly, so as not to wake and alarm their parents. The tailor shrugged.

'Look, Mario. Look what they've done to your brother!' he slurred.

Marios shook his head as many truths were revealed to him. He felt sure now what was meant by Saint Varnavas the Apostle's interventions. This act of violence on Andonis had to be the priest's final and most valuable lesson. Marios knew now that it was time for his direct relationship with God to begin. For only then could he hope to protect his family, without a middle-man to interfere with his prayers.

'Forgive me,' pleaded Marios, falling out of bed and kneeling before Andonis. He clasped his hands and lowered his head in shame. 'I'm the one who's brought this evil deed upon you. I prayed for it for my own selfish ends.'

Andonis found his brother's confession amusing. He tried to laugh, which made his bruised back ache. This in turn made him splutter for breath.

'Better stop all this praying, Mario. You'll end up killing me.'

'Please, Andoni. Don't mock me. I feel so guilty. All this has happened so that I might be recommended to the monastery at Jikos.'

Andonis was disturbed to see his younger brother's strange reaction, and felt obliged to offer words of comfort.

'Don't trouble yourself further. Never forget. For the love of God, all is permissible.'

Marios nodded. 'You must clean yourself up. We can't let mamma see you like this. Or babas. There's no telling what he might do.'

✳ ✳ ✳

Marios had got out of bed, dressed, and to his father's surprise and gratitude, announced that he would not be going to church that morning but accompanying him for a day in the fields. A day for digging up potatoes. A day when more than one pair of hands was needed.

'We should ask your brother to come too,' suggested Mihalis, making his way towards the brothers' bedroom. But Marios stood in his father's way and explained that Andonis had other important work to do today, and needed his sleep.

Some hours later, Andonis prised open his eyes and was blinded by the sun's rays streaming in through the window. He cursed himself. He'd wasted the whole morning asleep. He wanted to finish the captain's suit.

Andonis could feel his whole body aching. He tried to stretch, but the pain was too great. Slowly and deliberately he pulled himself out of bed. He gasped as he tried to manoeuvre himself to cause the least discomfort. There was pain all over his body. And in his heart.

He washed, dressed and hobbled out to his workshop. He looked over to the pile of untouched khaki shirts and shook his head. He resolved to ask the captain to take them all back. He couldn't do this job. And if the captain asked why, Andonis would point to the cut on his forehead.

He picked up the iron, opened the lid, and emptied the ash from inside. He filled it with fresh charcoal, which he then lit. When the charcoal glowed red, he would take the dark grey jacket from its hanger, place it on the work-top, and press it.

It would be agonising work.

✳ ✳ ✳

It was a wash day. Irini and the widow were in the front yard of Mihalis's house, bent over a round metal tub scrubbing at clothes with green bars of soap.

Earlier Irini had sprinkled ash into the water, which was then heated in the tub over a fire of small pieces of wood. The ash softened the water so that a rich lather could form, enabling the women to slide the soap effortlessly against the cotton fabric.

They scrubbed in silence.

First Irini had gone about washing Andonis's shirt. She'd rubbed away the black boot-marks, coaxed out all the red dirt, removed the dry blood stains. She'd scrubbed and scrubbed until no trace remained of the acts of violence committed against her son.

But though the shirt was now free from blemishes, Irini's worry remained. The widow sensed this worry, and though she was sympathetic she was also glad of the company. Andonis was in danger, there was no denying that. But so was Nigos. Only more so.

The widow broke the silence.

'You're the lucky one, Irini. You still have your husband and both your sons,' she remarked, gesturing at the tailor's shirt, now rolled into a tight white ball, waiting to be hung out in the sun to dry. There was a hint of resentment in the widow's tone, which Irini detected and resented in turn. 'Whereas my blessed husband's lost,' continued the widow, looking up to heaven. 'And only God knows where my Nigos is or when I'll see him again. And we all know what the Englezi will do if they catch him. Look what they did to Bambos!'

Both women shuddered.

'I realise my situation's nothing compared to yours, Xenu, but how can that ease my worry? I'm a mother. My child's in danger.'

The widow nodded. The eyes of both women met, both pairs filling. They embraced, neither caring that the other had soaking wet, foam-covered hands.

'We must be grateful for small mercies,' the widow advised soothingly. 'At least your Marios will be safe. Now that he's entering the monastery at Jikos. And my Yannis will soon be wed to Martha.'

'Praise to God,' Irini agreed, and both women crossed themselves. Both women were momentarily comforted.

Meanwhile Eros was helping to distract the women, darting about the tub, chasing soap-suds and dodging splashes.

'Stay away from my clean clothes, you dirty dog, or you'll be next in the tub,' warned Irini with a smile. She held up her bar of soap in one hand, began rubbing it up and down with the other and licked her lips. 'And I'll scrub that cucumber of yours so hard, I swear there'll be nothing left!'

The widow smirked a moment, then quickly remembered herself.

'Hush, Irini, with such talk, or God will surely find cause to punish us,' she chastised.

'You hush yourself!' retorted Irini, splashing the widow with foam. 'What's the point in washing if we're not allowed to be a little dirty too?'

Both women fell silent again, scrubbing with renewed vigour. Finally their sulking was interrupted by the loud shrieks of approaching children. Irini looked up, and recognised two young boys of the village coming along the road, chasing a small lizard with sticks. It was Yoda's young sons.

'Kill! Kill! The Englezos is getting away,' cried one.

'Don't be afraid. The battle will be won. For I am the famous Yorghos Ghrivas, leader of Eoga,' assured the other.

The boys swung their sticks, but the lizard eluded them, and only the red dust of the road received their blows, wafting into the air like wisps of smoke. The widow observed the boys as they drew nearer, and tutted.

'The holidays haven't started yet, Irini. Shouldn't they still be in school?'

'All the schools are shut, Xenu,' explained Irini. 'Governor's orders.'

The widow huffed. 'May the governor have my curse. What right has he to shut our school?'

'Because the governor wants the Greek flag to be taken down from the classrooms, and the teacher refuses.'

The widow raised her hands in a gesture of helplessness. 'What madness is this, Irini?' she asked.

'Eoga orders the flag up, and no one dares argue with Eoga. So the flag stays up and the school stays shut,' huffed Irini.

'How can a piece of blue and white cloth upset everyone so much?' asked the widow. She gave Irini a look of bewilderment to show that she couldn't fathom the actions of the governor, nor the teachers, nor indeed the organisation her son had run off to join. It was a look which invited Irini to reciprocate, to show solidarity.

But Irini merely shrugged and resumed her work. She reflected a moment. 'England doesn't want her step-children weaned onto another mother's milk.'

The widow nodded, but then raised a disapproving finger.

'But a mother who won't let her children progress is unworthy of the name.'

Irini frowned. 'How can the children progress when our teachers are too scared to teach? When all they can do is wash young brains with ancient stories of ancient glories?'

'Children need to learn their history,' remarked the widow.

The boys in the road were still within earshot, and continued to torment the lizard.

'Forward, brave Eoga warriors. We must smash the enemy,' declared one.

'I follow you. We'll deliver Cyprus to our beloved mother. We'll rid ourselves of these Englezi and their Turkish dogs,' added the other.

Irini glanced at the widow and raised her eyebrows.

'It's not history they've been learning, Xenu,' she announced. 'It's hatred.'

The women heard the sound of a vehicle approaching. The boys turned and looked to see who it was, and once they had seen, dropped their sticks and fled in the opposite direction. Today was not a day for being real heroes. The women exchanged nervous glances. Only one thing could inspire such panic in the children of the village.

The army jeep came to an abrupt halt outside the front yard. Two young soldiers in red berets descended.

'Christ and my All-Holy Virgin! What do they want from us now?' cried the widow, wiping her wet hands on her apron.

Irini, however, carried on with her washing.

'Stay calm, Xenu. We've nothing to fear. We've done nothing wrong.'

Irini was not comforted by Eros's response. Normally he was happy to greet guests with angry growls, but this time he sensed real danger and could only cower behind the tub.

The soldiers marched into the yard. Englezos number one removed his beret.

'Good morning to you, ladies,' he said pleasantly.

'What does he say, Irini. What does he say?' demanded the widow. Her voice was bordering on hysterical, and both soldiers grinned at each other.

Irini breathed in and pushed out her still firm bosom as a gesture of defiance.

'No speak English,' she announced, only just in the tongue of the soldiers.

Englezos number one stared back lecherously, then rubbed his chin. Irini noted that the young man's face was completely smooth, not due to shaving but through lack of any discernible growth.

'Skeelo,' said the soldier. 'We want skeelo.'

'What's he say? What's he say?' demanded the widow.

'I think the asprogolos means wood. Xilon,' suggested Irini, in an attempt to calm her distraught friend. Irini now bent down to pick some uncharred twigs from the fire underneath the tub and offered them to the soldier, who shook his head angrily, pushing them away. The twigs fell to the floor.

'You stupid bitch. It's your dog I'm after. Skeelo! Why can't you speak English?' demanded Englezos number one.

Irini slapped her cheek with her hand.

'By God, I can't understand you, you demon!' she yelled.

Now Englezos number two stepped forward.

'Come on ladies. Where's that beautiful little doggy?' he enquired politely.

As he drew nearer, he caught sight of Eros, curled up behind the tub. Carefully, he crouched down, grabbed hold of one of the dog's front legs and pulled the animal towards him. Eros released a terrified yelp. Irini was now in shock. She knew what they had come for. Her dog. Her shhillos.

'Easy, boy,' said Englezos number two, wrapping his arms round Eros before standing upright. He turned and carried the dog away. Eros managed to free his head, and stretched over the man's shoulder to give his mistress a look of despair. Irini observed helplessly, her eyes now pools of water.

'That's our dog, sir. Our dog, I tell you!' she pleaded in her own language, but the soldiers had already retreated from the yard and were now getting back into the jeep. The engine roared, and a moment later the vehicle, the soldiers and Eros had disappeared in a cloud of red dust.

Irini grabbed her head with soapy hands, coating her hair in white foam. The widow tugged at Irini's dress.

'They've taken Eros, Irini. Do something!' she screamed.

'What can I do? Tell me? What can I do?' retorted Irini.

A devastated widow dropped to her knees.

'My All-Holy Virgin. They've stolen Eros. The stinking Englezi criminals. May they have one thousand and two of my curses. May Eoga kill each and every one of the red-haired devils.'

Irini dropped next to the widow. 'They go too far, these Englezi. They go too far.'

The women embraced. The widow was wailing uncontrollably, and Irini noticed tears were rolling freely down her own cheeks. And with their grief came a shared dread.

'What will I tell Mihalis?' muttered Irini between sobs.

✳ ✳ ✳

Andonis, with his good command of English, had charmed his way into the British army base. The young tailor was known to some of the guards after his previous visit. Now he burst into the captain's office, cursing at the annoying private who was trying to prevent his entry. The captain's initial reaction was that of outrage at being disturbed with such insolence. This soon passed, however, as he recognised the angry young Cypriot, holding a large brown parcel and struggling to free himself from Williams's clutches.

'Tell this barbarian to let go of me!' screamed Andonis, now getting the better of the less athletic guard. The captain's anger had turned to amusement and also admiration. Andonis had somehow managed to place the guard's head in an arm-lock.

'My apologies, sir,' gasped Williams, addressing the captain. 'He just pushed through before I could stop him. Says he's a tailor with a suit to deliver. But who knows what's inside that parcel? It could be a bomb.'

Andonis looked at the captain and grimaced.

'Request permission to shoot him,' added Williams, in no position to shoot anybody.

'Request you shut up,' threatened Andonis, tightening his grip, and making the guard moan with pain. The captain glared at the tailor, and noted with concern, and not a little professional curiosity, the cut on his forehead.

'How dare you barge into my office like this and manhandle my staff,' he said curtly.

'I'll break his neck, sir. See if I don't,' vowed the angry young Cypriot, extracting more moans from Williams.

'I can't allow that, Tony,' cautioned the captain. 'You're of no use to anyone dangling from the end of a rope.'

He then addressed the red-faced Williams. 'It's all right, Williams. I'll take over now. Thank you.'

'Are you sure, sir?' spluttered Williams.

'Quite sure,' replied the captain. 'This man is indeed my tailor. He gets a bit passionate about his work.' He gestured to the Cypriot to release his man. Andonis did so.

'Very good, sir,' said a relieved Williams, now trying to straighten himself out. Andonis turned him around and pushed him out of the door.

'I'll be outside if you need me,' advised the guard. 'Just say the word and he's a dead man,' he added, tapping his revolver in its holster.

'Thank you, Williams, but that won't be necessary,' assured the captain. Williams nodded and pulled the door shut behind him.

Now the captain turned to the Cypriot. His face displayed a cold anger. 'You stupid fool. You're lucky to be alive!'

'Am I?' screamed the angry tailor, throwing the parcel to the floor.

'Have you gone totally mad, man?' demanded the captain, slapping his desk. There was a teapot on it, which jumped. There was also a rattling fan, which now moved precariously close to the edge.

'Too right I go mad, captain. Mad! Mad! Mad!' retorted Andonis slapping the desk repeatedly to punctuate his words. The fan dropped to the floor. The captain launched himself from his chair.

'Will you calm down or, so help me, I'll shoot you myself!' he fumed, making as if to withdraw his revolver.

'Go on then, shoot! Kill me now. For I no longer wish to live under British rule,' retorted Andonis, and breathed in deeply to expand his chest and offer the captain a bigger target.

The captain reflected a moment, then shook his head. He stooped and placed the fan back on the desk, before sitting down and pouring himself a cup of tea.

'Fancy one?' he enquired, and Andonis shook his head. The captain took his first sip, the tea seeming to calm him. 'What happened to your head?'

'Don't worry about that, captain,' replied Andonis. 'Worry about who's going to finish off your precious army shirts, because I'm afraid it won't be me!'

'What is all this, Tony?' asked the captain.

'This,' announced Andonis, taking out a five-shilling note from his pocket, the down-payment for the suit, and throwing it at the captain, 'is this.' The captain shrugged, to indicate he hadn't understood.

Andonis continued, 'You steal with one hand, give back with the other, then steal again with the first. And like fools we fall for it. But no more, captain. No more. Take back your shirts. And take back your thirty pieces of silver.'

The captain picked up and examined the note, before shaking his head. 'I recall we agreed a fair price for your tailoring services. What's the problem now?'

'What's the problem? You English are the problem! You're always the problem. Two of your thugs in red berets came by the village this morning and snatched our dog. They make my mother cry. She's put on black like she's lost a son. And my father is a broken man. Eros was his pride and joy.'

The captain frowned and took a second sip of tea. 'I don't believe this, Tony. Our men are being butchered by EOKA terrorists, the situation's spiralling out of control, and you come to me about a dog?' he enquired.

'I thought maybe you'd understand, captain. I'd heard you English were a nation of animal lovers.'

The captain clasped his hands, and spoke with only a hint of regret.

'Look, Tony. I'm really sorry to hear of your family's loss, but what do you expect me to do? I can't be held responsible for the actions of one or two unruly servicemen. There must be upwards of twenty thousand troops stationed on this island.'

'That's twenty thousand too many,' yelled Andonis. 'I've heard you like our sayings, captain. Well here's one: "A fish rots from the head". You and your troops could learn from that.'

The captain took a third sip, and shook his head.

'Get over it, Tony. These things happen,' he said, and looked down at his papers to indicate that important army work beckoned.

Andonis refused to take the hint.

'But these things always seem to happen to us,' insisted the tailor. 'So we come to the captain, the man who supplies, and ask him to track down our dog. Five shillings is a fair price for your services, don't you think? And what's more, you at least can be sure it's money earned honestly.'

The captain took another sip and looked back up at the Cypriot.

'Officers of the British army have more important things to do than go in search of missing dogs.'

'Really? Like what? Searching the hills for EOKA terrorists?'

'Indeed,' agreed the captain. 'Amongst other things.'

'Only they're not terrorists, captain. They're no different from me, no different from my father. Simple men. Of honour and principle. Fighting for freedom. Fighting for what's been stolen from them,' added Andonis. He clenched a fist and shook it at the captain.

'You know what, captain? You asprogoli really make me sick,' he declared before turning to leave. The captain tapped his desk.

'Wait,' he called. Andonis turned back, and the captain got up and pressed the five-shilling note back into the Cypriot's hand. Then he reached down, pulled out the completed suit from the brown bag, and admired the tailor's handiwork.

'I'll do what I can,' he assured, taking out his wallet and counting out some more notes for the tailor as full payment for the suit. Then the captain retook his seat. 'Pull a few strings if I'm able.'

Now he raised a hand to indicate that it really was time for the Cypriot to go.

'Thank you, captain. It's important. For all our sakes,' advised the Cypriot before leaving.

Alone in his office, the captain drained his cup of tea and was filled with sadness. Where would all this anger and violence lead?

30
The coup   *Do braxigobiman*

Arriving back to my room from the library, I put the radio on. I was waiting for the time when I could retune my wireless to the appropriate station and receive more up-to-date news.

As it transpired, I wouldn't need to. The news on Radio 4 was talking about Cyprus. My little island was on the BBC!

Makarios is dead, they were announcing. Makarios-is-dead.

That morning, while his beatitude was entertaining a group of schoolchildren from Egypt in the presidential palace, tanks had burst through the main gates and started pounding the walls with shells. The palace guards had stood their ground, but after a few hours they had been overwhelmed, and the palace had been set ablaze. There were reports from a capital city in a state of disarray, with soldiers and armoured vehicles, sirens and explosions. Forces loyal to Makarios were rising up to resist the coup d'état orchestrated by the fascist junta in Greece and carried out by the extremist madmen of EOKA B. The island faced a bloody civil war and, I knew, much, much more.

I took out the harmonica Ruth had given me and placed it to my lips. I found myself playing the music to an ode to liberty which an old departed friend had once demanded I play. I played with irony. It was another country's national anthem.

Then I rolled myself a cigarette. A strong one. So others controlled the destiny of my homeland. What had changed? Nothing. Except I had a daughter. So another tragedy was about to befall my people. What was new? Nothing. Except I was a father.

My own father had once told me that when I was older, with children of my own, I'd see things differently. I took a long drag of my cigarette. Now at last perhaps I could. A woman, pregnant with a child I now knew to be mine, had once told me she had to learn to endure. I took another drag. Now at last I too would have to learn.

I thought of Ruth. Life was cruel and unfair, but she'd found a way to keep going, to keep strong. I thought of the captain. He was retired from the army, but he too had found a way to keep going, to keep up the fight. They had shown that there could still be hope and meaning, and now more than ever I needed that hope and meaning. I felt for the thimble in my pocket, took another drag of my cigarette, and prayed I might be filled with both.

31

The olive tree *I elia*

When, unexpected and unannounced, a bearded Nigos had appeared at the workshop early one sweltering morning, the tailor was overjoyed. He was also a little concerned, as Nigos had seen the pile of untouched khaki army shirts and frowned. Nigos didn't even look at his brother's suit, now finished and on its hanger, awaiting collection for the forthcoming wedding.

Nigos had crept into the village the night before, to visit his mother. He'd come to have a bath, to have his clothes washed, to have his belly filled, and to feel more human again.

Now he'd come for Andonis. Nigos had orders to report to the muhtaris for details of an important mission. A mission which, it had been decided, would involve the tailor.

Andonis went to embrace his friend, but Nigos stepped back and gave the tailor a cold stare. Nigos had no time for such childish displays of affection. Not now he'd grown a beard and slept under trees with his new comrades. Not now he hunted rabbits and birds. Not now he accepted gifts of food from supportive villagers from around the district. Not now he'd learnt how to use guns and make bombs. Not now he had turned into a ruthless fighter.

Nigos looked at the cut on his friend's forehead and nodded.

The tailor was both confused and concerned when Nigos instructed that they should go to the shop of the muhtaris. Andonis nevertheless agreed and promised he would follow in a short while. First he wanted to pack the shirts back into their boxes for the Englezi to come and retrieve.

'Come soon,' Nigos urged.

※ ※ ※

Nigos arrived at the shop of the muhtaris, and was ordered to bolt the door.

'Where's Andonis?' snarled the muhtaris, who was sitting at his table. He eyed the young man sternly, in a way meant to convey that the tailor's absence indicated a lack of obedience on Nigos's part. Nigos raised his eyebrows.

'Stay calm, sir. Andonis will be here soon,' he replied, and was surprised at himself for not being intimidated by the muhtaris, as once he would have been. Nigos had changed. He was used to the company of really fierce men. 'He's just finishing off at the workshop.'

'It's he who'll be finished off,' warned the muhtaris, before beckoning Nigos to approach him. Nigos did so with head held high. The muhtaris couldn't help but be impressed by the young EOKA warrior.

'Tell us, Nigo. How is life in the hills?'

Nigos felt himself swell with pride.

'I can't tell you how tough it is, sir. Living from day to day. On your wits. In fear of being captured by the Englezi. But I also can't tell you how good it is finally to be free.'

The muhtaris nodded. 'And we can't tell you how much we envy you. How much we wish we could join you. If only…' he hesitated, 'if only we were younger.'

'You have important work to do here in the village, sir,' noted Nigos, and looked around at the jars of olive oil, at the packets of rice and macaroni. The face of the muhtaris reddened.

'So, you visited your poor mother last night?' he enquired, in a bid to regain some authority. The EOKA warrior nodded. 'Good,' continued the muhtaris. 'Your visit will have comforted her.'

Then, after a pause, the muhtaris asked accusingly. 'Is it true your brother is still going ahead with his wedding to Martha?'

It was Nigos's turn to be embarrassed.

'Yes he is, sir,' he conceded, 'though I did caution that now was not the time to be making such frivolous plans.'

'Indeed,' confirmed the muhtaris with a nod. 'Still, for you at least the plans must be interrupted. Sit, sit.'

Nigos did so, on a chair in front of the counter. The muhtaris leant forward, and spoke quietly and deliberately.

'If someone in our village was thought to be a traitor, Nigo, how would you advise we deal with him?' he asked. Nigos hesitated. Was the muhtaris referring to Andonis? Was this a test of Nigos's loyalty to the struggle?

Nigos picked his words carefully. 'My advice would depend on the nature of the treachery, sir,' he suggested.

The muhtaris slapped the table, and Nigos frowned.

'Nature of the treachery? Doesn't your brain cut?' fumed the muhtaris. 'Treachery is treachery. People who work for the enemy must pay.'

Nigos nodded an apology. He felt certain now that the muhtaris was referring to the tailor.

'If you mean the uniforms, sir, please understand, Andonis is an ambitious tailor. I'm certain no disrespect was intended when he accepted the order,' explained Nigos.

'Your loyalty to your friend is touching but misplaced,' declared the muhtaris haughtily. 'The work that lackey of the Englezi has been doing isn't the treachery to which we refer at this time.'

Nigos nodded. 'You mean, then, his liaisons with the Turkish girl?' he asked. 'As I understand it, this episode is now over.'

The muhtaris clasped his hands. 'We're aware of this, Nigo. The Turk-lover's dalliance is not the treachery to which we refer either. Rest assured, Nigo, Andonis is to be given the opportunity to redeem himself. It's the least we can do for our cousin Irini.'

The muhtaris noted Nigos's relieved expression.

'Clearly your friend's lack of judgement is a source of concern,' continued the muhtaris, and Nigos shrugged. 'Be mindful, Nigo, it's a concern we share. And we know it's down to having a father who, despite a Greek mother, seems to hate the motherland. But no, the treachery of which we speak involves a Turkish goatherd.'

Nigos was confused. 'What, simple Erden?' he asked.

The muhtaris nodded. 'Too simple, it seems, to know who the enemy is,' he said. 'We're informed that the goatherd witnessed the Englezos who bothered your sister getting his just rewards. It appears he recognised the car Bambos was driving, and informed the authorities. In short, Nigo, he's the traitor responsible for your cousin's arrest, torture and execution.'

'The filthy Turk. So he's the one,' fumed Nigos, clenching his fist.

'Bambos was a brave young man. He lived a hero and died a hero. Unlike your friend the tailor, Bambos gave nothing to the Englezi. Unlike the simple goatherd, he kept his mouth shut to the last.'

Nigos was consumed by anger. He was now a man capable of killing, and knew it.

'What do you propose we do, sir?' he pressed impatiently.

The muhtaris smiled. He opened the drawer of his table and pulled out an object wrapped in white cloth. He handed it to Nigos. It was heavy, and Nigos immediately guessed what it was. Then the muhtaris pulled out a second bundle and placed it on the table. Nigos glanced up at the muhtaris, to intimate that he was unclear why there was a need for two.

The muhtaris pointed to the one on the table. 'This one's for the deed, Nigo. Your one's to ensure the deed is done.'

At that moment they heard a knock at the door of the shop. The tailor had arrived. The muhtaris nodded to Nigos to let Andonis in.

'You've asked to see me, sir?' enquired Andonis politely. Under normal circumstances the tailor would have been irritated at being summoned in this manner, irritated at having his work interrupted. But these weren't normal circumstances.

'Indeed we did,' said the muhtaris in an ingratiating tone, beckoning the tailor to pull up another chair beside Nigos. 'We wish, if we may, to speak to you about certain activities in which you've been involving yourself of late.'

Andonis shrugged. 'You've spoken to me already, sir. Surely you recall coming to my workshop,' he pointed out defensively.

'We do recall. And we also recall that it was you who suggested further instruction might be necessary. Instruction on why politics must interfere with trade.'

'Don't worry, sir, I'm beginning to understand for myself,' conceded the tailor. 'The uniforms are packed and ready to go back untouched by this tailor's hands. I now know not to do work for the Englezi.'

'Good, good,' said the muhtaris encouragingly. 'You'll be glad to know we've an important lesson to enable you to understand even more fully.'

He gestured to Nigos with a finger, and the EOKA warrior unwrapped the revolver in his hand and pointed it at Andonis.

Andonis felt sick. For a moment he thought he was going to be shot there and then by his friend. He would have thrown up over the table, but somehow managed to hold back, for fear that any sudden movement might be his last. The blood pumped through the veins in his head. Horror swept through his mind.

Then suddenly the horror passed, and Andonis felt as though he were no longer inside himself. He was now a dispassionate observer of events in the shop of the muhtaris. He could sense the muhtaris talking. About a treacherous goatherd, about a task in hand, about a getaway. But to Andonis it seemed like a eulogy in an unfamiliar tongue about a life that had ended. His life.

He turned to his friend. 'Is this sense, Nigo?' he whispered.

Nigos nodded. 'Liberty or death,' he proclaimed, pushing his revolver into Andonis's chest. 'It's your choice.'

Andonis felt the cold metal pressed against him. Slowly and deliberately he moved a hand and eased the revolver away.

'May God help the whole world, Nigo. And then us,' he said, picking up the other revolver from the table.

The muhtaris instructed the young friends to pull their shirts out of their trousers, and to conceal their weapons by tucking them into their belts. One friend had a look of resolve on his face, the other a look of dread.

The muhtaris ushered them out into the blistering heat of the day.

'Now do what you have to do. And do it quickly,' he commanded, pulling the door shut.

Andonis and Nigos walked in silence across the square. Anjela, who was wiping tables outside the coffee-shop, saw them and waved a greeting as they passed. She stared at the bearded Nigos. She barely recognised the stern-looking young man who'd once charmed her into lending him the coffee-shop van. How livid she remembered Vasos had been. Then she looked at Andonis; the face of the young tailor was drained of colour. She feared for him.

'And where are you two off to?' she enquired. Her tone was one of real concern rather than idle curiosity.

Nigos spoke. He had the demeanour of a proud soldier addressing a helpless civilian in a time of war.

'The tailor has work to do, Mrs Anjela,' he declared. 'Someone needs measuring.'

Anjela understood, turned to Andonis, and looked at him fearfully. 'You must take care,' she pleaded. Andonis went to reply, but Nigos interrupted.

'You take care of your communist husband and his coffee, Mrs Anjela. I'll take care of Andonis,' he said, and pulled the tailor away and onward.

Anjela thought to call Vasos to come and do something, but realised that her husband could not alter what was to be.

※ ※ ※

It was a fair walk to the goatherd's hill, off the main road and up a dirt track. Under the sun's relentless glare.

Nigos set the pace. Whenever Andonis slowed a little to take out a hand-kerchief and wipe his face, Nigos would grab the tailor's arm and pull him forward. They continued to walk in angry silence. They'd been through such rituals before during the course of their friendship, with a variety of causes. Now both suddenly became conscious of the absurd situation.

They glanced at one another, and this time it was Andonis who was to speak first.

'That was some performance you and the muhtaris put on,' he mumbled.

'I see no point in us having this conversation.'

Andonis smiled. 'Isn't that my line?' he enquired. A hint of a smile appeared on Nigos's mouth.

'Are you afraid?' Nigos asked.

Andonis shrugged. 'Do the wet fear the rain?' he rejoined, his face dripping with sweat.

They clambered up the hill. Nigos was beginning to sweat too now. Andonis could make out the figure of a young man under the shade of an old olive tree, surrounded by grazing goats.

The goatherd had seen the friends approaching. Their presence at such a time could only mean trouble. Perhaps Andonis was jealous. Perhaps the tailor wanted to have it out with him over Funda.

Erden felt for the knife tucked under his belt. Then he raised himself and spoke to his goats.

'Come on, my beauties. Time to go.'

'Wait,' called Nigos, rushing forward to block the goatherd's path. 'We want to talk to you.'

Erden froze on seeing Nigos's look of violent intent. 'But what could two fine men of the village want with a poor, harmless goatherd like me?' he enquired nervously.

'We've been told an animal's gone astray,' advised Nigos threateningly, the beads of perspiration now merging on his brow.

Erden shook his head. 'No, sir. All my goats are accounted for. Even my little Yasmin is fit and well now, due to Mr Andonis's generous act of kindness.' He turned to the tailor with grateful eyes. 'So thank you, sirs, but you're mistaken.'

'You're the one who's mistaken, goatherd,' countered Nigos. 'One stupid animal has got himself into trouble. Real trouble.'

'Please, sirs. What do you want from me?' pleaded the goatherd, but his face showed signs that he now knew exactly what this was about.

Andonis spoke calmly, and his tone helped put the goatherd at ease.

'Erden,' he said. 'Remember that moonlit night some weeks ago? Did you see a soldier get a beating? Down there along the road to the town?'

Erden looked down to where Andonis was pointing, and shuddered. He did not want to be reminded of that horrible incident. The punching, the kicking and the moaning. Then he looked at Nigos and shuddered once more. He did not want to share in that poor man's fate.

'Come on, Andoni, let's get on with it. We both know he's guilty,' urged Nigos, the sweat now rolling down his face and dripping from his chin.

Andonis, shirt drenched, addressed the goatherd once more.

'There are people in the village, Erden, who believe you told the Englezi what you saw.'

Erden shrugged with resignation. Of course he'd told the Englezi. They'd been swarming around like angry bees in the days and weeks following the attack, and had forced him to tell them everything. About the man on the bicycle. About the car following. About two young men who'd come out, about how ruthless they'd been.

Then all at once he recalled Funda's warning, about not saying anything to anyone. Her warning had come too late. Instinctively Erden felt for his knife again. The goats sensed danger. A few now abandoned their goatherd and made their way down the hill to a safer place.

'Please. I am a poor goatherd. Funda, my betrothed. She's pregnant,' pleaded Erden. Andonis's mind was now spinning out of control. Funda? Carrying the goatherd's child? This and the heat was more than he could bear.

'Come on, Andoni. Do what you have to do or else!' demanded Nigos, pulling out his gun and pointing it at the tailor. Shocked at the sight of the revolver, Erden stepped back. Nigos now shifted his weapon and trained it on the goatherd.

'Stay where you are. You have to answer for my cousin, you filthy animal,' he screamed. Then he glanced at the tailor.

'Come on, Andoni. Do it!'

Andonis could think only of Funda. Nigos trained the revolver back on the tailor. Erden saw his chance. He pulled out his knife, lunged forward and plunged it into Nigos's abdomen. Still gripping his weapon, Nigos fell backwards onto his buttocks, gasping with pain and with blood streaming from his wound.

As he fell, Nigos aimed his revolver at the goatherd. Andonis withdrew his weapon and did likewise.

'You filthy Turk!'

Bullets crashed into the goatherd. The knife fell from his hand and he fell to his knees, before collapsing to the ground in front of the olive tree. His blood flowed into the dirt. Nigos writhed in agony. Erden lay still, barely breathing.

Andonis blinked the sweat from his eyes and crouched down. With a trembling hand, he found himself putting the revolver to the goatherd's head.

Andonis stared at the weapon, which grew heavy in his outstretched hand. A hand which trembled.

'Finish me too, Andoni,' moaned his wounded friend. 'I won't make it out of here alive.'

'I won't leave you to die among the animals.' Andonis was still staring at the revolver.

'Andoni, listen to me,' implored Nigos, his voice no more than a painful wheeze. 'There's no time. Go quickly. There's no choice.'

'There is a choice, Nigo,' countered Andonis. 'Liberty or death. Remember?'

And with those words Andonis stood upright, pulled back his arm, and threw his revolver as far away as he could from the old olive tree and into the brush. He tried to do the same with the revolver still gripped by his friend, but Nigos wouldn't let go.

Andonis looked at his friend's abdomen. There was a gash of several inches across it. If he could just stem the flow of blood, Nigos might have a chance. Andonis pulled out a needle and thread from his shirt pocket. The screams, accompanied by the ringing of goats' bells, carried down towards the village.

Andonis sewed up his friend. Then, with great care, Andonis lifted the blood-drenched, semi-conscious Nigos into his arms and carried him down the hill.

32

The resurrection   *I anastasis*

Not long after hearing the news about the coup, I was contacted by Ruth, or a woman who could only have been Ruth. I told the fellow lodger who took the call to say I wasn't in. It was good of her to want to offer support, but I wasn't able to face her, or anyone, in the state I was in. I felt guilty. About Ruth. About everything.

I thought sewing might help. It didn't.

My thoughts returned to the president. Our president. I'd always had little time for priests and bishops and archbishops, but felt that somehow this man had been different. He had enjoyed the trust and respect of the people; well, Orthodox Christians at least. Makarios had led the quest to be free of outside domination. And now outsiders had returned, to wipe him out, and with him any chance of liberty. And I knew what the alternative to liberty might be.

I switched on the radio to see if I could tune in to more news. To my utter disbelief, I heard his voice.

'I am Magarios. I am alive. And as long as I live the mob that has rebelled will never rule Cyprus,' it said.

I was in awe. Makarios had, by some miracle, escaped the plotters. I learnt that the broadcast was live from the monastery at Jikos. Jikos! I sensed my brother Marios's presence, and at that moment thought I understood what it might be like to experience his faith. To believe, as he believed, in a resurrection. To believe that a man of faith could suffer for the sins of others. That such a man could overcome death to deliver a message of hope, that all who believed in him might yet be saved.

And I cried and cried. And I scratched the back of my hand on the bristles of my face as I fought to wipe away those unrelenting tears.

I took out the old thimble from my trouser pocket and stared into the tiny indentations. If ever I needed my brother's faith it was now. I recalled how Marios had found his. As a child he had fallen ill with a terrible fever. Huge boils had developed all over his body. Even the village doctor was at a loss.

As a last resort, and against my father's better judgement not to move him, my mother's will was done to save their younger son. The whole family made the long journey to the monastery of Saint Andreas the Apostle, a place where miracles happened.

Once at the gates, my mother and frail brother fell to their knees and shuffled inside. Marios kissed the icons and crossed himself. Within days, the fever was gone and a new fever had consumed him. The fever of the Church. His symptoms were severe.

I remembered Marios's reply when I questioned whether our visit to the monastery and his subsequent recovery had been nothing more than a happy coincidence.

'Only God knows. All I know is that He's with me now. What had to happen on the way is His business. Just accept, Andoni. As I accept.'

Now, at last, I was ready to accept, and as I did so I felt a glorious energy surge through me.

I accepted the news that Makarios had once more been forced to flee his country. I accepted the news, soon after, that a fleet from Asia Minor was heading towards Cyprus. I accepted that aircraft were dropping hundreds of bombs and thousands of paratroopers onto the island. I accepted that operation 'Attila', the preordained invasion of Cyprus, had begun.

What had to happen on the way was His business.

33

The wedding   *O ghamos*

Andonis was slumped on a rickety chair, outside an abandoned old farmhouse far from anywhere. His elbows rested on his knees, hands supporting his head, as he stared into the ground. He wished he could believe, like his brother Marios believed, in the miracle of God's love. For only a miracle could save Nigos now. And only a miracle could save Andonis.

The friends had been picked up on the road by a waiting car with three EOKA men inside. They had been brought here. One EOKA man had now driven off to fetch a doctor. All suspected, though no one suggested, that a priest should be fetched too.

Andonis could hear Nigos inside, groaning for the All-Holy Virgin. Andonis wished he was Nigos. At least he was paying quickly for his sins, with blood and with pain.

Andonis mourned: for the goatherd; for his friend; for a love which could never be. He mourned for the innocence which had made life worth living. He mourned for the rest of his existence.

An EOKA man emerged from the farmhouse shaking. He took out a packet of cigarettes from his pocket and offered one to Andonis. Andonis refused with a slight raising of the head.

'The doctor will come,' the man tried to reassure Andonis, patting him on the shoulder, before leaning against a nearby fig tree to calm himself with the tobacco. 'We must hope and pray that God may spare him.'

Andonis closed his eyes and shook his head. Someone who'd taken another's life had no business with hope or with prayer. God had His plans. They could not be altered by those unworthy of forgiveness.

A second EOKA man came out of the farmhouse and addressed the tailor.

'Your friend is asking for you.' Andonis took a series of short breaths before rising slowly from his chair.

He entered the sparse room where Nigos lay, curled up on a makeshift bed of old sacks. His middle had been wrapped with another sack. This one was stained red.

With eyes barely open, Nigos had observed his friend's entrance, and made an effort to compose himself. The pain could wait a moment. Nigos spoke, his voice no louder than a whisper.

'Come closer.'

Andonis crouched down by his friend. He hardly recognised the contorted bearded face drained white of blood before him. The tailor took his friend's hand and gave it a squeeze. There was now no strength left in Nigos to reciprocate. His hand hung limply in the tailor's lap.

'You sewed me up real good, didn't you, Mr Tailor?' whispered Nigos.

The tailor nodded. Nigos eased his hand away from Andonis and let it flop against the sodden sack that covered his wound. Then slowly, he turned the bloody palm towards his friend.

'Look, mamma. Blood!' croaked Nigos, and tried to laugh, but failed through pain. Nigos's face now grew stern. His head rose and his eyes strained in their sockets, trying to make contact with Andonis's. Andonis leant forward to make it easier.

'You're sure we killed the Turk?' asked Nigos, this time using his lungs, which Andonis could see was agonising work.

'I'm sure,' replied the tailor in a whisper, and felt a terrible shame as Nigos used his diminishing energy on a proud smile.

'That's good. I knew I'd make a patriot of you,' Nigos whispered. His eyes focused on the intense sunlight streaming in through the door. 'Now you're a real hero.'

Andonis shook his head. 'I don't feel like a hero.'

Nigos glanced back at his friend and frowned. 'You've always been a hero to me. I always looked up to you. Always wanted to be like you.'

It was now Andonis's turn to look towards the light. Tears were forming in his eyes.

Nigos continued. 'You were always that little bit stronger, faster, wiser. And I knew, so I followed you.'

Andonis put his finger to his friend's lips, stopping the blood trickling from them.

'Don't talk, Nigo,' he advised.

Nigos rejected the finger with a movement of the head.

'But today, for once, we did something *I* wanted.'

Andonis reached for his friend's hand once more, and squeezed it tightly.

'And look what happens?' whispered Nigos. He attempted to laugh once more, but coughed blood. Andonis wiped it away with his free hand.

'In God's name, Nigo, hold on to yourself. They've gone for a doctor,' he implored.

Nigos raised his eyebrows dismissively. 'I won't make it, Andoni. But don't worry, I'll die content, knowing I did my duty. And that I got you to do the same,' he whispered. His eyes were becoming heavy. They started to close.

'Nigo,' cried Andonis, grabbing the stained collar of his friend and pulling him forward. 'You call this doing your duty?'

Nigos's eyes reopened and focused on the tailor. He spoke with a struggle.

'Liberty or death. That's the choice our people have, remember? God wills that I choose death. You must choose liberty,' he insisted, clutching at Andonis's hand with what remained of his strength.

'Stand in for me as best man at my brother's wedding,' he instructed.

Andonis nodded.

'And when the wedding's done, explain things to my mamma. In ways she might understand. Tell her how much I love her.'

Andonis breathed in deeply and nodded. A serenity appeared on Nigos's face.

'And promise me you'll look out for my sister,' he whispered as his eyes shifted from his friend to the door to catch the light from the sun for the last time.

'And never forget our homeland, Andoni. It matters more than life,' he whispered.

Andonis leant forward to kiss Nigos on the cheek. A tear dropped from the tailor's eye and merged with the blood trickling from his friend's mouth.

※　※　※

They dug a grave outside the farmhouse, under the fig trees, and there they buried Nigos. Andonis had wanted to take his friend's body back to the widow, back to the churchyard where Nigos's father rested. The EOKA men had explained that under the circumstances it would be better if Nigos's body did not go back to the village. Andonis could not go either. Not for a while at least. It would be too dangerous.

The men invited the tailor to leave with them, to join EOKA and live like a bandit up in the hills. Andonis declined. When they asked to be given Nigos's revolver, he refused them, as Nigos had refused him. When they tried to insist, Andonis pointed it at them and said he knew how to kill a man.

They calmed the tailor by telling him he could keep the weapon. Then they gave him a roll of bank notes; to compensate the widow, when the time was right. And then they left Andonis, miles from anywhere, to live amongst the blood-stained sacks.

Andonis stayed at the farmhouse. He survived by drawing water from a nearby well and shooting birds with the revolver's remaining few bullets. He plucked and gutted them, the way he'd seen his father pluck and gut his mother's precious chickens, and cooked them on a makeshift fire. And when the bullets were done, he buried the revolver near his friend and lived off the figs which fell from the trees.

He remained unshaven, and thought of his dead friend. And of Funda and Erden. And of Marios. The Maronite too. He sat up all night and counted shooting stars, until sleep overcame him, and with it a hope that he might never wake again. He spent hours sitting by his friend's grave doing nothing. Nothing came easily to Andonis now. He wondered whether he could live the rest of his life like this. He thought he could. It felt good to be free.

And the days passed, and slowly some of Andonis's senses returned. A sense of duty was one. The wedding of Yannis and Martha was imminent. A sense of foreboding another. Were the tailor not to attend, all would know him guilty of Erden's murder. Then Andonis could never return to the village. His parents would never see him again.

By going back now there was a chance people might believe that it was Nigos alone who'd finished off the goatherd. After all, Nigos was the EOKA man. Andonis? He was just a tailor. Away looking for work in the town. It was a chance worth taking.

Andonis took off his shirt, stained brown with other men's blood, and went to draw some water from the well. Then he scrubbed and scrubbed until no trace remained of the terrible acts of violence.

❋ ❋ ❋

Andonis set off for home in the early dawn. It took him several hours, but it was a walk that did him good after so many days of doing nothing. Now, ahead of him, he could make out the whitewashed houses of the Muslim neighbourhood. He would have to pass through it to get to his father's house. Which would be the bigger ordeal? Facing the Muslims or facing his family?

It was mid-morning, and there were a number of women outside in their colourful dresses and headscarves, picking grapes or hanging out washing in their respective front yards. Such everyday activities did nothing to disguise the tense atmosphere. No one interacted. No one talked. The tailor's approach ensured no one talked.

As the nervous Andonis drew near, he saw two Muslim villagers about his own age. They were dressed in ill-fitting police uniforms. They observed, with anger and suspicion, the unshaven tailor as he approached them. When he reached them, they gestured to him to stop. They began to speak to him in the Cypriot vernacular. Not wholly fluent, but enough to be understood, and with some Turkish words thrown in.

'Who are you? What is your business here?' growled the shorter of the two policemen. He held a wooden baton in his one hand, slapped it on the palm of the other.

'It's me, Andonis the tailor. Son of Mihalis the farmer. I live a few hundred yards up the road. I've been away in the town, staying with relatives and working. What's the problem here?'

'What's the problem here?' repeated the baton-wielder, his face reddening with rage.

'Haven't you heard?' interjected the other, taller policeman, scrutinising Andonis's facial growth. 'There's big trouble in the village. Some days ago Erden the goatherd was shot dead.'

Andonis put his right hand against his face and shook his head. It's what a man who'd been told of murder would do.

'They make us police. To help control you murderous Greeks. To help find the killer. You know him, don't you?' added the shorter man accusingly.

Andonis could feel the sweat building on his brow. 'Erden? No, not really. He kept himself to himself. I did help him once, when a goat of his was ill.'

The taller man nodded. Andonis's compassionate act was well known among the Muslims.

'Not Erden. Your friend, Nigos. The widow's boy. He's the killer,' declared the shorter man. 'Everyone knows it was him.'

Mindful not to show it, Andonis was relieved that Nigos was the suspect. Relieved and guilty. He took a step back.

'Did Nigos commit such a crime?' he enquired with what he hoped was alarm. 'My God. Are they sure?'

'Everyone knows your friend's with Eoga. Do you know where he's hiding?' asked the taller officer.

Andonis's mind raced.

'No…I don't. I've been away, as I said. Working in the town. I'm a tailor. You know how it is. Business has been slow in the village.'

'You're lying,' declared the shorter man, poking his baton into Andonis's stomach. 'We'll have to arrest you. Let the Englezi beat the truth out of you!'

'Leave him,' advised the taller. Then he addressed the tailor. 'If you've been away working you'll have brought back some money, yes?'

Andonis felt for the roll of notes intended for the widow in his trouser pocket. He felt his needle and thread. He pulled these out first.

The taller policeman nodded. 'See? He's the tailor. Let him go.'

But his friend was not finished.

'Where's the money?' he insisted. Andonis hesitated, then reached into his pocket and pulled out the money. The shorter Muslim snatched the roll of notes and began leafing through them.

'Take it all. It's yours,' offered Andonis with resignation. 'What use is money in this village of mistrust and hate?'

The shorter Muslim nodded distractedly, and signalled to Andonis to be on his way. As he did so, the taller officer nudged at his comrade and, with a nod of his head, gestured at someone behind Andonis. Instinctively, Andonis turned. A young Muslim woman with her head bowed was approaching, carrying a clay jug. Andonis could not see her face, as it was concealed by her black shawl, but as she walked she sang. And her voice was unmistakable.

Off she set, Miss Yeragina,
To the well to fetch cold water.
Drun-drun, drun-drun-drun-drun.
As her bracelets rattle on.

'She still sings. She's with child, her betrothed is murdered and she still sings. Why?' questioned the taller officer. Andonis understood why.

'She won't be denied that.'

As Funda neared, the two policemen removed their caps and lowered their heads. Funda looked at Andonis, but the face he saw had changed. The glowing smile seemed a distant memory. Only the voice remained. And the green eyes. The three men stood watching her in silence. She continued singing. And as she sang she stared at the unshaven and dishevelled young man in front of her, a man she thought she knew, a man she thought she loved.

And she fell into the well.
And she gave an almighty yell.
Drun-drun, drun-drun-drun-drun.
As her bracelets rattle on.

She put down her jug and spoke to the two policemen in Turkish. They shrugged, and she indicated that they should leave. They nodded. Before moving off, the taller policeman took the roll of notes from his colleague and handed them back to Andonis.

'We're only doing our job,' he said apologetically.

When the two policemen were out of earshot, Andonis spoke.

'Funda. I'm so sorry,' was all he could think of to say. His face had reddened, and sweat was now dripping from his brow. Funda shook her head dismissively.

'Don't be, Andoni. Life's cruel. Perhaps it's better to find out early and learn to endure,' responded Funda.

Then there was silence. Funda and Andonis stood there in the dusty road looking into each other's eyes, oblivious to the people and the atmosphere around them. Funda knew her tragedy made her immune to criticism, for the time being at least. As for Andonis, the urge to be near Funda again, even for a few moments, was too strong to resist.

'It must be terrible for you,' he said eventually, for want of anything better to say.

'Yes. Terrible. For me and for this whole damned country when a decent and honourable man has his life taken.'

'A real loss,' agreed Andonis, again for want of anything better to say.

Funda shrugged, and then pulled out a thimble from a pocket in her skirt. The tailor's thimble. Andonis felt a lump come to his throat. She made to offer it to him, but he raised a hand to refuse. The thimble fell from her hand and rolled along the ground.

'Only with real love can there be real loss,' mused Funda.

Andonis nodded. Both stared down at the thimble.

Then Funda looked up at the tailor.

'You need a shave,' she said, with a hint of a smile, which made her face glow.

'I long for one,' replied the tailor, smiling back, but Funda's smile was gone.

'Will you be all right?' he continued.

Funda sighed. 'I'll find a way. There's a life inside me for which I must be strong,' she replied, patting her abdomen.

Now she picked up her jug and made to move away. Andonis placed a hand on Funda's shoulder.

'Perhaps I can find a way to help,' he offered, but realised from her expression how pathetic he sounded to her.

Funda shook her shoulder free.

'Leave me alone, Andoni. Please. I must have no more foolishness from you,' she commanded.

Andonis nodded. He stooped and picked up the thimble.

'Please accept this,' he said, separating the bank notes and placing half of them into Funda's hand, together with the thimble.

He was afraid she wouldn't accept, but Funda hesitated for only a brief moment before stuffing his offering into her pocket.

'I will,' she declared. 'After all, I must learn to endure.'

He wanted to tell her that he loved her, that he'd always love her, but she was gone.

※　※　※

Andonis walked through the village to the house of Mihalis. The nearer he got, the more apprehensive he became. How was he to face his father?

Andonis recalled an occasion when, as a boy, he'd been sent home early from the village school for arguing with his teacher. The teacher had been twisting the ear of an ever-errant Nigos, and Andonis's protestations on behalf of his friend had been made a little too forcefully.

When Mihalis learnt of his son's misdemeanour he brought out a brown leather belt with a shiny gold buckle from a cupboard. Despite the fear of his impending punishment, Andonis's eyes had lit up when he noticed the new belt. It was like ones he'd seen American cowboys wear in picture-books and at the travelling cinema. Mihalis took hold of Andonis and bent him over his knee.

'That's.' Wallop. 'For.' Wallop. 'Disrespecting.' Wallop. 'Your.' Wallop. 'Teacher,' yelled the farmer.

Andonis screamed out with each lash of the belt.

'And this,' added Mihalis with a smile, now presenting the new belt to a sobbing Andonis, 'is a present from the town, for standing by your friend.'

Andonis shook his head. This principle thing had got out of hand.

He passed a number of Christian villagers on the way home through the square. They greeted him respectfully with a nod of the head, but saw from his expression that it was not appropriate for them to stop and talk to him. The village understood. The village would wait for all to be revealed. With trepidation.

As he drew nearer to his father's house, Andonis could hear the sound of a violin accompanied by singing. It was a traditional wedding song always performed at the ritual shaving of the groom. The voice belonged to Vasos. Andonis could now make out the words:

Barber, your blade its sharpness heed.
To shave the groom not make him bleed.

He entered the house. Yannis was sitting on a chair in the middle of the room wrapped in a towel, and with his back to Andonis. Vasos was leaning over him with a razor-blade, and Simos stood by them playing his violin. Mihalis was also present, observing proceedings. Vasos looked up and saw Andonis. The blade slipped from his hand and struck the floor. The music stopped abruptly.

Yannis looked round from his chair.

'Andoni!' he cried. 'Thank God, you're back.' Then his glad expression vanished as he saw that Andonis had returned alone. 'And my brother? Where's Nigos?'

Andonis lifted his hands. The expression on his unshaven face told all present that he knew but would not say. The older men exchanged glances, but no one spoke. They waited for the brother to speak.

'What's going on, Andoni?' Yannis implored eventually.

Andonis shifted uncomfortably. He looked at his father, and searched deep into Mihalis's eyes for guidance. Mihalis glared back, and almost imperceptibly his head twitched from left to right. With his eyes still firmly fixed on Andonis, the farmer put his other hand on Yannis's shoulder.

'Hush!' he whispered.

Under normal circumstances Yannis would have acquiesced, but these were not normal circumstances. He became conscious of the other two men in the room. They also wanted news of Nigos, but neither dared ask. It was up to Yannis to extract answers about his brother. If he didn't, what kind of man was he? What kind of husband would he make?

Yannis launched himself from his chair, and the towel fell to the floor.

'No, sir, I won't hush,' he retorted. Bits of lather flew out from around his mouth as he spoke. 'I want news of Nigos. This thing is driving us mad. All the gossip and rumours. Some say he's a hero. Others, I know, think differently.' He glanced at Mihalis. 'But everybody says shame. Shame for the widow and shame for me and Stella. That we'll not see Nigos again. Not today of all days. Not ever.'

Now Yannis stared at the tailor. 'Please, Andoni. I have a right to know. What's happened to my brother?'

'Sit down and prepare for your wedding!' yelled Mihalis, taking control once more. There was an authority in his voice that Andonis and Yannis knew only too well. And Vasos and Simos too. An authority that few men in the village would dare challenge.

Mihalis turned to Simos. 'Why have you stopped? Come on, play!'

Simos did so immediately. Vasos gently eased Yannis back into the chair and began to sing again. He picked up the towel and the razor from the floor, and resumed the shaving of the now silent bridegroom.

Call his mother to come, to smoke him as well.
To give him her blessing, to bid him farewell.

Andonis retreated into the bedroom he shared with Marios. His father followed and shut the door, leaving the music and the wedding preparations behind them.

'So?' prompted Mihalis.

Andonis looked around the room and was saddened to see that his brother's clothes and books and possessions were gone.

'Where's Marios?' he asked.

Mihalis sighed. 'He's left us. Joined the monastery at Jikos, with the priest's blessing.'

'Without waiting to say goodbye to me?' asked Andonis. His father nodded with resignation, and Andonis shook his head in disbelief.

'No one knew what was going to happen or when you'd return. Baba-Ghlioris thought it best for Marios to get away. Baba-Ghlioris thought all this might get out of hand.'

'Marios has left us?' cried Andonis. 'He's chosen God above his family?'

Mihalis nodded. 'It was always so with Marios,' he explained, and the two men found comfort in each other's pain. 'Now, please, tell me about Nigos.'

Andonis conveyed all that was necessary with his eyes.

Mihalis slapped his cheek and rocked his head. 'So it comes to this?' he asked, his voice now quivering. 'I bring you up to think for yourself and it comes to this? My God.'

Andonis frowned. This was not the time for accusations.

'Thank your God that it's the widow's boy who's gone, baba, and not yours,' he pointed out coldly.

'Ah, so I'm meant to be grateful?'

Andonis nodded. 'You wouldn't want to change places with the widow, would you?'

Mihalis felt guilty, and rubbed the thinning hair on his shaking head.

'Be grateful then, baba, but know that I'm not. Because I'd gladly change places with Nigos.'

A surge of emotion swept through Mihalis, and he did everything to prevent it from flowing out of his eyes. He placed a hand on his son's shoulder, but Andonis brushed it away.

'We both lost our lives, Nigos and I. But only one of us is dead,' he said. Mihalis nodded.

'Shave and clean yourself up. Your mamma and the others will be waiting. We have a wedding to go to,' the farmer instructed, and Andonis, recalling his dying friend's requests, nodded.

'And then you'll speak to Mrs Xenu,' instructed Mihalis.

Andonis shuddered.

'I'm not sure I can go through with it, baba.'

He hoped his father would nod. To show he understood. To say he would take his son's heavy burden on his older shoulders. But instead Mihalis's face filled with rage. Some years ago he had been the one to inform Xenu that she had become a widow. It was the hardest thing he'd ever done in his life.

'You can't go through with it?' he bellowed, punctuating each word by poking his finger into the middle of his son's chest. 'You're a man now, Andoni. Start acting like one!'

✳ ✳ ✳

The wedding of Yannis and Martha in the village church seemed more like a funeral.

All the Christians of the village were there. Heads bowed. The widow, Stella and Irini. Vasos, Anjela and their family, including old man Haji-Markos in his breeches, washed specially for the occasion. Simos was there too, though not his golden smile. A watchful but sombre Yoda was of course present, along with her daughter and young sons, and her tall thin husband; for she had a husband, a quiet man who usually went unnoticed.

Only the Muslims stayed away. And those young men now living in the hills. And the muhtaris.

And when father and son entered, the mother saw them and screamed. She screamed as only a mother whose missing child had suddenly and unexpectedly reappeared could scream. She screamed her son's name. The widow, at Irini's side, looked up. The momentary euphoria in Xenu's eyes disappeared when she saw that Nigos was not with Andonis. The women wanted answers, but the ceremony was about to begin.

The now clean-shaven tailor took his place before the ever-bearded priest. Andonis stood to the right of the groom, who was looking uncomfortable in the perfectly fitting suit the tailor had made him. Martha stood to Yannis's left, in her white flowing wedding dress. She should have looked radiant. She looked resigned.

And to the left of the bride stood Stella, the maid of honour, with that unmistakable mole on her cheek. Her lips were full and red, her black hair shiny, in a bun tied with a white ribbon. She'd lost weight through worry for her brother and the man she couldn't help but love. Now she felt attractive, shapely and slim in her red dress. And guilty too for doing so.

And Baba-Ghlioris chanted the ancient words, but there seemed to be no conviction in his voice, nor in the voice of the psalmists. The young people before the priest went through all the necessary motions, with the crowns made of pearls, the silk ribbons, the silver-plated goblets of wine and the rings of gold.

And on a number of occasions the eyes of Stella met those of Andonis. And she imagined a better world, where she and the man she had always loved might be the ones exchanging crowns and rings in a traditional religious ceremony. And he imagined a better world where hatred borne of religion did not exist.

And when it was over, the widow came to the front of the church. As tradition dictated she was wearing a black shawl. She had wrapped it tightly round her head to hide a face devoid of joy. The bride and groom stooped to enable the widow to kiss their respective crowns.

Then she kissed Martha on both cheeks.

'May you live, my daughter,' she whispered.

Then she kissed Yannis on both cheeks.

'May you live, my son,' she whispered. 'And how I wish your father were here to see you. And your brother also.'

Then she pulled her shawl forward again and stepped away to enable others to approach the newlyweds and to wish them a long life.

And Stella was next. And after she'd kissed the newlyweds, she went over to kiss her mother.

'May God keep them safe, mamma,' she said. 'And our Nigos too, wherever he is.'

The widow nodded. 'And next year, God willing, will be your turn,' she whispered.

And Irini was next. And after she'd kissed the newlyweds she went over to kiss her friend.

'May both your sons live long, Xenu,' she said. 'And your daughter and daughter-in-law. And may God help us all.'

The widow nodded. 'God help us all,' she agreed.

And Mihalis was next. And after he'd kissed the newlyweds he went over to kiss his late friend's widow.

'May you be granted grandchildren, Xenu,' he said.

The widow nodded. 'And you also,' she whispered.

And Andonis was next. And after he'd kissed the newlyweds he went over to kiss his best friend's mother.

'May your children find peace, Mrs Xenu,' he said, and reached out to wipe the tears rolling down her cheeks.

The widow nodded. 'Where is my Nigos, Andoni?' she demanded, as only a mother could demand.

Andonis stared at the woman for a moment. He felt like he'd once felt when, as boys, he and Nigos had been standing on the edge of a cliff, staring at the deep blue sea below them. His friend had dared Andonis to dive in, was chiding him for not doing so. And Andonis had built up the courage to jump.

And the whole church fell silent.

'Nigos has left us, Mrs Xenu. He asked me to tell you how much he loved you.'

'What are you telling me, Andoni?' cried the widow, knowing full well from the look in the tailor's eyes. 'My God, my God. My golden son. He's gone and left me behind. He's gone and won't return. Just like his father.'

'What are you saying, Andoni?' demanded Irini.

Mihalis raised his hand.

'Enough,' he commanded. 'It's the truth.'

The widow had lost control of her body and had fallen to the floor of the church. She began kicking and punching it. A wail was now emanating from deep within her. The priest was alarmed to see such a display at a wedding. He thought to intervene, to pull the widow up and console her with words of God. But Mihalis stood in his way. And the priest knew his place, and disappeared into the ieron.

Stella and Yannis knelt down with their mother, and all three hugged each other tightly. At that moment they became as one flesh, as one blood.

'Why? Why? Why?' shrieked the widow releasing her grip on her children and turning to Irini. 'Wasn't taking my husband enough? God had to take my son also?'

'God wants those He loves close to Him,' Irini sought to comfort, kneeling herself to stroke the widow's hair.

'That's right. God. The Great One. He who knows it all,' shrieked the widow. 'All except how to help me. How to show me mercy.'

And with that, the widow resumed her wailing. And the wailing echoed round the church of the village as villagers within stood in sorrow. Then the wailing subsided, and slowly Irini helped Xenu to her feet.

Irini led Xenu outside, so that she might feel the warmth of the sun, breathe the fresh air and hear the song of the birds. And Mihalis and Andonis followed. And then the newlyweds, with Stella and all the wedding guests behind them. No rice was thrown.

The widow stood before her late husband's grave, and called to Andonis to come to her. She stared into the tailor's eyes.

'We want you to tell us everything, Andoni. We need to know,' she demanded.

'Nigos is gone, Mrs Xenu. That's all I'm able to tell you. That's all you need to know,' replied the tailor. He felt for the roll of remaining bank notes in his pocket.

'But is it true what they're saying, Andoni? That he was responsible for the death of the goatherd?'

Mihalis spoke next. 'Xenu. It's best we don't speak of this,' he warned.

'Best for whom?' shrieked the widow. 'For Andonis? For you? So you won't get into trouble? So your lives won't be destroyed? What about me? Why does no one ever consider what's best for me?' She pointed at the grave. 'My husband didn't. My son didn't either. I just have to live through it all. Years and years of torment. Now doubled. Tripled.'

'I know, Mrs Xenu. Believe me, I know.' The tailor's tone had a strangely calming effect on the widow. She reached out to squeeze his hand. He slipped the roll of notes into hers.

At that moment all present heard the ominous sound of vehicles approaching. And soon three army jeeps full of soldiers had arrived outside the churchyard. And then they were rushing in. Five, ten soldiers shouting at the frozen Cypriots. Shouting at them not to move.

And the priest now rushed out of his church with rosy cheeks, squinting from the bright sunlight, and shouting at the soldiers.

'Out of my churchyard, you demons! Out of my churchyard!'

But the soldiers ignored him. Three of them came for Andonis and grabbed him, while a fourth informed the tailor that he was under arrest. Andonis showed no resistance, indeed he cooperated as they put handcuffs on him. There was a look of calm acceptance on his face. He had already come to terms with others making decisions for him, with others controlling his destiny.

Irini was now screaming at the top of her voice.

'In God's name, Mihali, do something!'

But there was nothing that Mihalis could do, and the soldiers marched Andonis away.

'No!' implored Stella. 'Let him go! Let him go!'

Irini addressed her husband once more. 'My God, Mihali. The asprogoli came and took our Eros, and now they're taking our Andonis as well!' she sobbed.

Mihalis looked up to heaven, and was momentarily blinded by the sun. 'And the Church took Marios. What colour does that make God's arse?' he asked, struggling to contain his emotions.

At the gate Andonis wanted to stop, and the soldiers allowed him to. He looked back towards his parents.

'Mamma. Baba. I love you both. Please forgive me for causing you such pain. Please forget you ever had me as a son,' he said before letting himself be pushed into one of the waiting jeeps.

Irini, Xenu and Stella were now crying as they had never cried before. And Mihalis joined them. The rest were mortified. Even Yoda was lost for words. Only old man Haji-Markos moved. He lit himself a rolled cigarette and took a long drag, hoping it might be his last.

No wedding festivities were to follow.

✳ ✳ ✳

There was a new arrival at Jikos. Ever since he was a little boy the new arrival had dreamt of entering the famous monastery to devote his life to prayer. And now his dream had come true. He was so full of faith and so calm of spirit that he hoped before long to make a favourable impression on the elders.

All would be well for the new arrival, in this world of peace and piety, even if all wasn't well in the world he'd left behind. A world of anger and hatred, violence and suffering.

The new arrival wanted to pray and pray for the world, but first he needed guidance on how to pray. So he prayed and prayed for guidance. And his prayers were answered. And he sat down to write a letter to his beloved elder brother.

My dear Andoni

I hope my letter finds you and finds you well. Your brother is so filled with happiness to be here serving our Holy Orthodox Church. I left the village in search of the ultimate truth and my prayers are being answered. Being exposed to the supreme knowledge of the holy men in this great monastery is opening my eyes to the true challenge facing our people in their quest for liberty. It's all becoming clear to me now.

How I wish I could share my joy with you, my brother. For it is certain that you would understand. We are not so dissimilar, you and I. All that differs is the way we choose to express our love.

Our leader, Archbishop Makarios, took a holy oath to work for the birth of national freedom, a holy oath never to waiver from the goal of uniting Cyprus with Mother Greece.

For it is God's will that our Cyprus, precious jewel of the Mediterranean and coveted gateway between Europe, Asia and Africa, be delivered from the yoke of foreign domination. The people of our sacred island must be allowed to take their rightful place, helping to build a modern Greek world. United, strong and free.

God willed that, despite centuries of struggle and oppression, the glory of the Greek people would not be allowed to fade. Our brave priests took great risks and were prepared to sacrifice even their lives to sustain our special awareness of God, of self and of each other. In so doing, generation upon generation were immersed in the Greek way of life. To this day, the flame of our divine heritage still flickers in the hearts of the people of Cyprus. Until such time as liberty enables that flame to burn brightly once more.

For not only is Cyprus peopled by Greeks. Cyprus is one with Greece, as the hand that writes these words is one with me. The whole is greater than the sum of its parts. And Greece can only regain her rightful place as the true custodian of human civilisation when all her constituencies are reunited into one glorious realm of Orthodox Christendom.

And what great destiny does God have for His cherished people? What further strides has our liberated soul to make in the fields of arts and science, mathematics and philosophy, politics and religious thinking? What great knowledge has our great civilisation yet to impart to the world? What glorious potential is there to be fulfilled?

Meanwhile the western powers tell us that it is not appropriate to adopt a resolution on Cyprus which accepts our right to self-determination. And so the British presence on Cyprus has become an unwelcome occupying force. Britain plays games and creates diversions to maintain a grip which should have been relinquished many years ago. Britain deludes and demeans herself while America runs the world. But America is to Britain what Rome was to ancient Greece. An intellectually and morally bankrupt heir.

When Rome faced destruction, from within as well as from without, only a Greek-inspired spiritual re-awakening through the teachings of Christ could rejuvenate, reinvent and reunite the empire and safeguard European civilisation.

History is repeating itself. In desperation, the western powers make a pact with the infidel. They invite him to play a role in deciding the future of Cyprus. The door is open to those who, when presented with the opportunity, seized the holy city of Constantinople and desecrated the great cathedral of the Holy Wisdom. The door is open once more to those who, for centuries, were allowed to close the door on ancient enlightenment.

They cannot succeed. They will not succeed. Destiny calls us once more. Cyprus, the first Roman province to convert to Christianity, has been summoned by God to lead the world out of the wilderness. The path of righteousness is lighting up once more, leading our brave Christian warriors onward. Onward to a new beginning.

For it is clear to me now, Andoni. Our struggle is not and never has been against the converted Muslim minority of Cyprus. They will be free to pursue a new life in the new island of love, encouraged to make their contribution to the *glory of the new Greece which we will all help to build. They will be immersed in the language, culture and philosophy of the greatest civilisation the world has ever known. And they will be welcomed back with open arms, as compatriots, as brothers, as fellow Greeks. They will be welcomed back with love.*

They will be welcomed home, Andoni. For Cyprus is their home too.

Yes, my brother. I have found true happiness here serving our Church. I pray that you will also find the happiness you deserve. I pray that one day you can believe as I believe.

For love truly can conquer all.

Kiss our mamma and our babas and send them all my love.

Your loving brother,

Marios

Andonis had been interrogated, but refused to answer. Then he had been beaten, but still refused to answer.

There were no answers. Only questions.

Then he was left in a cell for days on end, until he began to miss the questions; miss the accompanying pain that might distract him from the pain he felt within. The real torture was there.

Then one day the cell door creaked open, allowing bright sunlight to flood through. It took a moment for Andonis to recognise the figure looming over him. It was the soldier he'd once manhandled outside the captain's office.

Williams looked down at the broken, dishevelled Cypriot curled up on the floor, then threw a canvas army bag over to him. Andonis stared at the bag a moment, then fumbled to release the straps. Inside he discovered clothes. His own clothes. And soap, a razor, a small jisves and coffee. Cypriot coffee. Then Williams handed him papers and passes, tickets and money. English money. And also a letter. From Marios.

'I've been told to give you these,' explained Williams. 'You're a free man.'

The words echoed in Andonis's head. A free man. About to start a life sentence.

'The best of British,' added Williams, and led the Cypriot away.

✳ ✳ ✳

And so Andonis's aimless journey began. And as the boat set off from the harbour, one man had turned up to wave him off. And he held a dog in his arms. A dog that was lost and then found. The dog Irini had christened Eros.

34

The mother   *I mamma*

Irini sat alone on her bed in her small home, which had once been her elder son's workshop. As bombs thundered in the distance and people much nearer screamed in terror, she thought of him. She had done so every day since he'd been taken by the Englezi.

Her thoughts were happy ones. She was recalling a moment long, long ago when a young Andonis had dived into the sea to retrieve the cross which the village priest had thrown in. How her heart had quickened as her son disappeared beneath the waves. How relieved and then how proud she had been when, finally, her son's fist was to break the surface of the water, clenching the silver prize.

Now she clenched her own crucifix on a chain round her neck, and prayed.

'My God, help all the world,' she whispered. 'And then us.'

Irini's small transistor radio was on. It kept her company, now that her friend Xenu was too busy helping Martha to pay Irini attention. Not that Irini begrudged the other widow for neglecting her. Xenu's duty was to her son's family. And besides, not that anyone needed to know, Irini had a duty of her own.

A man's voice declared, in an irritating mainland accent, that the brave Greek Cypriot home guard was standing its ground and, against overwhelming odds, was hitting back at Attila's advancing troops. Irini raised her head and eyebrows. Meanwhile the bomb blasts felt as though they were drawing nearer. The room shook, the door shifted on its hinges, photographs on the old sewing machine next to the bed rattled. Irini trembled.

She gazed longingly at the photographs, and at one in particular, an old black and white one, which shifted closer towards her with each new explosion. It was of her and her late beloved Mihalis, on the day of their wedding.

Irini's mind returned there. How dashing the young Mihalis looked, in his fine new breeches, his white silk shirt, his black velvet waistcoat embroidered with gold decorations, his red satin waistband. Now she looked down and could see his shiny new boots as his feet stepped expertly forward and then back, back and then forward. Now she looked upwards, past his dark brown moustache and into his hazel-green eyes. And there he was, holding her in his big strong arms. And they danced round and round. And the whole village had encircled them, and people whistled and clapped. And the violins played. And the old wedding song rang in Irini's ears.

And these two who are dancing, they will be joining soon.
The one he is the sun, the other she's the moon.

And Irini's eyes became like glass marbles. And the right one overflowed, and a single tear trickled down through the grooves of her leathery cheeks, soaking the delicate grey hairs of her chin before falling onto the bed. And she recalled the love in her young husband's eyes as they turned and turned and turned.

And new bride how it suits you, a watch that's for all time.
You've chosen well your love, one from a blood so fine.

And somewhere not too distant was the cracking of artillery. Women of the village were shrieking.

'The Turks are coming! The Turks are coming!'

But Irini could hear only cheers and laughter from her wedding guests, and the firecrackers they were setting off.

But new bride, your new husband, take care not to alarm him.
Always with your sweetest words, make certain that you calm him.

Irini closed her eyes tightly, forcing back the tears. She wiped her face with a handkerchief before lifting her bones off the bed. She carefully placed the wedding photograph face down to prevent it from falling off the edge. Then she moved towards the open door of her small home.

Outside she could see neighbours loading their cars with whatever possessions they could carry. Clothes and televisions. Tables and kettles. Plates and ironing boards. And children with dolls and balls and teddy bears. And fathers shouting at everyone to hurry up. And mothers herding their children. And grandmothers in black, crossing themselves. And everywhere dread. But no time for reflection or sadness. Nor even anger.

Irini shook her head before noticing her frame reflected in the long mirror by the door. She looked old dressed in black. She pulled at the fasteners that held her hair in a tight bun, and let her long grey locks fall down to her waist. She picked up a brush and, observing herself in the mirror, ran it through her hair.

Suddenly, Yannis appeared at the door. His face twitched, and he was dripping with sweat.

'Come on, godmother. Martha, the children and my mother are ready to go,' he urged breathlessly. His eyes darted round the room in search of anything of value. He saw nothing. He put his arm round Irini in an attempt to steer her outside.

Godmother gave godson a curious look. She moved out from under his arm and back towards her bed. She reached down, and took out an unopened envelope from beneath the pillow.

'Yanni, I have a letter. Please read it for me.'

'What letter, godmother?' asked Yannis with distraction. 'There's no time now, please. We must go.'

Irini passed the envelope to Yannis. Godson had been taught to read, godmother hadn't. No village woman of Irini's generation had.

'It came recently. From England. From Andonis,' she announced.

'Andonis?' cried Yannis in disbelief. His interest was aroused. He stared at the handwritten envelope with stamps displaying the head of a foreign queen. 'Why didn't you tell me before?'

Irini shrugged. 'I was afraid, Yanni. And so I've been saving it. Waiting for the right time. And now that time has come.'

Yannis shook his head. 'But not now, godmother. We'll go through it once we're safely away from here.'

'No, Yanni,' said Irini forcefully. 'You will read it now.'

Yannis sighed. He knew his godmother well enough to realise there was no point in arguing with her, any more than with his late godfather. He wasted no time in tearing open the envelope. Irini sat down on her bed as Yannis read out the letter.

My dear mamma

I pray that this letter finds you and finds you well. I must first thank the person you have tasked with reflecting the contents of my heart. I ask for patience and understanding.

But don't think I'll hold back, mamma. Your son must speak to you without inhibition. There are too many unexpressed feelings inside me. Passions that once defined me have been locked away for too long. My thoughts must be freed and allowed to find their way back home.

Too many years and miles now lie between us, but I feel a closeness through a deeper understanding that comes with experience. It's a closeness that was rarely possible when we were together. I left as a young man who thought there was nothing more that you or anyone else in the village could teach me. Now, as I grow older, I realise how wrong I was. Age brings with it one certainty. That all other certainties are an illusion.

Forgive me, mamma. Your son took a man's life, an innocent and good man, and this exile is my penance. Worse than any prison, it is a solitary confinement created by my own mind.

England is a land of endless opportunities. An ordinary man with drive and energy can achieve extraordinary things here. There is cold. There is darkness and rain. But there is a society of people who have overcome such natural obstacles to create a world of comforts. But your son shies away from opportunities. They are not for me.

It is every man's duty to work, and I have worked. But I've had no reason to strive. I merely exist from day to day. Yes, mamma. This strange land has transformed your son. He is a man you'd barely recognise. A foreigner. I hope the money I've been sending to the village has been of more use to you than it would have been to me.

I live alone, in a small room in a big house high up on a hill. I have one or two friends, including a woman I met recently who reminds me of you, but I've not married. The circumstances that led to my leaving the village made me realise that such a goal was not for me. I'd had too much love. Too much hate. I regret not having been able to give you the grandchildren you deserved. I am sure our Marios has made you proud. Who knows? Perhaps he is a bishop now. But you expected more earthly rewards from me, and I have failed you.

Yes. I still love her, mamma. I won't ever stop. Her face is all but faded from my mind. I can barely remember her voice or her smile. All I feel is a presence. A reminder of better, happier times, when the world was there to be challenged, when a young man could still dream the impossible.

Don't condemn me, mamma. Don't shake your head and sigh that deep sigh of yours. My dream must live on. For without it, I too may as well be dead. You have your cross and your icons, mamma. All I have is the memory of a beautiful love. I would rather have that memory endure than allow hate to consume me as it did our village.

I think of you often. I imagine you baking bread in the clay oven. Throwing grain out for our hens. Washing bedsheets in the tub. I so wish we could be together once more. That I could taste your fasolia. That you might chastise me for not showing enough respect to Mrs Xenu or for misbehaving with Nigos, God rest his soul. Sometimes I dream I have woken up back in my bed next to

265

Marios in our house. I'd be so overjoyed. I'd even accompany you both to church on Sunday.

I learnt what happened to babas, God rest his soul. His absence from the world leaves a void which can never be filled. I'm so sorry I wasn't able to be there to hold you and to comfort you. Perhaps not as Marios would have comforted you, with his fine words about heaven and the mysterious ways of God, but as a son who knows what real pain can mean, who could have shared your grief for a man who was a rock to us all.

Please don't wait for me any longer, mamma, for I will not come. I couldn't bear to see your face repainted to reflect babas's absence, to be in a village that couldn't accept his wisdom and his love. I prefer the village I knew as a child. When we were happy. When we still dreamt we could be free.

As I write these words now, I wonder whether you'll ever get to hear them. Whether you'd want to after all these years of silence. I can only hope that a mother's eternal bond with her son will allow some glimpse of me. Sometimes the role of a parent is just to be there. A source of comfort for an unsure child. And so I kiss you, mamma, and let you know that, while my brother may always have God in his heart, I will always have you.

And her too.

Till we meet again in another paradise.

Your loving son,

Andonis

Yannis replaced the letter into the envelope. Tears were trickling down his cheeks. He turned to the woman.

'We have to go now, godmother. We don't have much time. The Turkish soldiers will be here any moment,' he implored.

'Go, Yanni?' enquired Irini. There was a faraway look of serenity in her eyes. 'Go where?'

A burst of gun-fire could be heard not too far away. There was now a look of panic in Yannis's eyes.

'We'll head south, for the bases. The Turks won't dare attack us there. We'll be safe with the Englezi.'

'The Englezi?' enquired Irini. She smiled and shook her head. 'I'm not going anywhere, Yanni.'

'Godmother, please. The soldiers are ruthless. They'll kill anyone they find. I can't let you stay here,' insisted Yannis.

Irini rose from her bed.

'Yanni, listen to me. This is my home. I married your godfather in the church, gave birth to his children in the house. I baked him bread in the oven outside, fetched him water from the village well. When they took his life, I buried him in the churchyard, and since then I've lit a candle at his grave every day. So please don't ask me to leave. Take your mother and your wife and your children and go. Make a new life for yourselves. But my life is here. My life will always be here.'

Irini embraced her godson, kissing him on both cheeks. Then she clenched him tightly, and Yannis was awed by the woman's strength.

'Go, Yanni,' she urged, refusing to release her grip. 'But first I must ask you one thing.'

Yannis nodded helplessly.

'Keep the memory of this place alive in your heart and in your children's hearts. Until one day, when all this pain and misery and madness are over, you will return.'

Yannis was now sobbing like a baby, and tried to pull himself away.

'Never forget,' boomed the old lady. The force in her voice hit Yannis like a bolt of lightning. It was as though the late Mihalis had returned from the grave to issue this final command. Yannis nodded, and as he did so, Irini released him.

He grabbed his godmother's hand, kissed it, and stared deep into her eyes. 'I will never forget,' he vowed, and was gone.

35
The guest   *O xenos*

What now, Tony? Writing that letter to my mother, saying I'd never return, was the latest of a long list of regrets. I didn't want any more. What now, Andoni?

I felt compelled to phone the one man who'd been there before in my time of greatest need, and he told me he would come. To stay calm and he would come. And there was emotion in his voice.

And while I waited for him to make the journey up to London from Hove, I busied myself finishing off my sewing before preparing my lodgings for his arrival. I swept the floor, dusted down the surfaces, changed the bedclothes, cleaned the sink with some scouring powder which I'd once bought for such a purpose. I was mindful also to empty all the ashtrays. I even popped out again to buy some flowers, and also a vase. And some fresh milk and Rich Tea biscuits. And cloves and cinnamon sticks. After all a guest was coming. A xenos.

And when he arrived we embraced. We'd never done so before, but it felt right to do so now. He patted me on the back, and I felt a warmth from him that I didn't think he or any other man like him was capable of generating.

'So this is your home?' he enquired sympathetically, looking my room up and down with what I could tell was disappointment. At first I was a little put out. I'd made such an effort to make the place appear presentable. But then, as I looked around, to see how he saw, I shared his disappointment.

'It's where I live,' I replied, and he nodded, as if to appreciate the distinction.

I made a pot of tea. I dropped cloves and cinnamon in with the tea leaves. I put the teapot and cups in a tray, which I placed on my bed. Then I sat next to it while he sat facing me, having been offered the only chair in the room. We sipped our teas. He told me he liked it this way, just as he liked his coffee the Cypriot way.

'I'm grateful, captain. You came when I needed you. But your country hasn't come. Britain stands by and does nothing,' I admonished. I knew I was being unfair to him.

'There were clearly other considerations,' he offered uncomfortably.

I shook my head. 'Ones more important than justice, morality and humanity?' I fumed.

The captain shook his head, before finishing his cup of tea and replacing it on the tray. I lifted the pot to pour him another, but he raised a hand to indicate he'd had enough.

'So, what about that thimble I gave you?' he enquired, to change the subject.

'The thimble,' I repeated, and took it out from my trouser pocket, clasping it with fingers from both hands. We both stared at it a while.

'What now, captain?' I asked eventually. I felt like a soldier awaiting orders from a trusted officer. I knew my life might be in his hands once more.

'You're going to have to tell *me*,' prompted the captain.

I smiled at him. 'You're going to help me return, captain,' I announced. 'You're going to help me find my loved ones. Please. You have to reunite us.'

The captain picked up his empty cup, and indicated that he was now ready for more tea. I filled it.

'I'll do what I can,' he assured with a wink, before taking a sip. 'Pull a few strings if I'm able.'

It was raining. I descended from the back of a black taxi holding a brown parcel. The driver glanced at me and then at his meter. Behind him was the captain, sitting there, waiting for me. He was mindful to look away, out of his own window, to allow me a moment's privacy. Before me was the Muswell Hill Centre.

I rang the bell, and presently Ruth appeared at the door.

'Tony,' she gasped with what I could see was pleasant surprise. She glanced back to check on her young people. I could see them sitting patiently at the back of the centre, beyond the sports area. They'd begun chatting quietly to themselves, but appeared to be behaving.

'You have them well trained,' I remarked, and she turned back to me and smiled a warm smile which I realised I'd become rather fond of. I felt for the harmonica she'd given me. It was in my trouser pocket.

'Ruth,' I said, and then paused a moment. 'I've come to say goodbye.' The last word hadn't come easily.

She looked beyond me towards the waiting taxi. I did likewise, and noticed the tiny droplets of rain falling through the beams of its headlights.

'Where are you going?' she asked, though I could tell the answer was already apparent to her.

'Home,' I replied, and the word sounded strange to me. 'Esso mu,' I found myself repeating under my breath, and then added with a grin, 'You can tell Dave that the foreigner's finally going back to his own country.'

Ruth shook her head, ignoring my attempt at humour.

'But it can't be safe, Tony. There's a war on.' She looked embarrassed at having to state the obvious.

'I'm needed there,' I explained soothingly. Ruth nodded, and looked down.

'You could have been needed here,' she replied, almost in a whisper.

I shrugged, and looked down at the brown parcel in my hands. Then I looked up again, beyond Ruth and the sports area. I smiled.

'Keep teaching those kids to respect their differences, Ruth,' I urged.

I could see tears forming in her eyes before she shut them, forcing a single drop to fall.

'And take good care of that lovely daughter of yours.'

Now Ruth's eyes reopened, and I saw this as my opportunity to lean forward and kiss her tenderly on the forehead.

'I really hope you find what you're looking for,' she said.

I thought to tell her that in many ways I already had. I thought to tell her that in many ways it was down to her. I presented the brown parcel to her.

'This is for you,' I said.

She took the parcel and, with tears now rolling down her cheeks, she tore at the paper. She revealed the white silk blouse I'd made for her, and let it hang against her bosom.

'My goodness, thank you,' she declared, smiling at me through sodden lashes.

'I hope it fits. I only had my imagination to go on,' I explained with a wink.

She laughed and she cried. 'It's wonderful.'

'So are you,' I observed, raising a hand.

'Please take care, Tony,' she urged.

'You too, Ruth,' I said before returning to the taxi to escape the rain.

'Ya su,' she called to me as the taxi drove away.

36
The refugee   *O brosfighas*

As we were driven round a wet North Circular Road heading towards the airport at Heathrow, the captain and I sat in silence and in thought.

Turkey had interpreted the ambivalence of an otherwise preoccupied American administration as a licence to claim more land and finish the job she'd set out to do. After all, wasn't partition in everyone's best interests? The Turks could have their piece, the Greeks could have theirs. And someone more powerful could control them both.

I stared through a window specked with raindrops at the passing suburbs of north-west London. I wondered whether I'd live to see the captain's homeland again. A place I realised I was going to miss. One which had offered a number of distractions to fill an otherwise empty life. A place I'd remember with affection. Love even. For BBC radio and fish and chips. For double-decker buses and Alexandra Palace. For summer rain.

For Dave and his cousin.

When we arrived at the airport, I felt in a trance as my military friend, drawing on his experience, got where he meant for us to be. Airport personnel were put in their place, formalities waived, doors opened, barriers crossed, areas accessed. Eventually, we were riding on an electric float, heading towards a waiting aircraft.

'Unbelievable, isn't it?' noted the driver, addressing the captain. He pointed to the large sacks being loaded aboard.

'Clothes, blankets, towels. Many brand new. Some with notes in the pockets sending love and best wishes. The generosity of the British public, eh?'

I nodded. I couldn't help but feel a certain gratitude. The captain turned to me and shook his head.

'Most of these items are from your own community, Tony. Your people have shown themselves to be resourceful and well organised in a time of crisis,' he explained as the float came to a stop before the steps leading up to the aircraft.

I nodded with pride.

We were to share the aircraft with assorted people, young and not so young, female as well as male, all of whom looked to be English. Some waved a greeting to the captain as we entered. On taking our own seats, he explained that these were Red Cross colleagues. Some were medically trained, others, like the captain, were retired members of the armed forces.

'Some of us at least know we have a duty to do something,' he explained.

As the aircraft prepared for take-off, the captain assessed what our moves should be after we had landed at the British base on the island. How, by then, it would be early morning. How, with help from his Red Cross contacts, we'd try to reach the refugee camp to where people from my village might have escaped. How we'd need to assess the situation again before working out the best way forward from there.

I listened with only half an ear. I'd never flown before, and was too apprehensive to concern myself with what I might do if ever my feet touched the ground again.

As the aircraft accelerated along the runway, fear consumed me. My hands became clammy and I began to shake.

✳ ✳ ✳

Fear gripped me throughout the flight, and particularly during the aircraft's descent and landing. Fear prevented me from preparing myself properly for how I might feel back in my homeland. Only when the plane had come to a halt and the doors had been opened, only when the heavy Cypriot air met my nostrils, only then did it hit me. A familiar sickly sweet smell, of fields and of the sea, of dry heat and of the past. And smells of things that I'd hoped to forget, but which now grabbed me by the throat. Of violence. Of pain. Of death.

And inside the base, mayhem. People screaming and shouting. People crying. Cypriots as well as British. The former, men and women, the very old, the very young. Relieved that their lives were no longer in immediate danger. Shocked that, in the blink of an eye, their yesterdays had been swept away. Dismayed that their tomorrows were now in the hands of those who had let them down before. The latter, army personnel, desperately trying to create a semblance of order, yet unable to come to terms with their complete loss of control. I felt for them all.

The captain pulled strings and got to speak to a charming though intimidating army officer at the base, who ended up being charmed and intimidated himself. I was proud of the captain. And then we were in an armoured vehicle being driven through the Cypriot countryside in the early dawn. I felt exhilarated, seeing familiar landscapes and vegetation, feeling the growing intensity of the heat, filling my lungs with sea air. I felt nauseous. I could sense that much had changed. For the worse.

Then, when I knew us to be a few miles south of the village, the driver brought the vehicle to an abrupt halt outside a large lemon grove. In better times a farmer would have made a living from the fruit growing from the trees. But no more lemons would be sold this year. Our driver wished us the best of British and left the captain and me there, among the citrus trees.

The captain wanted to march straight into the camp, but I raised my hand to indicate that I needed a moment. I couldn't bring myself to look at the people. I had to look over them, at the tree-tops. I noticed the wind breezing through the leaves. And beyond the trees was the blue sky, interrupted here and there by the odd fluffy white cloud. And there beyond the clouds was the intense ball of fire. And I stared into it through eyes almost shut, happy to be blinded momentarily by its glare.

I remembered how, as a child, I'd always imagined God to be a majestic being in the sky, in blue robes, with a long white beard, and with a golden face, beaming down on me and everyone else. Keeping us together. Keeping us safe. Where was my God now?

Still looking up, I walked forward, reached up to the first tree, and pulled at some lemon blossom. I breathed in its sweet aroma, and found myself filled with His love. The smell reminded me of Funda. I put the blossom in my shirt pocket, next to the thimble.

The captain was businesslike. He told me he would find someone in authority to establish whether it would be possible for us to travel on into the village.

I nodded, and built up the courage to look down and around. Hundreds of people were gathered round makeshift shelters. Some I could hear were sharing their experiences and sense of helplessness. Some busied themselves trying to make a home out of what few possessions they had carried and what few items they'd been given. Others cried or sat in silent contemplation.

And there were children, playing, exploring, making friends. For many of the young ones, I imagined, this was the start of a new adventure. Some even played fighting and shooting games in and out of the trees. They'd learnt such games from an early age.

And there, not far from me, was a bus with a sign in front bearing the name of my village. An old bus, though not as old as the one I remembered. And leaning against it, one foot resting on the front wheel, was a man I recognised. Older, with a face lined by the sun, but whose gritted teeth revealed an unmistakable flash of gold. I made my way over.

'Mr Simo. It's me. Andonis,' I called, approaching with open arms. He turned towards me with an uncertain look, and called out to two young boys playing nearby. I could tell he'd recognised me, but also that he had no desire to embrace me. Instead he wrapped his arms round the boys, as though to protect them from a foreign invader.

These had to be his children, which meant he must have found himself a wife. Better late than never, I thought, and smiled. There was no golden smile in return.

'My God, you're alive!' he declared, staring at my forearms, no doubt noting my untanned skin. I nodded.

'You've come from England?' he enquired. I nodded once more.

'Welcome, then,' he added, rolling his eyes skyward. 'Look what's happened to us, Andoni. We've become the pity of God. Like fools we sat there, listening to the lies on the radio. That's all we've ever been told. Lies. All lies!'

'What news of the village, Mr Simo?' I asked. He shrugged.

'What news can I tell you?' he replied. 'We've been chased out of our homes, in only the clothes we wear. We've lost everything.' He spoke as though it were my fault. 'Everything! And you know what? It's no more than we deserve. All of us!'

'Please, Mr Simo. Try and be calm,' I urged, and then felt guilty. Simos glared at me.

'That's easy for you to say. Running off to England. Everything of yours is safe,' he countered. The younger of his two sons started whimpering in his embrace. I reached out and stroked the boy's hair to soothe him.

'It's all right, son,' I advised, before returning the glare of the boy's father. 'Your children are safe, aren't they?'

Simos nodded and tightened his grip on them.

'And your wife?'

He nodded once more. 'She's here. She's gone to fetch water,' he explained with relief.

'If your family's OK then you've lost nothing of value.' My voice was uncompromising. Yet again he nodded, this time more humbly. Many others, we both knew, had not been so fortunate.

'It's just that you've no idea what we've been through, Andoni,' he said. 'You don't understand.'

I was hurt; as though all those years of torment and solitude counted for nothing; as though, in his eyes, I was no different from an Englezos.

'It's my village too, Mr Simo. My people too,' I insisted. 'So please. Tell me. What news of my mamma? What news of Yannis and his family?'

Simos now looked at me with compassion.

'I think Yannis's family headed south, for the bases of the Englezi. His mother Mrs Xenu was with them,' he offered.

'And my mamma?' I pressed. 'Was she with them too?' I didn't get an answer. 'What's happened to her?' I pressed again, and he lowered his head.

'I don't know,' he replied in a way which indicated that perhaps he had an idea but would not say. I rubbed the bristles of my chin.

'I'm going back. I'm going to find out.'

Simos's eyes filled with fear, as did the eyes of his sons. All three shook their heads.

'No. No. No. Don't be stupid, Andoni. I fought in Crete against the Germans, but that was nothing compared to this. I've seen with my own eyes,' warned Simos, and he was shaking. I felt myself shake too.

He closed the eyes that had seen too much.

'My cousin. Yoda. Her family have had a terrible tragedy.'

I remembered that scheming, interfering gossip of the village, and found myself doing so with affection. Now I feared for her.

'My God. What's happened to Mrs Yoda? Is she…'

'Yoda's here somewhere, with her husband,' interjected Simos, and I was relieved. For only a second.

'What about her sons?'

Simos squeezed his own sons tightly.

'Her two fine National Guardsmen? Only God knows what's happened to them. Fighting, like all the rest, I expect, against Attila. Always fighting! But what chance have they now, with their old-fashioned rifles? No tanks. No aircraft. They don't stand a chance.'

That left Yoda's daughter, Anna. I remembered the plump girl, friend of our Stella. I feared for Anna. And I feared once more for her mother.

'So what of Anna, Mr Simo?'

Simos's eyes filled with sorrow, and the first signs of tears. He released his grip on his sons and ushered them off to find their mother.

'When we heard the bombs, Andoni, when we saw the forest fires, we finally knew the truth. We knew we should flee. I piled my family into the bus. Many villagers piled in with us. Yoda, her husband and Anna too. She still lived with her parents. Anna never married.'

I nodded. Like me, I thought. But unlike me, Anna had stayed close to those closest to her.

'And as we left the outskirts of the village the bus was stopped by soldiers. Turks from Anatolia. You could tell, because ours know some words of our language. But these people, they knew nothing. They shouted at us all to get off the bus. Then they tied up the men and the older women, and took Anna and the younger women away into an empty animal shed. Yoda was calling out in what little Turkish she knew for them to take her instead, but the soldiers just laughed.'

Simos was speaking faster and faster. As though it might be less painful if he could tell it quickly. But it was already too painful for me.

'It's OK, Mr Simo. I don't need to hear any more,' I interjected, but he frowned at me.

'Well, I need to tell it, Andoni. So listen well. England and the world must know what has happened. You must tell them what comes from lies,' he retorted. 'They took the women, Andoni, and they raped them. And when these poor creatures emerged from the animal shed, one by one, they were like ghosts. But our Anna didn't come, Andoni. We waited and waited, but she wouldn't come. And when we asked the other girls where Anna was, they told us she had kicked and bit and screamed so much the Turks got angry and finished her.'

Simos wiped the tears from his cheeks.

'And one of the violated women whispered that Anna was the lucky one.'

I wiped the tears from my eyes.

'And then, Andoni, they untied us all and told us to go. And I went inside the animal shed with my poor cousin and her poor husband. And we saw Anna lying there in a pool of her own blood. It was awful, Andoni. And Yoda came out and screamed at the Turks to finish her too, but they just laughed again. Laughed, Andoni, and told us to get back on the bus and to be gone from there. Get out and be gone for ever!'

Simos broke down. I embraced him.

'We weren't even allowed to bury her,' he bawled. I hoped the captain, wherever he was, whatever he was doing, would be a while longer. For I knew not even his soothing words nor his reassuring touch could offer me comfort at this moment.

And when the captain did return, he nodded recognition at Simos before tapping me on the shoulder and gesturing that I should follow him. I tried to pull away from Simos, telling him I had to go now. Go back to our village. But he was unwilling to release me.

'Don't worry, Mr Simo. Nothing I face can be worse than what I've been through already. Only not knowing. That's worse. Take care of your wife and your children, Mr Simo. May you all live.'

Simos nodded, and as he loosened his grip tried to give me one of his golden smiles, but it just wouldn't come. I waved Simos goodbye, and left him by his bus.

It was then I noticed the captain was holding a bottle of whisky he'd clearly managed to procure. The reason was not so clear.

The captain explained that he'd spoken to UN personnel, who'd informed him of the reported atrocities that had taken place in Cyprus. Mass killings, men being shot in front of their wives, women being raped in front of their husbands, people being tortured, punished, degraded.

I nodded. I knew.

'It's an orchestrated policy of population removal, Tony. On both sides. And worse than anyone could have imagined,' he added, shaking his head.

'Are you saying it's too dangerous? That we should give up now?' I asked.

'On the contrary, I won't let anything stop us now,' he replied, shaking the bottle of whisky at me.

The captain had asked at the camp if we might borrow one of the UN's jeeps for 'humanitarian reasons'. He'd been told to wait until a higher authority could be contacted for permission.

'In the circumstances, surely all we need is God's permission,' I declared. The captain looked at me, closed an eye and nodded.

'You're right, Tony. Follow me,' he ordered with irresistible resolve, and I followed.

We crept over to where half a dozen jeeps were parked. Without permission we clambered into one with a key in the ignition, and without permission the captain started it up. UN soldiers nearby noticed us. All had guns, but true to form no one acted. Just observed.

And as we made our way through the lemon grove and back onto the main road, I noticed one more familiar face queueing for water. It was the fat face of a sad, broken old man. The muhtaris. I thought to call out to him from the jeep. To accuse him and his ilk of bringing about this enosis with Turkey, but I didn't. It was clear he was suffering enough.

I gestured towards the bottle of whisky the captain had on his lap.

'I didn't know you drank, captain,' I said.

'I don't. But perhaps others might want to, up ahead,' he explained, slipping the bottle under his seat.

37

The village   *Do horkon*

We were drawing ever closer to the village. I was able to make out the bell tower of the church of Saint Varnavas the Apostle. The landscape before us hadn't changed from the one of my memory. Still the same vegetation sprouting out of the same red soil. And the same birds, flying overhead.

The captain now thought it safer to avoid the main road, so we detoured through fields and along dirt tracks, steering clear of trouble wherever he sensed it might be lurking. A soldier's sixth sense. And we found ourselves approaching the hill of Erden, and a feeling of horror overcame me. The captain gave me a curious look. He had noticed my cheeks redden, observed the beads of sweat now gathering on my forehead.

'We never did find out for sure, Tony. About the incident with the goatherd. Were you really responsible?' he enquired. He slowed the jeep, and turned to look at me as though assessing whether I was indeed capable of taking a man's life. I gave no answer, and the captain knew not to press.

'Please stop,' I said, and he brought the jeep to a halt.

To the captain's dismay, I got out and started to make my way up the hill. He called after me, asking where I was going. I didn't reply, so he followed me. When I reached the old olive tree I knelt down before it. I noticed the letters carved on the bark. Two names.

E-R-D-E-N and F-U-N-D-A.

I removed the white flower from my shirt pocket, breathed in its sweet smell, then placed it carefully on the ground by the tree.

We returned to the jeep and continued our journey in silence. Back on the main road, on the outskirts of the village, we approached the old well, long since disused. How I yearned to taste what it had once offered.

It was then that a handful of soldiers appeared from nowhere on the road ahead, training their guns on us. I could make out on their helmets the small red insignia, with white crescent moon and star. I was gripped with an ancestral sense of dread.

The captain grabbed my arm, and instructed that I should stay put and remain calm. On reaching the soldiers, the jeep came to a halt.

The soldiers were unshaven, and their eyes were glazed. With their Anatolian features, they looked different from our own Muslims, who after all looked like Cypriots. I sensed that the soldiers were as afraid as I was. Afraid of what they were capable of.

One, evidently the man in command, raised his hand and shouted something at us in Turkish. The captain showed no fear. He exuded an air of indignation at having his freedom of movement restricted. He jumped out of the jeep.

'So, who's in charge here? You?' enquired the captain, addressing the soldier, who was now noting the UN signs on the jeep. He appeared both confused and intimidated, and could respond with no more than a feeble nod. Then he frowned, as though remembering that he and his men were the ones with the power.

'Who are you, please?' he demanded, in broken English, swinging his gun menacingly at the captain.

The captain raised his eyebrows defiantly.

'I'm not prepared to answer any of your questions until you and your men put your weapons aside.'

The man in charge maintained his frown a moment, but realised it was getting him nowhere. He turned to his men and gestured that they lower their weapons. He lowered his own too. Then he repeated his question, and this time the captain answered.

'I'm here with the Red Cross. I'm a retired officer of the British army,' he stated, before pointing to me. 'I've brought a local guide with me. There are one or two items in the village we've been asked to return for. You know, sentimental stuff. If it's all right with you, of course.'

It was evident from the soldier's puzzled expression he hadn't fully understood. As though to help clarify matters, the captain reached into the jeep and pulled out the bottle of whisky from under his seat. The soldier's eyes widened, and he smiled with delight as the captain handed it to him.

'Have a drink with your men. We'll be through with our business before you're done,' offered the captain with a wink. 'Sorry though, no glasses.'

There was a hint of contempt in the Englezos's voice which, after many years in London, I could recognise, but the Anatolian could not. The soldier had already unscrewed the cap and was enjoying his first swig from the bottle. He gave a satisfied gasp, wiped his mouth with his sleeve, and spoke.

'Go quickly,' he ordered, gesturing to the captain to be on his way. 'And then leave quickly, yes?' he added.

The captain raised his head and eyebrows, got back into the jeep and turned the engine back on. But before we could pull away, the soldier had raised his hand and was coming round to my side of the jeep.

He took another swig of whisky, then his grubby hand reached out and grabbed my face. The sense of dread returned. He spoke in English.

'And say goodbye, yes?' he gloated. He released me and I smiled. In my language the words for goodbye and hello were the same.

'Ya su,' I said as the jeep rolled off.

We approached via the village's Christian neighbourhood. It was deserted but for a few stray dogs rummaging around big bags filled with household items and children's toys. Possessions that had evidently been abandoned during the escape.

We drove past the church. A little further on, the captain brought the jeep to a halt outside what was once my father's house. There it stood, as it had always stood, only with no one to greet me, no father smoking on the veranda, no mother hanging out washing.

There too was my old workshop, its door wide open and with clothing strewn on the ground outside. Invaders had been.

On my way in I bent down to gather up the clothing as I made my way inside. I could see my workshop had been transformed into my mother's home. I recognised her lace embroidery. I recognised her smell. And there on the bed, in an opened envelope, was a letter I also recognised. I shut my eyes a moment as I recalled some of what I'd written. Then I took a moment to look at the photograph of my grandmother on the wall among the icons. My yaya smiled at me. I tried to return her smile, but wasn't quite able.

Then I glanced over to the old Singer next to the bed, and noticed three framed photographs on it, two upright, one face down. One upright was in colour, of a man I recognised, older, dressed in the garb of an Orthodox bishop. I nodded at my younger brother Marios proudly. The other was an older, black and white photograph of two young men on bicycles, faces full of fun and mischief. I sighed and shook my head. Then I reached over to pick up the third frame. My parents' wedding photograph. I could contain my tears no more.

'Mamma! Baba!' I cried, turning to the captain.

And when my childlike sobbing was done, he helped me out of the workshop, back into the sunlight. We got back into the jeep, and he suggested that we should continue our journey, but I wasn't yet able. I told him we had to return to the church.

I walked through the gates of the churchyard, and the captain followed at a respectful distance. There was only silence. I remembered the last time I'd been here, when the soldiers had come for me. I had the same feeling of resignation.

I searched among the gravestones until, at last, I found what I was looking for. I fell to my knees when I read my father's name. The captain had ventured inside the church and, after an appropriate period, had returned with some thin candles and a box of matches. He handed a candle to me. I thought a moment before reaching for another. After removing the existing spent candle, I planted two new ones into the soil in front of the gravestone. I then struck a match to light them both. The air was still, and each flame grew.

And then, after I'd wiped my cheeks, I wiped the dust from the gravestone. Finally, with my bare hands, I turned over the red earth to mark off some space. This small piece of land, at least, could be significant only to me.

The captain helped me to my feet, and with one arm around my shoulder, led me back to the jeep. We took our seats once more.

'You've seen to your dead, Tony. Now it's time for the living.'

The jeep made its way back along the main road towards the square, towards what used to be Vasos's coffee-shop. I saw the big carob tree, and recognised the old building. I had half-expected Vasos himself to appear at the door to greet us in his apron, like he always used to, but instead we were met by suspicious stares. Groups of men had gathered round the tables outside, occupying unfamiliar territory. The shop itself was shut.

Amongst the Muslim faces were ones I vaguely recognised, and which appeared vaguely to return that recognition. I felt guilty. I sensed the Muslims shared my guilt. I was content to keep things vague, and so it seemed were they.

Then, looking further ahead along the road, I recognised someone else, walking away from the square. He was approaching barricades and barbed wire, and blue and white signs saying 'Halt'. Beyond was the Muslim neighbourhood. At some point the village must have been partitioned, just as Stella had said. But now that the soldiers had arrived, the partition wasn't needed here, and a gap had been cleared.

The figure had reached the gap. He walked with a slight limp, and on hearing the jeep's engine quickened his pace. To my joy, there were no crutches to support him.

'Zeki!' I called as the captain stopped the jeep just behind him. Zeki turned slowly to face us. He was no longer a delicate young teenager, but a fully grown man. He scrutinised my features until the inevitable recognition. And then surprise, followed by confusion, and finally alarm.

'Andoni? Is that you? Andonis the tailor?' he asked. I nodded.

'What are you doing here?' he demanded, concerned, I could tell, for my safety.

I wanted to get down from the jeep and wrap my arms around him, to squeeze out all the years and events and experiences that lay between us. But I didn't. Somehow it felt inappropriate.

'I've come back, Zeki,' I announced with a smile.

Zeki shook his head.

'You've come back? Christians have fled in fear of their lives, Andoni. I can't tell you what horrors have been done for our sake. For our sake! It's not safe for you. Please, get away from here.'

It was my turn to shake my head, and with it a finger at him. 'I'll not leave, Zeki. Not now. This is my home.'

Zeki rubbed his chin while looking at me intently. Then he looked back at the sullen faces of the men outside the coffee-shop, in the abandoned Christian neighbourhood. He laughed ironically.

'Welcome home, then,' he said, and limped up close to the jeep to offer me a hand of greeting, which I accepted. He also gave the captain a salute, which was returned in good humour.

'Look at you, Zeki,' I enthused staring down at his legs. 'I think it's amazing.'

'Isn't it! I'm not the poor old cripple you used to know, eh?' declared Zeki with pride. 'And I'm married now, with three rascals!' he added with joy.

'May they all live for you.'

Zeki's pride and joy disappeared. He shook his head.

'Live, Andoni?' he asked, pointing to the barricades. 'For what? This? What world are we creating for our children?'

I shook my head too.

'Never give up hope,' I replied, pointing to his legs. 'So, tell me. Who fixed you?'

'I had an operation, over in England, some time ago. The doctors there can work miracles,' he explained before adding. 'My sister paid. She got the money together somehow, may Funda always be well.'

Now he hobbled around a bit, as though performing a dance, to show off the extent of his mobility. I felt the urge to jump out of the jeep and dance with him at news of Funda.

'So, how is she?' I asked. Zeki gave me a knowing smile.

'Why don't you ask her yourself?' he replied, gesturing ahead in the direction of the barber's shop. I nodded, and my heart began to pound. Now Zeki raised a parting hand and began to walk through the gap in the barricades.

'Need a lift?' asked the captain, starting the engine.

'No, that's all right, sir. It's not far,' replied Zeki. 'I can walk.'

❋ ❋ ❋

And as the jeep passed into the Muslim neighbourhood, women in colourful dresses and headscarves interrupted their chores and waved. A few children had formed a line along the roadside and were saluting. The captain smiled and saluted back.

As we drew nearer to the barber's shop I was both surprised and pleased to see the old wooden sign still dangling there, still displaying the word for barber in two languages. I could see also, however, that the shop had been transformed into a modern hair salon, for men and women. And there, below the old sign, another surprise awaited me.

A beautiful vision of someone who, unlike all the rest, somehow hadn't aged. And as the jeep slowed I could make out she was singing as she swept outside the shop. A beautiful voice.

The Funda of my memory.

And then she stopped her sweeping and her singing. She stared up at me, confused and suspicious.

'Funda?' I called doubtfully. I turned to the captain for guidance. He realised what I'd yet to realise and smiled. And slowly, the suspicion and confusion faded.

She smiled at me and spoke in Turkish.

'My mother?' she asked, and gestured to the door behind her.

But the woman dressed in black who emerged was not Funda. It was another whom I loved, and my heart nearly exploded.

'Mamma!' I screamed. I fell from the jeep and ran towards her.

'My son!' she replied as we embraced. I felt like a little boy as my tears soaked into her black cardigan.

'I tried to find you, mamma, but you weren't there!' I cried. 'My God, I thought you were dead.'

She pulled back my head and wiped the tears from my eyes. Then hers, flooded, burned into mine.

'Now you know a little of how it feels, you rascal,' she chastised, and I joined my hands and begged forgiveness.

People were now gathering outside the barber's shop, and I feared for my mother's safety. I looked up at the captain, now standing by the jeep, but he remained calm.

'What are you doing here, mamma? Why didn't you get away with the others?' I demanded, and my mother raised her eyebrows and shook her head to chastise me once more.

'And leave my village, Andoni? And leave the only family I have?' She grabbed the hand of the beautiful young woman, who had greeted me. 'And leave my Afrulla?'

Granddaughter smiled at grandmother. And grandmother went over to hug the man of principle who'd once retrieved her dog, who'd now retrieved her son. The captain. The Englezos.

Now daughter smiled at father. Her father smiled back. Then her mother appeared at the door.

'What wind has blown to bring you here?' she whispered, as if to herself as much as to me.

'The one that led to you,' I replied with a smile.

Then we all heard the ominous sound of an approaching armoured vehicle. Soon soldiers had arrived outside the barber's shop. They were shouting at the frozen Cypriots. Shouting at us not to move.

One soldier, gun in hand, descended. I recognised him, red-faced with eyes bloodshot, as he lurched angrily towards me. Calm acceptance replaced ancestral dread as the soldier aimed his gun at me.

'No!' screamed Afrulla. The soldier hesitated, and turned to look at her.

'What are you doing?' she demanded in the Anatolian's language. He appeared disarmed by her fearless beauty.

'This man is a Greek spy,' he slurred.

'He's no spy,' she proclaimed. 'He's my father.'

After a moment, confused and self-conscious, the soldier responded in the only way open to him: by lowering his weapon and withdrawing with his men.

38

The thimble   *I dhahtilistra*

Andonis and Funda were alone in the moonlight.

'You called her Afrulla,' he announced proudly.

'Afrodhidi,' she replied, giving their daughter's full name. 'The goddess of love.'

Then Andonis remembered something he'd brought with him from England. He removed the harmonica from his trouser pocket, before placing it to his lips.

Andonis began to play, unaccompanied at first, hoping that Funda's beautiful voice might join him. Unable to resist his call, she soon began to sing.

Off she set, Miss Yeragina,
To the well to fetch cold water.
Drun-drun, drun-drun-drun-drun.
As her bracelets rattle on.

And she fell into the well.
And she gave an almighty yell.
Drun-drun, drun-drun-drun-drun.
As her bracelets rattle on.

Yeragina, I'll save your life.
And I will make you my wife.
Drun-drun, drun-drun-drun-drun.
As her bracelets rattle on.

'Will you be my wife, Funda?' Andonis asked softly when their song was done.

'You'll give up everything for me and Afrulla, Andoni? Live here among the soldiers?' Funda's beautiful green eyes were framed by sodden lashes. 'For they won't budge now,' she warned, stroking the tailor's receding hair – hair now flecked with grey.

How she still loved his hair.

'I've already given up everything for the sake of our love. For I know liberty can mean nothing without it,' explained Andonis. 'Share my faith, Funda, that one day the troubles will go away for ever. When we've shown the world we love each other. That we've always loved each other.'

The tailor reached into his shirt pocket, pulled out the thimble once gifted to him by his late grandmother, and presented it to Funda, just as he had done all those years ago in the village square.

Funda stared at the tailor's precious offering. She knew it meant everything to her. It made her a woman who knew no fear. Funda lifted her hand, and Andonis slipped the thimble onto her finger.

Then they fell into each other's arms and, as their lips met, the years melted away. And all at once they were transported back to a magical, mythical time. A time when all things were possible. A time of joy and hope, laughter and song, wisdom and love.

A time that passed.

Acknowledgements

The author is indebted to the following organisations:

ABCtales
Arts Council England
Cypriot Academy
Cypriot Who's Who
Exposure Organisation Limited
Friends of Cyprus
Social Spider
The Literary Consultancy